Alternate Gettysburgs

Edited by Brian Thomsen and Martin H. Greenberg

Fiction by

Harold Coyle
Doug Allyn
William H. Keith, Jr.
James M. Reasoner
Brendan DuBois
Jake Foster
Robert J. Randisi
Jim DeFelice
Simon Hawke
Denise Little
Kristine Kathryn Rusch

Essays by

Abraham Lincoln
Steve Winter
William Terdoslavich
Paul A. Thomsen
William R. Forstchen

ALTERNATE
Gettysburgs

Edited by Brian Thomsen
and Martin H. Greenberg

BERKLEY BOOKS, NEW YORK

The stories herein are works of fiction. Names, characters, places, and
incidents either are the product of the authors' imagination or are used
fictitiously, and any resemblance to actual persons, living or dead,
business establishments, events, or locales is entirely coincidental.

ALTERNATE GETTYSBURGS

A Berkley Book / published by arrangement with
the authors

PRINTING HISTORY
Berkley edition / February 2002

Visit our website at
www.penguinputnam.com

ISBN: 0-425-18377-7

BERKLEY®
Berkley Books are published by The Berkley Publishing Group,
a division of Penguin Putnam Inc.,
375 Hudson Street, New York, New York 10014.
BERKLEY and the "B" design
are trademarks belonging to Penguin Putnam Inc.

PRINTED IN THE UNITED STATES OF AMERICA

10 9 8 7 6 5 4 3 2 1

CONTENTS

WHY GETTYSBURG?

Brian Thomsen

★ ★ ★

The Battle of Gettysburg is one of those hallowed moments of American history rivaling the Battle of Bunker Hill ("Don't shoot until you see the whites of their eyes"), Custer's Last Stand (jokes about Arrow shirts not withstanding), and of course, the Attack on Pearl Harbor ("A day that will live in infamy") that literally everybody remembers and respects.

But the question is, why?

Is it the truly wonderful job that the National Parks Service has done restoring the battlefield (not to mention the inspired presentations ranging from those of amateur reenactors to the early hi-tech presentation of one area museum's electric map)?

Is it the literary excellence of *The Killer Angels*?

No.

Though these after-the-fact preservations have helped to keep the memory alive, there has to be more than just that.

Let's look at the exclusionary facts:

- Sumter began the war and Appomattox Courthouse ended it, so it was neither first nor last

- Antietam was bloodier

- it lacked the head-to-head combat of the best versus the best (though it featured Lee, Grant was absent, and though Meade was a player, he was no U. S. Grant)

- it wasn't the longest

- it wasn't the shortest.

Then the question remains: Why Gettysburg?

I recall studying the battle back in grammar school, as part of fourth grade history. I was fortunate as I had been to Gettysburg the summer prior and had actually seen the battlefield and all of the related sites of interest. Sure, I read the textbook and listened to the teacher (Mrs. Alessi of St. Camillus grammar school). But I already knew about the battle.

The time for the test came.

Question eight: What was the significance of the Battle of Gettysburg?

I thought, and answered: It was the farthest north the Army of the South ever reached as part of their invasion.

No problem . . . until I received my test back with the answer marked wrong.

The correct answer (according to the textbook) was that it was the number of men who were killed.

No, I thought to myself, it must be a mistake.

The same question came up on the final, and once again I got it wrong (or more correctly, I got my answer marked wrong—I guess in grammar school great minds are not allowed to differ in their opinions).

The moral of this childhood memory: Neither answer is the proper reason why Gettysburg has taken its hallowed place in history any more than everyone having to memorize the Gettysburg Address as some part of their early schooling.

I guess the answer is really not any more important in the overall scheme of things than why Columbus went off course or why Washington didn't opt to be a Tory.

Gettysburg is a part of history, and a provocative and fertile part it is.

The rich pantheon of characters, the sequence of events, the epic tragedy of men at war—and it was all real.

In *Alternate Gettysburgs,* other aficionados have raised their own questions about the battle, invoking an intriguing variety of what-ifs, from Harold Coyle's variation on Pickett's Charge to Simon Hawke's surprise supplies uncovered in the nick of time to James Reasoner's blood-drenched alternative to the Gettysburg Address—all tales of a battle that might have gone differently, might have changed history, perhaps might even have given the South the often-decried last chance for victory.

Great minds can differ . . . but the memory and awe of the Battle of Gettysburg shall not vanish from the face of the earth.

Ever.

Sedgwick's Charge

Harold Coyle

PART ONE
Afternoon, July 3, 1863

THE GREAT CANNONADE

For nearly an hour and a half Southern gunners flailed away at the Union line across from them with shot and shell. The batteries engaged in this endeavor had been drawn from each of the three corps belonging to the Army of Northern Virginia, and the men hailed from almost every state belonging to the fledgling Confederacy. With few exceptions, they were veterans of a war that was now in its third year. Even if their commanders failed to tell them so, the lowliest private shuttling ammunition from limber chest to gun understood that their efforts were but the prelude to what most believed to be the final act of a long and bloody three-day struggle.

Whatever they had been in a former life mattered little to them or their officers at this particular moment. Amidst the din and choking dirty white smoke generated by their labors, the Southerners who manned the 142 guns scattered along an arch that described some one point three miles went about their routine without pause, without hesitation. Fire. Roll the gun forward. Swab the piece. Load.

Prime. Aim. And fire yet again. Once every one to two minutes, the gray-clad artillerists repeated this drill. Once every one to two minutes, they stepped forward and executed assigned duties in much the same way that factory workers slave away at their machines. Were one to look at the entire process with a clear head and objective eye, he would have been able to argue that each of the two-ton guns was little more than a machine, an engine of death.

Such philosophical dalliances had no place on the gun line. Few of the Confederate gunners entertained any thoughts other than those necessary to maintain the deadly drum beat upon a foe that was often masked by their gun's own smoke. The sanguine words of politicians didn't clutter their consciousness. Nor did any of the sweet sentiments, expressed by family and friends in rare letters from home, come to mind. The gray-clad artillerymen knew what was expected of them. Their officers had no need to mouth patriotic sentiments or set an example through false heroics. In silence they went about their tasks with the same detachment to the world around them that a sleep walker experiences as he makes his rounds. Fire. Roll the gun forward. Swab the piece. Load. Prime. Aim. And fire yet again.

Few manning the guns paid any attention to the long ranks of infantry that lay tucked away in the woods behind them. They knew that those soldiers would soon be called upon to rise up and cross the open field before them. They knew that many an infantryman would die out there as they traversed the rolling farmland in the face of Union guns like the ones they themselves were servicing. When those pieces came into play, the advancing ranks of Southern infantry would be exposed to the same devastation the Confederate gunners were working so hard to inflict. Unlike their gray-clad brethren, however, when the line of attacking infantry was within 250 yards, the Yankee gunners would be able to use canisters—tin cans stuffed with thirty-one-inch iron balls that turned each cannon into a huge shot gun. If this were allowed to happen, the grand assault would become little more than a slaughter.

Twenty-eight-year-old Colonel Edward P. Alexander understood this. West Point and two years of war had taught him well. After all, little more than six months before, the role he and the Union guns he was so desperately trying to silence had been reversed. In December of '62 he had commanded a battalion of artillery on Marye's Heights. While enemy guns sited across the Potomac strove to put his batteries out of action, his gunners had stood their ground as wave after wave of Union infantry sallied forth from the streets of Fredericksburg and onto the open plain before them. With the detached eye of a professional soldier, Alexander had watched as the dense columns of Yankee infantry were shredded by the combined weight of his guns and the galling rifle fire of Cobb's brigade of infantry. Time and time again, fresh brigades surged forward into the open where they were pummeled by shot, shell, and minié. Time and time again, the once-proud regiments of the Army of the Potomac broke and withdrew, leaving in their wake the dead and those who would soon be dead. By the time night brought an end to that nightmare, the snow-covered ground before Alexander's guns was covered by a blood-stained blanket of blue.

That the same thing could very well happen here within the next hour or two to the soldiers of Pettigrew's and Pickett's divisions was never far from the young colonel's thoughts. So the immediate task at hand was clear—as clear as anything could be in the midst of a battle. He *had* to silence those Union guns. But that was the simplest of his duties that day.

What was not so straightforward was the role he had been assigned in deciding when to unleash the infantry assault. The young colonel was already feeling a bit uneasy at his selection to command the Grand Battery over more senior artillery officers then present on the field. While he could easily ignore the bruised egos this appointment would cause, not so easily side-stepped was the additional responsibility that he had been saddled with by the officer who had been designated as the overall commander of the attack, Lieutenant General James Longstreet. Though he would give the order to open the bombardment, the commander of the First Corps not only left it to the colonel of artillery to determine when the time was right for the infantry to go forward, but also to actually issue the order to General Pickett to do so. While this in itself was highly unusual in Alexander's eyes, even more disconcerting was the exchange of notes that he and Longstreet had engaged in just prior to the commencement of the great cannonade. One in particular struck Alexander as inappropriate, yet very telling. In it, Longstreet advised the colonel of artillery that if, in his judgement, his fire did not have the desired effect upon the enemy, he, Alexander, was to advise Pickett not to make the assault.

Understanding what was at stake and already unsure if his guns could achieve the task assigned them, Alexander fired back a note to Longstreet. In it he made three points. First, he tried to make it clear to his corps commander that the only way he had of telling if his bombardment had silenced the enemy's artillery was by gauging the volume of their return fire. Second, he attempted to pass the responsibility for the final decision to launch the attack back to Longstreet by stating that the army would have insufficient ammunition to make a second effort if the one he was about to initiate did not achieve the desired results. "If there is any alternative to this attack," Alexander wrote, "it should be carefully considered before opening fire. . . ." Finally, Alexander pointed out that even if his gunners did silence or chase off the Union guns, it was his personal opinion that the attack would succeed only "at a very bloody cost."

In his response Longstreet persisted in leaving it to Alexander to judge when to send the infantry forward. Sensing that his commander was not going to relent on this point, shortly after the noon hour, Alexander rode over to where Pickett waited with his troops. During the visit the young colonel of artillery was impressed by Pickett's confidence. Though he still felt a keen sense of uneasiness, Alexander was sure of one thing as he made his way back to his guns: Once they did open the cannonade, the twenty-eight-year-old colonel of artillery concluded that the infantry would have to attack.

It was not until the grand bombardment was well under way that Alexander's resolve on this point began to ebb. Rather than stand by and take the beating that the Confederate gunners were metering out, Union guns replied in kind without letup. Though most of these rounds sailed harmlessly over his gun line and into the woods where the infantry waited, it was obvious to Alexander that his efforts were having little, if any, effect on his foe. Like the stocks of long-range ammunition in the caissons, what little confidence he had concerning this enterprise was dwindling with each passing minute. Desperately, the colonel of artillery scanned the ridge across from him, searching for a sign that his guns had inflicted sufficient damage upon the enemy. Twice an aide dispatched by Pickett had ridden up to inquire if the time to advance had come. Both times Alexander had sent the aide away wanting. It wasn't until the third visit that the colonel of artillery, ever mindful that his gunners would soon be firing off their last rounds, responded with a note that was somewhat ambiguous and quite desperate in tone. "If you are to advance at all," Alexander wrote, "you must come at once."

Alexander's note found Pickett with his commanding general. The man who would soon be leading over 10,000 men into battle was passing the time by writing a letter to his dear Sally, a woman to whom he was betrothed. After reading the note he had been handed by his aide, Pickett immediately passed it on to Longstreet.

The terrible moment had arrived. As he read the note, the man General Lee had charged with the responsibility of organizing the grand assault did little to hide the dread he harbored concerning the enterprise which had been entrusted to him. The tenor of the note only added to his anguish. Though he saw and understood this, Pickett was anxious to have a decision one way or the other. When Longstreet had finished reading the note, Pickett asked if he should advance.

Overcome by the terrible consequences his pronouncement would have, Longstreet found that he could not find the words necessary to send Pickett forward. Turning his head away and letting his chin drop until it almost touched his chest, he merely nodded. Sensing that this was the best that his commander could manage by way of response, Pickett drew himself up. "I shall lead my division forward, sir," he announced before leaving to rejoin his command. To all who had witnessed the unfolding drama, it seemed that the die had been cast.

While their corps commander found it impossible to muster up any enthusiasm for the pending attack, the Confederate infantry who had been waiting in the woods behind Alexander's gun line were galvanized into action. Some 10,500 fell in, as officers shouted orders, drums rolled, and sergeants used whatever means necessary to "encourage" those who hung back. The two and a half divisions assembling for the advance consisted of 4,600 Virginians, 3,600 stubborn North Carolina Tar Heels, 1,100 Mississippians, 550 from Tennessee, and 350 men who claimed Alabama as their home. Like the men on the gun line before them, the vast majority of these men were hardened soldiers, veterans of many a hard fight and desperate struggle. They knew what was coming. They understood that once they stepped off and began their advance, nothing would stand between them and the same terrible punishment their own guns had been laboring so hard to inflict upon their foes. Most appreciated the terrible fact that the execution they were about to face would be terrible. Even if they themselves managed to survive the carnage, many a messmate and companion who had become their brothers would not be alive that night. Still, most of the men belonging to Pickett's and Pettigrew's divisions took their place without hesitation, for they shared the belief expressed by Robert E. Lee himself—that victory was within their grasp.

Having dispatched his note to Pickett, Colonel Alexander continued to scan the Union line searching for a manifestation of any sort that would support the decision he had already made. Slowly, almost painfully, the seconds slipped away. One by one his own batteries began to run out of ammunition and go silent, adding to the apprehension the Confederate colonel already felt.

Then it began to happen. Above the din generated by his own artillery, Alexander perceived an unexpected slackening of fire from the Union guns. He had no sooner noted this when he saw it—the sign he had been so desperately seeking. Across the open fields, over on Cemetery Hill, Alexander watched with growing excitement as several enemy batteries that had been firing from there limbered up and began to withdraw. While he had no idea what was behind this sudden maneuver, he took heart and immediately scribbled another note to Pickett, urging the general to commence his assault as quickly as possible. Having done this, the colonel of artillery turned his attention to the task of bringing up nine howitzers which he intended to send forward with Pickett.

He was still waiting for these guns to appear when Longstreet rode up to him. Alexander lost no time in reporting the situation to his commander. He explained that while he was encouraged by the withdrawal of the Union

guns he had observed scant minutes before, he feared that
his batteries now had insufficient ammunition remaining
with which to support Pickett's attack.

Stunned by this revelation, Longstreet did not hesitate.
Whether he saw this as one last opportunity to avoid an attack which he did not favor will never be known. What is
clear is that he immediately ordered the commander of his
Grand Battery to stop Pickett and send his caissons back to
the army trains to refill them.

Now it was Alexander's turn to be shocked. Though he
understood the order, the young colonel of artillery made
no move to carry it out. Instead, he countered by explaining that the army's supply trains had but a little long-range
ammunition left. Furthermore, Alexander pointed out to an
alarmed Longstreet, even if there were sufficient stocks
available, it would take him an hour to carry out the resupply, an hour which the enemy would surely use to im-
prove their own situation.

For the longest moment the two men considered what
the other had said. It was Longstreet who spoke first.
These words came slowly, almost mournfully. "I do not
want to make this charge. I do not see how it can succeed."*

Again there was a pause as Longstreet weighted the
consequences of what would happen if he let Pickett go
forth. For his part, Alexander waited for his corps commander to either repeat his last order or rescind it. Finally,
drawing himself up, Longstreet reached out, grasping
Alexander by the shoulder with one hand while pointing to
the ranks of Pickett's infantry now making their way forward. "There is no time to discuss this further. Go and stop
him before it is too late."

Having gone forward but a few yards, Brigadier General
J. J. Pettigrew looked back and discovered to his horror
that only two of the four brigades belonging to his divi-

sion's first echelon were following. Those commanded by Brigadier General Joseph R. Davis and Colonel J. M. Brockenbrough were nowhere to be seen. He barely had time to wonder what had become of his two errant subordinates before an aide added to his alarm. "Sir, Pickett's division had halted! They're not advancing!" Pivoting about in his saddle, Pettigrew watched in utter amazement as the Virginians who were supposed to be advancing in line with his division faced about and marched back into the woods from which they had just emerged.

Shaken by these unexpected developments, the division commander of two days reigned in his horse and turned to face his own command. Though he had no idea what was going on, he was keenly aware that those men who had followed him this far were visible to Union gunners. Somehow, he had become the victim of an order gone astray. Frantically he looked this way and that, trying to take everything in while searching for a solution. One thing quickly became clear to the former college professor. If the division that had been entrusted to him the day before remained where it was, they would soon begin to draw fire from every Union gun that could be brought to bear upon them. Finding that he had no other choice, Pettigrew threw his right hand up and ordered his men to halt, face about, and go back.

As if sensing his master's confusion, the horse Major General Winfield Scott Hancock rode shook his head and looked back at him. The commander of the Second Corps of the Army of the Potomac paid no heed to his mount. Rather, the Union general continued to gaze across the open fields at the woods from which two enemy brigades had emerged. Having prepared himself for what he expected to be a desperate struggle, Hancock was taken aback when the line of gray infantry stopped after cover-

ing but a few yards, executed a right about-face, and
calmly marched away.

Puzzled by this, no one along the crest of Cemetery
Ridge moved. Many a man hardly drew breath as general
and private alike stood watching and waiting for the Confederates to make their next move. To a man, they searched
for any sign of the lines of gray infantry that each and
every one of them expected to reappear and surge forth
like an onrushing wave. For an hour and a half they had
been subjected to the most awful cannonade they had ever
beheld or endured. The effort required to maintain that
bombardment and the enormous expenditure of ammunition consumed by it could only be justified if the Rebel
infantry exerted themselves with equal vigor and determination.

Yet nothing happened. Even the Rebel gunners, barely
visible to the naked eye in the distance, seemed to be waiting for their own infantry to sally forth and commence the
attack. Though he had managed to preserve an air of calm
during the Confederate cannonade, Hancock now found
that this most unnatural lull was unnerving. Overcoming
the inertia that seemed to have set in, the Union general
spurred his horse on and began to move along the crest of
the hill at a trot, like an impatient cat pacing back and
forth. All the while he cast a wary eye out across the va-
cant fields that lay before his positions. Slowly, his anticipation began to give way to hope—hope that the enemy
infantry would appear. The impatient Union general now
found himself praying that Lee would foolishly send his
infantry forward, exposing them to the same sort of punishment that had been wreaked upon his division at Fredericksburg.

That thought caused Hancock to reign in his mount. Lee
was no fool. He was too good a soldier to mount such a
desperate attack and was far too wily a foe to make such
an obvious move. But if the enemy was not going to come

at them in the center, then where? Lee was up to something, that much was obvious. If the cannonade that had
mesmerized everyone for so long had not been the prelude
to a frontal attack, then it had to be a demonstration, a ruse.
Tearing his eyes away from Seminary Ridge, the commander of the Union center twirled about and looked to the
south toward the two hills where so much of the previous
day's fighting had taken place. As he vainly searched for
any sign that something was amiss, the name Chancellorsville crept into his consciousness.

With this thought now firmly planted in his mind, Hancock once more turned to the west. Even without using his
field glasses, the Union general could see that the Confederate gunners were busily limbering up their guns and
scampering away. Whatever they had been trying to do, it
was obvious that they were finished. That much was clear.
What was not at all apparent was what, exactly, that was.
Unable to stand by idle and wait for Lee to reveal his purpose at a time and place of his choosing, Hancock jerked
the reigns of his mount till he faced east and dug his spurs
in as he took off in search of the army's commanding general. He had no intention of allowing General Meade to
wait as Hooker had done in May.

Traveler was pleased that they were in no particular hurry.
The reins were loose and his rider made no effort to spur
him out of the leisurely pace they had settled into. Like his
master, the horse let his head droop. He was tired, very
tired. It had been a busy day, one the pair had spent riding
this way and that, sometimes at a walk, sometimes at a trot.
Late in the afternoon, shortly after the great storm had
passed and the warm summer day had grown quiet once
more, he had even been spurred into a dead run.

Like his bruised flanks, the memory of that incident still
pained Traveler, for his master had been quite excited. The
animal himself had been whipped up into a state of near

frenzy by the harshness of his master's voice and the force
with which the spurs had been repeatedly applied. In all
the years he had served him, Traveler could not recall a
time when his master had been so agitated. All the other
horses were affected as well, as the two of them danced
about while sharp words were exchanged between his
master and the men gathered about. That something was
wrong was clear. That he was not at fault was of little con-
solation to Traveler. He loved the man he carried upon his
back. He enjoyed the attention that was lavished upon him
and the excitement the pair generated when they rode
along among the soldiers. It was good, the war horse
thought, that this day would soon be over. He looked forward to the grooming, watering, and feeding that awaited
him. Perhaps tomorrow his master would be himself again.
Perhaps he would ride him out to a spot where Traveler
could enjoy the lush green grass. Or maybe the pair would
ride among the soldiers. That, the horse thought as he
made his way along, would be grand. He loved hearing the
soldiers cheer.

At that moment the man riding Traveler wanted nothing
to do with those soldiers. With his eyes downcast, Robert
E. Lee avoided any contact with those who cared to look
his way. He had failed them, and they knew it. Though
none would ever imagine saying so out loud, Lee felt their
disappointment and bewilderment.

Behind him his aides and staff officers rode at a distance which would allow them to be at the general's side
in a flash if beckoned, yet far enough away to give Lee the
solitude he seemed to need at this moment. In the gathering shadows of late afternoon, the commanding general of
the Army of Northern Virginia went over the tally of
missed opportunities that his army had endured during the
course of the past three days. None of them, in and of itself, had been fatal to the army or the enterprise upon
which it was embarked. While disconcerting at the mo-

ment, each had not only been survived but seemed to give way to another, more inviting possibility.

Yet each new stratagem that Lee had come up with in the wake of a disappointing performance by one subordinate had been frustrated by another who had, for one reason or another, not carried out his assigned task as he should have. Lee had been able to overlook Heth's error in bringing on a battle that they were not prepared to fight. He understood how the recent loss of a leg could cause Ewell to hesitate when he had held the advantage at the end of that first fateful day. The general had even mustered the strength needed to set aside his anger with Stuart for that officer's dereliction in not providing the intelligence that would have made all the difference. The commander of the Army of Northern Virginia accepted each of these failures, put any thought of remonstration aside, and moved on.

Longstreet's performance that afternoon, however, was another matter. Even now, Lee could feel anger mounting as he reflected upon that general's decision not to launch the infantry attack. Though every point his senior corps commander made was valid and his explanation plausible, Lee could not escape the fact that the man whom he had come to rely upon had failed him. It had been, Lee found himself repeating over and over again, almost as if the failure had been willful, perhaps even malicious.

Reining in Traveler, Lee paused, lifted his head, and gazed up at the sky. Behind him his attentive staff followed suit, halting as they braced themselves to respond to whatever instructions their beloved commander passed on to them. But the general made no effort to call any of them to his side. Rather, Lee simply sat astride his mount, staring up at the heavens.

Jackson would not have failed him. Once the decision had been made, his trusted right arm would have moved heaven and earth to carry out his orders. Jackson had never given Lee any reason to mistrust him or be concerned. After today, he feared he would never be able to trust Longstreet in the same way.

Lowering his eyes, Lee looked about at the growing shadows. This day was over. The promise of victory that had shone so brightly just scant hours before was gone for good. Tonight he would have to make some very hard decisions. Tonight he would have to prepare his army for their return to Virginia. As much as he would like to try once more to break the Union army before him, Lee knew that he could not stay where he was. Unlike his foe, he did not have access to railroads with which to resupply his army. Even if he could detach foraging parties, which he could not do while standing face-to-face with the enemy, there was no way that he could replace the artillery ammunition that had been expended that afternoon. To continue this campaign without doing so was a gamble that even he was unwilling to make.

Pulling in on the reins, he gave Traveler a gentle nudge with his heels and continued on. Tonight he would send off his wounded using all the empty supply wagons his quartermaster could muster, guarded by those brigades belonging to Hill's corps that had been so roughly handled on the first day. He would remain here with the rest of the army one more day, just as he had done at Sharpsburg. Perhaps, Lee thought, Meade would do what McClellan had not. Perhaps the Army of the Potomac would come to him as it had at Fredericksburg. While his guns would not be able to lash out at them at long range, each battery still had ample stocks of canister. And his men, his beloved soldiers, were still unbeaten and unbowed. Given a chance, they would do whatever he asked of them. Anything. Of this he was sure.

What he was unsure of was how best to overcome the failure of leadership that had plagued him these past three days. He had once told Jackson that he believed that the Army of Northern Virginia would be invincible if it could be properly organized and officered. That he had yet to achieve this had been made painfully clear to him that very day. Equally clear was that he would not solve those problems tonight or during the course of this campaign. Changes would need to be made, changes that were best made when heads were clear and wounded pride had been afforded an opportunity to heal.

So for the moment he would have to content himself with dealing with those issues which needed to be tended to. Uppermost was the preservation of the army and its pride. They might have to go back to Virginia, but they would do so because they had chosen to and not because they had been compelled to do so by their enemy. Though this was a small victory, Lee knew that wars are won in the hearts and minds of men.

PART TWO
Almost Midnight, July 3, 1863

THE COUNCIL OF WAR

In a few minutes it would be July 4, a day of national celebration. But it was not recalling their country's past glories that brought the circle of general officers together for a second time that night. Rather, it was to determine what they would do when dawn came again to ensure that their children would have cause to celebrate this day in years to come.

The men who commanded the seven corps which made up the Army of the Potomac listened in silence as Major General Alfred Pleasonton apprised George Meade of

what his cavalry had discovered. Much of what the troopers had found as they rode through the early evening darkness, probing and prodding in search of the enemy, was
already known. Skirmishers deployed all along the section
of the Union line between Cemetery Hill and Culps Hill
were quick to pass on word that their Confederate counterparts had begun disappearing shortly after sunset. General Sykes, commander of the Fifth Corps at the other end
of the line, reported that the same thing was happening to
his front. So the intelligence Pleasonton was providing
with regard to these movements merely served to confirm
something everyone in the room already suspected: The
Rebel army was in the process of redeploying.

The revelations which the army's senior cavalryman
was able to supply concerned what was going on behind
the thin line of pickets that screened the Confederate front.
Detachments dispatched to seek out and harass the
enemy's rear sent back word that large columns of wagons,
accompanied by substantial bodies of infantry, were moving west through Fairfield and away from Gettysburg.
This, Pleasonton pointed out, clearly indicated that the
Army of Northern Virginia was in the process of withdrawing. "Though the Rebels may still be on Seminary
Ridge in strength," he ventured, "Lee is preparing to retreat. Of this I am sure."

What Pleasonton could not discern from the reports rendered by his patrols was just how long those Confederate
troops on Seminary Ridge would remain there. Nor could
he completely assuage the fears expressed by some that
Lee was up to something. Like the massive cannonade the
Union center had been subjected to that afternoon, there
was concern that the westbound columns of wagons were
but a demonstration designed to distract their attention
from some grand maneuver that they had yet to discern.
General O. O. Howard, commander of the Eleventh Corps,
was especially transfixed by this possibility. "At Chancel-

lorsville, Hooker convinced himself that Lee was retreating just hours before Jackson fell upon my corps," he pointed out. "What makes any of you think that he will not try to do the same here?"

Just as he had done on each night after the fighting had died down, Major General George G. Meade held a council of war early on the evening of the third. Though the final decision as to what the army did ultimately rested with him, Meade had adopted the custom of soliciting the opinions of his subordinates as well as asking them to vote on various questions and courses of action he was considering. To some this came across as a lack of moral courage. Others saw it as a means of using the collective wisdom of the army's senior leadership.

During the course of the earlier gathering it had been decided that the army would continue to defend the ground they held. While fears that Lee was attempting to outflank them diminished somewhat with the coming of night, that possibility had not been totally dismissed. Every man in the room had fallen victim to one of Lee's stratagems in the past. With little more than 57,000 men available for duty the next day and the need to protect Washington, Philadelphia, and Baltimore, none of the corps commanders had pressed very hard for going over to the attack. The only thing Meade decided to do at that time was order the assembled corps commanders to return all the units he had taken from Sedgwick's Sixth Corps. Having done that, Meade instructed that general to be prepared to move his reconstituted corps forward in support of Pleasonton's cavalry.

Rather than a full-blooded assault, this action was meant to be little more than a continuation of an effort made against the Confederate's right, late in the afternoon of the third by Kilpatrick's division of cavalry. Lacking infantry support, they had been unable to make any headway. Still, Pleasonton held the opinion that this flank was quite vulnerable, and had managed to convince Meade of this during the course of the earlier meeting. Now, with solid evidence that Lee was, in fact, in the process of disengaging, several of the corps commanders led by Hancock sensed an opportunity. Spurred on by the commander of the Second Corps, they pressed Meade to act. "If nothing else," Hancock stated, "send the whole of Sedgwick's Sixth Corps forward to drive that flank in. If he's successful, Fairfield and the pass to the west of it will be uncovered."

As July 3 gave way to a new day, Meade relented, revising his earlier plan by increasing the number of troops involved and the scope of the operation. While this maneuver was aggressive in nature, its ultimate goal was not to deliver a crushing blow. Rather, Meade saw this as an opportunity to place the Army of the Potomac in a new position, one which his Confederate counterpart would have no choice but to attack if he wished to escape. Though not as aggressive as some back in Washington would have preferred, the commanding general in the field was in no mood to throw away what he saw as a perfectly good victory.

"Your's is the only fresh corps I have," Meade reminded Sedgwick. "If it turns out that the enemy is determined to hold his ground, you are to refrain from squandering your men in futile attacks."

"But if I do manage to break his line or find myself standing on his flank?" Sedgwick countered.

"Then you will push on to Fairfield. The Fifth Corps will support you," Meade replied. Turning to Major General George Sykes, the commanding general motioned with his hands as he explained. "The Sixth Corps will go forward. If the situation warrants it, you will advance on the flank of that corps in echelon. Once you have begun your advance, Slocum and his Twelfth Corps will follow on your right."

"And the rest of us?" Hancock asked.

"I dare say the rest of you could use a bit more time to sort out and rest your troops," Meade stated in a most deliberate and purposeful manner. "You will continue to hold your ground. So long as a sizable portion of the enemy's force remains on Seminary Ridge, we retain enough of a force here to keep him in check. But," he added quickly when he saw the look on Hancock's face, "be prepared to move on a moment's notice. With Sedgwick and Sykes at Fairfield, we will have Lee between us. If he moves against Sedgwick, you will go over to the attack using the Second and Twelfth Corps. If, on the other hand, Lee attempts to escape by using the northern route through Cashtown and on to Chamberburg, you will pursue while I will push the Sixth Corps west to Greencastle and the Fifth to Waynesboro to cut his line of march. Either way, he will find himself in a most difficult position. Just be sure," Meade added, "that you do not expose your commands to surprise or permit them to become separated from each other. If Lee perceives he has a chance to destroy this army in detail, he will seize it."

Whatever enthusiasm their commanding general had whipped up while outlining his plan was dashed by this last cautionary note. For despite the success that they had enjoyed thus far on this field, every member of this council of war stood in awe of a foe that had not only frustrated every effort that had been mounted against him, but seemed to have an infinite ability to turn a defeat into something of a victory. That their luck might be changing never occurred to them. Perhaps they were too tired. Or perhaps they had lost too many battles. Whatever the reason, the senior officers of the Army of the Potomac returned to their various commands in order to prepare them to avoid defeat rather than secure victory.

PART THREE
Dawn, July 4, 1863

THE GLORIOUS FOURTH

Longstreet's personal staff were quite adept at reading their commander's mood. On this morning both his manner and expression served to warn those officers that they would need to give him a wide berth. The only words that he had spoken after emerging from his tent were to inquire if there had been anything further from General Lee. After Moxley Sorrel, his adjutant, replied that nothing had been received, Longstreet sighed and turned away. With head bowed, he made his way to where his horse was tethered. Without a word, he mounted up and trotted off, forcing his attending aides and staff to drop their half-eaten breakfast and scramble for their own mounts.

Slowly, Longstreet made his way north along the ridge occupied by his soldiers. He had not heard directly from Lee since the previous afternoon. Even the written orders he had received later during the night had been delivered by a courier and signed by Lee's adjutant. As difficult as it had been to endure the dressing down that his commanding general had subjected him to in the aftermath of Pickett's aborted attack, the thought that Lee was still angry with him was intolerable. Perhaps, Longstreet thought as he slowly made his way among his troops, he would meet Lee and the two would have an opportunity to mend the disaffection between them that had manifested itself in the course of the previous three days.

The heavily wooded terrain feature the commanding general of the First Corps was riding along was called Warfield Ridge by the locals. It was separate and apart from Seminary Ridge to the north, where both Hill's and

Ewell's corps had taken up positions during the night. The Emmitsburg Road, which ran from Maryland into Gettysburg, dissected the ridge at a sharp angle. It was from the cover of these woods that the divisions belonging to McLaws and Hood had begun their assault on the afternoon of the second. And it was back to this place that those two divisions had retired on the night of the third without Hood, many of their comrades, or victory.

At the moment, the soldiers of those two bloodied divisions were arrayed along the crest of the ridge more or less in line of battle. The northern end of the ridge was occupied by McLaws's division, made up of two brigades from Georgia and one each from South Carolina and Mississippi. To their left, Hill's corps held the center of the Confederate line. Hood's battered division was spread along the other half of Warfield Ridge. Now commanded by Brigadier General E. M. Law, this division held the Confederate right with only two brigades of Stuart's cavalry screening to the south. Like McLaws's, it was comprised of a fair number of Georgians as well as Law's old brigade of Alabamans and a brigade Hood had once commanded made up of the First, Fourth, and Fifth Texas as well as the Third Arkansas. Pickett's division was behind the line of ridges. While it was said that they were being held as a reserve force for the entire army, many of the men who had stormed the round-topped hills and gone into the wheat field on the second complained bitterly about the preferential treatment that Pickett's Virginians always seemed to enjoy. Though they grumbled amongst themselves and took every opportunity to taunt their rivals in other units, the men who made up Longstreet's corps soldiered on, if not out of dedication to their cause then out of habit.

As they did every morning, those who were not required on the line made their way back to where they gathered in small groups around fires to cook their morning meal, socialize, and swap the latest rumors, news, and gos-

sip. None of them needed to wait to read a newspaper to
discover what their army had achieved. They all sensed
that they had failed to humble the Yankees and guessed
that they would soon be going back to Virginia. Like all
old soldiers, they had developed a sense about certain
things. And like Longstreet's staff, they could read the
mood of their officers. Unlike their superiors, the men felt
no need to hold their opinions in check. Lacking anything
else to occupy their time, they freely exchanged views on
any and everything that went on around them.

On this morning the main topic being discussed concerned the incident between their commanding general and
Lee. Though only a handful of people had actually witnessed the confrontation between those two men after
Pickett's division had been recalled, and few heard what
had been said, everyone had thoughts concerning the matter. The majority of the old campaigners felt that
Longstreet had been justified in stopping the attack. The
Yankees, they pointed out, had been in position too long
and had been afforded too much time to throw up earth-
works. Having gone against entrenchments before, they
pointed out that even God himself could not muster
enough artillery to make a difference. While there were
those who felt that Longstreet should have at least given
the Virginians a chance, their arguments were more often
than not shouted down. These contrarians were reminded
that they themselves had failed against a foe who had been
less prepared than the Yankees Pickett's division would
have gone against.

The appearance of their corps commander riding among
them brought many of these discussions to an abrupt halt.
All sensed that he was feeling the effects of their failure,
perhaps more than they themselves did. While some had
cursed him when he had all but marched their legs off during punishing marches, they all revered and respected
him. If he had faults, they forgave him. And if he desired

to be left alone, they afforded him the solitude and quiet he craved.

Longstreet had gone but a little way away when the early morning calm was shattered by the crack of musketry to the south. Reining in his mount, the Confederate general spun about and peered off into the distance while listening to the sound of a growing battle. Without needing to be told, his adjutant was already in the process of dispatching an aide to investigate. Like their commander, the soldiers stopped whatever they were doing, put aside their frying pans, and came to their feet. Some reached over and gathered up their rifles and equipment. All who could alternated between looking off to the south where the sound of gunfire was growing at an alarming rate and glancing up at Longstreet in an effort to gauge just how serious this was.

He was well aware of this. Though concerned by the exchange of gunfire that grew in intensity with each passing second, Longstreet knew that his every action and expression was being watched. Whatever he did would set an example. If he gave way to his own fears and began to dash about like a madman, the soldiers of McLaws's division would become rattled. So he fought the urge to dig his spurs in and gallop off. Instead, Longstreet gave the reins a slight snap as he eased his heels into the flanks of his mount. With a measured pace that belied his concern, he made his way toward the sound of the guns.

Writers tend to exaggerate about the enthusiasm with which soldiers rush forth into battle. They often mistake the mass hysteria that men are often able to whip themselves up into for an eagerness to cast aside all thought of self-preservation in the name of a noble cause. The simple fact is that men, especially those who have already tasted the bitter fruit of battle, harbor all the fears, dread, and sheer panic that any rational person would experience when faced with the imminent prospect of death or dismemberment.

Yet for centuries men have willingly gone into battle. The reasons for this contradiction are as numerous as the combatants themselves. Sometimes a single man can go into battle time and time again propelled to do so by a different reason on each occasion. In the case of the soldiers belonging to Sedgwick's Sixth Corps, the impetus that drove them on with such élan that morning was the simple fact that they were tired of waiting. They had waited on the outskirts of Richmond in the spring of 1862 to go forth and bring an end to the rebellion that divided their country. They had sat in the East Woods at Antietam while a broken Confederate army stood its ground and then was permitted to slip away in the night. At Fredericksburg the corps had taken its place in the line of battle but done nothing while those elements of the army to their right impaled themselves upon a stone wall and the other half was thrown back after breaking the Confederate line. Even when they had finally been afforded an opportunity to strike a decisive blow against their hated foe in May of 1863, a failure of nerve on the part of their army's commanding general had forced them to throw away a victory that was theirs for the taking. So despite the fact that none of the 12,000 soldiers who wore the Greek cross of the Sixth Corps were anxious to embrace a glorious death in battle, even the most reluctant warrior in the ranks was primed and ready to go forth that morning.

And on they did come. Like a flood tide, the dense columns of blue-clad infantry emerged from the shadows of a wooded hill named Big Round Top and surged forward. There had been no preliminary bombardment by the corps guns, no timid probing and jabbing by clouds of skirmishers thrown out in advance. Relying on the intelligence that had been provided to him by Kilpatrick's cavalry, General John Sedgwick decided to use the same bold tactics that had served him so well in May when his corps had stormed the dreaded heights above Fredericksburg. His men would advance at the quickstep with muskets unloaded. Though this added to the already considerable trepidation that all soldiers feel before stepping off into battle, it denied them the temptation to stop and fire before they closed with the enemy. "If we are to succeed," a regimental commander shouted to his men as they prepared to step off, "we must rapidly cross the open ground and smash into the Rebel line as one would use his fist to strike down his foe. Let no man hesitate. Today we will drive into them with all our might. We will run them through with the bayonets to the muzzle. Today we will break them. Forward!"

Whipped up to a frenzy by pronouncements and speeches such as this, the Sixth Corps came on. In the lead was Horatio G. Wright's First Division made up of regiments from New Jersey, Maine, New York, Pennsylvania, and Wisconsin. Striking southwest until they hit Plum Run, the various brigade columns deployed to the left and into line of battle with Bartlett's Second Brigade on the left, Tolbert's First New Jersey Brigade on the right, and Russel's Third Brigade following the First.

Brigadier General Frank Wheaton pushed his Third Division forward on the heels of the First. Wheaton also waited until they hit Plum Run before deploying into line of battle. His lead brigade was made up of three Massachusetts regiments and one from Rhode Island, and was commanded by Colonel Henry L. Eustis. When this brigade hit the Run, it moved at an angle to the right and began the complex task of changing formation from column to line of battle. Even before those units had completed their evolutions, the First Brigade commanded by Alexander Shaler surged straight ahead and into the gap that had opened between the First Division on the left and the New Englanders to the right. Wheaton's old brigade, made up of troops from Pennsylvania and New York, followed the first two, prepared to reinforce either of the lead brigades or exploit any opportunity that presented itself.

Led by the corps commander himself, the two brigades of Howe's Second Division remained in column. Ever mindful that battles were fickle affairs, Sedgwick wanted to maintain control of a substantial portion of his command to deal with any unexpected eventualities. So Grant's Brigade of Vermonters and the men from Maine, New York, and Pennsylvania who followed Neill were held back.

When all was set, the Sixth Corps would move against the Confederates on Warfield Ridge with four brigades abreast. The Second Brigade, First Division on the far left served as the base with the First Brigade, First Division coming next. Then there would be the First Brigade of the Third Division, which was actually the last of the four units that would reach its assigned position. Finally, the Second Brigade of the Third Division would serve as the right flank for the line of battle. Once the officers redressed the ranks and all the regiments were aligned, the Sixth Corps would present a front made up of 2,000 men and measuring 1,200 yards from left to right.

The doctrine of the day measured the speed at which infantry moved using the term "pace," which was equal to twenty-eight inches. Common step, or normal march speed, was ninety paces while quick time was established at 110 paces. Officers could use double-quick, which varied between 165 to 180 paces per minute, but not for long. Troops forced to use double-quick time became winded. When exhaustion began to take hold, formations tended to fall apart as individuals unable to keep up fell out or collapsed.

Since the distance between Plum Run and the southern end of Warfield Ridge is a little over one half mile or a thousand yards, the time needed to cover that ground at quick time was something like thirteen minutes. Of course, that is the time for the first man or unit. Only the lead brigade of Wright's First Division would be able to use quick time throughout the entire attack. If the forward momentum of that attack was to be maintained, everyone else behind that lead unit would have to move at double-quick while deploying if they hoped to catch up. The further back in the line of march that a brigade was, the longer it would need to run in order to reach its assigned place in the line of battle. Sedgwick understood this. He expected that all of the brigades that were assigned to the corps's first echelon would not be in place until almost the last minute. But he was confident that they would be, and that the weight of this force, the speed at which it came on, and the ferocity with which it hit would overwhelm the Confederates, just as they had done two months before at Fredericksburg.

It was not their numbers or the stature of the soldiers that made their advance irresistible. They were, after all, mere mortals. Except for their uniforms and the regimental standards they followed, there was little difference between them and the startled Confederates who manned the picket line. It was the collective spirit that permeated the packed ranks, the energy of their officers, the fact that they had been afforded the opportunity to make their peace with their God, and a burning desire to do what they could to bring this terrible war to an end that made the Sixth Corps a force to be reckoned with.

Having executed a sharp oblique movement to the left as soon as they had passed out of the shadows of Big Round Top before going into line of battle, the two brigades of Wright's First Division swept past the southern tip of Warfield Ridge. Astonished by the sudden appearance of the advancing Union line, those Southerners who had remained along the crest of the ridge were slow to respond. Several critical minutes slipped away before the

first drummer boy beat the long roll and the efforts of those
officers who had been at their posts began to take hold. By
then it was too late to do anything but fire a few wild volleys at the fast-moving ranks of Union soldiers as they
came on.

It was the Third Division under Brigadier General
Frank Wheaton that struck the Confederate line head-on.
Unlike those in the First, Wheaton's lead brigades were
unable to align themselves in line of battle before they
plowed into the Rebels. Colonel Eustis of Massachusetts
never hesitated as he drove his Bay Staters and Rhode Islanders forward. It was Shaler's responsibility to bring his
New Yorkers and Keystoners up to him and take their
place on his left. Eustis was in the lead, and therefore set
the pace.

Even if their brigade commander had tried to stay their
advance, the soldiers of Wheaton's Second Brigade would
not have obeyed. The weapons they held were unloaded.
Other than their eighteen-inch bayonets, these men had no
way of striking at an enemy that they could clearly see
scurrying about in an effort to form line of battle. The
steady, irresistible advance was quickly becoming a race,
one being run by men determined to cover as much ground
as possible before their foes had an opportunity to fire
upon them. Though a handful of individual Confederates
did manage to do so, striking down some of the New Englanders that were coming at them, their efforts had no real
impact. The Yankees took the gentle slope in stride and
slammed into those dazed Confederates who had not already taken to their heels.

The sound of battle to their front had the effect of causing the soldiers of Shaler's First Brigade to redouble their
efforts. Suspecting that they had blundered by not reaching
their assigned position in the corps' line of battle in a
timely manner, every officer from the brigade commander
down to the most junior lieutenant spurred their men on.

Red-faced and flashing their swords madly above their heads, they did everything in their power to push their men forward and close the gap that they were supposed to have been filling.

The Confederates who had the misfortune of facing this oncoming horde of screaming Yankees were the same men who had thrown themselves against Little Round Top two days before. That effort had cost some regiments fifty percent of their total strength. Companies that now numbered less than a dozen men commanded by sergeants found themselves confronted by another, totally unexpected crisis. Unable to muster the determination needed to make a stand against such a terrible host, most soldiers quickly took the only course of action that made sense to them: They ran. No attempt was made to prevent them from doing so, for many an officer joined the spreading rout rather than stand his ground. Within minutes, the brigade anchoring right of the Confederate line was swept away like so many dried leaves.

Sensing that victory was theirs for the taking, Shaler's brigade roared with a mighty huzzah that was heard for miles. Onward they rolled, tucking their heads down as they broke into a dead run. Already on the verge of losing its cohesion, this uncontrolled lunge caused the brigade to fly apart as it turned north and began to sweep up Warfield Ridge.

Of all the scenes that could have greeted him, Longstreet could not have imagined a more terrible one than that which he came across. The fleeing men hit him in waves. Reining in his horse, the general had no time to raise his voice in an attempt to arrest their flight. Even if he had the presence of mind to do so, he needed both hands to control his mount as the soldiers of Law's division made their way as fast as their feet could carry them to what they assumed was safety. Beyond them Longstreet could hear the deep-throated roar announcing that the enemy was near at hand.

In an instant the commanding general of the First Corps determined that no power on earth could arrest this rout. He was still mulling over what to do next when Moxley Sorrel reached his side. Shouting more as a result of the excitement of the moment than the need to be heard, the young officer asked Longstreet what his orders were. In a flash the general turned and faced his adjutant. "These men are lost to us. I will go to McLaws and have him refuse his right. His division will serve as a fire break. I want you to go to Pickett and order him to form his command to the rear of McLaws's division facing south. On my orders Pickett's men will pass through those of McLaws and hit the Yankees while they are still milling about trying to sort themselves out."

"What about General Lee?" Sorrel asked. "Pickett's men are the only reserve the army has."

"There is no time!" Longstreet snapped. "If we do not check those people and soon, there will be no army. Now ride to Pickett and bring him up. I will tend to McLaws."

With a mighty jerk, Longstreet yanked his horse's head about and spurred the animal on as he headed off in search of Major General Lafayette McLaws.

Riding along at a steady pace, General Sedgwick watched as Wheaton's Second Brigade continued their wild charge up Warfield Ridge and turned north in pursuit of their fleeing foes instead of maintaining their advance to the west. Concerned that Shaler's men, obviously out of control, would become hopelessly intermingled with those of Eustis, Sedgwick prepared to ride over to the right and do what he could to sort things out. Before leaving, he turned to Brigadier General Albion Howe, the commander of the Second Division, with whom he had been riding. Segdwick pointed to the rear of Wright's First Division.

"We seem to have succeeded in slipping past their flank, just as Pleasonton predicted. Send one of your aides up to Wright and tell him to continue on to Fairfield. You will follow him. I'm going to go over and get Wheaton back on track."

Standing up in his stirrups, Howe looked above the heads of his own men back toward the Round Tops. "What of our right?" he asked. "I do not see any sign of the Fifth Corps."

Sedgwick didn't bother looking back. "That is not our concern at the moment. I will send word to Sykes to bring up his corps once I have Wheaton's boys in hand. Just make sure you keep up with the First Division." With that, the commanding general of the Sixth Corps dug his spurs into the flank of his horse and took off at a gallop.

Every attack reaches a point at which it is in danger of going too far, or overextending itself. The trick is for a commander to gauge when he is approaching that limit and reign his command in before crossing that line, provided that he has the ability to do so. In the case of Shaler, he never had a chance to regain control before his brigade stumbled into McLaws's waiting men. Unlike the unfortunate Alabamans that they had sent scurrying, the Georgians of W. T. Wofford's brigade had been afforded ample opportunity to form their line of battle and prepare themselves for the coming fight.

As the Union horde drew near, the Georgians leveled their weapons with measured ease and waited for their officers to give the order to fire. Drawing upon every ounce of willpower that they could muster, regimental commanders calmly cautioned their men to remain steady in voices that belied the excitement they felt mounting with each passing second. They would have but one opportunity to bring an end to an advance that would, if they guessed poorly, sweep their men away as well.

Having entered a patch of heavy woods that covered much of Warfield Ridge, the jostling mass of Union soldiers eager to run their fleeing foe to ground did not perceive the danger they were in until the very last minute. Those who had taken the lead during the wild chase were the first to see the waiting wall of grim-faced Confederates. Though they did their best to arrest their mad rush, those who were coming up behind them did not. Anxious to keep going, they pushed those who were doing everything they could to escape the terrible fire that was about to be delivered. It was this moment that the Rebel officers had been waiting for. In quick succession each regiment cut loose with a devastating volley at a range of less than fifty yards.

The effect on Shaler's men was devastating. The slow-moving one-ounce minié balls literally threw the men they hit back into the arms of their companions coming up from behind. The whole confused mass of Yankees recoiled from this sudden turn of events. Officers who had been content to simply follow along now found themselves faced with a crisis. Turning this way and that, they began to push and shove men into some sort of semblance of order. These efforts, however, were quickly cut short as Wofford's Georgians brought their rifles up again and unleashed a second volley that cut through the Union ranks like a scythe through ripe autumn wheat.

The entire Union line staggered, then began to melt away. While not every unit broke, even those that retained some modicum of order had no choice but to retrace their steps. Though the crisis for the Confederates had passed, the contest was far from over.

Even before Shaler's First Brigade received its bloody check, his division commander found that he was having to adjust his line of battle to accommodate the rapidly changing situation he found himself confronted with. As serious as it was to have one third of his entire command slip out from under his control, even more disconcerting was the failure of the Fifth Corps to advance. Throughout the entire movement forward, Wheaton had kept a wary eye over his shoulder. By the time his Second Brigade began their ascent of Warfield Ridge, it was clear to him that he was on his own. His first adjustment to deal with this new set of circumstances entailed a wheeling movement by Eustis's brigade designed to bring that unit into alignment with Shaler's, which had veered to the right and was now facing north. Almost immediately, the Second Brigade made contact with skirmishers McLaws had thrown out to delay and harass the Union advance. Though their fire was accurate, it was not enough to keep the three regiments from Massachusetts and the Second from Rhode Island from coming about and facing that portion of McLaws's line that stretched across Warfield Ridge from east to west.

When completed, the division commander had hoped that he would then be able to drive the Confederates north, along the crest of the ridge. But the sudden reversal of fortunes suffered by his errant brigade and the line that McLaws had established put an end to that. This now forced Wheaton to extend his right flank by bringing up his Third Brigade. While this made up for the missing support that should have been provided by the Fifth Corps, it left him in contact with a determined foe and no reserve, a circumstance that could be tolerated so long as the Confederation did not mount a serious counterattack and Sedgwick did not commit Howe's division elsewhere.

Only when he was satisfied with the deployment of the brigades belonging to Eustis and Colonel Nevin, commander of the Third Brigade, did Wheaton begin to make his way over to where Shaler was doing his best to restore order to his command. He was met halfway by Sedgwick, who demanded a full accounting of his actions. Riding side-by-side just behind the newly established line of bat-

tle, the two general officers discussed the situation while
Wheaton's men exchanged fire with Confederate sharpshooters and skirmishers. When they came across Eustis
standing against a tree, Sedgwick reined in his horse and
asked how things were going. The brigade commander informed his superior that the Confederate fire appeared to
be picking up. "I suspect," he casually mentioned, "that
they will be testing us before too long." Then, taking note
that Sedgwick was mounted, Eustis commented that it
might not be a bad idea for the general to dismount and finish his tour on foot.

The Sixth Corps commander bristled at this suggestion.
Looking out over the heads of his own men in the direction
of the enemy, he made light of the precariousness of his
position. "I would not worry about that," he stated calmly.
He then added in a rather cavalier manner, "They couldn't
hit an elephant at this range," before being shot out of the
saddle.

Stricken with horror, every man who saw their beloved
corps commander go down dropped whatever he was
doing and rushed to his aid. Though hit squarely in the
chest, Sedgwick was still alive, but barely. The gushing of
blood and the rapidity with which color drained from the
general's face was all Wheaton and Eustis needed to see.
The general was dying.

This horrible fact had not taken hold before the entire
Rebel line erupted in a massive volley. Even before the
deafening roar of rifle fire had faded, the familiar high-
pitched shriek that sent chills down the spine of even the
most hardened veteran was raised. Without having to see
it, both Wheaton and Eustis knew that the Rebels were attacking.

After firing, the soldiers of McLaws's division stepped
aside as best they could to make way for Pickett's Virginians. Denied an opportunity to strike a decisive blow the

day before, the soldiers from the Old Dominion were just as anxious to go forward as Sedgwick's men had been less than an hour before.

The Confederates didn't have all the advantages that the earlier Union assault had enjoyed. The regiments belonging to the two brigades leading this counterattack were in the process of redressing their ranks after passing through McLaws's men when they were struck by a devastating volley. Scores of men went down, either shot dead or reduced to a withering heap on the ground. Here and there some units, shorn of their company commanders or thrown into confusion, hesitated. But not all. Some took the pelting in stride and went forward without missing a beat. Others managed to quickly shake off the effects of the galling fire and press on.

The net effect of this uneven response meant that various sections of the Union line were hit by the attacking Rebels at irregular intervals. Some Union units managed to let loose a second volley but not enough to make a difference. This was especially true on the Union left, along the section of the line held by Shaler's jumbled command. There, many a unit had been rattled by the sudden reversal of fortunes they had experienced when checked by the fire delivered by McLaws, leaving them unable to mount an effective defense against the vicious attack being delivered by Pickett's men. While none of the regiments belonging to Wheaton's First Brigade were routed at this time, all gave way and began to withdraw along the axis of their advance.

Sensing that he was gaining ground on his right, Pickett brought up his third brigade, commanded by Brigadier General Lew Armistead. As that officer was passing by, Pickett motioned over to the left, where the units belonging to the Union center were still holding their ground against repeated efforts by Kemper's brigade to break them. "See what you can do, Lew, to help out over there."

Because of the nature of the terrain and patches of thick woods, it took time for regiment commanders holding the center of the Union line to realize that the entire left flank was being thrown back. Hard pressed to hold their own against continuous pressure from Rebels to their front, none were prepared for the raking fire that took them in their own flank as elements of Armistead's men entered the fight. Like dominoes, each of Eustis's regiments was hit and fell away, joining Shaler's men in what was now becoming a general retreat. Only the Second Rhode Island managed to wheel those companies on the left of its line in sufficient time to meet this threat. Wheaton took refuge in the lee of this bulkward together with his staff and that of Sedgwick.

The latter were doing their utmost to protect their mortally wounded commander. While laudable and noble, this concern over the welfare of a man who was on the verge of dying blinded those staff officers to their duties. No one had gone off to inform the next senior officer in the corps, Brigadier General Wright, that he was now in command and that the situation to his right had dramatically changed. Ignorant of what was befalling the rest of the corps on Warfield Ridge, Wright continued to advance his command westward, toward Fairfield, pursuant to the last orders he had been issued. Nor did Wheaton or any of Sedgwick's staff dispatch a rider to bring up a brigade from Howe's Second Division to support the Third Division as Sedgwick had intended to do before being struck down. All of these responses were forgotten as the leadership of the Third Division struggled to deal with the immediate threat they faced, and Sedgwick's attending staff dragged their stricken general about in a desperate search for sanctuary.

Lee found Longstreet with Brigadier General J. B. Robinson of Hood's division. Though his brigade was but a shadow of its former self, the Texans belonging to Robinson were eager to redeem themselves after their shameful flight earlier that morning. With the advance of both Kemper and Armistead checked by the desperate stand being made by the Rhode Islanders, Longstreet explained to his brigadier that it would be up to his men to break the deadlock. "If we can unhinge that unit, the rest will fall away. We'll then be free to sweep down the ridge and fall upon the exposed flank of the enemy divisions as they cross Marsh Creek."

Drawing himself up, Robinson saluted his corps commander. "Sir, my men are Texans. We will not fail you."

Longstreet forced a smile as he returned the salute. With nothing more to do, he stepped aside and watched as Robinson drew his saber, waved it once over his head, and dipped its point to where the standards of the Second Rhode Island fluttered above the thick, dirty white smoke of battle. "Texans, those colors will be ours!" he yelled. "Forward at the double-quick step."

Even Robert E. Lee, sitting serenely astride his favorite horse, could not remain unmoved by the unfolding drama before him. By the time Longstreet had remounted his own animal and trotted over to where his commanding general was waiting, Lee's blood was up. "You have done well, General," he stated before the commander of his First Corps could say a word. "I think if we can punish those people moving against Fairfield, when it comes time for us to go back to Virginia, we will be able to hold our heads up and be proud of what we have achieved here."

Both Lee's demeanor and his words almost brought tears to Longstreet's eyes. At that instant he realized that whatever disappointment his commanding general had harbored over his conduct over the past three days had been forgiven. He was, once more, Lee's most trusted and faithful lieutenant. "There is still much work to be done,

General Lee. And we cannot at all be sure that the day will be ours."

All business now, Lee nodded in agreement. "This is true. But we have them on the run. I will go over to General Hill and have him dispatch Pettigrew's division to your command. Use them to finish what you have started." Then, rising up off his saddle and leaning forward toward Longstreet, Lee raised his hand and brought his fingers together until they formed a tight fist. "Hold on to them, General. Hold on to them and drive them. Grant them no respite. God has given us another chance. Do not squander it as we did on the first day. Pursue them and crush them." Having made his point, the gray-bearded general eased back in his saddle and looked up at the heavens above. "God willing, we will put an end to this terrible affair." With that, he gave Traveler a tug with the reins and trotted off in search of A. P. Hill.

November 2000

History would record that the fourth day of July, 1863, was indeed a glorious day. The ensuing rout of Sedgwick's corps and subsequent retreat from Gettysburg by the Army of the Potomac was hailed in Richmond as a victory without equal. But it would not prove to be decisive. The contest that spelled the end of the Confederate States of America did not take place in Pennsylvania. In fact, the battle that would later be seen as the beginning of the end had already been fought. All that remained to be done on that particular Independence Day to bring a long and frustrating campaign to an end was for an indifferently dressed Union commander to accept the final surrender of all Confederate forces in and around the town of Vicksburg. This capitulation, and not the repulse of Sedgwick's Charge, would be remembered as the turning point of the Civil War.

HISTORICAL NOTES

1. Until the reader comes across the asterisk (*), all events are true. It is at that point that I deviate from fact. Longstreet did order Alexander to go off and stop Pickett. But Alexander did not go, and Longstreet did not repeat the order. Instead, the two men stood there waiting for the other to say or do something. But neither did anything as Pickett's Grand Division came up, and passed through the Confederate gun line and into history.

2. Since Pickett's Charge never took place, on July 3, Winfield Scott Hancock was not shot or wounded that day. One of Meade's more aggressive corps commanders, it is well within reason to imagine that Hancock would have urged a more aggressive response. As it was, Meade did contemplate the exact maneuver described. Hancock's role in this alternate history is simply to expedite that decision.

3. In May, 1864, at Spottsylvania, General Sedgwick was killed in action in an incident very similar to the one described here.

Custer's First Stand

Doug Allyn

As it happened, they were the first Union troops to enter Gettysburg. June 28, 1863, the Fifth and Seventh Michigan Cavalry of the Wolverine Brigade trotted up the Emmitsburg Road on a sleepy summer afternoon, riding easy but alert, the eyes and ears of Fighting Joe Hooker's main Union force.

They looked parade-ground sharp and battle-ready, weapons gleaming, horses fresh and frisky, blue uniforms dusty but dapper.

In addition to sidearms and sabers, each man in the brigade had a spanking new Spencer seven-shot repeating carbine, a gun you could load on Sunday and shoot all week long.

As the Wolverines approached the town, the locals poured out of their homes, lining the streets, applauding, yelling, waving flags, treating their arrival like a holiday. Church bells added to the din of the cheering, and milk-fed lasses sprinted out to drape flower garlands over the men and their mounts.

Freckle-faced Lieutenant Archie Standen glanced at his company commander, Colonel Rivers T. Giles.

"Damn Colonel, if I'd known war was this much fun, I'd have enlisted sooner."

"These same townies will be bitching to Stahel if we commandeer a single damned chicken without paying top dollar for it, Arch. Something's up. They're way too happy to see us. See that the men stay alert. I don't like the feel of this."

As Standen dropped back to pass the word, a local merchant approached Giles and quickly stammered out an explanation for the warm welcome. A ragtag Rebel corps had marched boldly through Gettysburg a few days earlier—Ewell or Jubal Early, he thought. The townie described the Rebs as Attila's Huns reborn, but it sounded like normal foraging for food and supplies to Giles. The Rebs had to live off the land, just as the Yanks did in the South.

Still, it was clear the body of infantry were more than a scouting party. Flankers for a larger force? Giles quickly jotted a note and sent a dispatch rider galloping to the rear to inform General Stahel of what the Wolverines had found and ask for orders.

They came by return messenger. Move out of the town, sweep the area, then await further orders. A pity. Townsfolk were distributing giant slices of steaming fresh bread slathered with apple butter to the riders, Michigan boys hastily stuffing their mouths as they wheeled their mounts and headed out the York Pike.

And away from destiny. If they'd lingered in Gettysburg one more day, the Wolverines would have won the honor of opening the big show. Instead, Buford's cavalry replaced them in the town, and in the history books.

After crossing Rock Creek, the Fifth and Seventh scouted a five-mile sweep to the northeast. They found no sign of Rebels, so they regrouped and camped a few miles from Gettysburg in a field south of the York Pike. An elysian field. Apple and maple groves perfumed the air and provided shade for the men while their animals grazed, knee-deep in clover.

At dusk they were joined by the other half of the Michigan Cavalry Brigade, the First and Sixth Wolverines. Of the four regiments, only the First had seen hard fighting.

Blooded in the Shenandoah Valley campaign, its first
colonel, Thorton Brodhead, had been blown to pieces by a
canister round at Second Manassas. Along with his horse.
The two corpses were so mangled and entangled, the burial detail couldn't be sure where man ended and horse
began, so they simply interred them together. And as
Colonel Charlie Town quipped in his commander's eulogy,
it was only right and proper that a horse soldier journey to
the next world with a good mount beneath him.

Stationed in Washington during the winter of '62
through '63, the First had been refitted, then reinforced by
the other three regiments.

General Stahel's first order was to distribute officers
from the First throughout the command, hoping to stiffen
their green leadership with experienced fighters. An unpopular move. Soldiers prefer to fight and die among
friends.

Colonel Rivers T. Giles, a tall, saturnine lumberman
from Detroit, had been among the officers transferred.
Training with the Seventh throughout the winter had eased
some of his doubts about the new troops.

Few Wolverines had enlisted for the bounty money.
Michigan was hardcore Abolitionist country, the final leg
of the Underground Railway. Rowboats were moored at
regular intervals along the Detroit River, reserved for the
use of runaway slaves fleeing to Canada. Slavehunters
foolish enough to venture into the north country after run-
aways were lucky to get off with a beating. A few had been
lynched. Publicly. Others simply disappeared.

These troops were tough, working-class men—loggers,
storekeepers, schoolmasters. They might be green, but
they believed in the Cause. They'd do.

After an easy spring of minor skirmishes with Reb pickets, new friendships had formed and the brigade was once
again a unified fighting force, the largest all-Michigan unit
in the war.

Still, Giles felt more comfortable with the officers and men of the First Wolverines, his original outfit. After seeing that his men were properly camped, arms at hand, sentries posted, he sauntered over to the First Cavalry's tents and accepted a cup of coffee from its commander, Colonel Charles Town, who was talking to a huge, red-faced Dutchie in soiled farming clothes.

"Any luck today, Rivers?" Town asked.

"Fresh bread, pretty girls, and rumors," Giles replied. "The townsfolk in Gettysburg say a fair-sized Confederate force moved through the area two days ago. Ewell's infantry, or so they believe. Could have been Jubal Early, though."

"Infantry? Interesting," Town smiled. A college boy who could charm a crow off a dead calf, Charlie Town was the perfect staff officer: genial, witty, well-dressed, and well-connected. But no fool. "This gentleman . . . what did you say your name was, sir?"

"Schwimmer. Kurt Schwimmer. I got eighty acres over to—"

"Of course," Town said, cutting the older man off politely. "Mr. Schwimmer tells me he and his neighbors have spotted riders in the distance for several days. To the southeast."

"How many?"

"Many," Schwimmer said, nodding energetically. "Couple dozen each time, and more than one unit. Regular cavalry, not scouts."

"Mr. Schwimmer here is originally from Bavaria," Town added. "Served in the Prussian army before emigrating. He knows cavalry, I think."

"Jeb Stuart?" Giles asked.

"Possibly," Town nodded. "Not the main force, though. But with Ewell to the west of us and Stuart to the east . . ."

"Lee has to be nearby. Southeast, maybe with Stuart

raiding ahead of him. But what's his objective? Harrisburg? Baltimore?"

"Perhaps we can ask him. We've been ordered south to Emmitsburg at first light. From there we'll reconnoiter in force with orders to contact and engage the enemy wherever found. General Stahel intends to direct the search personally."

"From the Emmitsburg Inn, no doubt?" Giles asked dryly.

"Of course," Town grinned. "The general can see a damn-sight farther from a rocker on a hotel porch than from the back of a horse. Good hunting, Rivers, but I'll wager a Reb dollar I spot Jeb Stuart's plume before you do."

"Be careful what you wish for, Charlie," Giles said.

Stuart's cavalry turned out to be the least of their problems. When the brigade arrived at Emmitsburg, they were greeted by baffling new orders, but not from General Stahel. These orders came all the way from Washington.

With Generals Robert E. Lee, Jeb Stuart, Ewell, Longstreet, and half the Confederate army prowling the Pennsylvania countryside, General Pleasonton decided it was the ideal time to reorganize his command, top to bottom.

Fighting Joe Hooker was out as boss of the Army of the Potomac, fired. Replaced by Major General George Meade, the fifth new commander in less than a year.

The Wolverine command had been reshuffled as well. Judson Kilpatrick, a West Pointer originally from New York, was promoted from colonel to brigadier general and given overall command of the division. Even more surprising, active command of the Michigan Brigade went to a junior officer from Monroe who'd been leapfrogged up five grades, from lowly lieutenant to brigadier in one fell swoop.

His name? General George Armstrong Custer.

After meeting briefly with General Meade, Kilpatrick took charge of the division immediately, dismissing General Stahel with a brusque handshake.

As for Custer, no one even knew where he was. On route from Washington, they said.

"Sweet Jesus, what are we in for, Colonel?" Lieutenant Standen asked Giles that night as they sipped chicory coffee in front of their tent. "Do you know any of the new commanders?"

"Served under Kilpatrick in the Shenandoah. Bony little Irishman with big sideburns. His nickname around headquarters was 'Kill Cavalry.' He's hard on animals, harder on men. Sloppy soldier but at least he's game for a fight. I guaran-damn-tee he won't be hunting Jeb Stuart from any rocking chair."

"And Custer?"

"Cinnamon," Giles said grimly. "Custer oils his hair with the stuff. You can smell him at duelling distance. He was a staff flunky in Washington but a fine horseman, or so I was told. By Lieutenant—excuse me—Brigadier General Custer himself. He was a shavetail lieutenant at the time. Met him at a Washington Christmas ball. A firebrand, they say. Talks a good fight but I'm not sure he's ever smelled powdersmoke. All in all, Arch, this war just got a helluva lot more interesting."

Giles was dead right on all counts. At first light, General Kilpatrick rode east out of Emmitsburg at the head of a column to begin the hunt for the legendary General Jeb Stuart.

A damned brief hunt. By late afternoon, scattered units of Wolverines were already tangling with elements of Stuart's cavalry. Fierce skirmishes were exploding along the Hanover Road and points southeast.

With their units dispersed all over the countryside in small search parties, the Wolverines hadn't men enough to

confront Stuart's cavalry head-on. Instead, they exchanged
fire with his scouts wherever they met. And for the first
time in the war, they had an advantage in these fights.

Stuart's horsemen favored the revolver. Some carried as
many as six pistols, two in saddle holsters, two in gunbelts,
and two more in shoulder holsters, giving each rider thirty-
six rounds of rapid fire. But only at short range.

Armed with new seven-shot Spencer repeating carbines, the Wolverines could dismount, touch off a fusillade
of accurate firepower outside of pistol range, then remount
and withdraw, well able to defend themselves even when
outnumbered.

Their tactics were new to the Rebs. In the first years of
the war, the poorly mounted and trained Union cavalry had
no belly for battle. Jeb Stuart dismissed them as plowboys,
and the contemptuous joke among the Yanks was "who's
ever seen a dead cavalryman?"

Both sides were seeing dead cavalrymen now. Leader-
less, with General Kilpatrick miles away, scattered Wolverine units were simply galloping toward the gunfire, wading
into the fighting where they found it. And as more Yanks
continued to arrive, Stuart was forced to send out stronger
forces to drive off the haphazard bands of Wolverine skirmishers.

Ordinarily, Stuart would have formed a front to sweep
the pesky Yanks aside or ride them down. Not today. The
South's grandest cavalier was paying the price for a very
profitable raid.

Thundering past Washington, D.C. (and scaring the hell
out of its politicians), Stuart's cavalry had swept up
through Maryland, commandeering supplies by the cart-
load as they came. Out of touch with Lee for days, Stuart
intended to present his general with an early Christmas
present: an entire wagon train of desperately needed supplies.

But now those same precious supplies were slowing his

advance. For once, it was the Union horsemen who could hit and run while the usually mobile Southerners were forced to defend their lumbering loads of loot, slowed to the snail's pace of their draft animals.

Lieutenant Archie Standen spotted him first.

Standen's squad of ten Wolverines had just exchanged fire with a dozen of Stuart's flankers, dropped two with the first volley, then fled when twenty more Rebs charged down a low ridge, whooping their battle cries.

Wheeling his troop smartly, Standen galloped his men to a clump of aspens on a high knoll a half mile from the road. Piling out of their saddles, the Wolverines hastily formed a tight defensive perimeter, kneeling, shielded by the trees.

The Rebs wisely pulled up just out of rifle range, hooting and catcalling, daring the Yanks to lay down their long arms, to come out and fight with pistols like gentlemen.

Glancing to his rear, Standen saw a rider approaching at a trot, calmly observing the fight. And even with stray slugs whining through the leaves overhead, Standen rose to get a better look.

"What the hell is this?" The rider looked like a circus ring master, with flowing blond locks, a crimson kerchief knotted casually at his throat, and a black velvet cavalry jacket garishly gilded with gold braid on its sleeves. His boots were over the thigh, and one side of his wide-brimmed hat was pinned up by a rosette, giving him the rakish look of a Royalist cavalier straight out of a sixteenth-century painting.

Standen was tempted to blast the rider out of his saddle on general principles, but he held off. And as he drew nearer, Archie recognized the twin rows of brass buttons, the insignia of a brigadier general. Custer. Had to be.

Standen stepped into the open as his new commander reined in his mount. Custer returned his salute with a nod.

"Who's in charge here?"

"I am sir, Lieutenant Archie—"

"I don't mean in charge of this particular hill, Lieutenant," Custer said patiently, as if talking to a child. "Where are your officers?"

"Scattered from hell to breakfast, sir. The brigade divided into search parties to look for Stuart this morning. We found him. I sent riders to inform General Kilpatrick a couple of hours ago. Might take them awhile to locate him though; he's riding with the First."

"I see," Custer nodded, nudging his horse forward to the firing line for a better look, ignoring the snap and whistle of bullets ripping through the foliage around him.

"Sir, you might want to step down," Standen cautioned. "Even at this range a Reb could get lucky."

"I'll wager my luck against Jeb Stuart's any day," Custer said calmly. "Napoleon said 'war favors lucky generals,' Lieutenant. And I intend to be a very lucky general." Rising in his stirrups, Custer doffed his hat and bowed to the Southerners in a mock salute. And drew an angry fusillade of gunfire in return.

"Hey, get down you idiot!" one of the Wolverines yelled from the end of the line. "You'll get us all killed!"

"Take that man's name, Lieutenant," Custer said, then grinned to show he was joking. "I'll see you at the officers' call this evening, Mr. Standen, if not before. Carry on, and good hunting."

Wheeling his mount, Custer trotted off to the northwest as calmly as he'd come.

"Who the hell was that clown?" a trooper asked.

"You don't want to know," Standen replied.

They found out soon enough. Perhaps because he'd been a mere lieutenant the week before, General Custer was all business. At officers' call that evening he accepted introductions just long enough to get each man's name, then asked for reports. When Colonel George Gray of the Sixth launched into a detailed account of his units' running gunfight with the Rebels, Custer cut him off with a curt wave.

"Skip the heroics, Colonel. I assume your men fought well. They're Wolverines, they're supposed to fight well. But Stuart still owns the damned road and he's still moving. Where is he going?"

"I assume he's headed for Hanover, sir," Gray said acidly. "It *is* the Hanover Road after all."

"There's nothing for him in Hanover," Custer countered, ignoring Gray's sarcasm. "Division has informed me that Rebel troops are moving into Gettysburg in force, so I believe we can assume that will be Stuart's ultimate objective. What are your estimates of his strength? Each of you?"

Colonel Gray's educated guess put Stuart's numbers at fifteen thousand, Colonel Russ Alger of the Fifth raised the ante to twenty thousand or more.

"Much too high," Custer said, frowning. "He couldn't feed that many. I doubt very much that he has more than twelve thousand, probably closer to ten. We have five thousand, and since Gregg's been ordered to Gettysburg, we're on our own for the moment. If we face Stuart openly, we'll be crushed to no good purpose. So we'll harry him into Hanover, gentlemen. And make a stand there."

"Hold the town against ten thousand or more?" Colonel Giles of the Seventh asked doubtfully.

"Obviously not," Custer shrugged. "But Stuart can't attack the town in force without leaving his wagons undefended. He's fought hard for those supplies and Lee needs them. I'm betting he'll avoid a pitched battle in order to protect his loot."

"You're betting the whole brigade," Giles pointed out. "Shouldn't we consult General Kilpatrick?"

"He's in Gettysburg, conferring with Meade," Custer

said, a red tinge creeping above his crimson neckerchief. "The decision is mine, Colonel Giles. But you needn't worry; I won't throw you to the wolves alone. I'll be riding with the Seventh tomorrow. And from here on."

"The Seventh?" Charlie Town echoed, frowning. "Sir, the First Cavalry has—"

"—more experience, I know," Custer interrupted curtly. "But seven is my lucky number, Colonel, so the Seventh it is. On the morrow, we'll brace Stuart in Hanover. Assuming the general doesn't choose to slaughter us to the last man, he'll probably veer north toward York. If he does, we'll encourage him. He's a brilliant commander. Without him, Lee is deaf and blind. We can count every minute we keep them apart as a small victory. Any questions?"

There were none, except for the one Archie Standen voiced to Giles afterward. The one they'd all wanted to ask.

"*Assuming* Stuart doesn't choose to slaughter us to the last man? Was General Custer joking?"

"Damned if I know," Giles said. "But he definitely wasn't smiling."

Jeb Stuart dodged Standen's question the next day. And dodged the Wolverines as well. On July 1, after a fierce, probing skirmish on the outskirts of Hanover, Stuart decided against trying to fight his way through the town to reach Gettysburg. He swung his wagon train north instead, toward York, with the Wolverines snapping at his heels all the way.

To Jeb Stuart, the hero of a dozen victorious campaigns, the Michigan Cavalry was little more than an annoyance. Far more troubling was the rumble of guns in the distance. He'd hoped to link up with Ewell well to the north of Gettysburg, in Carlisle or even Harrisburg. The thunder of artillery told him the fight had already begun to the southwest, probably at Gettysburg, and from the sound of the barrages it was no skirmish.

Slowed by his wagons, Stuart's pace was anything but brisk, and Custer and the Seventh easily outraced him to York. Late that afternoon Stuart was again faced with the choice of fighting for a town he didn't want or bypassing it. Again he chose to veer north, this time toward Carlisle.

By continuing his march through the night, Stuart blunted the Wolverine's effectiveness. Sniping in the dark was futile, and as they drew closer to Carlisle, it was Custer's turn to make a choice. He couldn't be sure where Ewell's infantry was, and Stuart's Cavalry already outnumbered the Wolverines. If they were trapped between the two Rebel forces, the brigade would be smashed like a fly on an anvil. It was time to back away.

Leaving four squads of the Seventh to trail and harass Stuart, Custer led the Wolverines south to link up with Gregg and Kilpatrick to shield the Union left at Gettysburg.

While Stuart's long caravan continued its slow march south from Carlisle, the battle of Gettysburg was well into its second day. A bad day for the South.

Early in the afternoon Longstreet attacked Meade's left in front of the Round Tops while Ewell simultaneously attacked on the right. It almost worked. Sickles, commanding Meade's Third Corps had been driven off the Emmitsburg Road and nearly routed. Only the last-second arrival of reinforcements kept Meade's entire left flank from collapsing.

But in the end the attack failed and the Confederates were driven back to their original positions with heavy casualties. Wounded men were left in the open, moaning, crying for mercy in the sodden July heat.

And late in the day, Jeb Stuart finally came trundling into Lee's camp, hauling his overloaded wagons of loot.

Stuart expected General Lee to be thankful for the sup-

plies. He wasn't. Stuart and his cavalry had been missing
in action during two crucial days of the fiercest fighting of
the war. He had come late to the dance, his exhausted men
had been in the saddle nearly forty-eight hours, and his
horses were spent, ridden nearly into the ground.

Bobby Lee was so enraged he almost asked Stuart to
deliver his damned supplies to the men dying in the peach
orchard or the Valley of Death. But Southern gentleman
that he was, General Lee only remarked that it was good of
General Stuart to join them. At long last.

Coming from the impeccably courteous Lee, the mild
rebuke stung Stuart like a slap in the face. He tried to apol-
ogize, but Lee waved it off. Stuart had missed two days of
hard fighting, but perhaps he had arrived in time to finish
this battle for good and all, to destroy Meade's army and
the Northern will to fight, with a single, bold stroke.

Lee's plan was brutally simple. Pickett's division would
strike the Union center on Cemetery Ridge, supported by
elements of Hill's and Longstreet's brigades, an irresistible
assault force of nearly fifteen thousand men. Ewell would
attack Culp's Hill at the same time. And in the confusion,
Stuart would circle wide around Meade's right, smash into
the thinly defended Union rear, and tear it apart. Forced to
defend two fronts, Meade would surely surrender. Or be
destroyed.

An elegant plan, Stuart agreed. And it would work. He
would see to it. He would not fail his general again.

But the best laid plans . . .

Shifting fifteen thousand troops at once is tricky business. In the morning, Lee had considerable difficulty moving Pickett's men and the supporting troops into position.

Dick Ewell couldn't wait. His men had infiltrated
halfway up Culp's Hill in the night, and as dawn broke,
they found themselves well within range of Union riflemen. Both sides commenced firing as soon as they could
see each other.

Forced to begin his attack early, Ewell's Rebs made a valiant charge for the summit. But the Union troops on the hilltop had been reinforced during the night and were firing from the cover of trees and trenches. The Confederates were driven back to the foot of Culp's Hill with heavy losses. By mid-morning Ewell's part in the fight was already over. And Lee was still doggedly moving Pickett's massive assault force into place.

It was an eerie time. As noon approached, the sprawling battlefield fell nearly silent. A tense silence. On Cemetery Ridge, Union troopers dug in deeper or rigged tents for shade, waiting, listening to distant shouted commands and the squeak of Confederate gun carriages as Lee assembled his overwhelming assault force. And then even those noises faded away.

Satisfied that his men were properly placed, Lee rested them for an hour. Meade joined Brigadier General John Gibbon for a leisurely lunch with General Hancock and a few staff officers on the reverse slope of Cemetery Ridge. Hardbitten old soldiers, hats off, lounging in the shade, eating boiled chicken, chatting. Waiting to fight. To kill or die.

A few miles to the southeast, Custer and the Wolverines were also waiting, but not quietly. Still new to his command, Custer spent the morning inspecting his troops, shifting their positions to no particular purpose. Fidgeting. Eager for a fight.

At noon Stuart led the brigades of General Wade Hampton, Fitz Lee, and Jenkins out of Gettysburg, heading east on the York Pike. Three miles out, he suddenly veered south off the road, leading his men up Cress Ridge.

Leaving his men concealed in the trees, Stuart rode out to scout the ground personally.

Peaceful. Only a few Union pickets in the distance. No threat to his forces. From the ridge, Stuart could see for miles: All the roads, supply wagons, and defenses of the

Union rear stretched out before him like markers on a battle map.

Directly ahead were the house and barns of John Rummel. Beyond them? Nothing. Flat, open fields that
stretched three quarters of a mile to the Hanover Road. Undefended. Perfect terrain for cavalry action. Satisfied, he
rejoined his troops, ordered his field guns to deploy, and
then waited.

Near the center of General Lee's line at the peach orchard, a single Confederate gun fired, white powder smoke
wafting slowly toward the clear sky . . . and then the entire
universe suddenly erupted in thunder.

All along the Rebel line, from the orchard to the slopes
west of Gettysburg, 140 Confederate cannons fired in one
long, rolling barrage, the heaviest bombardment of the
war.

The unearthly din was so stunning, so utterly overpow-
ering, that Union gunners who attempted to return fire
could scarcely hear the roar of their own artillery. To the
Yank troops cowering on Cemetery Ridge, it seemed that
hell itself had opened to rain down fire and destruction.
The entire valley below was a mass of roiling smoke,
pierced by flashes of gunfire from invisible cannons.

On Cress Ridge, Stuart heard the cannonade, understood what it meant, and ordered his own gunners to prepare to fire a single round each to the four points of the
compass to signal Lee that his cavalry was in place and
ready.

But even as his artillerymen made ready, Stuart realized
that most of the distant Confederate barrage wasn't achiev-
ing the desired effect. The Rebel gunners had aimed just a
bit too high. Instead of sweeping Cemetery Ridge, the
shells were falling on the far side, crashing to earth amid
the supply wagons and ambulances.

Terrified, the sutlers, corpsmen, and observers whipped
their teams to a gallop and fled for their lives in a panicky

rout, leaving the roads and fields to the rear of Cemetery Ridge empty and practically unguarded. The Confederate barrage may not have softened Cemetery Ridge for Pickett, Stuart noted grimly, but they had blown the back door to the Union rear wide open for General Jeb Stuart and his cavalry brigades. He couldn't have planned it better himself.

On the far side of the ridge, through the smoke of the incredible cannonade came the most magnificent Confederate advance of the war. Fifteen thousand Rebels in triple ranks, battle flags fluttering overhead, sunlight gleaming on bayonets and gun muzzles, moved forward in a line that stretched more than a mile.

Flowing irresistibly out of the trees into the open, the Rebs paused to dress their lines as though marching on parade. Once aligned, they surged forward into the Valley of Death in almost complete silence.

The Rebel artillery held their fire as the infantry passed through their lines, the Union gunners held theirs to conserve ammunition, and the massive front was still out of rifle range. So they advanced in an eerie hush. The only sounds were the crunch of their own boots and occasional muted commands of Rebel officers.

And it was in this silence that Robert E. Lee heard the distant discharge of a single field gun, firing to the four points of the compass.

General Lee wasn't the only one who heard the Confederate signal. Russ Alger's Fifth Michigan were dismounted, concealed in a grove, shielding the Union rear just beyond the Hanover Road. Running toward the sound of the Confederate gun, they swarmed out of the woods, taking up positions along the stone and split-rail fences of Rummel's Farm.

General Kilpatrick had inspected the area earlier, but then had received orders to move the Wolverine brigades around the Union left to reinforce Round Top. Kilpatrick left straightaway, leaving Custer to gather up the widely dispersed Wolverines and follow. But shortly after Kilpatrick pulled out, word came that Stuart had been spotted on the York Pike headed east, leading a considerable force.

Custer, pacing nervously in front of his tent, dismissed the trooper who brought the news, thought a minute, then turned to Colonel Giles.

"Tell the men to hold their positions, Colonel. We won't be joining General Kilpatrick."

Giles blinked in surprise. "But our orders—"

"The situation's changed. Stuart isn't leaving this fight, he's circling. If we follow Kilpatrick, there'll be open ground between Stuart and Cemetery Ridge. I intend to counter that move, on my responsibility. Is there any part of that order you don't understand, Colonel?"

"No, sir," Giles said, saluting. "I'll see to it."

"Do that. And we'll dispense with the discussion next time," Custer called after him.

Giles had just passed the word to Charlie Town when gunfire erupted near Rummel's Farm.

"That's the Fifth," Giles said, wheeling his horse, "and it sounds like a helluva lot more than a scuffle. Hold your men here, Colonel. I'll find Russ and get word back to you as soon as I can."

Galloping off to locate the Fifth, Giles spotted Custer in the distance, leading the Seventh Cavalry toward the fighting. As they neared the farm, they began meeting troopers from Alger's Fifth, pulling back, out of ammunition. The Fifth's orderly retreat promptly dissolved into confusion as Custer and the Seventh blundered into them. Blocked by the stone fences, with no room to maneuver, the tangled Wolverine units made perfect targets for Rebel skirmishers who were moving up, sniping from the fences.

Red-faced and cursing, with men dropping all around him, Custer somehow reassembled the Seventh amid the confusion, then led a charge toward the fences, forcing the Rebels to give up their positions and pull back.

Giles found him in the open, methodically firing his pistol at the distant Confederate positions though they were well out of range.

"General, new orders have come from General Kilpatrick. The Rebels are making an all-out assault on Cemetery Ridge. The Wolverines are to deploy on foot here and fight a delaying action. We're to hold to the last man if we must, but above all, we're to keep Stuart out of the fight."

"I believe you've misunderstood General Kilpatrick's orders, Colonel."

"No, sir, I—"

"You've misunderstood!" Custer snapped. "Or Kilpatrick has. We're horse-soldiers, we don't make *last stands*!" He fairly spat out the words. "We'll keep Stuart out of the fight all right, but not by turning ourselves into infantry. Stuart's not the only cavalryman who knows how to circle. Tell Colonel Town I'll join him with the Seventh on the road. We'll form a battle line and prepare to charge. Stuart will think he's seeing our entire force. When he moves against us, you and Alger will strike him from the rear with the Fifth and Sixth. With luck, we'll end his threat once and for all."

"With luck?" Giles echoed in disbelief. "Sir, we're greatly outnumbered here. Firing from the cover of the stone walls, our new carbines will give us the only advantage we have."

"Advantage be damned! This will be a cavalry battle, the biggest of the war! We're better armed, better mounted and we're by-God Wolverines!" Custer roared. "I can lead the Seventh Cavalry through any army on earth, Colonel, and you'll either carry out my orders in the next five seconds or I'll see your brains on the ground, sir! Now move!"

For a moment, death was in the air between them. Giles

was facing a jumped-up lieutenant with delusions of
grandeur while Custer saw a battle-weary mossback made
timid by fear of Stuart. A single word, an incautious movement, and they might have killed each other. But the moment passed. They were both soldiers, after all.
Wolverines.

"I'll see to it . . . General," Giles said, swallowing the
bile rising in the back of his throat. Snapping a proper
salute which Custer ignored, Giles wheeled his mount and
galloped off to find Alger.

On Cress Ridge facing Rummel's Farm, Stuart was
growing impatient.

"Those damned skirmishes at the walls are slowing our
advance, Wade," he said to General Hampton. "Take your
brigade . . . wait! Good lord, what have we here?"

Nearly a mile away on the Hanover Road, a single regiment of Union cavalry, the First Michigan, was deploying
in line. When their ranks were dressed, a second unit, the
Seventh, moved in front of them to form a forward rank.
At Charlie Town's order, the two regiment lines drew their
sabers, then settled in their saddles. Waiting.

"I'll be damned," Stuart said softly. "I do believe they
mean to challenge us in the field." The two hard-bitten
generals glanced at each other, grinning as gleefully as
boys on Christmas morning.

"Well, sir," Hampton nodded, "shall we accommodate
them?"

"We aren't seeing their whole force," Stuart cautioned.
"There are only fifteen hundred or so at the road. I expect
their reserves will attack us from one side or the other. No
matter. Tell the men to draw sabers and save their sidearms
for Cemetery Ridge. I mean to carve my way through these
country plowboys, strike the Union rear like Jove's thun-
derbolt, and win the damned day for Bobby Lee."

Taking tactical command, Hampton quickly deployed
his own and Fitz Lee's brigades into a column of

squadrons, facing south toward the Union line on Hanover
Road. It was perfect ground for a cavalry fight, flat and un-
obstructed for nearly three quarters of a mile, bordered by
stone fences and trees, as neatly arranged as a Roman
arena built for blood sports.

For a moment, the two lines of armed men faced each
other in silence. Then, as if signaled by the God of War,
both sides began to advance at a walk, the seasoned veterans of the Confederate cavalry facing the fresher but relatively untested Wolverines.

Screened by the trees along the fence, Giles watched
Fitz Lee and Hampton come. After delaying his entrance
as long as he could for dramatic impact, Custer rode out of
the trees and placed himself at the head of the advancing
Seventh.

Slowly the two sides drew nearer. Half a mile. Then
less. At the quarter mile, again as if by the same signal,
both lines of horse soldiers spurred their mounts to a trot.

"My God, Russ," Giles whispered to Colonel Alger.
"What a magnificent sight."

And it was. The grandest spectacle of warfare, twin
lines of cavalry moving toward each other in perfect alignment. In the distance, Lee's artillery barrage fell silent, as
though the whole world had stopped fighting in order to
watch.

"Custer may be a maniac," Alger muttered, "but by God
he's no coward."

Out in front of his troops by at least four lengths in his
circus-rider regalia, Custer was easily the most visible target on the battlefield. Yet no Rebs sniped at him. In this
arena, it would have been sacrilege.

With the distances rapidly narrowing, Custer rose in his
stirrups and raised his saber. "Bugler! Sound charge!
Come on, you Wolverines!" And he was off.

Across the field, Wade Hampton's bugler answered,
and the entire Confederate line surged forward at the gal-

lop, their thundering hooves drowning the battle roar from Gettysburg as Pickett's men were nearing the crest of Cemetery Ridge.

Both battle lines were sweeping toward each other at full gallop now, men crouching in their saddles, howling like mad dogs, raised sabers gleaming in the afternoon sun.

As Giles wheeled his mount to lead the strike at the Confederate rear, he suddenly turned to Alger. "Hold your men here, Russ. Dismount them, get them to the walls where they can do some good."

"But Custer—"

"—wants his obituary in history books! Get the First to the walls! If they break through us, the road to Gettysburg is open for them!"

Without waiting for a reply, Giles spurred away, joined George Gray at the head of the Sixth, and began leading them in a wide circle around the trees.

In the center of the field, the Blue and Gray lines smashed into each other with a horrendous impact. Screaming horses were bowled over like tenpins, trampled to death with their riders.

Sabers rang, men shouting and cursing, wheeling their lathered animals, desperately pivoting in their saddles to slash at each other like barbarians.

A roiling cloud of gray dust rose, turning the battlefield into a hazy welter of blood and iron. The first Confederate surge nearly carried them through the Union lines, but amid the confusion and carnage of hand-to-hand combat, their superior numbers didn't mean much. There was no way to bring them to bear.

Then, just as it looked as though the Wolverines would have to give way, Giles and the Sixth broke out of the trees onto the battlefield. With the fight a whirling maze of mad-dened hand-to-hand combat, Giles had no clear target to charge. Instead, his troopers spurred forward at a gallop and threw themselves into the battle, one-on-one.

More evenly matched now, the fight swayed back and forth over the field, the advantage first tilting toward one side, then the other. Smaller groups were spinning off from the main like eddies near a whirlpool, men fighting to the death in single combat like knights of old, wounded, dying, falling to be trampled by the crazed animals. Or killing without a whit of mercy or even a moment's triumph, then spurring back into the fray to kill again.

And now Alger's dismounted riflemen began to have an impact. As the combatants spread out, they made better targets, and the Fifth began to pour accurate fire into the fight, reducing the odds against the Wolverines one dead Rebel at a time.

Here and there wounded men tried to surrender, but for the most part, no quarter was asked or given. This was no duel, there was no honor at stake on Rummel's Farm, only butchery, warriors reduced to their basest denominator, hacking each other to pieces.

But as the clash wore on, Hampton's horsemen were wearing out. His troopers had been in the saddle for three days with only a few hours' rest. Jaded mounts and road-weary riders began to fade under the ferocity and firepower of the Wolverine Brigade. The Rebels simply hadn't the stamina to continue fighting hand-to-hand much longer.

They'd begun the battle with the advantage of greater numbers, but those numbers were quickly melting away as Alger's regiment, shielded by the stone fences, continued to pour a withering fire into the Confederate ranks with their new Spencer repeating carbines, the fusillade growing more furious as they were joined by stragglers from the rear guard of Cemetery Ridge.

From his observation point on Cress Ridge, Stuart watched the battle seesaw, hoping for a breakthrough but knowing his exhausted men couldn't sustain the pace much longer. The rolling thunder of distant guns told him the fight for Cemetery Ridge must be nearing its peak while he was stuck in this damned field. He was failing Bobby Lee again, but if he didn't withdraw his men soon, there'd be none left to save.

Suddenly, in the thick of the fight, Wade Hampton took a saber cut across the head and went down. And seeing his friend fall was the final straw for General Jeb Stuart.

With an oath, he spurred his mount down the ridge, drawing his saber, heading for the fight. In an instant, his staff officers, reserves, and even the artillery, were in full flight behind him, whooping their war cries, gladly following Jeb Stuart's plume into battle or to hell, if need be.

The noise and dust raised by the gun carriages made the little Confederate force seem much larger than it actually was, and its approach lifted the spirits of Fitz Lee's and Hampton's brigades. And froze the guts of Custer's cavalry.

Shouting "To me! To me!" Stuart and his officers tore a swath through the middle of the swirling fight, galvanizing his troops, pulling them together by the sheer force of his passage and personality. Custer was a courageous leader, but Stuart was a true chieftain, an avatar on horseback, scion of an unbroken line of warriors from the dawn of time. And his men rallied to him, knowing his presence meant they would somehow win, their courage and fighting spirit soaring as the sparks flew upward.

Dazed, exhausted, thinking they were being overrun by Rebel reinforcements, the Union cavalrymen began to disengage, retreating toward the shelter of the stone walls for protection.

Their swirling, milling withdrawal kept Alger's regiment from firing at the Confederates as they hurtled past, and then it was too late. Stuart's brigade vaulted the last low fence and rolled over the Hanover Road, galloping cross-country in an unruly mob, headed for the rear of Cemetery Ridge.

Both Custer and Giles instantly realized what was happening, but Stuart's desperate charge had scattered the Wolverines and their officers wasted precious moments gathering the regiments before sounding the charge and setting off after Stuart.

They were only a quarter mile behind, but their rifles were useless now. Stuart's mounts and gun carriages were raising so much dust, the Yanks couldn't see well enough to shoot.

General Jeb Stuart, meanwhile, was reorganizing his veteran cavalry command at the gallop, reforming his units, dressing his lines. By the time they splashed through Rock Creek and thundered onto Baltimore Pike, Stuart's brigades were once again in near-perfect order.

Swinging northwest on the pike, the Rebels raced down the open road for a mile before swinging sharply west again, riding to the sound of the guns.

At the Taneytown Road, Stuart halted his mad gallop just long enough to redress his lines, then the bugler sounded the charge and his brigade was off, whooping their battle cries, racing through the supply depot, sabering the sentries and drivers, seizing the wagons with their precious ammunition, then sprinting on to smash into the lightly defended rear of Cemetery Ridge.

Slashing through the thin line of skirmishers, Stuart's Rebels goaded their stumbling mounts to the top of the ridge and into the climax of the fiercest fighting of the war.

Pickett's men had reached the summit only moments before, drawing a swarm of Union skirmishers toward them. But as Stuart's brigade, some three and a half thousand strong, swept onto the road atop the ridge, firing their pistols point-blank into Yank troops whose defenses were facing the wrong way, the Union realignment turned into a rout.

Already deafened by Lee's cannonfire and shaken by Pickett's tenacity, Meade's infantry was shattered by Stuart's sudden appearance. Boiling out of their useless firing pits, they fired hastily into the milling whirl of the fight, then scattered for their lives to keep from being sabered or ridden down.

Heartened by the sight of Stuart's battle flags on the crest, the usually wary Lee threw the last of his reserves into the fight, ordering Longstreet and Ewell to renew their attacks on the flanks.

From the north end of the ridge, Meade saw not only Stuart's brigade but a second train of riders behind him, covered with the gray dust raised by Stuart's guns.

Assuming the Wolverines were more Rebel cavalry, Meade hastily gave the order to withdraw and reorganize. Moments later, when the Wolverines began exchanging fire with Stuart's rear guard, Meade realized his mistake and tried to rescind his order. His sudden reversal threw the Union command into total disarray, officers screaming contradictory orders at troopers streaming down the ridge, running like rabbits from cavalry where there could be no cavalry.

As his troops swept the Yanks from Cemetery Ridge, General Jeb Stuart swiveled in his saddle to peer down into the swirling roil of Wolverines who were desperately trying to fight their way through the firing line of his rear guard at the foot of the ridge.

Stuart tried to spot the outrageously garbed officer who'd led the initial Union charge at Rummel's Farm. But amid the confused carnage and dust, men looked so much alike that some were killing their own by accident. Perhaps Custer was dead already.

He wasn't. When Meade's bugler sounded recall, both sides gradually stopped fighting, disengaging by an unspoken agreement born of honor and exhaustion. Men who'd been slaughtering one another like rabid wolves a moment before backed warily away, arms at the ready.

Atop Cemetery Ridge, Pickett's men ceased firing without an order. They'd seen slaughter enough. Let the Yanks take their wounded and go.

It was over. They'd won.

Retreating east on the Taneytown Road, Giles saw Custer trotting his lathered, dusty mount away from the battle. He expected a tongue-lashing for violating his orders but didn't get one. The baby general rode by him without so much as a glance. Jaw clenched, eyes still glazed with the madness of battle, Custer was staring into some unimaginable distance. As though he was still locked in a faraway fight against an unseen enemy.

The rain thrumming softly on General Kilpatrick's tent provided a mournful accompaniment to the squeaks and groans of springless carts carrying the Union wounded south on the road to Emmitsburg.

The Union rout at Gettysburg was an unmitigated disaster. Countless dead, perhaps twenty-thousand, and twice that number wounded. So many prisoners the Rebs were paroling them to save their supplies.

Meade had been recalled to Washington. Rumors had Fighting Joe Hooker being reinstated as commander of the Army of the Potomac, but it didn't matter. He had damned few troops left to command.

Peace was in the air. With Baltimore and Washington itself threatened by Lee's triumphant forces, Lincoln would have no choice but to recognize the Confederate States of America as a reality. And soon. President Jefferson Davis was said to be traveling north to congratulate the victors at Gettysburg.

Perhaps he would confer with Lincoln on his return journey and it would all be over by the fall.

*   *   *

Brigadier General Judson Kilpatrick and his staff were poring over a drastically revised battle map when Custer strode in and saluted smartly. If Kilpatrick was surprised by Custer's outrageous regalia—the velvet jacket, buccaneer boots, and slouch hat—he managed to conceal it. He motioned to his aides to leave them, but when they were finally alone, Kilpatrick simply stared at Custer for a time, his face unreadable.

"You had bad luck in battle yesterday," Kilpatrick said at last.

"Yes, sir, I—"

"Luck should never have been a factor!" Kilpatrick snapped, cutting him off. "Your orders were to make a stand, not divide your force and take on Stuart hand-to-hand. You risked not only your own life and those of your men, you gambled away the Army of the Potomac and the cause for which we fight! We were not yours to toy with, Custer. Nor were the Wolverines chips to be wagered recklessly just because you felt lucky."

"Napoleon said 'war favors lucky generals,' sir."

"Napoleon died defeated and disgraced!" Kilpatrick snapped. "And you're no Napoleon, sir. What you are is a damned reckless, insubordinate . . ." He turned away, swallowing hard to control his rage. "Hero," he finished.

"Sir?"

"Oh yes, Custer, you're one of the heroes of this fight. If it were up to me, I'd order you shot for flagrant disregard of orders in the field, and I'd gladly take a place in the firing squad myself. But shooting you would only inflict further damage to morale which is at rock bottom already. If we're to salvage anything from our reverses at Gettysburg, we'll need heroes. There's no question you and your Wolverines fought bravely, so for the moment at least, you're a hero, sir."

"Thank you."

"Don't thank me, Custer. Pack your bags instead. I intend to transfer you out my command at the first opportunity. To the west, if I can. Your schoolyard tactics are better suited to fighting red Indians than real soldiers."

"I will, of course, serve wherever my country needs me," Custer said mildly. "With the grand actions of this war nearly over, the west might suit me better at that. There's still adventure to be had there. But if I'm a ... hero of this fight, as you say, I wonder if I might ask one favor?"

"I owe you no favors, sir! Now get out, and see to your men."

"Yes, sir." Custer snapped to attention, gave Kilpatrick a perfect parade-ground salute, and wheeled to leave.

"Custer?"

"Sir?" Custer paused in the tent doorway, his garish costume outlined against the gray drumming of the rain.

"What favor?"

"If I'm to be exiled to the west, sir, would you see to it that my new cavalry outfit has a seven in its title? Seven is my lucky number."

"My God, sir, you haven't heard a word I said, have you?" Kilpatrick sighed. "You don't even understand what you've done. Well, sometimes it's better to be lucky than competent, Custer. You're living proof of that. And since luck is your only edge, far be it from me to dull it. I'll get you command of a seventh cavalry unit somewhere. But God help you when your luck runs out."

"He will, sir," Custer said with a grin, "I'm sure of it." He wheeled and stalked out.

Kilpatrick stared after him, shaking his head. "God help you, sir," he repeated softly. "And God help the Seventh Cavalry."

Author's Note

On the third day of the battle, General George Armstrong Custer and the Michigan Wolverine Brigade did indeed meet Jeb Stuart's warriors in one of the most spectacular cavalry battles of the war. Savage as the fight was, it has been largely dismissed by historians as a mere footnote to the larger battle. It ended in a standoff, and what were a few thousand dead horse-soldiers compared to the carnage on Cemetery Ridge?

But, as General Charles King noted at the time, if Stuart's cavalry had "come charging furiously at the rear of our worn and exhausted infantry even as Pickett's devoted Virginians assailed their front, no man can say what scenes of rout and disaster might have occurred."

But they didn't. Out of ammunition and about to be overrun, Custer mounted a reckless saber charge, fought Stuart to a standstill, and kept him out of the big show. The action forged Custer's reputation as a firebrand and made him one of the media darlings of the war.

But if a man's character determines his destiny, George Armstrong Custer's fate at the Little Bighorn was probably carved in stone on that sunny July afternoon in 1863, at a small farm three miles from Gettysburg.

—D. A.

In the Bubble

William H. Keith, Jr.

Thursday, July 2, 1863, 8:50 P.M.

Under the mercifully advancing darkness, he rode up the
Emmitsburg Pike from the south, drinking in the impres-
sions, the flavor, the heavy, smoke-tasting atmosphere of
battle. His aides and the scout assigned to guide him across
the unfamiliar terrain, sensing his mood, perhaps, hung
back a bit, granting him a respectful privacy.

Nothing at West Point, nothing in twenty-one years of
military service, nothing of his experiences at First and
Second Manassas, at the Peninsula or Fredericksburg, not
even the bloody horror of Sharpsburg, had prepared him
for *this*.

Lieutenant General James Longstreet guided his horse
gently around a tangle of smashed cannon, splintered tree
trunks, and broken-down fence rails. Along the roadside,
small groups of dazed and weary scarecrow soldiers
looked up from their evening cook fires as the party
passed. Some, recognizing him, stood and saluted; others
simply stared, numb with exhaustion and shock.

"We whupped 'em, Gen'ral!" one ragged veteran called
out. "We done *whupped* 'em!"

Longstreet managed a smile at the man . . . one of
Barksdale's Mississippians, he thought. Poor Barksdale—
dead or captured in the mêlée this afternoon, along with so

many of his men. But the spirit of those who'd survived that day was still unshaken. *Unconquerable.*

"That we did, boys," Longstreet replied. "Well done! Well done, all of you!" And someone in the gathering crowd whipped up a cheer.

Perhaps the victory had been less than he'd hoped for, but it *was* victory, nonetheless. And if there'd been a failure of coordination at the highest levels of the Army of Northern Virginia, there'd been nothing whatsoever lacking in the zeal of the men who'd fought here this day.

Thunder continued to mutter and rumble to the northeast. That would be Ewell, throwing his corps against the enemy's right . . . but late, too late. Old Dick might yet succeed against the hills anchoring the Yankee right, but it wouldn't help *here*, where the army had come within the proverbial hairsbreadth of crushing the Federals in a victory capping a year of victories, and this time on their home soil.

Scant hours before, the Confederate legions had swept across this ground, unstoppable, unconquerable, a headlong rush smashing with fire and bayonet through the perilously extended and unsupported left flank of the Union army, storming patches of ground and woods and farmland bearing names immortal from this day on—the Peach Orchard, the Rose Woods, the Wheat Field, Trostle's Farm.

The arms of the Confederacy had come so *damnably* close to complete victory this day. By every reasonable measure, the Army of Northern Virginia had triumphed, smashing the exposed left wing of the Army of the Potomac and driving it back in tumbled disarray nearly a mile to the high ground to the east. And for a tantalizing few hours late this afternoon, his forces had clawed at the bloody slopes of those hills. Evander Law's Alabamians had been within an ace of sweeping the Federal forces from one rocky, half-naked eminence that would have put them in a position to roll back the entire enemy flank.

And just an hour ago, with the sun slowly setting on the tangled, crimson horror of this day's carnage, Wright's Georgians had battled all the way to the crest of the low ridge marking the center of the Yankee line. Unsupported and exhausted, the Georgians had been nearly cut off by the last-second arrival of Union reinforcements and had had to cut their way out.

That same pattern—of initial success, with complete victory thwarted at the last moment by enemy reinforcements hurried in from other portions of their line—had dogged the Confederates time after time as they'd hammered at the southern end of the Yankee line. How many times had complete victory been within the Confederates' grasp? If Anderson had supported the attack on the Union center, if McLaws had succeeded in storming the hills anchoring the Union right, if Ewell had just attacked when he was supposed to, if, if, if . . .

We came so close. So very close . . .

This was the bend in the Emmitsburg Pike where the party should have borne off to the left, to pick up the long, north–south rise of Seminary Ridge. General Lee's forward command post was there, just opposite the enemy's center across the valley on Cemetery Ridge. He'd intended to seek the general out, to raise again the prospect of a flanking march. Put half of the army astride the trio of roads leading south from the town toward Washington, and the shaken Federals would *have* to come down off those heights.

It would be Fredericksburg all over again, and a victory that might well end this savage conflict and win independence for the South.

But other soldiers were crowding around now, drawn by the cheer, momentarily blocking his way. They looked up at Longstreet in the gathering dusk, the haggard faces of men who'd given all that had been asked of them, and far, far more.

"We'uns almost had the damned blue bellies t'day, General," one called out. "Give us the word and we'll hit 'em agin t'morrow and send 'em all a-scamperin' clean back to Washington!"

Longstreet reined up his horse, studying the faces, the eyes of the men around him. Their spirit was strong, yes, but what he noticed now was their eyes . . . their *eyes*, glazed and haunted with having seen too much.

How could he order such men, men who'd given so much, to charge into the maelstrom of hellfire again? Gunfire continued to rumble in the distance as Ewell's attack gained momentum. He hesitated.

"General?" his adjutant said, walking his horse up alongside. "Aren't we going up to find General Lee?"

Longstreet knew the battle, his career, the survival of the army, of the Confederacy itself, all hung in the balance. So much depended on what decisions were made next.

"No," he said at last. He'd been riding north to rejoin General Lee, who should at this moment be at his command post on Seminary Ridge, to discuss with him the successes—and failures—of this day. He'd been determined to make one last appeal, even though Lee seemed unshakable in his determination to fight this thing through on *this* line, on this ground.

But the faces of these men . . .

"No," he said again, deciding. "These men have done their part. The final victory must be left to others."

He pulled his horse's head back around, facing south.

"But it ain't finished yet, sir," an aide said. "General Lee should've followed your advice, General. He—"

Longstreet silenced the man with a look. He would tolerate no criticism of the army's commander and his friend.

"We have not been so successful as we'd wished," he said after a moment. Strange, having made his decision, he felt almost at peace. "But for now, we have *done* our part."

He shook the reins and urged his mount forward.

"I'm in the bubble," he muttered, more to himself than to any of the others. "I'm *in the bubble*. . . ."

"What did he say?" the aide asked, scratching his head.

"Beats th' hell out of me," another officer replied. "C'mon. It's been a hell of a long day."

Longstreet ignored them. Part of him was musing on the words he'd just uttered. What *had* he meant by those enigmatic words, which had surfaced unbidden from his melancholy thoughts? What bubble?

Another part of him, though, was too excited to care. . . .

Friday, July 2, 2038, 9:25 P.M.

"Yeah, man, when I'm in the bubble," John McIntyre said, "nothing else exists for me. It's like I'm *there*." He tossed back the last of his rum and Coke, and signaled the waitress for another.

Moments before, he'd emerged from the simlink in the basement of the Student Union Building, blinking at the sudden fall from the virtual reality simulation playing in his brain to the mundane reality of his leather-padded recliner and its array of sim connects and bundled fiber-optic feed cables. After logging out with the student manning the desk in the Union computer cluster, he'd emerged into the warm July evening and walked across the quad to the Lee's Arms, just off-campus.

The place was crowded tonight. Years ago, the Lee's Arms had become a watering hole and social rally point for the Greater Washington Area Gaming Society, and it was always full after an event, but this weekend the place was insane. McIntyre and his circle of gaming buddies from Georgetown University had managed to grab their usual booth, but only because their day's contributions to the festivities were finished now and they'd arrived early.

"So. What's this 'in the bubble' stuff I keep hearing?" Randy Stuart wanted to know. He was a new recruit to the ranks of wargaming and was still wrestling with some of the specialist language.

"It's an old simmer's term," Christine Dell told him. She'd pulled her chair around to snuggle against McIntyre. The two had been lovers for some months now and still reveled in the warmth of intimate touch. "I used to hear my dad talk about it when he was into this, back when they were called recreationists. It means you're so into the scene, the history, the atmosphere . . . it's all so realistic, that you really do think you're there."

McIntyre grinned as he gently stroked the back of Dell's head. "Yeah, I've heard the old-timers could get pretty caught up in it all, even without VR and God!" The waitress brought his drink, and he disentangled from Christine long enough to take the glass and have a sip. "It's better nowadays, though. More real than anyone could imagine. Nothing like it in the world!"

"Shit," Greg Howarth said, laughing. "I thought simmer recreationists were always pining for the good old days when they had to hand sew their uniforms and spend a few thousand dollars on authentic hardware!"

"Ha! You think I'd do this if I *really* had to sleep on the cold ground and eat chunks of beef half-warmed and half-charred over an open fire? That's just nuts!"

A loud cheer went up elsewhere in the pub. "Ah-ha!" Howarth said, turning in his seat. "There goes Toby's right!"

"About damned time," McIntyre said. "What's he been playing at all day?"

On the big, floor-to-ceiling wallscreen on the back wall, knots of men in gray rushed up a steep and naked slope, the flash of their musketry stabbing and sparking in the deepening gloom. The computer was adjusting light levels for the viewers, of course, so that they could see what was

going on. The time readout in the upper right corner read
9:42 P.M., Thursday, July 2, 1863, and in the Reality, twi-
light had long ago given way to night. The voice of a news
commentator droned on above the crack and rattle of muskets and the deep-throated boom of massed artillery.

Toby was Toby James, a member of the Georgetown
group, and tonight he was simming General Jubal Early of
the Confederacy. The troops depicted on the big screen
were Hays's brigade of Early's First Division, the
Louisiana Tigers, and they were rushing the Federal guns
emplaced atop Cemetery Hill. In the background, just visible through the thick smoke and the gathering darkness,
were the twin brick towers connected by an arch: the gate-
house to the Evergreen Cemetery with its many windows,
most now shot out.

The news commentary was revolving around the fact
that Early's attack had come so late in the day, and on the
usual list of human-interest stories connected with that part
of the battle. Visible on-screen now was the famous Cemetery Hill sign: *Any persons found discharging firearms on
these grounds will be prosecuted to the full extent of the
law.* The Sports Channel reporter was having a lot of fun
with that proclamation, posted originally to discourage
kids from hunting squirrels within those normally quiet
and sacred precincts. The battle lines were surging toward
the flat plateau of the hilltop now, as Union soldiers struggled to hold against the oncoming Louisianans.

"Go, boys!" McIntyre said, leaning forward and thump-
ing the table with his fist. "*Go!*"

"Five gets you ten they don't make it," Howarth said.

"Hey! Whose side are you on?" Stuart exclaimed.

"My own, of course. The Union line is just too strong
up there. Just like in the original fight."

"I'll take your money," Dell said. "Meade's been bleeding those hills dry to support his left trying to hold John

here off. The ones that are left are shaken. They got mauled yesterday, remember."

"Yeah, but they've had time to dig in."

"Shit! You're talking about the Eleventh Corps! Most of them are Dutchmen who don't even speak English! They routed when Early hit them yesterday, just like they routed two months ago when Stonewall hit 'em at Chancellorsville! And they're still flighty!"

"It's not just Dutchmen. The Iron Brigade's up there."

"What's left of them!"

"It's enough!"

"Says you!"

"Quiet down, you two!" McIntyre told them. "I want to hear this!"

The announcer was talking about the failure—as had happened in history—of Lee's attacks against both Union flanks to coordinate with one another. He was making a lot of the fact that Dick Ewell's corps had failed to seize that critical high ground yesterday after the initial staggering victory of the Confederate forces over the broken and scattering remnants of the crumbling Union line.

And today, ordered to support Longstreet's attack far around to the south by hitting the eye end of the fishhook-shaped Federal line, he'd delayed so long before striking at the fishhook's barbed point that he might well have actually thrown away a second chance at grabbing the twin hills anchoring the Yankee right—the thickly wooded eminence of Culp's Hill and the lower but strongly defended Cemetery Hill just south of the town of Gettysburg.

"Why do you think Toby waited so long?" Dell asked.

"I don't think it was Toby," McIntyre replied. "I think it was Kirkpatrick."

"C'mon, John. Just because you hate the guy's guts—"

"No, it's not that. The guy's an asshole. He's had it in for me ever since I stopped him in that sim we did of Sharpsburg at U of C last year. He just didn't want to see me as Longstreet take the Round Tops and turn the Yankee flank!"

Thomas Kirkpatrick was the president of the South Carolina Wargamers' Association and a long-time rival of McIntyre's in the regional competitions. In this event he was simming the Confederates' Second Corps commander, General Richard S. Ewell.

"So you think that by delaying his attack . . ." Dell said.

"He let me divert the Yankees, pull them off to their left to face me," McIntyre said, completing the thought. "Gave him a better shot at breaking their right and center."

"Aw, *shit*!" Stuart said, watching the screen. "Another commercial!"

An ad for Coldstream Lite was coming on.

The Games broadcast was real time. The date was July 2, 2038, the one-hundred seventy-fifth anniversary of the Battle of Gettysburg, and the Electronic Reenactment Historical Society was gaming out the battle over the course of three days, playing the fight out hour by hour, even minute by minute. The Games had attracted interest enough in the general public that the Sports Channel and SNN both were covering them, with live feeds off the Net showing what the sim-gamers themselves were seeing and hearing in the hook-up.

That meant big money from big sponsors and the chance to simultaneously link in with ten thousand other gamers from all over the world in the largest real-time battle sim ever attempted. But it also meant that those sponsors got air time, with interruptions for commercials more often than not breaking in at the *damnedest* times.

McIntyre sighed and took another sip of his drink. Military recreationists had been around for sixty years or more, since the days when, if they wanted to experience life in another century, they bought or made all of the equipment and uniforms and accoutrements of their particular period and spent summer weekends camping out with fellow enthusiasts under the eyes of a bemused public, sleeping in tents, cooking over open fires, and engaging in mock, meticulously choreographed skirmishes in the fields of obliging farmers. McIntyre's grandfather had been a Civil War recreationist, a member of the First Virginia Cavalry, back in the late '80s.

Military gamers had been around for even longer, starting with commercial boxed games like *Gettysburg* and *Tactics II* all the way back in the 1960s. The earliest versions had been played with small, cardboard counters representing different military units, played across a square or hexgrid map of the battlefield, with booklets of rules describing how to move, how to engage in combat, how to calculate losses. As the computer revolution had taken off in the '80s, it had been inevitable that computer programs would appear, allowing gamers and armchair generals to refight the wars and battles of history, to play what-if with Hastings and Cannae, Waterloo and Bastogne, the Formosa Strait and, of course, Gettysburg. From their humble beginnings with *Pong* in the early '60s, computer games had become increasingly more detailed, more realistic, richer in their simulations of historical reality, until the Georgetown University server nexus, known unofficially as "God of Battles," could mediate the virtual realities of nearly ten thousand participants worldwide in a colossal merger of computer simulation and historical reenactment. Participants jacked in through the link connects, accepting cortical feeds through micro implants in their scalps and the backs of their necks. The God of Battles computed the odds, estimated the interactions, calculated the variables, and fed the compromise of virtual realities back to the participants. The illusion was so complete in all five sensory modalities that enthusiasts insisted it was better, sharper, more *real* than real life.

Internet VR battles had grown increasingly popular in the past ten years, especially those with the Civil War as a venue. Gettysburg had been the most popular, the most oft-refought battle of that war, and it was only right that Gettysburg would be the climactic engagement chosen by the Electronic Reenactment Historical Society as the first such battle to be opened to the general public.

The last estimates McIntyre had heard suggested that eight point two million people worldwide were tuning in through the Internet, vicariously experiencing the battle as it unfolded live across the electronic hilltops, ridge crests, valleys, and farmland of the far-flung simulation. It was a bit eerie when he was actually linked in, playing the role of General James Longstreet, to know that that many people were looking over his electronic shoulder, as it were, watching him, feeling him wrestle with the same tactical and logistical problems the historical Longstreet had faced 175 years ago.

Reenactment had become big-time entertainment, with a bit of live theater thrown in.

But then, when he was in the bubble, he rarely even remembered that he wasn't Longstreet, or that the Battle of Gettysburg had been fought and decided a long time ago.

The litany of commercials—for beer, for Toyota's newest hydrogen-turbine car, for Levi's smartsuits, for the IBM-Toshiba Quantum IV—played itself out. The sportscaster reappeared beneath the Sports Channel's sleek Battle of Gettysburg II logo, describing the action to date.

And when the netfeed returned, showing that night-darkened hilltop just south of the town . . .

"Son of a gun!" Howarth exclaimed as the patrons of the Lee's Arms burst into wild cheering. "He *did* it! He took Cemetery Hill!"

It was true. The Louisiana Tigers had rushed the Union guns, capturing many of them and scattering the gunners. Fierce hand-to-hand fighting continued to rage in the flame-shot darkness.

"Look at the troop numbers," Dell said, referring to the

line of statistics scrolling down the right side of the screen. "Meade pulled so many people away from his right to support his left against Longstreet, the brigades left to hold Culp's Hill and Cemetery Hill are down to skeletons. It looks like Early was late, and that gave him his chance!"

The others at the table groaned at her pun.

"Well," McIntyre agreed, "if they'd managed that attack earlier, when they were supposed to, I might have been able to break through at the Round Tops or even Cemetery Ridge." He slapped the table top, furious. "Damn it! I was so close! . . ."

"Yeah, and those boys on the screen now would've walked into a deathtrap," Dell said. "The casualties would've been completely unacceptable."

"I've been noticing a number of interesting digressions from history so far," Stuart said. "It'll be fun to see how this plays out."

"Well, it can't turn out *too* different," Howarth said. "I mean, the sponsors have paid how many millions of dollars to broadcast a complete replay of the battle with a really big climax, right? We have to give 'em their money's worth."

"Sure, but there's still the question of who's going to win this time around," Dell said. "Nobody would bother watching if that was a foregone conclusion!"

"I just mean the battle won't end today because Longstreet managed to turn the Yankee's left . . ."

"Yeah, I wish," McIntyre grumbled.

". . . or Early manages to hang on to Cemetery Hill," Howarth added.

"I just wish the media weren't so wrapped up in it," McIntyre told them. "It's turning a friendly little sim into a real circus."

" 'Friendly little sim'?" Dell asked. She arched an eyebrow in her best oh-come-now look. "You know there's no such thing! Not since gaming went big-business on us!

Sponsors. Advertising." She made a face. "Way too much input on too little bandwidth. I'm surprised they haven't started asking the troops to wear corporate sponsor logos on their uniforms!"

"Now *there's* an idea," Stuart said, grinning. "I wonder how much someone would pay us for that idea? We could wear big patches saying 'Eat McBurgers' on our haversacks! . . ."

McIntyre guffawed. " 'Have a cold Coldstream' on our canteens!"

The news feed zeroed in on one Confederate soldier laying his hands on the carriage wheel of one cannon, shouting "C'mon, boys! This gun is ours!" A burly Yankee gunner, a private in the heavily German Ninth Corps, bellowed the reply, "Nein! This gun ist *unser*," and laid the Confederate soldier out cold with a swing of his ramrod.

Stuart laughed. "That really happened! I remember reading an account . . ."

"Of course it happened. The God of Battles incorporates everything about the real Gettysburg that its search engines can find." Dell shook her head. "But there are differences, too. The real Early didn't get *nearly* as far up that hill. His division was mangled by those guns, then driven back by reinforcements arriving from elsewhere along the Union line."

"Well, it looks like that's what's happening here," Howarth pointed out. "Look there. Those are Yankees coming up from the southwest, aren't they?"

"Hard to tell in the dark," McIntyre said. The shadowy line of troops fired, the flashes of their musketry popping and strobing against the darkness. Louisiana boys toppled and fell. "Ah! Must be Yankees! Damn it, why isn't Hays ordering his troops to fire?"

The Confederate line—Louisiana troops mingled now with a couple of regiments from North Carolina—wavered uncertainly but did not return fire. The approaching Yankees got off another volley, killing more men and wounding others, and still the gray-clad line did not return fire.

"Stonewall Jackson," McIntyre said, suddenly.

"What about him?" Howarth asked.

"Two months ago, at Chancellorsville. He was out riding reconnaissance ahead of his own lines after dark. Coming back, his party blundered into a North Carolina Regiment—"

"The Eighteenth North Carolina. And that was exactly two months ago tonight!"

"Right, right. The Confederate troops got spooked, opened fire, and shattered Jackson's left arm. He died a couple of weeks later from pneumonia." He nodded toward the hesitating soldiers on the big screen. "Hays might be thinking these are reinforcements coming up from Cemetery Ridge. He doesn't know that my boys—that Longstreet's boys, that is—didn't break through as planned. And he doesn't want to score on his own goal."

At that moment, the approaching line of troops halted and fired a third volley, this time so close that the flashes illuminated their blue tunics and the trefoil forage cap emblems identifying them as Second Corps. Dozens of Confederate soldiers fell, and the colors dropped. "*Fire! Fire!*" their officers screamed, and a ragged volley crackled from their ranks, but their spirit was already broken. Louisiana and North Carolina boys began falling back, abandoning those hard-won cannons, abandoning hundreds of dead and wounded from both sides sprawled among the guns. The Union troops gave a wild cheer and rushed forward. The Confederates tumbled back down the hill in a tangled, scattering mob. Musket fire continued to crack and snap, but the irresistible momentum of the Confederate attack had clearly melted away with the daylight.

The Union right and center were safe.

"Our boys sure missed a hell of a chance there," Howarth said.

"Well, it means the networks will be happy," Stuart pointed out. "Just like the original battle, we have one more day to go. The *big* one."

"Not bigger than today," McIntyre said. "More famous, maybe. More spectacular. Everything staked on one wild, glorious charge. . . ."

"Like I said, it'll make the networks happy. It promises to be quite a show."

"Assuming Bobby plays it like his namesake did in the original battle," Dell said. "So, John. He's your friend. What do you think he's going to do?"

The media had gleefully pounced on the fact that the man simming Confederate General Robert E. Lee was none other than Robert Lee Bolling, son of a Tyson's Corner lawyer and supposedly related to *that* branch of the Virginia Lees.

"He's keeping that a close-guarded secret," McIntyre said, grinning. "He wouldn't even tell me. But I don't think it's going to be what really happened!"

"It would be a bit pointless if it was," Stuart said. "I mean, this is a *re*-creation society, right? The idea is to explore the what-ifs and might-have-beens of history!"

"It's a hell of a lot more than that now," Howarth said. "We have people tuning in from all over the world. Hell, a couple of thousand of the simmers are foreigners. National pride's at stake. That and a few billion dollars in network contracts and advertising. I'm not sure gaming's ever going to be the same after this!"

"I know I won't be the same if I have to do one more interview," Stuart said.

The others laughed. Like Bobby Bolling, Phillip Randolph Stuart had a famous forebear, one intimately connected with the original battle 175 years before. His great-great-*great*-grandfather had been one General J. E. B. Stuart, commander of Lee's cavalry arm. The Sports Channel people had been all over him last week getting in-

terviews and perspectives . . . and to ask the inevitable
question: Why wasn't he simming for his famous ancestor?

The answer had been both simple and unpalatably mundane from the commentators' point of view. He was brand
new to war gaming and didn't have the tactical or strategic
experience necessary to command large bodies of troops
when he linked in. For the 175th Anniversary Gettysburg
Recreation, he was simming a sergeant in the Thirty-
Eighth Virginia. Perhaps when the 200th Anniversary
Games rolled around . . .

Besides, he *hated* horses, even computer-simulated
ones.

"Here's a question for you," McIntyre said. "Which is
more real . . . being inside the bubble? Or being out here
pretending to be celebrities?"

"We *are* celebrities," Dell reminded him. "Well, those
of us in command are, anyway." She grinned at Stuart.
"The ones who are giving orders instead of taking them!"

Christine Dell was also playing a general: General
George E. Pickett—*that* Pickett. Her division had only just
arrived on the field late today and would not be going into
action until tomorrow. Her big moment in the electronic
spotlight was still in the offing.

"Just look at Bobby," McIntyre said. "He's been glory-
ing in all the interviews!"

"That's okay, Christine," Stuart said, leaning back in his
chair. "Some of us don't want the responsibility or the
media attention. I'm in this hobby because I enjoy the experience. The bubble, like John says."

"We can't all be generals," Howarth said. His sim character was a private in the Fifty-Second North Carolina, one
of Dell's regiments. "There are only . . . what? A hundred
fifty, maybe two hundred generals being simmed in this
thing? And ten thousand active participants."

"Besides, this was a soldier's war," Stuart said, "no

matter what the history books have to say about generals and famous leaders. I'd rather experience the action from the ordinary soldier's point of view."

McIntyre knew what he meant. He felt the same and usually played ordinary soldiers or, at most, a junior officer. He'd accepted the role of Longstreet only because his old friend Bobby Bolling was taking the role of the original Lee. The two of them had been friends since high school, when they'd both first gotten into gaming. They'd endlessly debated the big Longstreet-Lee *what-if* and simmed it out a hundred times in GWAGS events and conventions. Ever since their big win against the SCWA last year, it had been inevitable that they would be asked to play Lee and Longstreet at this first-ever international event.

"John's got a point, though," Howarth said. "What's more real? Here?" He jerked a thumb at the screen, where the sports commentator team was breaking down the statistics of the day's action. "Or in there? In the bubble?"

"I guess that depends on your point of view," Dell answered. "It's as real as we make it in our own minds, right?"

"How very Heisenbergian of you, my dear," Howarth said. "I should have you come lecture my class." Unlike the majority of the members of GWAGS, Greg Howarth wasn't a student. He was a professor of physics at Georgetown University. McIntyre had met him three years before in an undergrad physics course, invited him to the Friday night warsim session, and they'd become good friends since.

"No thanks, Professor," Dell said, laughing. "That's not *my* idea of reality!"

"But we *do* manufacture reality," Howarth went on. "We observe something, it becomes real. So far as the universe is concerned, it *is* real."

"Ah, thus speaketh the prophet of quantum mechanics,"

Stuart said, raising his glass in mock salute. "All hail the great God Heisenberg!"

"No, all hail Microsoft and the God of the Internet," McIntyre replied. "Come on, people! It's virtual reality! Very good, very realistic, extremely detailed, and as accurate as a billion or so lines of code can make it, but it's not *real*. It's an electronic illusion playing itself out in our brains!"

"But what is real?" Howarth asked. "What do we mean by *real*? Schrödinger's equations tell us that what we perceive as real has to be described as a series of waveform functions. The cat in the box is alive *and* dead until an observer opens it up and the functions collapse into one possibility or the other."

"You and that damned cat, Professor," McIntyre said. "You know, in that whole course I took with you, I never really got that. How the hell can the cat be both alive and dead?"

"What grade did I give you?"

"A 'C.' "

"I'm surprised you did that well. Schrödinger's Cat is the defining parable of quantum mechanics. If you don't understand that, you don't understand the whole paradigm. Look, the cat in the box has a fifty-fifty chance of being alive or dead, depending on whether or not a radioactive particle decays and activates a trigger, releasing a poison. Heisenberg's uncertainty principle determines whether the particle decays or not, hence whether or not the poison is released and the cat is killed. Right?"

"Yeah . . ."

"I always felt sorry for the cat," Dell said, pretending a pout. "They should have put Schrödinger in the box."

"No one can see the cat," Howarth continued with a dirty look tossed in Dell's direction. "No one can observe it until they open the box and look inside. Until they do, quantum mechanics says the cat is defined by a complex waveform equation which doesn't collapse into a cat, into *reality*, until it is observed."

"So why doesn't the cat observe itself?" McIntyre asked. "What happens if the observer is in a box, watching a cat in a smaller box? Is the experiment real or not?"

Howarth sighed. "Fair questions. And I should add that the thought-experiment itself was Schrödinger's attempt to show how ridiculous it was to apply the uncertainty principle to anything larger than an electron. He didn't think his own equations made sense on a macro level. But every test we've brought to bear on his theories in the past hundred years demonstrate that there's no essential difference between the very small and the very large."

"But there're all kinds of differences," McIntyre said. He held his forefinger in the air. "An electron here can just vanish and reappear over *here*. I remember that much from your class, at least! Tunneling diodes and quantum computers couldn't work if subatomic particles didn't act that way. But you don't see that happening to people!"

"Because people are composed of more than one electron," Howarth replied. He rapped the table top with his knuckles. "This, what we call reality, is a kind of collusion between all of us. Unconscious, of course, but real." He thought for a moment. "You talk about being 'in the bubble.' Think of it as if we each manufacture a bubble of reality, a bubble that includes just what we can observe. For the four of us—and everyone else in this crowd—our bubbles overlap. We're going through a constant process of unconscious compromise as we all agree on what's real. By observing what's around us, we create the *reality* of what's around us. Understand?"

"No," McIntyre said. "I didn't get it in Physics 440, and I don't get it now. Look, Greg, if what you say is true, what are we doing when we link-connect to a sim? We're observing what's around us. We're being fed highly complex and detailed information about our surroundings, as realistic as the God of Battles can make it, right down to the smell of cordite and the tickle of grass beneath bare feet. We talk about being 'in the bubble,' but that's not the same as what you're talking about. The bubble represents what we feel when we're inside. We're not creating the world. The world, or a computer-generated description of it, is being fed to us through the link connects. We're observing it, experiencing it . . . but it's not real."

"John has a point," Dell said. "If we create the world by just observing it, wouldn't we change history when we sim? I mean *really* change it?"

"Huh," Howarth said. "Cool idea. But the past has already taken shape, been given form. Reality. The future hasn't been created yet. It's just possibilities and probabilities, waiting to be called out of all the formless mights and maybes."

"Ahh, how can you be so sure of that?" McIntyre said, teasing. "The future doesn't exist. Neither does the past, right? I mean, you can't touch it, can't reach it. Different people remember it in different ways." This time he rapped the table top. "Only *now* exists. We remember the past, what we've experienced of it, anyway, but if yesterday has no more solid existence than tomorrow, why don't we recreate it when we . . . recreate it?"

"Jesus," Dell said as the others groaned, "and you guys think *my* puns are bad!"

Howarth looked thoughtful.

"Hey," McIntyre added. "I was joking!"

"I know. But it's an intriguing idea. *Now* as an instantaneous wavecrest of reality, moving from past to future in a sea of possibilities. Observation shapes the future. Maybe it shapes the past as well!"

"But it *doesn't*!" Stuart pointed out. "Otherwise, we'd get a different now every time we refought a historical battle!"

"How do we know we don't?" Howarth said with

earnest seriousness. "Our memories would change. Maybe before our big event with the SCWA last year, the Confederates *lost* Sharpsburg. Or maybe McClellan got his act together, Lee's army was destroyed, and the Civil War ended right then and there, in September of 1862. But then John here beat Kirkpatrick down in Charleston last year, and everything we know, everything we thought we knew, changed!"

"But it *didn't* change," McIntyre said. "The real Sharpsburg was a draw."

"Maybe it takes a certain number of observers to have any real effect," Dell suggested.

"No, I just don't buy that at all!" Stuart said. "You guys are turning physics into magic!"

"And that," Howarth said with a smile, "is as perfect a definition of the field as we understand it today as I've ever heard!"

"Watch it, Greg," McIntyre said, gesturing with his hand. "I'll stop believing in you, and *poof!* you'll disappear!"

It was almost 10:30 P.M. On the screen, the sportscasters were continuing their commentary on the day's battle and what was in store for the morrow. In the background, a lone, baritone voice could be heard singing a melancholy rendition of "Rock of Ages." The voice was rich and deep and inexpressibly beautiful.

"I remember reading about a guy singing that night," McIntyre said.

"You know," Dell said, "maybe that's the true reality. Not battles, not generals making decisions . . . but the things that matter to ordinary people, life and love and the human spirit. Hear that singing? *That* is what creates worlds. Not dates and cold numbers."

Across the torn and bloodied ground between the two armies, stretcher bearers were seeking out the wounded as the moon rose and an informal truce descended over the battlefield. The singer, a Confederate soldier in McLaws's division near the infamous bloody Wheat Field, was singing hymns to comfort the hundreds of wounded boys within reach of his voice. Men on both sides fell silent, listening.

He sang several songs, ending with "When This Cruel War Is Over." At the end, applause, cheers, and whistles broke out from the nearby Union lines, and the Confederates joined in.

Perhaps, McIntyre thought, Christine was right.

People were the reality, not the battles, dates, or histories. He held her close that evening as he walked her back to their apartment.

Friday, July 3, 1863, 5:10 A.M.

General Robert E. Lee had risen while the stars were still bright in the Pennsylvania sky. Astride Traveler now, as the dawn slowly brightened beyond the Federal lines, he made his way south along Seminary Ridge, searching for the man he often referred to as "my war horse," James Longstreet. To the east, the sound of heavy gunfire and cannonade thundered and boomed and rattled, the cacophony muffled by intervening hills but not blocked.

The day was not off to a good start. He'd sent a message to Ewell ordering him to coordinate his attack on the Union right with Longstreet's assault today, but either the messenger hadn't reached Ewell in time or the Yankees had moved first, forcing him to fight before he was ready. The thunder over beyond those hills had begun at a quarter to four this morning, and was continuing to build in fury, with no sign of abatement.

Well, he reasoned, it would all work out. Ewell might yet pull off more Union troops from other parts of their line, leaving them vulnerable. He might even tempt *those people*, as Lee thought of them, to go onto the offensive, and that meant a major shift in the weight of their forces, from the center and left to the right. *Good.* . . .

As the morning light strengthened, he took the time to study the Union lines just a mile to the east, across a broad, shallow valley. Cemetery Ridge the locals called it, running south from the flat-topped eminence called Cemetery Hill which Jubal Early had come so close to taking and holding last night.

Southeast, the field was dominated by two hills, the Round Tops, rising above the fields, woods, and orchards overrun by Longstreet's men yesterday afternoon. They were the key to this part of the battlefield, and they were still in Union hands. South of that, the land undulated away in gentle ridges, hills, and forested valleys all the way to the Maryland border five miles away.

From here, he could see the Federal positions along the crest of the rise all the way from Cemetery Hill to the Round Tops. Massed batteries and troops, black against the sunrise. Through his field glasses, he could make out individual men resting behind walls of stone and split rail, the picket lines alert near the base of the ridge beyond the Emmitsburg Pike, the battle flags and regimental colors bristling in the early light, the officers looking back at him through their field glasses and telescopes.

Wondering, no doubt, what he was going to do this day.

He was pleased to note, however, that the enemy did not seem to have strengthened his position during the night.

One strong, decisive thrust, he thought. *Break those people's lines here, and the issue of Southern independency will be settled once and for all.*

He needed to confer with Longstreet.

The sun was just fully up when Lee found his second-in-command in a field a mile west of the Round Tops, close by the Emmitsburg Road, seated on a stump. Longstreet stood as his commander-in-chief rode up.

"Good morning, General." He seemed in good spirits, a contrast from their parting yesterday morning, when he'd been morose and depressed.

"General Longstreet," Lee said, dismounting and handing Traveler's reins to an aide. "It is good to see you."

"Sir, I have had my scouts out all night," Longstreet told him, "and I find that you still have an excellent opportunity to maneuver around to the right of Meade's army and maneuver him into attacking us."

Lee frowned. His second-in-command, apparently, was determined to continue the disagreement of yesterday. Perhaps he assumed that his corps' failure to take the high ground of Cemetery Ridge had changed his commander's mind. He pointed northeast, toward the center of Cemetery Ridge and its bristling emplacements. "No, General Longstreet. The enemy is *there*, and I am going to strike him."

Longstreet's face fell, his expression behind the long and thick beard he affected darkening. The two of them had clashed several times yesterday over this same issue, and Lee had thought they were beyond that question now. Old Pete was uncharacteristically verging on insubordination.

Lee wanted Longstreet to strike the Union line north of the Round Tops, in the same vicinity where Wright's Georgians had come so close to breaking the enemy line the night before. At the same time, Pickett's fresh division, just arrived on the field yesterday evening, would advance east across the mile-wide valley between Seminary and Cemetery ridges. He intended to throw a full quarter of his army at that one point in the Union line, a do-or-die effort to win the war this day.

Since early yesterday, Longstreet had been urging a different strategy, a division of forces and a march south and east around the Union line's left flank. Take up a position astride the three major roads leading south from Gettysburg, Longstreet insisted, and the Federal lines of supply and communication with Washington, D.C., would be broken. Meade would have to go onto the offensive, would have to charge Confederate troops dug in on high ground of their choosing. It would be a repeat of the Federal disaster at Fredericksburg seven months before, when Longstreet's divisions had crouched four-deep in a sunken road behind a low stone wall atop Marye's Heights as General Burnsides had launched six major charges against them, one bloodily after another.

Nine thousand men, three quarters of all of the Federal losses that bloody day, had been shot down in front of Marye's Heights.

Longstreet was correct in his assessment of one key aspect of the Confederate army: His soldiers were nothing less than superb on the defensive. At Fredericksburg, General Jackson, none less than the redoubtable Stonewall himself, had remarked, "My men have sometimes failed to take a position, but to defend one, never!"

How Lee missed the man he'd once called his right arm. . . .

Lee began discussing how he wanted Longstreet's corps deployed in support of Pickett. Longstreet, almost sullen now, resisted. "To withdraw my two committed divisions from beneath the Round Tops, General, would mean exposing the right flank of our attacking column. It would be the Union troops who flank us, rather than the other way about."

Lee considered this. "You make a good point, General Longstreet."

"My divisions have been reduced by nearly a third by their efforts yesterday. They are exhausted. To throw them again against the same objectives they spent themselves against yesterday would, in my opinion, be futile."

"Very well, General Longstreet," Lee replied. "Have McLaws and Law hold their ground. If we shift the point of attack slightly to the north, Pickett can be supported instead by two of Hill's divisions. You will be in overall command of the attack."

Longstreet sighed. "General Pickett has less than five thousand troops in his division, sir, the smallest in the army. Hill's divisions number no more after their heavy engagement of the past two days."

Lee could feel the man's inner struggle, emotions warring with one another. "Yes, I estimate that we will make this charge with 15,000 men," Lee said.

"General," Longstreet continued, "I have been a soldier all my life. I have been with soldiers engaged in fights by couples, by squads, companies, regiments, divisions, and armies, and should know as well as anyone what soldiers can do. It is my opinion that no 15,000 men ever arrayed for battle can take that position."

This was, Lee thought, a defining moment in the command of this battle. He could read the anguish in his subordinate's manner, bearing, and thoughts, heard the earnestness with which he spoke.

He was tempted to reverse his earlier decision, to agree with Longstreet's plea. It wasn't too late. . . .

Saturday, July 3, 2038, 6:40 A.M.

Robert Lee Bolling was tempted by the passion of his subordinate's argument. God, but John was playing his role to the hilt!

Turning, he stared across the shallow valley, at the ridgeline to the northeast. A small copse of oak trees marked the center of the Union lines, the point which he had already determined would be the guide for the advancing divisions. The thunder from the hills beyond continued to shiver the still, summer-morning air. He was keenly aware of his audience, though he couldn't sense them directly, of course. This was the defining moment in the command of this battle. . . .

"I appreciate what you are telling me, General Longstreet," he said in his soft, Virginia aristocrat's drawl, "but we will strike the enemy there, where his center has been weakened by our efforts thus far. Come. Let us find General Pickett and confer with him."

Friday, July 3, 1863, 6:41 A.M.

James Longstreet could be moody at times. Always taciturn, always stolid and undemonstrative since the death of three of his children from scarlet fever the year before, he often seemed withdrawn, but his men loved him. He was devoted to Lee and devoted, too, to the men under his command.

And now he felt torn between those two devotions. The man he revered was determined to follow a course of action that could only prove disastrous for the men who followed them. Repeatedly over the past two days he'd urged Lee to play to the proven strength of the Army of Northern Virginia, to take up a position that would force Meade to go onto the offensive.

The enemy would not survive another Fredericksburg. The Union soldiers were brave, there was no question about that. But they were ineptly led, and another military disaster, this time on Northern soil, would ruin the enemy *politically*, if not militarily. That seemed to be the essence of war—to hurt the enemy, and hurt him, and *hurt* him until his political will was broken, until he no longer had the political support necessary to continue the fight.

It seemed so damnably clear. This was a time for a conservative approach, a time not to risk all on a single throw of the dice. General Lee was a superb commander—in Longstreet's opinion there was none better—but if he had a weakness, it was his blind conviction in the infallibility of his own soldiers, and, just possibly, his gently aristocratic disdain for his opponents.

He'd seen his commander in this mood before, however, and knew that further argument would be fruitless. He signaled an aide to bring his horse.

The contest was in the hands of Providence now.

Saturday, July 3, 2038, 6:41 A.M.

McIntyre was horrified. He'd known Bobby Lee Bolling for years, known that he tended to be flamboyant at times, known that he could be a glory hound, but he'd never expected anything like this. All of the media attention, the interviews, the lead stories about the descendent of General Robert E. Lee simming his famous ancestor, had certainly put Bobby under the spotlight on center stage, but McIntyre had never expected his celebrity status to go to his friend's head like this.

He was making the wrong decision.

Until this moment, he'd felt as though he were riding the crest of history. Events in the battle so far had differed here and there from those described in the history books, but there'd been no major change.

McIntyre had been completely confident that this wargaming sim would prove to be more or less a reprise of the original battle. But Bobby was throwing a major wrench in the works by departing from his ancestor's strategy.

Focusing his thoughts, he brought to mind the mental code that allowed him to access options within the game. A menu bar appeared in his mind's eye, and he held the code word in his thoughts until the communications icon was highlighted.

By reciting Bolling's name, he opened a link to his

friend, a private back channel that let them chat without affecting the game's play.

While not a breach of the rules, chat lines were frowned upon in serious game play. Most simmers felt that the characters being represented should work out their strategies and tactics under the same limitations their historical counterparts had enjoyed. Close cooperation by several players on a back channel could easily upset the balance of play and, therefore, the realism of the sim.

But, damn it, this was different.

Bobby! He screamed into his friend's thoughts. *What the hell do you think you're doing?*

Hey, John! Bolling's voice answered in his head. *What's the problem?*

I thought we were sticking to the historical script!

Oh, that. Bolling's thought was dismissive. *No reason we can't put on a show for the networks, is there? They expect it.*

Is that what this is all about? A show?

Sure it is. What else? McIntyre could sense the man's shrug in his mind. *Besides, this is our chance to check the big what-if, right? See what would have happened if things had gone the other way. If things had gone Lee's way.*

Damn it, Bobby, we agreed to follow the historical line!

What's your problem? It's just a game. An abrupt mental snick marked the closing of the line. Bobby had just cut him off.

It's just a game.

Well, it was, of course. Just a game.

During his celebrated sim match with Kirkpatrick and the SCWA at the University of Charleston last year, he'd pulled some surprises out of his tactical hat when he'd simmed the Union commander, George B. McClellan. In the historical battle the fight had been pretty much a draw; Lee had saved his divided and weakened army from total annihilation at the hands of the much larger Union force, but he'd left McClellan in possession of the field and the battle had ended the Confederacy's first attempt at a campaign on Union soil. In the recreation at U of C last year, McClellan had feinted at Lee's left, beginning the battle as it had actually unfolded, but then with most un-McClellanlike daring, had thrown the majority of his forces across the Middle Bridge and cut the Rebel army off from its Potomac River crossing. McIntyre had certainly rewritten history that time, by forcing Lee's surrender at Sharpsburg.

If Howarth's notion was correct, that victory in the wargame sim should have rewritten history. The South would have lost the Civil War in the autumn of 1862.

So . . . why was his heart beating faster, his stomach twisting unpleasantly at the realization that Bobby Lee Bolling was departing from the tried-and-true historical recipe for Gettysburg?

He was in the bubble. That was all it was. He was getting so caught up in the sensory reality of the sim that he was confusing a computer-generated illusion with mundane reality.

He would have to focus on Bobby's new orders and do his best to carry them out.

It's just a game. . . .

Friday, July 3, 1863, 2:48 P.M.

Longstreet sat on a snake-rail fence, staring into white mist with a morose intensity he'd rarely felt before in his life. Thunder rolled, a steady, drumming crash and boom that pounded the earth and sky and hammered the senses until the brain grew numb and the will failed. The bombardment had been ongoing since precisely 1:07, when the first shot had banged out from the 140 Confederate guns arrayed in a two-mile arc of steel from northwest of the town of Gettysburg to just west of the Round Tops in the south.

The vast majority of that incredible weight of artillery was being directed against a relatively slender portion of the Union line, concentrating on the northern portion of the long, north–south ridge where Meade had anchored the center of the Army of the Potomac. The purpose of this savage bombardment, the most intense that Longstreet had ever witnessed, was to force the retreat of the Northern batteries on that portion of their line—there were at least eighteen guns on that part of the ridge alone—and to demoralize the troops crouched behind the stone walls that stretched along the crest of the ridge.

It was impossible to tell how effective the bombardment had been thus far. Within minutes of the firing of the opening gun, guns and target alike had been wreathed in an impenetrable white battle fog of roiling smoke. He could see the nearest battery, ghosts in the mist, four Napoleons bucking and leaping with each flash and crack, as the crouching, human shapes about them toiled with ramrod and swab, powder charge and ball, serving their wheeled, barking masters.

Would it make the necessary difference in the effort yet to come? *Could* it make the difference?

General Lee, Longstreet reasoned, was relying overmuch on the judgment of his lieutenants in this battle . . . except, of course, in his steadfast refusal to consider Longstreet's alternative to a direct attack on the Union center. Lee had the reputation for relying heavily on his corps commanders, giving them general directions, suggestions, recommendations . . . but rarely telling them how he wanted his orders carried out.

This, in fact, was one mark of a good commander—one who delegated to his officers and refused to be bogged down by the extraordinarily broad and complex minutiae of the deployment and management of an entire army. At times, though, Lee carried that delegation to extremes. Two days ago, for example, when he'd directed Ewell to take a hill south of the town "if practicable," he'd missed a grand opportunity to utterly smash an already smashed and routed enemy before they had a chance to dig in along that fishhook curve of hills and ridges they now occupied. Lee, ever the Southern gentleman, rarely issued an order as a demand, relying instead on his subordinates' own discretion.

Would to God he'd shown that same reliance and trust with Longstreet's suggestion of a flank march.

"General Longstreet?"

He looked up and saw Major General George Pickett dismounting from his sleek, black horse, shouting to be heard above the din. He could only nod in greeting.

Pickett saluted, then handed him a piece of paper, carefully folded. "I am in receipt of this message from Colonel Alexander, sir."

E. P. Alexander was the twenty-eight-year-old Georgian, a West Point graduate, who commanded the eighty guns of Lee's First Corps and was in overall command of the bombardment. The hastily scrawled lines read, simply, *For God's sake, come quick. The eighteen guns have gone. Come quick or my ammunition will not let me support you properly.*

Longstreet read the message carefully but said nothing. Alexander, he knew, had been given the responsibility, by Lee himself, to decide if his bombardment had been successful and whether the center attack should be carried out. Alexander knew his guns and what they were capable of; there was no doubt about that. But, God in heaven, to lay such responsibility on that young man's shoulders . . .

He looked again toward the center of the Union line, wondering if the bombardment had, indeed, driven off the Yankee batteries emplaced there. He could see nothing, however, but the drifting, clotted banks of smoke.

"General!" Pickett exclaimed. "Shall I advance?" He sounded intense . . . even eager. Pickett *wanted* this to happen.

George E. Pickett, Longstreet knew, was desperately anxious not to miss the war, though things had conspired thus far to keep him from the glory he sought. Fifty-ninth out of fifty-nine in the West Point class of '46, a classmate of both George B. McClellan and the immortal T. J. Jackson, he'd become a hero as the first American to scale the castle wall at Chapultepec and later defied a British squadron in a confrontation at Puget Sound. When he'd resigned his commission, however, to fight for his beloved Virginia, he'd arrived too late to fight at Manassas and been wounded at Gains Mill just *before* the charge that had won the battle. His wound had kept him out of action until after Second Manassas. He'd been in the reserve at Fredericksburg and deployed elsewhere during the Chancellorsville campaign. Bringing up the rear as the Army of Northern Virginia converged on Gettysburg, he'd almost missed this fight as well, arriving with his division only last night.

He would have his chance at glory this day, however. His divisions, plus two of D. H. Hill's divisions, would carry the assault to the enemy's center.

But Longstreet had to give the order.

He still didn't trust himself to speak, however. Any spoken word now would betray his lack of confidence, and that would be unthinkable.

Was there any other way? He'd tried to get General Lee to accept the obvious alternative, tried and failed. . . .

Pickett, leaning forward, eyes ablaze with the power of the moment, waited for the order. There were times when even the second-in-command of an army could do nothing but watch events unfold with nightmare surety and the inevitability of implacable fate. Slowly, reluctantly, Longstreet nodded.

"I am going to move forward, sir!" Pickett announced,

the curled and perfumed ringlets which were his trademark dancing to either side of his face. He saluted, remounted, and rode off toward the head of his waiting division.

Longstreet closed his eyes, unable to watch.

Saturday, July 3, 2038, 3:05 P.M.

McIntyre raised his field glasses to his eyes and peered across the valley, searching the far ridge for some sign that Alexander's artillery had, indeed, worked its magic against the enemy, had given them a chance for success.

The smoke blanketing both sides of the battlefield had begun to thin and lift as the batteries on both sides fell relatively silent. Before him, the Confederate legions in close order had passed the line of their guns and were striding now into the sunlit valley beyond, rank upon rank of them, battle flags aflutter in the breeze. The Union guns, silent for a moment, began to speak once more. It did appear that they'd been silenced in the center, but cannon remained ranked to either side, on the flat-topped Cemetery Hill to the north, and along the southern crest of Cemetery Ridge, and beyond on the heights of the smaller of the Round Tops, and these guns began thundering anew, firing into the flanks of the advancing gray formation. Solid shot smashed down whole rows of walking men in bloody confusion; case shot exploded in the sky overhead in deadly, blossoming puffs of smoke and shrapnel, or sent geysers of smoke, earth, and dust bursting from the earth. Men fell alone, in twos, in small and tangled groups.

But they kept pressing forward.

The Confederates were advancing in two blocks of men, Pickett's division in the south and the divisions of Trimble and Pettigrew to the north, with a quarter-mile gap between them. The entire advancing force, McIntyre knew, included eighteen Virginia regiments, fifteen North Carolina regiments, three regiments from Mississippi, and two apiece from Tennessee and Alabama. All told, they numbered perhaps 12,500 men, well short of the 15,000 of Lee's estimate. Some of the regiments from Hill's corps had been badly chewed up already—some had suffered casualties already of forty percent—but the full extent of their losses had not been known to the Confederate command.

Partway down the eastern slope of Seminary Ridge, Pickett's division—the brigades of Kemper, Garnett, and Armistead—shifted into a left oblique march which would close the gap between them and Hill's people to the north. Further down the slope, almost midway down the valley, they stopped to dress their ranks, taking casualties all the while. After an agony of moments, raked by deadly fire, they continued their march.

And still men died, or fell shrieking and writhing to the earth, with every yard advanced.

This is a game, a simulation, McIntyre told himself, clinging to the thought for comfort. *This is only a computer simulation. . . .*

Saturday, July 3, 2038, 3:21 P.M.

In her role as George Pickett, Christine Dell was having the time of her life. The simulation was perfect . . . *perfect.* Moments ago, her division had paused under the vicious, sleeting fire a second time to tear down the fencing along the Emmitsburg Pike at the bottom of the valley, and now it was advancing once more up the long and gentle slope toward the enemy positions.

The Union cannon fire had been joined now by volleys from the ranks of blue-clad infantry packed onto the ridge crest, shoulder to shoulder behind the low stone walls. As far as Dell could see, the intense Confederate bombardment had hurt them not at all, and they were rising now rank upon rank, regiment upon regiment, to shoulder their rifles and pour volleyed fire into the advancing gray ranks.

She reined up her horse at a barn just beyond the Emmitsburg Pike—the Codori Farm, if she remembered her history aright—to wait out the charge with her staff. George Pickett might have been enamored of glory, but he was also a major general, and division commanders simply did not expose themselves at the head of their troops.

In the historical battle, of course, Pickett had died on July 3, killed by a Union sniper firing from a house east of the Taneytown Road, just before the first of the immortal Union charges against the entrenched Confederates. Bobby Lee Bolling had completely changed the scenario, however. Pickett might die . . . or he might live. Either way, Christine Dell felt the inexpressible heady rush of excitement, awe, and joy as she watched those boys, *her* boys, storm those flame-laced heights. . . .

Saturday, July 3, 2038, 3:28 P.M.

Almost there . . . almost there . . . *almost there* . . .

Greg Howarth raced forward with his comrades of the Fifty-Second North Carolina, crowding one another, jostling, pushing ahead, reaching for the stone wall only scant yards in front of them now. A part of Marshall's brigade, the Fifty-Second had been aiming for that part of the Union line just north of the angle in the stone wall, but in the thunderous cannonade, the hellfire fury of the enemy rifles, the orderly regiments of Pettigrew's brigade had dissolved into a seething, forward-struggling mass of screaming, yelling men, impossible to distinguish by regiment, brigade, or division. He found himself leaning forward as he walked, as if pushing forward into a sleeting hail, and the men around him did the same, the wild, tumbling rush of their charge spent, so that now each step took every bit of strength and will they could muster.

Fifty feet from the stone wall, they paused, unable to move further. Instead, they huddled in a ragged, seething crowd, yelling above the thundering roar of gunfire, aiming their rifles, firing, reloading with rapid, spasmodic jerks of their ramrods, driving home cartridge and ball as dozens of their number collapsed around them, placing the percussion caps, aiming, firing again, all the while yelling like demented spirits. . . .

Saturday, July 3, 2038, 3:28 P.M.

More than anything else, Randy Stuart was aware of the sheer *noise* of that charge. At the beginning, he'd been in ranks with the others of the Thirty-Eighth Virginia, on the extreme left of Armistead's brigade, following in the trampled-down path of Garnett's brigade just ahead. Unable to see much save the backs of the men in front, the stubble beneath his feet, the deadly puffs of smoke from exploding shells above, he'd focused on the sound . . . the swish of trousered legs striding across the gently sloping ground, the clink and jingle of equipment, the slap of haversacks and canteens on thighs and rifle barrels on bowed shoulders, the incessant and fast-building roar and crack of the guns, the snap and thutter of shells whipping overhead. . . .

The ranks of Virginians were almost eerily silent; the shouted command when it came, "Left oblique . . . *march*!" seemed preternaturally loud against the thunder.

Down the valley slope, through the fence and across the road, then up the opposite slope, the ranks maintained good order, but in that final insane rush, regiment had merged with regiment and brigade with brigade into a single boiling, shouting, screaming, struggling tangle of men.

Just to the left of the copse of oak trees that had been their goal, the stone wall formed a sheltered angle where it ran north along the crest of the ridge, then cut sharply away to the east for a couple hundred feet before resuming its original orientation. Within that angle, hundreds of blue-clad troops were massed in close-packed ranks, firing wildly into the advancing mass of ragged gray.

A young lieutenant to Stuart's left waved his sword, shouting "Home, boys! Home! Remember, home is over beyond those hills!"

"Make ready!" another officer shouted, as though drilling his men on parade. "Take good aim! Fire low! Fire!"

The command was taken up and echoed up and down the Confederate line, as sheets of flame stabbed and flashed uphill, knocking down scores of the defenders.

And then the Yankees were dropping back from the wall, streaming toward the rear, as the Rebels surged forward, up, and over. Beyond the corpse-draped wall, a handful of gunners clustered around some cannons arrayed thirty feet beyond the wall, still working their guns as the gray tide swept up to the stone barrier and began lapping over. Not all of the enemy guns, then, had been withdrawn, and those that remained were savaging the oncoming Rebel ranks with canister.

But on they came, defiant, triumphant, unstoppable. Stuart saw General Armistead just in front of him, leading his brigade on, his black felt hat perched atop his sword, clambering over the wall, leading his men on with a shouted "Follow me!"

The sheer intensity of the moment, of the simulation, was overwhelming—the close-packed mob of Confederate soldiers spilling across the low stone wall, screaming and yelling and venting that peculiar high-pitched, battle-lust ululation that steadied them and unnerved their foes; the tumbling, close-pressed feel of men crowded ahead and

behind, to left and to right; the pounding of his heart; the
dry rawness in his throat as he added his voice to the
swelling Rebel yell around him; above all the booming,
thundering, keening, brain-numbing roar of musket and
cannon fire. For just a moment, Stuart was no longer in a
sim. He was *there*, crouched behind the stone wall, firing
at the retreating mass of Yankee soldiers on the other side.
They were running . . . running! *We're winning!*

In the bubble. . . .

He followed Armistead, whose hat, slit open by the
point of his sword, had now slipped down the blade almost
to the hilt. The general laid a hand on the wheel of the
nearest cannon, hesitated . . . fell . . .

A regimental color-bearer to Stuart's left screamed and
fell backward, his skull split wide open in gory spectacle.
Stuart grabbed the flag as it fell, leaped atop the stone wall,
waving it madly, balanced precariously there for just two
pounding heartbeats . . . and then something slapped him
hard in the chest, then again in the left side of his head.
There was no pain, no sensation at all save that double tap,
but his vision turned red and seemed to freeze in place for
a moment, and he wondered what had happened. . . .

Saturday, July 3, 2038, 3:45 P.M.

McIntyre watched in cold anger from his vantage point on
the snake-rail fence across the valley. The ridge crest opposite was shrouded now in battle smoke. He could see little but struggling shadows and the dip and wave of battle
flags dimly visible. From here, it was possible to believe
that the charge might be succeeding . . . but a courier had
already returned from that seething chaos with a message
for Longstreet from General Pickett. Unless those men
were stoutly reinforced, and fast, Pickett had reported, they

were not going to be able to hold on to what they'd won thus far.

There were troops in reserve—two of Hill's divisions to the north and Longstreet's own corps in the south—but McIntyre knew that those men would be needed to repulse a Union countercharge, should it come. Sending more men across that deadly valley and into the mêlée opposite would merely seal the fate of the Army of Northern Virginia.

How could Bobby have done this? *How?*

"General Longstreet, sir?"

He turned. Colonel Freemantle, an observer of Her Majesty's Coldstream Guards, was there, a look of rapt excitement on his young face. This, McIntyre knew, was Freemantle's first taste of battle, and he was clearly enjoying it. He wondered whether he was facing a mere computer simulation of the historical figure, or if someone was simming the British officer.

"General Lee sent me here," Freemantle said a bit breathlessly, "and said you would place me in position to see this magnificent charge." He stared across the valley at the struggle a mile away, as if seeing it for the first time. "I wouldn't have missed this for anything!"

A sim-visitor, McIntyre thought, disdainfully. A gamer who'd never participated in a sim as a reenactor before, who'd been assigned a minor historical role to play for this event. Or a curious observer—a member of the press, perhaps, who hadn't wanted to take a combatant's role.

"The devil you wouldn't," McIntyre growled through the bushy beard of his Longstreet persona. "I would like to have missed it very much! We've attacked and been repulsed. Look there."

In truth, there was still little to see but smoke and shifting, tangled, mist-shrouded shadows, and the rag-doll sprawls in gray and brown scattered all the way across the valley in the wake of the marching divisions.

But stragglers were dribbling back from the fighting, some walking, some running, many crawling or limping or helped along by companions, and as the minutes passed, more and more Confederate soldiers, the shattered wreckage of three divisions, began streaming back down the western slope of the far ridge, recrossing the near-mile of open field they'd marched across in such splendid order a few moments before.

"The charge is over," McIntyre said. He then added to himself, bitterly, *game over.*

Saturday, July 3, 2038, 3:55 P.M.

Bobby Lee Bolling sat quietly atop the simulation of Lee's horse, Traveler, watching the broken shards of the assault flowing back across the blood-drenched valley. *Man, I really screwed up this one. John is going to have me for breakfast. . . .*

Across the valley, as the firing slowly died away, he could hear the Federal soldiers shouting and hurrahing. And something else . . . like a chant. He had to strain to catch the word . . . *"Fredericksburg! Fredericksburg! Fredericksburg! . . ."*

He had to shake his head in admiration for the program running this sim. It had extrapolated from its database, drawing on the history of the bloody multiple repulses of the Federal divisions below Marye's Heights, and was having the simulations of the Union troops now shout the name of that battle back at the fleeing survivors of Pickett's, Trimble's, and Pettigrew's charges.

"It's all my fault," he called out to a group of ragged survivors as they streamed back past the lines of waiting Confederate artillery. "All this has been my fault."

"We'll whup 'em yet, Gen'rul!" one ragged soldier called out. "You'll get us into Washington yet!"

He shook his head. "I've lost this fight, boys. Now you must help me all you can."

Turning, he saw George Pickett, eyes dark and hollow, ringlets awry, and sighed. Even in defeat, the game had to be played out, the amenities observed. Besides, the game wasn't over yet. The Harvard professor role-playing General Meade might yet decide to counterattack, to make complete and absolute this disaster of Confederate arms. "General Pickett," he called out. "Place your division in rear of this hill, and be ready to repel the advance of the enemy should they follow up their advantage." Damn. He was always careful to use the phrase "those people" rather than "the enemy," but in his excitement he'd slipped a bit out of character.

"General Lee," Pickett replied coldly, "I *have* no division."

He sighed. "Come, General Pickett. This has been my fight, and on my shoulders rests the blame. Your men have done all that men can do." He paused, then added, "The fault is entirely my own."

Across the valley, the chant continued. "*Fredericksburg! Fredericksburg! Fredericksburg! . . .*"

Saturday, July 3, 2038, 4:40 P.M.

The legions of reporters, media personalities, and news anchors in the lobby of the Student Union had seemed as formidable as the massed ranks of Union troops and artillery atop Cemetery Ridge, but McIntyre, Dell, Stuart, and Howarth managed to tunnel their way through the mass of people and vidcorders, past the shouted questions. Most of the attention, for the moment, at least, was focused on Bobby Lee Bolling, who was answering questions from a makeshift stage at the far end of the lobby.

"It was all my fault," he was telling the reporters. "For

a hundred and seventy-five years, people have been second-guessing my ancestor, saying that he relied too much on his subordinate commanders, that he won the Battle of Gettysburg only because he listened to his second-in-command and pulled the famous flank march that put him and Pickett between the Yankee army and Washington. I just wanted to show that he could have won on his own. That he could pick a daring course of action and stick with it! I still think he wasn't wrong. . . ."

"He's really eating this up," Stuart said. He still sounded a bit dazed after his simulated death in the charge.

"Glory hound," Dell said, shaking her head. "He threw those men away!"

"It *is* just a game, Christine," McIntyre said. He grinned at Howarth. "You had me going there last night, Professor. All that stuff about history changing?"

Howarth shook his head. He'd only just emerged from the simlink, with Dell and McIntyre, his character having managed to survive the long walk back across the valley. "I just keep wondering how many people saw Bobby rewrite the way the battle turned out today. Damn, it was so *real*!"

"You were just in the bubble," McIntyre assured him.

They pressed through the glass doors of the Student Union and onto the steps outside. It was a hot July afternoon with a crystal blue sky overhead, not too different from the simulation from which they'd just emerged. A flag hung limply from the flagpole in the courtyard outside.

McIntyre felt . . . strange. Out of place. For a moment he wondered about the aftereffects of a particularly trying simlink. Some people reported feeling a bit disjointed afterward, a bit out of sorts, like sailors trying to find their land legs once more.

The flag overhead was unfamiliar. A Federal Union flag, the Stars and Stripes . . . not the Stars and Bars.

He sensed an odd burning . . . no, a doubling within himself. Two sets of memories, intact, complete, and side by side. Beyond the courtyard, beyond a stone wall still bearing ancient iron cannons, the hill fell away toward the white, monument-cluttered sprawl of Washington, D.D.

No, *not* Washington, District of Dixie . . . but Washington, D.C., the District of Columbia.

Where had *that* thought come from?

That the fate of nations could hang upon the outcome of a battle, or even upon the decision of a single man, McIntyre had no doubt. But could nations fall with the changed observation of their history? . . .

Christine . . . where was Christine? And Randy Stuart? They'd been beside him a second ago. Both of them were simply . . . gone.

General J. E. B. Stuart—who'd harried the fleeing mobs of Federal troops after their repulse from Pickett's line south of the Round Tops, who'd been President of the Confederate States of America from 1875 to 1880 . . . *no.*

There were other memories of an alternate Gettysburg, an alternate history, one where the famous Confederate cavalry commander had died after a skirmish in 1864 at a place called Yellow Tavern.

Randy Stuart had never been born.

And Christine . . . who? . . .

McIntyre was confused. The landscape around him shifted, dreamlike. One set of memories was fading now, like the shadow memories of a dream overwritten by the harsher thoughts and memories of the waking reality.

The Battle of Gettysburg had been *won*, with Hancock's Charge failing to break the dug-in Confederates of Pickett's and Longstreet's divisions astride the Taneytown and Baltimore pikes, the surrender of the Army of the Potomac coming the next day, on the centennial of American independence. Confederate independence had been recognized with the accords signed four months later, on November 19, 1863.

The Battle of Gettysburg had been *lost*, the high-water mark of the Confederacy, the beginning of the end, which would come two years later at a place called Appomattox. . . .

And far off, within the math-coprocessing bowels of some cacodemonaic cosmic computer, the last of the Schrödinger wave functions collapsed into reality.

James McIntyre blinked in the afternoon sun. His friend, his lover, George Howarth, looked at him, puzzled. "Problem?"

"Nah. Just trying to remember . . . something."

"Couldn't have been important."

"I guess not."

Together, they walked across the courtyard toward their apartment.

The Washington Wargaming Society was planning a big recreation sim for next June, on the ninety-fifth anniversary of the D day invasion of Normandy, and the WWII Reenactors' Club was planning a major event for June 6. He and Howarth were on the planning committee.

There'd been a lot of media interest so far.

It promised to be quite a show.

The Blood of the Fallen

James M. Reasoner

"**G**ood morning, sir," I said to the President after entering the room in Mr. David Wills's house where our party had spent the previous night. Mr. Lincoln had bade me enter after I knocked discreetly upon the door.

He was fully dressed for the ceremony save for his coat, which was draped over the back of the chair where he sat, and the black stovepipe hat, which reposed upon the writing desk next to a piece of paper. Mr. Lincoln laid aside the pen with which he had been writing and greeted me with a slight smile.

"Good morning, Captain. I trust you slept well."

"Very well, sir. And yourself?"

Mr. Lincoln leaned back a little in the chair and sighed. "Not as well as I might have hoped. I've been worried about Tad, you know."

Well indeed did I know the President's concern. The previous morning, when he had arisen to prepare for the day's journey by rail to Gettysburg, Pennsylvania, he had found that his son Thomas, also known as Tad, was ill with a fever of some sort. Ever since the death of his son William ("Willie") the year before, Mr. Lincoln had lavished all his affection upon Tad and had grown quite attached to the lad. I had heard him say that Tad was the best, most true friend he ever had. So it was only natural that the boy's illness would be a matter of most grievous anxiety to the President.

Mrs. Lincoln had not helped the situation, either, since her own attitude concerning Tad's health bordered on hysteria. I had heard her beg Mr. Lincoln to cancel his trip to Gettysburg. She insisted that the new cemetery located there could be dedicated without his remarks. Mr. Lincoln had considered his wife's request, then decided to make the journey anyway, furthering the rift between them, for Mrs. Lincoln was never so concerned about other things that she could not find the time to coddle some new resentment against her husband.

Ah, but I speak of things which I should not. Were I a servant, the ability to keep silent concerning what I see of my master's and mistress's behavior would no doubt be bred into me. But I am a soldier, so naturally I speak in a more blunt fashion.

On the morning in question, after his greeting to me, Mr. Lincoln picked up his pen once again, dipped it in the inkwell, crossed out a short passage in what he had written, and inscribed new words above those which had been deleted. Then he nodded in satisfaction, got to his feet, and picked up the paper.

"This isn't very long, but I think it will do. I'll have a go at it for Seward and see what he thinks," announced the President.

Secretary of State Seward, who also had made the trip to Gettysburg, was housed in a room directly across the hall. I stepped back, opened the door for Mr. Lincoln, and waited in the corridor while he knocked on Mr. Seward's door and was admitted by the Secretary.

The time I spent waiting in the corridor allowed me to reflect upon my service to the President. He was quite close to his secretaries, Mr. John G. Nicolay and Mr. John Hay, because he spent a great deal of time with them. I daresay Mr. Lincoln thought of the two young men as friends, though they were so awestruck by him that they probably were incapable of returning the feeling in quite the same manner. As captain of the military guard detail that watched over him, I, too, spent a considerable amount of time in the company of Mr. Lincoln. I had seen him in all his moods: the robust cheer that was a legacy of his days as a backwoodsman; the black anger that could sweep upon him with little or no warning; the deep melancholies that threatened to draw him down into an abyss from which there was no escape. The President's mental state was like lightning, flickering here and there with no sense of where it might strike next.

This is not to condemn him; were I charged, as he was, with the monumental task of managing a war while at the same time avoiding the trips and snares of political life, I have no doubt that my mind would not be up to the chore. I was but a simple soldier whose only concern was keeping the President safe from physical harm.

Shortly, he and Secretary Seward emerged from the Secretary's room, and Mr. Lincoln returned to his own bedchamber to claim his hat and coat. As we went downstairs, he took a pair of white gloves from a pocket of the coat and drew them on. I thought they gave him an exceedingly dapper look, which was unusual for him.

Mr. David Wills, whose idea it had been to convert part of the battlefield near Gettysburg into a cemetery so that the brave men who had died there could be laid to rest with the proper dignity, in proper surroundings, met us at the door of the house. He said, "Your horse is waiting, Mr. President. The procession will be getting underway soon."

Mr. Lincoln nodded. "Thank you, Mr. Wills. And thank you as well for inviting me to speak. It is an honor to be here."

"The honor is ours, Mr. President," said Mr. Wills as he ushered our small party out-of-doors.

A military band was gathering to lead the procession.

The dignitaries who would occupy the speakers' platform were mounting up. I did not see Mr. Edward Everett, who was to be the principal speaker. Along with Mr. Wills, Mr. Everett had greeted us upon our arrival in Gettysburg the previous evening, but I was given to understand in a later conversation with one of Mr. Wills's friends that Mr. Everett suffered from a bladder ailment and was wont to disappear for short periods of time on frequent occasions. So I thought nothing of his absence now.

There was some delay before the procession began moving toward the new cemetery, and during this interval, members of the crowd which had gathered along the street pressed close to the President, eager to shake Mr. Lincoln's hand or simply to touch the hem of his coat. Mr. Lincoln was pleasant to one and all, but as one who knew him well, I could see and recognize the dark brooding in his eyes. He was worried about the remarks he was to make, worried about his son Tad, worried about his wife and her anxieties. Those things I knew, and though I sympathized deeply with the President, there was nothing I could do to alleviate his concerns.

Finally, with much pomp, to the strains of martial music, the procession got underway and moved out of Gettysburg to the south, heading toward the long, wooded elevation which had been known as Granite Ridge before the battle but which was now increasingly referred to as Cemetery Ridge. That would have been an appropriate name even before the great conflict, for at the northern apex of the elevation was located the old Evergreen Cemetery. Now, adjacent to it, the new cemetery had been established, and the work of reinterring the bodies of the soldiers from their shallow graves scattered about the battlefield was proceeding steadily, though there still remained many of the poor lifeless lads to be transferred to their new resting places.

The battle had taken place the previous July, and this

was late November. So nearly five months had passed, but still the smell of death hung over the fields. Many carcasses of horses and mules killed in the conflict lay here and there, rotting in the sun. They had been cleared away from the new cemetery, but some were close enough so that their unpleasant odor drifted to the speakers' platform.

There was no seat for me on the platform, of course..I stood near the steps at one end of the bunting-draped structure. Next to my position, a small tent had been erected, for what purpose I had no idea at the time. I watched Mr. Lincoln climb onto the platform and take his seat next to his friend, Mr. Ward Lamon, who would introduce him later. The band continued to play, and the huge crowd that had streamed out of Gettysburg in the wake of the official procession gathered in front of the platform. I looked along the ridge at the great semicircle of new graves that had been formed, each one marked with a small headstone. It was a peaceful scene, beautiful yet sad, but above all peaceful, as death is the ultimate tranquility.

I looked around but still saw no sign of Mr. Edward Everett. However, a few moments later, the tent flap opened and the man himself stepped out, clumsily buttoning the final button on his trousers. Remembering what I had been told about Mr. Everett's bladder ailment, I now realized the purpose of the tent. Mr. Everett nodded to me, then began to ascend the steps to the platform.

Someone tugged on my sleeve, and I turned to see one of the young officers assigned to my detail, Lieutenant Wallace by name. He looked quite agitated, so I said, "What is it, Lieutenant? What's wrong?"

"A telegraph message has just arrived from Washington," he informed me.

"For the President?"

"Yes, sir."

"Well, it will have to wait," I told him. "The ceremony

will soon be underway, and it will cause great upset if it is interrupted."

"But, sir—" Lieutenant Wallace broke off his protest and swallowed hard before he resumed, "I really think the President should be informed of this development, sir."

"Give me the message."

"You'll give it to the President, Captain?"

I fixed the lieutenant with the cold stare of command and repeated, "Give me the message."

Wallace was a good officer despite his current distraught state. He obeyed orders, handing me a telegraph flimsy. I glanced at it, then looked again as my heart began to pound in shock.

Though most of that fateful day I remember in vivid detail, time has blurred my recollection of the exact wording of that message. The gist of it, however, is still quite clear. During the night, the President's son, Thomas "Tad" Lincoln, had succumbed to the fever which had befallen him. The tragedy was a double one, for Mrs. Lincoln, who had been at her son's bedside and had insisted upon staying alone with him following his passing, with this new grief piled upon the sorrow which remained from Willie's death, had hanged herself and was also dead.

Before being assigned to see to the President's wellbeing, I had taken part in the Battle of Bull Run and had been wounded there, a Rebel bullet striking me in the left forearm but fortunately missing the bone. I can tell you in all honesty, the shock of being wounded in battle was not as great as what I felt when I read that message from Washington.

Lieutenant Wallace was right: Mr. Lincoln had to be informed of this dreadful news as soon as possible.

But when I looked to the platform, I saw that Mr. Edward Everett had already begun his address to the giant crowd. His ringing tones filled the air, and I was loath to interrupt him in his fulsome praise of the courageous men who had given their all at this spot to turn back the invasion of the raging Southerners. When Mr. Everett had concluded his remarks, I determined, I would then approach the President and inform him of what had happened. No doubt he would decline to issue his own speech and would instead return to Washington with all possible haste, but that could not be avoided.

I had forgotten, for the moment, the reputation Mr. Everett enjoyed as a prodigious speaker. Indeed, while the knowledge of the deaths of Mrs. Lincoln and young Tad gnawed at my vitals, the President sat on the platform blissfully unaware of the tragedy for two hours or more while Mr. Everett spoke. Those were, without a doubt, the lengthiest two hours of my life.

All things come to an end, and so, finally, did Mr. Edward Everett's remarks. As he turned to sit down, I went up the stairs quickly and moved behind the row of chairs until I reached Mr. Lincoln. From the corner of his eye, he saw me coming and turned his head slightly so that I might more easily bend and whisper into his ear. I did so, conveying the news to him, hating the fact that I had to be the bearer of such awful tidings.

Mr. Lincoln grew stiff, and his hands tightened on the hat he held in his lap. He turned to me and whispered, "There can be no mistake?"

"No mistake, sir," I told him. "I am so sorry."

Mr. Ward Lamon was looking at us curiously. He leaned over and asked in a quiet voice, "Mr. President, do you wish to postpone your remarks?"

To my great surprise, Mr. Lincoln shook his head. "I shall go forward with them," he said. His voice, never particularly strong, held a slight quaver, but he appeared to be determined to carry through with his obligation. My admiration for the man, already great, increased mightily at that moment.

After Mr. Lamon introduced him, the President stood

and placed his hat on his head, then stepped up beside the
desk that had been placed at the front of the platform. He
reached into his coat with his right hand and brought forth
the paper on which he had written his speech. His left hand
was slightly curled and hung at his side, the knuckles resting on the table. For a few seconds he gazed out at the
crowd, which was naturally restless after the lengthy
speech by Mr. Everett. Then, without looking at what he
had written, he began to speak.

"Four score and seven years ago . . ."

I must admit, though I have read Mr. Lincoln's famous
words many times since that day, I paid little attention to
his remarks at the time he made them. I was still standing
behind the row of chairs, watching the crowd as was my
habit on any occasion when the President appeared in public. It appeared that some of the spectators were trying to
make out the words of the speech, but others were talking
and laughing among themselves. Children ran about, and
their mothers chastised them. Near the front of the crowd,
a photographer was struggling with his photographic apparatus as he tried to set it up so that he could capture an
image of the President. The first words that really pene-
trated my consciousness since Mr. Lincoln had begun
were: ". . . government of the people, by the people, for the
people, shall not perish—"

Suddenly, he paused. As if in pain, he bent slightly at
the waist, still leaning with his left hand on the table, and
I saw a shudder go through him. He swayed momentarily
like a tree in a strong wind. I could not see his face, but
those in the crowd who were closest must have been struck
by his expression, for they fell silent and stared up at him.
Mr. Lincoln turned his head and muttered something. I had
difficulty distinguishing the words, but I believed then and
still believe that he said, "Not enough. No, not nearly
enough."

Then he straightened, his chest swelling with the deep

breath he drew into his body. He turned his head, his eyes meeting mine, and cast aside the paper he held. He thrust out his hand toward me and commanded: "Your pistol, Captain Stark."

I was struck dumb for a moment. I had no idea why Mr. Lincoln wanted my pistol. But he was, after all, my commander-in-chief. I unsnapped the flap of my holster and drew my pistol, reversing it so that I gripped the barrel. It required but a step to reach the President and place the weapon in his hand. Mr. Everett, Mr. Lamon, Mr. Wills, and all the other dignitaries on the platform, including the governor of Pennsylvania and the governors of several neighboring states, looked on in shock and horror. None of them knew what the President intended to do with the pistol.

Nor did I.

He swung around to face the startled crowd once more, the pistol gripped tightly in his upraised hand. His voice rang out with more power than I had ever heard in it before. I know now that he was returning to a theme already delineated in his speech as he said: "No, we cannot consecrate this hallowed ground, for the men who died here have already done that. The brave men who fell . . . *and the blood of the fallen cries out for vengeance!*"

I fear my jaw dropped in surprise. Though there was no doubt he was possessed of a volatile temper, I had never heard the President speak of vengeance on anyone, in any form or fashion. But now, his voice shaking with emotion, he continued: "Those who have brought us to this tragic pass must be punished. Those who will turn away from the bosom of the nation must be driven from it like vipers. They must be made to pay for their traitorous actions. Would that I were a soldier once more myself, that I might take this pistol and shed Rebel blood!"

He thrust the pistol into the air, and at that moment, the photographer who had been struggling with his equipment finally succeeded in arranging it to his liking. He threw the black shroud over his head and bent to his apparatus, exposing the collodion-covered plate in the camera so that the powerful image of President Lincoln, standing on the speakers' platform at Gettysburg, his face dark with anger and hatred, his hand brandishing a pistol as he swore vengeance on the South, was captured for all time.

Cheers began to rise from the crowd. I knew what they did not; indeed I knew what no one there was aware of save myself, Mr. Lincoln, and Lieutenant Wallace. The President was acting out of terrible grief for his wife and son, not out of his true nature. The twin demons of anger and melancholy had him in their grip.

But the motivating factors no longer mattered. The President had called for vengeance on behalf of those brave soldiers who had died at Gettysburg, and the crowd, as crowds always will when emotions are sufficiently high, embraced his wish. The cheers became shouts, the shouts became howls, and the tumult rose above the formerly peaceful hills.

By the time we returned to Washington that evening, news of the President's remarks had somehow preceded us. The city was abuzz with speculation.

Already in recent months there had been a great deal of talk in the capital concerning how the rebellious Southern states would be dealt with once the insurrection was concluded. Before the battle at Gettysburg, I would have said that such talk was putting the cart before the horse, that it was best to win the victory before discussing the terms of the peace.

However, as a military man, I could see now that the end was inevitable. The invasion of Pennsylvania was the high-water mark of the Southern states' efforts to break free of the Union. With a decided advantage in both men and material residing with the Federal forces, it was only a

matter of time until the so-called Confederacy was defeated. No one wishes more to see the end of war than a
soldier. To my way of thinking, the time had come to talk
of settlement and peace.

The Democrats wished to see a cessation of hostilities,
the withdrawal of the Emancipation Proclamation, and
amnesty for the Rebel states, which would be welcomed
back into the Union as if they had never left. A faction of
the Republican party was in general agreement with this
stance, with the sole exception that the freed slaves would
remain free. This, indeed, was the position which I believed was held by Mr. Lincoln. The radicals in the President's party, however, were much more vehement in their
insistence that the rebellious states should be punished for
their sins rather than forgiven. Some members of Congress, in fact, would have seen those states stripped of their
very statehood and reverted to the status of territories instead, governed by military governors, with no leaders and
no real power of their own. In order to assure equality for
freedmen, Southern landowners would be stripped of all
their property and possessions, which would then be distributed among those deemed deserving by the Federal
government.

The men who held these beliefs took heart when they
heard of the President's remarks. Mr. Lincoln had come
over to their side. Indeed, when sketches appeared in
Harper's Weekly of Mr. Lincoln standing on the platform
in Gettysburg with a gun in his hand, calling for
vengeance, the drumbeat of the radicals grew steadily
stronger.

No one was quite prepared, however, for the intensity
with which the President pursued this new goal. He proposed either execution, imprisonment, or banishment for
the leaders of the Southern government, as well as for any
officers above the rank of captain in their military. He proposed as well that all Southern assets be seized and held in

perpetuity by the Federal government, and that the owning of any sort of property by former members of the Confederate army be forbidden. These former soldiers would instead be forced to work in the fields and all the fruits of their labor would be turned over to a commission of freedmen and Northern managers and advisors. The white Southerners would, in effect, become slaves themselves.

Mr. Lincoln busied himself with these matters during the winter of 1863–64, urging Congress to pass resolutions calling for such arrangements, pending the surrender of the Confederate leaders. By occupying himself so strenuously, he was able to put aside the memory of that bitterly cold day in Washington when both his wife and his youngest son were laid to rest.

I remember seeing the yellow glow of a lamp burning in the window of his bedchamber in the White House, far into the night on many occasions as I checked the guard detail. Sometimes when I saw him at his desk, more gaunt and haggard than ever, I felt in my heart that I should speak to him, should urge him to put this remorseless effort behind him. But he was my commander-in-chief, and it was not my place to tell him how to conduct the affairs of the nation.

No one had informed the leaders of the Southern army of the inevitability of their defeat. With a fanaticism heretofore unseen, they fought on stubbornly through 1864, through Mr. Lincoln's overwhelming reelection to the presidency, through the terrible lean months of '65 when there was no food to be had in the South and they found themselves harried at every turn by General Grant, General Sherman, and the Federal troops at their disposal. The summer of 1865 found General Robert E. Lee and the pitiful remnants of his army pinned against the sea near Norfolk, having slipped past the Union forces that had earlier burned Richmond. There are times when I wish I could have been there to see that gallant, foolish final charge led personally by the great Southern general. I know, however, I would not have wanted to witness Lee's death, especially in such a lost cause. A soldier can find joy in the defeat of an enemy, but not in the death of good men.

With Lee dead and the Southern army defeated, Jefferson Davis and the other political leaders of the Confederacy were brought to Washington, tried, and hanged. I shall never forget the sight of Mr. Lincoln standing and looking in satisfaction at the row of gallows along Pennsylvania Avenue, with their grisly burdens swaying slightly at the ends of their ropes.

That should have been the end of it. The Southern territories were in utter subjugation. With the President supporting them, the radicals had a firm grip on power and policy, and they began to put their plans into effect. Anyone who opposed their harsh treatment of the conquered lands was brushed aside.

And there *was* opposition. In the spring of '66, a cabal composed of Southerners bitter at their defeat and disenfranchisement and Northerners who believed that the present course would ultimately result in the destruction of the nation, plotted the assassination of the President. Fortunately, one of the men intrusted with the details of the plan, an actor, was too fond of strong drink and said too much to the wrong person. I accompanied the detail that went to arrest them.

We climbed quickly up the stairs of the boarding house where the plotters were congregated and burst in upon them. My pistol—the same one that Mr. Lincoln had held above his head at Gettysburg—was in my hand when I rushed in with the other soldiers. The plotters were well armed and began firing on us. I saw the actor, a fellow called Booth, pointing a revolver at me and discharged my own weapon before he could fire his. He was thrown back against a wall by the impact of the bullet and then slid slowly down it, leaving a smear of blood on the paper. That was the first time I had seen combat since Bull Run.

But it was not to be the last.

By December of 1866, there were reports that an army was once again forming in the Southern territories. It was a different sort of army than had ever been seen before, however. These forces, supposedly led by a former Confederate cavalry general named Forrest, moved like phantoms, striking here to wipe out a garrison, then in another territory to burn down a supply warehouse, then in yet another territory to blow up a railroad bridge. These fast, hard strikes were the sort of thing that had been carried out during the war by irregulars, but that was all the South had left to carry on the fight. Forrest was a fugitive, facing imprisonment or death if he were caught, so he had nothing to lose by harrying the army of occupation. The movement he started, reportedly called by its adherents the Brigade of the New South, spread rapidly, but it would have remained little more than a minor annoyance had it not been for the British.

Always possessed of a certain sympathy for the Confederate cause, the British government, disturbed by the effect upon their economy of the destruction of the American cotton industry, decided to recognize the New South as the true government of the Southern territories, and the brigadier, as Forrest was now known, as its leader.

I well remember that day in the spring of 1867 when Secretary Seward broke the news to Mr. Lincoln. The President was sitting at his desk, more thin and drawn than ever, but his eyes burned like fire as he listened to the Secretary. Mr. Seward concluded by asking: "What shall we do, Mr. President?"

Mr. Lincoln looked up and said, "The British go too far. If they ally themselves with our enemies, then they are our enemies, too. We shall invade Canada and show them the folly of their actions."

Mr. Seward's eyebrows shot up. "Sir?"

The President's fist thumped down hard upon the desk. "This government shall not be trifled with! The world had best recognize that fact, and the sooner it does, the better."

Acting on Mr. Lincoln's orders, Mr. Seward summoned Secretary of War Stanton, and soon Generals Grant and Sherman were closeted with them as well as plans drawn to launch an invasion of Canada. The first strike would be across the Niagara River in New York, at the spot where the great falls of the same name thundered.

The attack was repulsed, and almost immediately, Great Britain declared war on the United States. For the third time in less than a hundred years, we found ourselves locked in a struggle with the former mother country. At the same time, the British continued sending aid to the brigadier and the New South, so that we were fighting on two fronts, and within a matter of months the strain began to tell on our army. Our forces began to withdraw from the Southern territories, but that withdrawal simply emboldened Forrest. According to the few spies we still had in his camp, the brigadier began making plans to march on Washington.

With the entire country threatened, Mr. Lincoln followed the only course of action that seemed open to him: He declared a state of martial law and suspended the elections that normally would have been held that autumn. The elections would take place, he pledged, as soon as the threats from north and south were dealt with successfully.

The howls of outrage from Congress were deafening, but at least half of the populace still supported Mr. Lincoln, rallying to the sentiments he had first expressed on that awful day at Gettysburg. And he still commanded the army, which was not an insignificant matter. So he was able to cling to power, however tenuously.

The Year of Our Lord 1869 was the turning point. One last bastion of Federal power remained in the South: that in Florida. It was wiped out by a two-pronged attack, an overland assault led by the brigadier combined with a seaborne invasion by the British. With that final obstacle removed, the entire former Confederacy was united again, save for the Republic of Texas, which had withdrawn to go its own way (a development which came as no surprise to anyone who had had the slightest dealing with the Texans). The British and Canadians had fought our troops to a standstill and forced them back south of the northern border; then, in a daring stroke, they swept down to take control of the Midwest and the Mississippi River. Just as when our forces captured the Father of Waters and dealt a severe blow to the insurrectionists, so did this British maneuver damage our chances of defeating them.

The fateful meeting between the brigadier and the British prime minister took place on one of the Caribbean islands. As was reported later, Forrest asked the prime minister to have the British forces merely hold their positions. He wanted the task of dealing with Mr. Lincoln's army himself. His foreign ally having agreed to this proposal, the brigadier began to move his forces up through Virginia, past the burned-out former capital of Richmond, following a path that would bring him ultimately to Washington, D.C.

The soldiers of the Union fought valiantly, but the long struggle that had never really ceased since the firing on Fort Sumter more than eight years earlier had weakened our army to the point that they could not hold back the Southerners. In a move that shocked nearly everyone north of the Mason-Dixon Line, the brigadier pledged that the slaves who had been freed by Mr. Lincoln's famous proclamation would remain free under the government of the New South and would indeed play a vital role in the society which he envisioned. This further weakened what little support still remained to the President. Men began to desert in droves from the army, no longer able to understand why they were fighting.

It was a warm night in August when the end came. The roar of cannons on the capital's outskirts had been heard for days, but on this day it had grown steadily louder. Now, as darkness fell, the night sky was emblazoned with red, a nightmarish reflection of the conflagrations that encircled the city. I could see the glare through the windows of the President's office as I entered.

"Sir," I said to Mr. Lincoln, "the carriage is waiting to take you to the station."

It had been decided earlier in the day that while the trains were still running, the government should be moved from Washington to New York. Many members of Congress had already fled. Mr. Lincoln had waited, however, loath to leave the city that had been his home for the past nine years, the city that had represented to him everything that he held dear about our nation. It was the city, as well, that held so many unhappy memories for him, but I believe he was as reluctant to let go of those as he was the recollections of his many triumphs. The pain was too much a part of him to relinquish it easily.

Now he looked up at me from where he sat at his desk and shook his head. He said, "I cannot go, Captain Stark."

"But, sir," I responded, "the city will likely fall before morning."

Mr. Lincoln nodded gravely. "I am aware of that, and I appreciate your concern, Captain, but the fact remains that my place is here." His back stiffened, and his bearded chin jutted defiantly. "I am the President of the United States."

Soon he would be president of nothing but a shattered dream, but I could not bring myself to speak those words. I merely nodded and said, "Yes, sir."

"But there is no reason for you to stay. Go on, Captain. Get out while you can."

"This is my assigned post, sir."

Mr. Lincoln clenched his hands into fists and leaned forward. "And I have ordered you to go!"

I allowed myself a slight smile as I said, "For the first time in my military career, sir, I find that I cannot obey an order from a superior."

A moment of silence passed as the President stared angrily at me, then, abruptly, he surprised me by laughing. He came to his feet, his long, ungainly form seeming to fill the room.

"Once I ordered you to give me your pistol, Captain. I wish to heaven I had never issued that order, but it is much too late to rescind it now. So now, once again . . ." He held out his hand. "I'll trouble you for your pistol."

Through the window behind him, I saw that the glow of the fires filled more than half the sky. The earth vibrated beneath our feet from the explosions of the artillery shells falling on the city. I said, "Mr. President, if I give you my pistol, I cannot protect you."

"I know, Captain. The time has come for me to fight my own battles."

A particularly loud explosion sounded somewhere nearby. I felt the hot sting of tears in my eyes as I unholstered my pistol and passed it across the desk to Mr. Lincoln. He took it and said, "The fight was the right one, Captain, but it was fought the wrong way."

I nodded in agreement, unable to speak because of the emotion that blocked my throat.

Mr. Lincoln raised the pistol and started to turn toward the window, prepared to face whatever might come, when suddenly a huge report sounded, accompanied by a blinding flash of light. I felt myself lifted and thrown back as if by a gigantic hand, and when I landed I was in an all-enveloping darkness; to its black embrace I surrendered myself without struggle.

*   *   *

I am an old man now, and in my time I have seen nations rise and fall and rise again. Our British allies could not be trusted, of course, and within a decade the brigadier's New South was fighting futilely for its life against an empire bent on regaining some of what it regarded as wayward colonies. The Texans united the western states, under their leadership, naturally, and by the turn of the century the Mississippi River was the boundary line between Texas and New Britain. Now there is talk that there may be a great war in Europe, a war that may well engulf the entire world. I think, as an old soldier myself, I am entitled to ask if there is no end to madness.

But the question is answered even before it is asked.

I have never told anyone, but on that day at Gettysburg, after the President cast aside the speech he had written and took up the gun instead, I sought out that crumpled bit of paper and rescued it from being trampled beneath the feet of the crowd. I have it still, carefully smoothed out and saved all these years, though the writing on it has faded quite a bit. I can make out how it was to end, though: "that this government of the people, by the people, for the people, shall not perish from the earth." Noble sentiments, forgotten in the pain of loss.

From that day forward, Mr. Lincoln fled from his grief but could never escape it. It grew and spread and affected the fate of nations. Without the grief there might have been forgiveness; with forgiveness might have come hope.

But the blood of the fallen cries out, and we answer. God help us all, we answer.

The High-Water Mark

Brendan DuBois

Alex Ruzdic parked the rental car at the visitors' center at the Gettysburg National Military Park, and waited impatiently for his son, Peter, to join him. His boy was tall and gangly and just barely thirteen. Peter could also hardly hide his dismay at spending a school holiday with his father and never failed to make some sort of stink about it. Alex tried to remember what it was like to be thirteen and whether he had disliked his father that much. Was it possible? His father had been a tractor mechanic, had worked hard and died young, and had been so proud that his only son had gotten into a university. Now, nearly twenty years later, he was at a university still, teaching American history, and he was sure Father would be even more proud of what he had accomplished in his life.

But Peter? "Pride of father" was probably never an expression that crossed his lips, and Alex knew the boy wished he was in some sort of hi tech business, making lots of money and piling up the stock options, but Alex was happy at the university, and happy to be here as well, on this hallowed ground. The airplane trip here had been a long one, and Peter's mother was spending the day shopping in Washington, but he was determined that he would show Peter this special place.

"Come along, Peter," he said. "I have to show you something—something important."

Peter sullenly closed the door to the rental car and came around. He had on blue jeans, black sneakers, and a black T-shirt that promoted some rock group Alex had never heard of. The boy's mood seemed to match the day's weather: cool and overcast, nothing like that awful hot July day so many years ago.

"And what's so important?" Peter asked, slowly walking over.

"If you hurry up, I'll show you," Alex said, trying to keep his impatience in check.

They took a path along a paved road that led deep into the park, and Alex noted all the rows of monuments, denoting places where farmed regiments had made their stand. Flags flapped in the breeze, and Alex hurried to a place where Civil War–era cannons were set up, near fences of wood and by a stone wall, pointing down toward a wide field. There. This was his fourth trip to Cemetery Ridge and it still brought tears to his eyes and made his hands shake.

He stood still and waited for Alex to join him. "There," he said, sweeping his arm across the field before them, a field that dropped down to a line of trees. "Imagine what it was like, more than a hundred years ago. It was a hot day, July third. This was supposed to be a quiet area. The forces for the Union that were here weren't expecting a fight, but the cannons opened up on them in the afternoon. The Union cannons fired right back, and for a while it was a cannoning duel, until Meade, the Union general, ordered the cannon fire to ease up, to make the Confederate forces think they had damaged the opposing batteries. Then they came, out of the woodline, tens of thousand of them, lined up and marching. It was like they were getting ready for a parade."

Peter leaned against a cannon barrel. "Uh-huh."

Never in his years at the university had Alex ever faced a more obstinate listener, and he pressed on. "The Confederate general in charge of the field was called Pickett, and what happened next would be forever known later as Pickett's Charge. The Confederate forces came up here, moving and moving, despite the fire and grapeshot and cannon fire that rained down on them. It was a fierce, fierce battle, and it happened, right here."

Peter folded his arms. "Uh-huh."

Now exasperated, Alex said, "Right here, Peter. Right here where we're standing was that crucial battle, and later, it would be called 'The High-Water Mark' of the Confederacy. And you know what else was important?"

"Nope," came the disinterested voice.

"Your great-great-grandfather, he was here. On this spot. Young Nicholas Ruzdic, far from home and his family, and here, he made his own stand, his own private stand."

For a moment, that seemed to get Peter's attention. "Really?"

"Really," Alex said, now hearing the pride in his own voice. "In fact, some historians think what he did that day, how he fought and what he achieved, won the day on the battlefield."

Peter unfolded his arms, now looked over at the grassy field below Cemetery Ridge, and looked back at his father.

"Cool," he said.

Never had he been so hot in his life, and even after filling up his belly with cool spring water, young Nicholas Ruzdic, a draftee in his nation's army, was thirsty again. They had spent the previous two days marching here, to this small town called Gettysburg in Pennsylvania, and he wasn't sure what he would find there, but he knew it would be terrible. He envied the other soldiers in his regiment, how they would relax and smoke smuggled tobacco and write letters home—those few who could read or write— and play games while in camp, but he could never relax, not ever. Even at night when he slept, he dreamed of the rich soil of his farm and his mother and father and sisters, and always, the dream ended the same way. The regimental army officer riding up, telling him that he had been drafted into his nation's service, and into the horror of war. And what a war! He had no fight with the Southerners, cared not what they did or how they lived, but his nation had plucked him from his simple life on the farm and brought him here, and it terrified him so.

He still got the shakes, remembering the first battle he had been in here, when he had arrived in this part of the country. A minor skirmish that probably merited a sentence or two in whatever dispatches were sent to Mr. Lincoln, but several men of his regiment had died that day, from bullets to the head or the gut or a sword thrust into the neck. The men hadn't died tidy, oh no sir; there was blood and screams and entrails oozing out, like when he helped Father butcher hogs back home, and he remembered how it was that horrible day. In one moment of time, someone he had trained with—like Boris, for example—with whom he had joked and swapped tales of growing up, had been alive and breathing, probably wishing to go back home as well to his own family farm. Then those Rebel yells, the gunfire, the thudding of hooves of the Rebel cavalry, and young Boris, about his own age, was sitting up against a tree, trying to hold in his guts with his bloody fingers. God in Heaven . . .

Didn't anybody else feel this way? It didn't seem so, for a day after that skirmish, most of the other men in the regiment, especially the officers, had shrugged it off. It was war, after all—even if it wasn't their war—and they were here to perform a duty. But Nicholas trembled with fear for days afterward, up to this day in Gettysburg, and knew what troubled him the most.

For he was a coward, there was no doubt about that, and the penalty for cowardice in his regiment was death.

Now, on this hot day, he was thirsty and was bivouacked with his regiment when the cannon fire opened up unexpectedly, and he ducked and felt his bladder let loose, and he knew he would die this day, either from the hands of the enemy or those who were supposed to be his comrades.

Alex was encouraged by Peter's response. "Cool, yes, I suppose you're right." He waved his arm out across the field again. "So there they were. This was Lee's last gamble, to try to crack the lines of the Union forces. For two previous days they had fought here, almost to a draw. But Lee knew if he could punch through this line here, on Cemetery Ridge, then the road to Washington would be open. And he was sure that Lincoln would sue for peace if he and his forces were starting to march on Washington. I mean, look around, Peter. Washington isn't that far away. A two-day march, if that."

Peter looked over at the wide field. "That's a hell of a distance to walk, Dad. You mean his troops came right up here?"

"Yes, they did."

"And the Union guys, they were here, firing at them, with their cannons and stuff?"

"Yes, they were."

Now it seemed like Peter was getting more interested and Alex tried to restrain his excitement at finally getting through that sullen exterior. "Man," Peter said, looking down at the field. "They must have been nuts."

Oops. Alex didn't feel so excited anymore, felt his voice rise. "Nuts? What do you mean, nuts?"

Peter shrugged. "I can't believe anybody would do that, that's what. What's the point? I mean, getting yourself killed, and over what?"

Alex eased his breathing. Remember, he thought, this is your boy. Not a grad student trying to needle his professor.

Just a boy, that's all, brought up in the lap of luxury, knowing hardly anything about the past.

He managed a smile at his son. "The point was, these men out here, they thought they were fighting for their country, that's why. They thought they were defending their homes. Oh, some were defending slavery and others were fighting because they had no choice, but most were fighting here for an ideal, for something greater than themselves. I know it's hard to believe, Peter, but there was a time when an idea was enough to make a man pick up a gun and defend what he thought was right."

Peter said, "And my great-great-grandfather, he was here?"

Alex looked back, past the paved road. "Yes, over there. The day of the battle his unit was kept in ready reserve to respond in case there was a breach in the lines."

Peter smirked. "So, when the battle started, he was just sitting back, having a cool one?"

Alex looked down at the line of woods where young Colonel Alexander's cannons had been placed, where they had been cascading shells into the Union lines.

"No, not really," Alex said. "Not really."

Nicholas slowly raised himself up, peering up the slope of the hill, past the smoke and debris. The crotch of his wool pants was wet, and he picked up a handful of soil, to rub it against himself, to hide from everybody else that he had panicked and had soiled himself like a child. But no one was paying him attention. Everyone else was hunkered down as the cannon fire was returned by the Union batteries on the other side of the hill. About them were trees and boulders and fields and a dirt road and some farmhouses. Horses in the distance stirred and pulled against their lines.

"Damn Rebs," someone muttered nearby. "I thought this was suppose to be a quiet place. No fighting here, the captain said. You heard him last night. No fighting here."

"Maybe somebody forgot to tell the Rebs," someone else said, and there was some laughter, and even Nicholas joined in for a moment, just to clear his head. Nearby there was a little white farmhouse where it looked like some of the Union generals and the others were meeting, for even at this distance, he could tell the officers by their hats and by the way they held themselves. More cannon fire erupted and shells exploded in the distance, and then the captain trotted up, his uniform and brass and piping nice and shiny, his beard clean and trimmed. Flanking him was his adjutant, also resplendent in his own shiny uniform, and on the other side of the captain was the flag bearer, carrying the staff with the regimental banner fluttering in the hot breeze.

The captain leaned forward in his saddle. "Hold on, lads. The Rebs have stirred up some trouble, but I'm sure we'll be in the thick of it soon enough. Just stay here and hold on. Don't dare move back or try to hide. No other place is as good as the one you're standing on. It's all chance, all a matter of God's will. But hang on and maybe we'll be in for some fighting, some chance for you to do your duty."

Then the captain rode off, his adjutant at his side, the regimental banner flying proudly, and even though Nicholas was frightened and thirsty and wished again for the thousandth time he were back home, the sight of the regimental colors did stir him some. A patriot, he thought with disgust. I'm just a simple farmer, nothing else. I'm no patriot.

Another burst of cannon fire off to the right, and some screams, and Nicholas hunched over. Damn captain, he thought. At least the bastard gets to ride away if the firing gets too hot and heavy.

*   *   *

Peter was sitting by a large elm tree, his long legs splayed out. "So, when do we get back to D.C., and see Mom?"

"When we're done here," Alex said, sitting down next to him.

Peter said something like "jeez" and folded his arms, and then Alex tried to pick up the pace. My word, can't the boy see what happened here, why it was so important? Alex thought. And to think that his own flesh and blood had been here more than a hundred years ago!

Other tourists were moving along the park roadway, stopping here and there to look at the regimental monuments. But Alex tried to ignore them, tried to get back to the tale.

"So, in the afternoon, at about 2 P.M., Pickett's Virginian troops and the others started marching out of the woods. They were lined up, almost in parade-ground formation, and then they started their long march. Tens of thousands of them, in gray and blue and red, lined up, one right after another. One Union officer said the sight was so terribly wonderful that he felt guilty ordering the cannons to open up on them. But open up on them they did."

Peter picked up a piece of grass, started chewing on it. "Uh-huh."

"The Confederate batteries kept on firing against the Union lines, right here, but they were running low on powder and shot. But no mind, the soldiers out there in the fields, ready to march up here, they thought they were the best in the world. And they were going to prove it to the Union forces that day, one way or another. So they started marching, right up to these lines, right up to all of the cannons and rifle fire, marching right into the mouth of Hell itself."

Peter looked at the wooden fencing and the Union cannon and back down at the field. "And where was my great-great-grandfather?"

"In the reserve, not very far from here," Alex said. "And pretty soon, he would be called upon to do his duty."

"He was, was he?"

Alex nodded. "Yes. And you want to know why? Because he was the bravest of the brave. That's why."

After about a half hour of cannon fire, Nicholas had pissed himself again and had thrown up as well, when a nearby shell had smashed into a neighboring company of infantry, blowing apart arms and heads and legs. Horses fell to their sides, screaming in a high-pitched noise, their guts spilling out onto the ground. Once again, the captain had come back with his two companions, the adjutant and flag bearer, calling out to them, raising his voice above the sound of cannon and rifle fire, "Hold on, lads, just hold on! We'll be going up to the line soon enough! Just hold on!"

One old sergeant next to Nicholas said, "You hold on yourself, you damn fool. Tonight we'll be sleeping in a dirt grave while you'll be in bed with some whore. Hold on yourself."

Nicholas kept his mouth shut, knowing that insulting an officer like that was a serious charge, serious enough for flogging or even death if the officer was in a particularly foul mood. Nicholas also kept his head down, watching everything unfold before him, up on the crest of the hill. Smoke was rising up in great, gray waves, like mist on a cold morning out on the farm. The sound of cannon fire was a constant, thundering hammering that made his head hurt. His hands were sweaty as well, holding on to the rifle, and occasionally, he would wipe his hands dry on his wool coat, and sure enough, they would be wet again.

He looked around, tried to think of something to ease the trembles in his stomach. The last time he had been this sick had been on the boat trip that had brought him here. The constant moving back and forth on the water had made him throw up every day, making him so weak that he had almost fainted during their first long march off the transport.

But now . . . He knew that this was a major battle unfolding, nothing like the little skirmishes they had encountered here and there. Oh, the spilt blood and guts were real enough, but in a small skirmish, you could always make a point of trying to be safe. Find a boulder or a tree to huddle against, fire your rifle every now and then. Let the ones who thought they were brave go out and prove themselves. Not Nicholas, no sir. He would do as little as possible and keep his head and behind down. Let somebody else be a hero.

Here, though, that was a problem. On the other side of this ridge there were a few trees and rocks, but mostly it was open field. And suppose the Rebs came pouring over that ridge, screaming that damn yell of theirs that made his hands shake? Where could he hide then? Where could he be safe?

Another cannonball whistled nearby, bounced once off the grass, and exploded. A Union soldier in blue grabbed at his chest and fell to the ground, and Nicholas tried to swallow. He knew what he would do. If the Rebs came this way, he'd drop his rifle and run, hide somewhere. Then come out after the battle, smear some blood on him from some poor dead bastard, and claim that he was knocked out by a cannonball explosion nearby or something. In the confusion after a battle as big as this one, he was sure he could get away with it.

For he was a coward, and he was comfortable with that. Why the hell not? This wasn't his fight, no sir.

Alex brought his boy over to a place on the line where there was a succession of monuments and additional cannons, all pointing down the gentle slope of the hill. "Here, this is where the Virginians and their allies almost broke through the lines. You have to remember that the Union forces, they had made a number of victories here and there, but they often thought of themselves as the underdogs. For the most part, the Confederate forces had better generals, better tactics, even though the Union had better arms and equipment. So the battle could have gone either way that day, once the Virginians came up here. Right here, Peter, right here."

Peter looked around blankly, and Alex had the same irrational thought as before: that the boy, dressed in his jeans and rock-and-roll T-shirt, was somehow showing disrespect to this place. But then Peter surprised him by saying, "Dad, this place . . . it feels strange. I mean . . ."

Alex tried to hide the surprise in his voice. "Go on. What do you mean?"

Peter shuddered, rubbed at his bare arms. "I don't know. It just seems spooky. It's such a nice day. It's hard to believe all that you were saying. About the rifle fire and cannon fire and all the men dying here. And here we are, nothing much going on . . ."

Alex knelt down on the grass, put his fingers in the soil, his voice getting thick with emotion. "Here. Put your hands in the dirt, Peter. Just like this."

His boy looked around, probably to see if anybody else was seeing his crazy dad, but no, it looked safe, so Peter did just that. His thin fingers probed through the grass and into the dirt. Alex continued, going beneath the grass, his voice now quiet. "Feel that, feel the soil?"

"Uh-huh," his boy replied.

"That's what's real up here on this ridge. The tree, the fence, these cannons, the grass. They weren't here when the battle was going on. They all came later, just like the visitors' center, that paved road, the monuments. All of it came later, except for this."

Alex pulled up a small handful of soil. "This ground, this earth. This is where the reality is, Peter. You hold this soil and you can almost imagine hearing the sounds of the cannon fire, the rifles firing, the shouts and yells. You can almost imagine smelling the stink of fear, the burnt gunpowder, the burning of the fences and brush. All right here in this dirt. This is real, this is what connects us."

Peter imitated his father, brought up a small collection of soil as well. "He probably walked on this, didn't he."

Alex nodded. "Yes. Right here. Your great-great-grandfather probably walked right over this soil on his way to his destiny. Right here."

He watched his son carefully, knowing that if the boy were to say something as insipid as "cool" or make a joke or toss the dirt down with a grimace, he would lose his temper. He couldn't help himself. But Peter surprised him, surprised him greatly, by taking his other hand and gently rubbing the soil, the blackness staining his young fingers.

The captain trotted down, waving his saber. "Up! Up, you dogs! We advance, and we advance now!"

Nicholas no longer tried to swallow, as his mouth had been as dry as cotton all these long minutes under siege. There was a ragged series of shouts and yells as the company bestirred itself and started heading up the ridge. More smoke was billowing up from the rapid roar of the rifle fire, and he kept his head down as he moved with the other soldiers. His breathing was so hard he thought it would drown out the noise of the battle, but he was wrong. If anything, the shouts and yells and booms and thunder seemed to grow the closer he ran with the others up to the ridge. Nicholas found himself almost crying with fear as he saw the swirling mob of bodies and flags and rifles in front of him. Out of this horrible mess he could make out the blue of the Union forces mixed in with the grays of the Confederates, plus a fair amount of scarlet and other blue uniforms. How could these men fight like this, so close you could touch the enemy, and he found himself wanting to turn and run, but it was like being in the middle of a stampede of cattle spooked by a thunderstorm, and he found himself forced to run up to the ridge with all the others, the shouting and yelling and firing now so loud he thought his ears would bleed.

Peter gently dropped the soil to the ground, rubbed it in amidst the grass. "What happened here, then?"

Alex also let the soil drop gently from his fingers. "This was the closest the Confederates came to breaking the lines here on Cemetery Ridge. There were soldiers here from Pennsylvania putting up a tremendous fight. But the Confederates pressed on and on, and when they crossed over that stone wall, the Union forces started to crumble and fall back. Imagine a dike, Peter—a dike made of Union bodies—holding back the Confederates. Just like an earthen dike holding back a flood. The dike is battered, the dike is weakened, and then the flood comes through. Just a trickle to start. But if you cannot hold back that flood right there and then, when it's just a trickle, then disaster strikes as the flood breaks through and sweeps everything before it."

He looked around again at the peaceful countryside, feeling a trembling of energy, knowing what had taken place here, how his ancestor had made the difference. "This is where the Confederates broke through, where they were about to reach their victory. But then destiny called upon your great-great-grandfather."

Then the whole line of their troops surged up against the Union forces, moving and bumping and jostling, and here and there, Nicholas made out the gray of the Confederates, pressing in, pressing in hard. Smoke made his eyes water, and the noise was now so loud he could no longer make out what was causing it, the yells or the blasts of the artillery and rifle fire. It was a maddening swirl of confusion, as a Union soldier stumbled by him, bleeding heavily from his head. He almost tripped over two other bodies, saw a knot of Confederate soldiers by the stone wall, and he raised up his rifle and fired into the mass, the jerk of the recoil barely noticeable. He tried to reload, but the jostling, the moving, made him drop his cartridge, and the growling and the shouting grew louder. Near him was the captain and the flag bearer, and the captain was using the flat of his sword, beating about the heads and shoulders of his own troops, urging them forward, urging them into the thick of the battle.

Then, like a demon, a demon his grandmother would warn him about in her dark stories told around the small fireplace back home, the Rebel yell started up, the curdling, high-pitched screaming that made his stomach seem to drop to the ground. The yell seemed to have the same effect on the others, for his fellow troops started to falter, seemed to halt in their attack. The Rebel yell grew louder and louder as the Confederate troops picked up the shout and redoubled their assault. The gray uniforms were no longer behind the stone wall, they were now clambering over the wall, hatless and bloody and waving their swords and rifles. The line broke, and Nicholas blinked as the blue uniforms started to disappear.

The cries of terror then broke out as his fellow soldiers began to falter, began to stream back, and Nicholas shouted, too, thank God, pleased that they were breaking away, were starting to run, for in such a running mass, it would be easy enough to hide. He dropped his rifle and started falling back as the Confederates came closer, much closer.

Then the captain moved in, raising his sword up, screaming, "Don't you dare run, you bastards! Attack, attack! Move on up, you bastards!"

Nicholas felt his legs weaken, move on their own, and the captain came right to him, like the captain had seen him and only him, and the sword was raised up to come down on him, and Nicholas knew instantly that the captain wouldn't be using the flat of his sword, he'd be using the sharp side, and he threw up his hand to defend himself.

And then the captain and the flag bearer both were blown out of their saddles.

Alex could not believe how well the day was going now that Peter was showing interest in the story. This was what he had hoped would happen, that his boy would connect with the history of this hallowed ground, not only from the historical perspective but from the family perspective as well. Peter was now looking at him with interest, and Alex said, "Imagine what it must have been like, Peter. To be here alone, far from your family and farm. He was only a few years older than you. Can you imagine, a young boy, not much older than you, in the midst of a war?"

Peter just shook his head. Alex wished for a moment that he had been recording what he was saying to his boy, for this was turning out to be one of his best lectures ever. Alex said, "For those of us who have never been in battle, it's hard to get a good grasp of what really happened. There is so much blood and death and wounding and confusion. So much terror. Some of the rifles they recovered from the battlefield days later showed that the barrels contained two or three or four cartridge loads; in the middle of the battle, the soldiers using those rifles didn't even notice that they had misfired. So it's hard to re-create what happened here, but as historians, that's what we do. We try to put the stories together, of what has occurred, how it occurred, and who was involved."

Peter rubbed again at the dirt on his fingers. "So this is where the Virginians broke through. What happened after that?"

Alex clasped his hands together. "This spot, this very spot, is where your great-great-grandfather stepped into history."

*   *   *

His arm still up in the air, Nicholas was stunned to see the captain and the flag bearer swept away, and stunned even more when the regimental banner, bloody and torn, fell on top of him. He pushed away the heavy banner, gasped as the wooden rod popped against his head. He quickly fumbled his way out from under the flag, knowing that the Rebs were so close that he'd be dead if he didn't start moving.

Nicholas freed himself, both hands now holding the long staff of the banner, and a breeze came up, flapping the banner before him. He turned in a half-circle, looking to where the rest of his fellow soldiers were racing away, but they weren't running. They were now looking in his direction, their faces still frightened but they were looking at him. What for? Why?

"Hoorah!" came the voice of a soldier, Kutzov if he was correct, and then another, and another. "Hoorah! Hoorah!"

What the hell . . . and Nicholas realized with horror that they were looking at him, looking toward him, all because he was holding on to the damn regimental banner. He thought instantly of dropping it, dropping it right now on the ground because he knew from experience that those carrying such banners were often targets of Reb sharpshooters and he wanted to get away from this battlefield as quickly as possible, not carry the damn banner!

Yet . . . Another "hoorah!" broke free and he looked at the design of the banner, the gold and red threads, the fancy script, and he knew he couldn't drop it. He couldn't. The shouting of the Rebs and the gunfire were still roaring in his ears, but there was something else now, the shouts from his fellow troopers, the shouts of "hoorah!" and the way they looked upon him, like they were relying upon him, just a lowly private, and he swung the banner about him and found himself yelling, "Come on, boys! Let's show them what we can do! Hoorah!"

He could not believe what he had just done, could not believe that a simple and cowardly farmer like himself could have done anything, but the shouts and yells of "hoorah!" seemed to fill him with a burning sense of energy, a sense of duty and honor and, damn it, to show those Rebs a thing or two. Before him was the swirling mass of men and arms and rifles raised up and swords flashing, more screams and grunts and shouts, a riderless horse screaming in fear, a Confederate soldier with his left arm gone, bleeding as he was splayed over a gun carriage.

"Hoorah!" came the voices behind him, and he surged up against the mass of men, waving the regimental flag, and it was like before, feeling like he was a piece of wood on floodwater, being jostled and carried and sent to God knows where, but this time, it was different. Holding the banner above his head, screaming and waving, feeling the energy of his fellow troops, he found his legs moving quickly, faster than ever before. Suddenly, there was a soldier in gray before him holding up a revolver, but Nicholas dropped the banner some and swung at the soldier, striking him in the head with the ornamental eagle at the top of the pole. The soldier fell and the shock of hitting the man strummed through the wood of the staff, thrilling him.

"Hoorah! Hoorah!"

Now they were pushing, forcing, jumbling their way up to the stone wall, and the gunfire seemed heavier, as the Confederates began to falter, began to move back. Nicholas was exhilarated, energetic, never in his life having felt so alive. The troops were behind him as he raced forward with the regimental banner, waving it back and forth, no longer caring if a sharpshooter or anybody could see him. Along the way he had lost his cap and was bareheaded and he didn't care, for now he was at the stone wall, the same stone wall where the Confederates had first come across. He stepped up on the stone wall, glanced behind him at the surviving members of his company, following him into this bloody battle, and he yelled back, "Come on! We're winning! We're winning! Follow me, for the motherland!" and the shouts came back in reply, a murderous eagerness in their voices, as they all sensed the Confederates were losing heart, were tumbling and running back down the easy slope of the hill, back to the faraway shelter of the tree line. Nicholas spared a quick glance to his left and right, saw masses of men locked in struggle, moving against each other, smoke drifting across all of them, and now he was on the grass, yelling again.

"Follow me! Let's chase them back to Richmond!"

Another series of yells and shouts, and then there was an ear-splitting crack, as the ground before him erupted in a burst of dirt and smoke, and he fell on his back, blinking his eyes, his mouth tasting blood and dirt, and he tried to stay awake, tried to keep his eyes open, for all he saw above him was the flag of his regiment, and the eagle, the double-headed eagle of his sovereign, Czar Alexander II.

Peter looked at him with doubt in his eyes. "One man? One man made that much of a difference?"

Alex nodded. "It happens in battles sometimes. There are moments when everything is fluid, when everything is in some sort of rough balance. If your great-great-grandfather hadn't grabbed the regimental flag and raced forward to block the breach in the lines, then the Confederates would have broken through. Just one little breach. That's all it would take. But Nicholas was there, saw what had to be done, and did it, proving his honor, his heroism."

Peter looked around him. "Right here . . . one man . . ."

Alex said, "We often read about the princes and presidents, czars and kings, prime ministers and queens. They may be the bright lights in history, Peter, but often it's the little man, the frightened, brave little man, who makes a difference. Who makes all the difference in the world. And

your great-great-grandfather was one of those men. Who
made it all possible."

Nicholas came to, his head hurting, the shouts and gunfire
and sounds of battle now having faded away. He rubbed at
the dirt in his face and then sat up in shock, touching his
arms and legs and his belly, looking for a wound, looking
for blood, looking for anything, but he seemed fine. Except
that his head was throbbing and his mouth tasted of old
things, he was fine. He rubbed at his eyes, looked about
him, felt his stomach begin to heave around. What in hell
had he just done? Was he crazy? Mad? Had he actually
grabbed the regimental banner and led troops into battle?
    He looked about him at the late afternoon of the battle-
field. There were moans and groans from the wounded,
still laying in clumps as far as he could see. Smoke still
rose up in wisps from the stone wall and wooden fence that
was now behind him. Horses were on their side as well,
their large shapes already beginning to bloat, their legs
sticking out. Rifles and rucksacks and belts and canteens
were strewn across the field as well, and Nicholas saw the
regimental banner laying there on the ground next to him.
He slowly got up, wincing at the pain in his arms and legs,
using the staff of the banner to help hold him up.
    The battlefield seemed to spin about him and Nicholas
had to grasp on to the staff with both hands to prevent
himself from falling down. He had lived. Good God in
Heaven, he had actually lived. But who had won? How had
the battle ended?
    He looked again around him at the scene, and there,
coming toward him, was a group of officers. He recognized the uniform of one of the Czar's officers, and the
other men—bearded and serious—were dressed in the dull
blue of the Union. They came toward him, talking to each
other, and he wiped at his face, realized he had no hat or
weapon, just the banner firm in his hands. He coughed as

they came forward, and one of the bearded Union officers came forward and said something in English. The man looked tired, his eyes red-rimmed, a half-smoked cigar in a dirty hand.

"I'm sorry," Nicholas said, shaking his head. "I don't understand what you're saying."

The Russian officer came to him and said, "Stand up straight, soldier, as the Union American general talks to you."

Nicholas bowed his head, his sweaty hands still holding on to the staff. The American general said something to the Russian officer, who nodded and said, "This general, named Meade, wishes to know if you are the soldier who fought here, in this place called the Angle. The place where the Confederates almost broke through the line. Is that so?"

Nicholas nodded to the officer. "Yes, your honor. That is true."

The officer, tall and trim, with his gold braid bright against the scarlet of his uniform, turned and talked to the Union general, who nodded with a half-smile on his grim face. He came forward and held out his hand. Nicholas looked at the outstretched hand dumbly until the Russian officer whispered harshly, "Shake the hand of the noble general, you stupid peasant. Shake it!"

Nicholas shook himself away from the staff and grasped the general's hand, squeezed it, and bowed. The Union general backed away and talked to other Union officers, and the group of men laughed. Out in the field, men were marching from the tree line, and Nicholas shuddered and started to step away to the safety of the stone wall until he noted that the groups of men were being escorted by Union soldiers. The groups of men were dressed in gray, red, and light blue. The Union general noted the group approaching and spoke rapidly to the Russian officer, who translated for Nicholas without looking at him.

"See?" the Russian officer said. "See the prisoners coming up from the woods? We captured those men thanks to you and your Russian brothers. Uh . . . those men were the heart of the Confederate attack . . . uh . . . the Virginians, members of the British Coldstream Guards, and part of the French Invincibles . . . all of them were defeated today, thanks to you and yours . . . uh . . . it was a moment of great courage, to rally your regiment and block this advance before the Confederates and their allies broke through . . . uh . . . and our nation owes you a debt of gratitude . . ."

The Union general stopped speaking, and so did the Russian officer, who glared at Nicholas. "Well? Say something back to the noble general!"

Nicholas coughed and cleared his throat. "It was my honor, noble sir."

The Union general nodded and said something in reply, and the Russian officer said, "The general wishes to know, where are you from?"

"Kaptov. A village near Moscow. Quite small."

The Union general nodded, spoke, and the Russian officer translated: "Are all the men in your village as brave as you?"

Nicholas thought for a moment. Brave? What he did wasn't brave! It was sheer idiocy, and only by the grace of God and the Blessed Mother was he still alive and standing. Brave! What do generals and officers know of bravery, Nicholas thought. He hadn't been brave. He had been berserk, insane, thinking only of chasing the damn Rebs back to Richmond, when he should have been running in the other direction. He was no hero, and he knew if another battle would break out tomorrow, he would be trying to hide, trying to avoid—

"Speak up, peasant!" the officer demanded. "Answer the noble general, or I'll have you shot when they leave the field."

The Union officer said something, and again, the same phrase from the Russian officer: "Are all the men in your village as brave as you?"

Nicholas looked about at the still figures of the dead, heard the moans and yelps from the wounded. He cleared his throat and spat out a word. "No."

The Russian officer's face turned the color of his uniform. He turned and spoke rapidly to the Union officer, and the general nodded and smiled again in his direction, as did the other officers. The Russian went on and on, and then the Union general nodded and again held out his hand. This time, Nicholas needed no urging, and shook the firm hand of the man named Meade. The other Union officers came forward as well, shaking his hand, and then they started walking up along the stone wall, pointing out items of interest to each other, as the Russian officer stayed behind.

Nicholas shifted his hands around the staff of the banner. "Sir, what did you say to the Union general?"

"What do you mean?" the officer replied sharply.

He wondered what foolish bravery was making him talk so to an officer of the Czar, but he went on. "Earlier, the general asked me if all the men in my village were as brave as I. And I said no to the noble officer. Yet your reply . . . excuse me, sir, your reply went on for a while."

The officer laughed. "Of course, you peasant. Did you think I would insult the great general by giving him such a simple answer from a simple serf? Do you? I told him that yes, the men of your village and your country are all so brave, and all are eager to fight for the great Czar and the great Lincoln. That you were glad to be on the field, to fight the Rebellious, the British, and the French. That you would fight until the rebellion is quelled and the British and the French go home. That's what I told him."

The officer laughed again and Nicholas stood up straighter. "Sir, I am not a serf."

"Huh? What did you say?"

His voice grew stronger, here on this foreign battlefield. "Sir, I am not a serf. The Czar Liberator freed me and my father and mother and family two years ago. We are free men; we are now landowners. We are not serfs."

Nicholas expected an explosion of temper, perhaps a cuffing about the head or the sword being drawn from the officer's scabbard and thrust into him, but no, the officer laughed again. He came up to him and slapped him on the shoulder. "So you are. We forget, we officers and noblemen, what the Tsar Liberator has wrought. From freeing you serfs to bringing us halfway across the world to get revenge against the French and British . . . these are changing times, very changing times."

The Russian officer looked around the battlefield with satisfaction. "And I am so glad to be part of them. A good fight you put on, soldier. A very good fight."

The officer started walking away to join up with the Union officers, and Nicholas called out, "Noble sir!"

"Yes?" the officer said, turning around.

Nicholas coughed again. "Where is my regiment? Where shall I go?"

The Russian officer pointed to the woods from where the attack had burst out so few hours and so many lifetimes ago. "Your comrades are in the woods, still fighting the Rebs, the British, and the French. They say the battle still rages. They say the war may be over in a fortnight. I would say you should join up with your comrades." The officer then smiled before turning and walking away. "But I would suggest you take your time in joining them. You've fought well today. You deserve your rest."

Nicholas nodded and waited there on the still of the battlefield. He waited until the officer and the Union generals went away, far from sight, and then he looked down to the woods. Now he could hear the faint sound of rifle fire and

cannon booming. He shuddered. Join up with that? Go
back to that horror?

He shook his head, started walking down the other side
of the hill, away from the ridge, away from the battle. He
walked until darkness into the woods outside of this odd
town called Gettysburg, and when he was tired, he removed the banner from the pole, wrapped himself in the
thick cloth, and fell asleep in the brush, dreaming of his
family farm, back home in Russia.

Alex checked his watch. Almost time to go. Peter was now
leaning against the barrel of a cannon, looking back to the
visitors' center and the parking lot where their rental car
was parked. Peter said, "You're not putting me on, are you,
Dad?"

"Excuse me? What do you mean, putting you on?"

Peter was now smiling. "This whole story of my great-
great-grandfather. It sounds too good to be true. Young
peasant soldier from Russia comes to America and saves
the day. I mean . . . you weren't exaggerating, were you,
Dad?"

His lips now tight with displeasure, he grabbed his
boy's arm and said, "Here. Follow me."

"Hey!" came a shout, but Alex would have none of it.
He pulled the boy away from the tree, headed to a small
plain stone monument near the stone wall. He had waited
until they were getting ready to leave before showing Peter
this stone, and wished his mood were better. "Here," Alex
said. "Read it."

Peter looked at the stone, words in English and in Cyril-
lic:

NEAR THIS SPOT

JULY 3rd 1863

NICHOLAS RUDZIC

FOURTH IMPERIAL RUSSIAN GUARDS

AND HIS REGIMENT

TURNED BACK THE ADVANCE OF THE
CONFEDERACY AND ITS ALLIES
HE FOUGHT FOR FREEDOM AND FOR THE NOBLE ALLIANCE

Erected July 3rd 1913
Grand Army of the Republic and the Empire

"There." Alex pointed. "Satisfied?"

Peter nodded, now looking embarrassed. "Yes, but I have one more question. Just one more."

Nicholas woke to the sounds of men marching nearby, the creaking of the leather, the movement of the horses. He got up and reattached the banner to the wooden staff. Two cavalrymen came trotting through, Russian officers again, and Nicholas called out, "Noble sirs, I'm afraid I've lost my regiment."

The horsemen pulled up their mounts, and one called out, "Then stick with us, farmer boy. We'll go find them for you."

Nicholas draped the staff and the banner over his shoulder, and started walking yet again, hoping that the battles and the fighting would be over by the time he got there.

A coward's wish, he knew, but one he was quite comfortable with.

Alex said, "Go ahead. What's your question?"

Peter looked at his father and then around the battlefield and said, "One man like our great-great-grandfather. Did he really make that much of a difference? Did this battle make that much of a difference? Honestly?"

Thoughts started racing through his mind, like a semester's worth of lectures back at the university, back in St. Petersburg where he taught. How the American Civil War suddenly widened when the Americans halted a British mail ship, the *Trent*, on the high seas in 1861 and removed two Confederate envoys. How opinion was inflamed, both in the Northern American states and in Great Britain. How the intervention of the British Prince Albert in an attempt to resolve the crisis peacefully failed when the prince fell seriously ill and British troop transports landed in Canada and marched south to intervene on the Confederacy's behalf. And once Great Britain recognized the South as a sovereign nation, Napoleon III of France followed as well and decided to cause mischief on his own part by marching north from Mexico. Oh, how grim it had been for Mr. Lincoln back then.

And then . . . and then . . . Czar Alexander II, seeing an opportunity to get a measure of revenge from the devastating Crimean War a few years earlier, sent over "volunteers" to help the Union, and how they tipped the balance right here at Gettysburg. And then the French and the British, tiring of fighting on the side of slavery—especially since Lincoln and the Czar were both seen as liberators of slaves and serfs—brought their forces home. Only months after Gettysburg, the War of Rebellion in America was over.

But that wasn't the end of the story, oh no, it wasn't. For Lincoln was reelected in 1864 and in 1866 made a triumphant tour of Moscow and St. Petersburg. Lincoln Societies were established in Russia, translating his words of freedom and justice for everyone. And the pressure came on Alexander II to reform society, reform government, and the Russo-American alliance strengthened and grew over the years, especially during Lincoln's three terms. Eventually the wounds over the war healed such that the French and British came to work with the Russians and the Americans in the League of Nations at the turn of the century, to fight down oppression, to keep the peace around the world—especially with China and Japan and the Prussian states and the freed colonies in South America, Asia, and Africa—so that now, almost a hundred years after this battle on this soil, mankind had known such generations of peace and prosperity that had never existed.

Alex looked again up at the flags flying near the visitors' center: the Union Jack, the French tri-color, the double-eagle of Imperial Russia, and the United States flag with its thirteen stripes and forty-nine stars. All marking this place, what was called the High-Water Mark, not only of the Confederacy but of the tyranny that had once chained mankind.

"Yes," Alex said. "All the difference in the world."

The Angle

Jake Foster

Couple times during the night, Raines had to get up and tend to Verne. That last fight had really taken it out of him. Raines spent nearly twenty minutes in the back of the hovervan until Verne seemed all right again. Then Raines went back outside to the grassy side of the rural road and climbed back into his sleeping bag. He liked the night breezes and the sight of the stars. He was a free black man, somebody to be envied in these Confederate States of America, and he meant to enjoy it. . . .

Sam Raines's destination was a Clean Town in the lower part of Mississippi, place named Helmsville after the popular president of this third of the Confederate States, the somewhat frog-faced Jesse Helms IV. No friend of the black man, Helms had increased the percentage of Clean Towns to fifty percent. Pure white. Pure Christian. And pure mean sumbitch if you tried to sneak in there.

One other rule: It was illegal for a black person to have a prizefight with a white opponent. Pure white, pure Christian had seen too many fine young white men grovel on the canvas after being knocked down—or out—by some arrogant black buck. Penalties were hefty and, in some circumstances, included death.

Naturally, this created a huge underground madly desirous of seeing such fights. Big crowds, big money. White guys wanting to see black guys knocked senseless. Such fights were especially popular in the South where, police estimated, ten such events were staged each and every evening somewhere.

Raines was a manager/promoter. Verne was his fighter. Raines had had three fighters before but never as hateful as Verne. For one thing, he was handsome in a way that pleased white girls and profoundly pissed off white boys, suspecting as they did that Verne would be all to happy to defile their girlfriends. For another, he was a tough bastard, and when he was winning, he tended to gloat a little, humiliate the other fighter. Wasn't right, a buck like Verne making fun out of pure white manhood like that. And finally, Verne wasn't exactly a fighter of true-blue character. The referee distracted for a moment, Verne would slam his opponent with a quick rabbit punch, or go downstairs and temporarily immobilize the guy, who'd end up clutching his crotch, tears streaming down his face. Wasn't right, a buck like that treating a white man that way. No sir, it sure wasn't. Of course, that's why Verne got steady work. White people hated him and they hated him enough to pay to see him over and over again. You had to have an angle in this business, otherwise white promoters wouldn't use your fighters. Till he'd found Verne, Raines had had a pretty sad career.

As they moved along about two hundred miles an hour, Raines noticed how congested the air was getting with hovercraft of all kinds. They were nearing Helmsville. He punched up the personal code he needed for Bob Tyme, the Helmsville area promoter, and said, "Hi, Bob. Raines here." Tyme's chubby face bloomed on the tel-screen. "I need the coordinates where we're supposed to land. We need some time to rest and all before the fight tonight."

"Got a big farm spread. Your boy can use the farmhouse. In the basement, of course. White folks upstairs. There's a cellar entrance."

"How're the tickets going?"

"Good. But it could be better. I got one more stop to make over to the church I go to. There's a committee of Concerned Fathers there—two hundred of 'em, huge choir they have—and that's about how many more seats I got left to sell in the bleachers." Then, "I'm lettin' everybody know that tonight is gonna be somethin' special. I didn't say what it was. I just hinted it was gonna be somethin' they'd like real, real good. How's Verne?"

"Oh, he's in great shape."

"He was a little off last time. Some of my regulars weren't too happy."

"They'll be happy tonight. He's his old self again." He looked over at Verne and smiled. "Right, Verne?"

Verne did one of his promo poses. Made a fist of his huge hand and sneered. Sneered cold and sneered bad. Real bad.

"That's what I like to see," Bob Tyme said. "Some uppity buck. Crowd goes crazy when they see somebody like him. Have to hold back some of 'em from getting in the ring and shootin' him. That's just what I like to see."

"Prick," Verne said when Tyme was finished giving Raines the coordinates and signed off. He spoke to a dark screen. "Wonder what it'd be like."

"What what'd be like?" Raines said, looking below at Helmsville. The screen displayed data: *Pop: 175,346. Temperature: 81° F. Eight hour forecast: Continued warm. No precip.* Raines hated cities—pollution, crime, drugs, rocket ports, androids, clogged air lanes, stench—even the so-called Clean Towns.

Raines headed right for the large farm. Easy enough for a sky copper to see two black men over a Clean Town air space. What they'd usually do in a case like that, the local gendarmes, was cut themselves in. Oh, you could have your fight, all right, but they wanted twenty percent of your end of it.

"What it'd be like to be white. And swagger around. And feel safe on the street. And not have to worry what's gonna happen to your kids when they grow up." Verne was an angry man and never angrier than when he spoke about how white folks treated black folks.

"Save that for the ring," Raines said. "Remember, Tyme said he promised 'em something special tonight. And we both know what that means. So just save that wrath of yours for the ring."

"Wrath," Verne said. "I like that word." He smiled. "That's a nice word. Feels good in the mouth."

"Yes, it does," Raines said, thinking of how the Confederates, white women duty-bound to cleanse the States of attractive young black girls who might later on tempt white men—how the Confederettes had hanged both his sisters one scream-crazed hot night in the little family shack by a dirty river. "Yes, indeed, it does," Raines said.

Choir singing always gave Bob Tyme the chills, just the way the brass bands affected other folks. And this choir of Concerned Fathers—dedicated to seeing that every boy and girl was tested on his or her knowledge of the events following the Southern victory at Gettysburg—this choir could just make you weep with its Stephen Foster numbers.

Bob was a good friend of the Reverend Sykes. He sat watching the reverend conduct the choir. *My Lord, what magnificent voices.* He'd asked Sykes earlier about coming here and talking to the men. And Sykes had agreed.

When they got to "Old Man River" and the man who'd later be in blackface for the actual performance stepped out front . . . Bob was afraid he was going to cry. Blackface was standard stuff on the holo networks, but when you came right down to it, very few entertainers really knew how to do it. You had to be a compassionate person to perform blackface well, Bob had always thought.

You had to be like Jesse Helms IV. As Jesse IV always said, just because Negroes aren't as smart or as ambitious or as trustworthy as white people, that don't mean they don't suffer and they don't have feelings. God created them, didn't He, as forerunners of the white race? The way I read the Bible, Jesse IV always said on the holo, was God experimented with the Negroes—He wasn't exactly sure what kind of species He wanted, so He tweaked the black folks till He saw what He *really* wanted to do—and then He created white people in His exact image.

They sang ten songs and then the Reverend Sykes, stern-stout-stubborn (and getting a ten-percent cut of the gate), addressed his two hundred men here on the splendid sparkling altar of his church. "Men, a friend of mine would like to talk to you today. Some of you know him, some don't. I'd just like to say that he is a devout member of this congregation and just as concerned a father as you all are. He has a great idea for how you can enjoy some time with your children and show them—in a symbolic way—how the white man has always had to struggle for what is right and just. I don't want to say any more because my friend Bob Tyme can explain this all a lot better than I can. So why don't I just turn it over to Bob right now?"

There'd been some sighing, some glancing-at-wrist-chronos, some melancholy glances in the direction of the parking lot. And Bob, not an insensitive man, had picked up on all of it. And he certainly got the message: Keep it short.

"The first thing I want to do is tell Reverend Sykes how much I appreciate him letting me talk to you." He paused. "I promote white-black prizefights. And you know and I know those are illegal. So anybody who has a problem with them should leave right now. No hard feelings." Nobody left. Too intimidated by the group. "I believe—as does Reverend Sykes—that a young white boy or girl seeing the white-black struggle in the ring will see why it's so important to keep our race pure. He'll see what one black man is willing to do to a white man to win a prizefight. He'll show his animal nature for sure. And he can imagine for himself or herself what *a couple million* black men could do if they got together. It's a lesson they'll never forget and a lesson they'll talk about for years afterward. The way I see it, you owe it to your children to see this fight tonight. There's no guarantee who's going to win. But I'll tell you one thing—I can tell you who those kids of yours are going to be rooting for."

He could tell by the nods and the smiles that he had them. Oh, not all of them of course. Such short notice, you couldn't expect everybody to buy a ticket.

But a good share of them started filing down off the altar to where he stood with his old-fashioned paper tickets. He had a hundred and three to sell and damned if he didn't sell them straight off.

The boy said, "You really a darkie?"

Verne smiled. "You ain't supposed to call us darkies, kid."

Farm kid. Maybe eight, nine. Bib overalls. Bare feet. Sun-bleached hair. Verne on his way down to the cellar. Dumb. Didn't mean no harm.

"How come?"

"Because it ain't polite."

"That's what my pop calls them."

"You're s'posed to call us Negroes."

"How come?"

"Because darkies isn't nice. It insults us. That's what white people used to call us when they had plantations."

"My pop says they should *still* have plantations."

Verne laughed. "I ain't sure I want to meet that pop of yours."

"He says the only reason they done away with plantations was because they couldn't find enough darkies with enough gumption to run 'em."

"I'm gonna go down to the cellar now."

"There's spiders down there."

"I think I can probably lick 'em."

"You think you can lick Brad Dane tonight? My sister said he's the handsomest prizefighter she ever seen."

"I think I can probably do pretty good."

"My pop says Brad killed a darkie once. Beat him so bad the darkie just laid down in the ring and died. Don't that make you scared?"

"What it makes me," Verne said, smiling again, "is sure that I don't ever want to meet that pop of yours."

He went down into the cold shadowy cellar. Alone. Where the spiders were.

Bob Tyme drove a huge, new, shiny hovercar. It put down with a purr in the open field next to where the bleachers were. The bleachers would be obvious to the air cops. He'd had to pay them a pretty penny, the corrupt bastards.

Raines was there to meet him. They went over the jerry-rigged ring. It wasn't very big and it wasn't very sturdy but it would do. There was only the one fight tonight.

"Yessir," Bob said, "a lot of my customers—you know I have one fight a month these days—they wasn't very happy with Verne last time. He just didn't look good."

"Well, I got a feelin' they're gonna be happy tonight."

"If they ain't, Raines, I'm afraid you and me can't do business no more."

"Just relax, Bob. Everything'll be fine."

Bob made a face. "Got this young punk from Memphis. Talking about movin' into town here. Says he can promote a lot better fights than I do. I ain't young anymore. I can't compete against some young punk from Memphis. Memphis is a big city, Raines. Punk like him'll know all the new angles and promo stuff. He could run me outta business, I don't keep my customers happy."

The farmer came out. Bib overalls. Sun-bleached hair. Except he wore shoes. "Everything ready to go?"

Bob nodded. "Another hour or so, the crowd'll start comin'."

"They weren't too happy last time Verne was here," the farmer said.

"I mentioned that to Raines here," Bob said.

Yeah, about three hundred times, Raines thought, give or take a couple hundred. He wondered if the two had co-ordinated their little effort. Bob ragged him for a while, then the farmer—Jesse somebody—comes out and rags him, too.

"Your folks're gonna go away happy tonight," Raines said. "That I can practically guarantee you."

Bob Tyme stepped through the ropes. Walked around. He was chunky enough to make the ring wobble a little. "You ever do any fighting yourself, Raines?"

"Just enough to know I didn't much enjoy gettin' hit."

The farmer looked surprised. "I was always told you people had thicker skulls than we did."

"Well," Raines said amiably, deciding to just swallow the insult—what you could do with so many against you?—"I musta been gone that day that shipment of thick skulls came in 'cause the times I fought, I sure was in a world of hurt."

The farmer smiled. "Yeah, I guess that's why I never had no desire to fight, either. I didn't get one of them thick skulls, either."

The bleachers started filling up an hour later. Pretty good cross-section of society—rich, middle-class, working-class. Old, middle-aged, young. Loners, couples, whole families. Bob got his two beer tents going. A blue-grass group started singing Confederate war songs. A very

young group of Confederettes put on a modest pageant
lauding the lifestyle of the South. Then a couple of beery
white old-time prizefighters Bob had hired stepped into the
ring and told all about what a great white champion Brad
Dane was and how the crowd should really support him
tonight because by all rights the darkie had a lot more
power, reach, and experience than poor young Brad who,
even though he'd killed a darkie, was really just starting
out. Several teenage girls got all wrought up when Brad
Dane was mentioned. They started screaming and a few of
them started crying.

He tried to act humble, but how could a guy with those
muscles and those teeth act humble? He passed among the
crowd and let the girls touch him and the boys shake his
hand. What he was doing, Brad Dane, was trying to build
himself a regional following so hot it would propel him
onto one of the national holo networks, which was where
the big money was.

Bob had a small trailer for Dane. Brad didn't spend long
in there. He liked it too much among the crowd. And they
liked him even better when he was in his gloves and
trunks. He did a lot of this—holding his hands together
overhead in the victory signal—and that—kinda running
in place and sending out some fast, smart jabs. Swooning
and crooning all over the place.

Bob went over to Raines and told him to go get Verne.

Verne lay awake on a blanket on the dirt floor of the cellar. He was in his boxing gear. His eyes were open, staring
upward.

"I heard them talk."

"Heard who talk?"

"The farmer and his wife and their kids. It was nice."

"What was nice?"

"They sounded like one of those holo shows where
everybody laughs a lot and then ends up hugging each
other."

Verne could be a crazy sumbitch.

"You don't worry about that now, Verne. You just pick yourself up and follow me. It's time to fight."

"You ever live in a house like that?"

"Where people laugh and hug all the time?" Raines said. He shook his head, remembering the two little rooms his mama had back in Louisville, two little rooms and six little kids. "No, never did and don't figure I ever will."

"Even after all the money I'm gonna make you?" Verne said.

"Yeah," Raines said, "right."

Black-and-white fights always ran the same way. You had two whites fighting or two blacks, you weren't sure who the crowd was going to applaud. But you had a white man and a black man, the crowd went for the white man.

Didn't hurt that Brad Dane's trunks and shoes were made out of Confederate flags. Or that when he was swaggering up to the ring, Bob was playing "Dixie" over the lone loudspeaker. Music like that, people stood up with tears in their eyes and their hands over their hearts.

Then came Verne and they started booing. It wasn't fake booing either—like you had at the big-time holo rassling matches, where the crowd itself was part of the entertainment, hamming it up just as much as the rasslers did—it was real booing. They hated the sumbitch, big buck darkie like this wanting to do damage to a good Christian man like Brad Dane, the sumbitch.

Verne strode around the ring with his hands over his head and they started catcalling. Real nasty names. Bob loved it. This was what a crowd wanted. Somebody to love, somebody to hate. And you take a handsome buck, nobody a white crowd hates more than a handsome buck, specially one that struts around like he's king shit or something. And that was just how Verne strutted, too—king shit.

* * *

Raines counted the house. It wasn't computer-accurate but it was close enough. He went over to Bob Tyme and told him the count he'd gotten. "Still don't trust me, huh?" Bob smiled.

"It's just our agreement is all," Raines said.

"If I was a darkie would you want your money before the fight started?"

"You a darkie, I'd want the money the minute I set my hovercraft down." That wasn't true but Bob being white and all, he liked a colored man willing to talk his own kind down. You made white men comfortable when you showed them that you considered yourself inferior. They didn't feel threatened by you and were liable to be a lot nicer as a result. It was like you'd become the family dog or something.

Bob laughed. "Well, here you go."

He cheated him, of course. That was standard business practice. You did business with the colored, you *expected* to cheat them and *they* expected it, too. It was all part of the boxing ritual. They never complained because if they did you'd never use them again and they knew it. It was just about the best kind of business arrangement a fella could have, him knowing you was cheating but not saying a single word about it. No sir, you couldn't find a better kind of business deal than that.

Raines looked over the money in the envelope. Close enough.

"Now," Bob said, still leaning against the trailer he had all rigged up for Raines, "that boy of yours better put on one hell of a fight."

Just when he said that, the crowd went *whoop*. A real big *whoop*. Bob wasn't sure why. He hadn't been paying attention. The truth was, boxing had started to bore his ass off. A fella could only see so many prizefights in his life and stay excited. It was like any other job. A fella just got

plain tired of it. The crowd *whooped* again. Bob decided
he'd better start paying a little attention.

"You don't worry about that. He'll put on a fight, all
right."

"That last one of yours pissed off the crowd. I almost
didn't want to work with you again. I want them bucks to
be tough but I don't want 'em to be arrogant, you know
what I'm saying, Raines?"

"Yep. That's why I sold off my four other fighters and
put all my money in bringin' Verne along."

"He must put on some show."

"You just watch," Raines said. "You just watch."

Verne knocked Brad Dane down twice in the first round
and once in the second. In the second round, Dane barely
made it up in time for the count.

The white crowd, as you might imagine, was not happy.
Several men were of the opinion that if the darkie continued to win like this, someone in the crowd was bound to
haul out a gun and relieve the colored man of his life.

Not to worry. Between rounds three and four a miracle
seemed to have taken place. The once awkward, tentative
Brad Dane found his rhythm and began to wade into Verne
with great skill and ferocity.

Rounds four, five, six and seven went to Brad Dane,
too. While he didn't knock Verne down, he did keep him
on the ropes for long periods, and he did pound away on
him twice in Verne's own corner. The crowd was celebrating his imminent victory.

Rounds eight and nine, though, things changed. It was
Verne's turn to find himself again. The footwork was fancy
once more, and the punches were on-target and powerful.
Brad Dane was starting to show some of the punishment he
was taking. His legs started to wobble and twice he looked
desperately to his corner, as if his trainer could call out
some magical advice.

But there was no magical advice to be had. The fight was once again Verne's. He not only used his left uppercut, his best punch, he even unloaded a few times with his right. He didn't have a particularly good right hand. At least, not until today.

The crowd turned sour again. The consumption of beer doubled every time the colored fella started winning. Even the Confederettes looked a little wilted when they led the crowd in a tired little cheer celebrating Dixie.

Round ten was even. The first minute-and-a-half went to Verne. But then Brad Dane abruptly started pounding blows into Verne's ribs. Body punches don't usually win a fight but these were bone-crunching body punches and they immediately began taking their toll. Verne began retreating. He'd been the aggressor. Now Brad Dane was the aggressor and remained so for the rest of the round.

But it was round eleven—the fight was scheduled for twenty rounds—when it happened, something so remarkable, so astonishing that folks in this part of Dixie would be talking about it for years afterward.

The round started slow. Both fighters were clearly tired. Brad Dane was gasping for air at certain points and Verne kept shaking his head to clear it. Even their punching was off, either not landing quite true or not having much power behind it.

That all changed with one minute and three seconds left to go in the round. Brad Dane had been holding Verne at bay with unimpressive little jabs. Dane was clearly getting himself a rest. And then—as if that miracle he'd been asking for earlier had just been dropped from the sky—he threw a hard right into Verne's jaw. It pushed Verne back several feet and staggered him enough that he didn't seem to know where he was for a moment.

Brad Dane was a killer. Not every fighter has that instinct, but Brad Dane had it. And he moved in on Verne instantly, body punches, uppercuts, roundhouse rights, even—when the referee was distracted—a couple of quick rabbit punches. The crowd, as one, was orgasmic, standing on its feet, stomping on the wooden bleachers with terrifying enthusiasm. Even the once-docile Confederettes were putting on a show of bouncing breasts and flying fannies that would have made a madam blush. Southern white Christian manhood was safe again in the form of handsome Brad Dane.

Verne tried to fight back but he couldn't. Brad Dane was hitting so hard and so fast, all Verne could do was cover his head with his hands and try to sway right to left so that he wasn't quite so much an easy target.

But Brad Dane had one last trick to pull. He leaned back just enough to be able to see under Verne's bowed head. And he used this moment to bring forth the most impressive, clean, true, Armageddon-like uppercut of his career. This was all being holo'd for the networks to see and when the nets saw this uppercut, they'd sign Brad Dane to a six-fight contract for sure. And at top pay.

It was kind of funny. At first, the uppercut didn't seem to have that much effect. While it landed true, it didn't cause Verne to move much. He just sort of stayed in place, his head still down, swaying a little right to left.

There were eighteen seconds left in the round.

And then he collapsed. That was the only word for it. Collapsed. He just fell straight down. If a body can become a puddle, Verne's did.

And the frenzy—the blood lust—the rage against the black man—all that was suspended for the time being in the awful silence that befell the crowd.

Because they knew. *They* knew and the referee knew and Raines knew and Bob Tyme knew and the farmer and his kid knew.

Verne was dead.

They stood in their silence and gawked and gaped and goggled at the ring where he lay. And a shadow of their mortality passed over them the way it usually does when one human sees another human freshly dead in some kind of accident or crime—*that could be me.* It makes you wonder if animals—cats and dogs and rabbits, for instance—have the same reaction when they come upon the fresh corpse of one of their own kind.

Raines got in the ring and so did Bob Tyme. Raines haunched down and talked to him and worked on him and shook his head and teared up and cussed a couple of times. Brad Dane, who was too much of a nice clean-cut boy to do elsewise, came over and looked down at Verne and then made a big display of saying a prayer out loud with his mouthpiece still in, which made it kinda hard to understand but you got the point anyway. He was the kind of young man you wanted for a son.

The first man who shouted, shouted alone. But he was quickly joined by two or three others. Then by six or seven others. Then by twenty or thirty others. And soon a quarter, then a half, then just about the entire crowd was cheering. It helped that Raines had quickly gotten help in putting Verne's body into a black plastic body bag. And it helped that Raines and a couple of white boys working for Bob carried Verne out of the ring and to Raines' hovervan. And it helped that the door was shut on Verne. And it helped that the body was now completely gone from sight.

And it helped that Brad Dane broke out with this big shit-eating grin on his face and jammed his gloved hands up in the air and started strutting around the ring.

And it helped that the loudspeaker started blaring "Dixie!" just then, too. That helped maybe most of all.

You'd have thought it was New Year's Eve, all that yappin' and yippin' and yayin'. New Year's Eve.

Raines had his money and his dead fighter and there wasn't much reason to wait around. He was just climbing into his van when Bob came up and said, "I don't s'pose you want to hear this but that was one of the best fights I ever promoted. Them folks're gonna be tellin' their grandkids about this one, way a darkie died in the ring." He shook Raines's hand. "You be sure to call on me again, Raines. You sure know how to put on a fight." Then he winked. Leaned toward Raines. "Best thing ever happened to my business. They'll be comin' out in droves now, hopin' to see it again. Every time now they'll be hopin' the black man dies."

"I'm glad it worked for you."

"It sure did, son. It sure did."

Raines nodded and climbed into his van.

They were in free air space before Verne climbed out of the body bag. Far away from Helmsville. They'd had the body bag specially made with a zipper inside. And Verne had gotten good at it. He got out nice and easy. He came up front and sat in the copilot seat.

"How much you get?" he asked Raines. And Raines told him. "Nice." Then Verne said, "You know, someday we'll run out of places to pull this little trick."

"I'll be an old man and retired before we run out of places," Raines said. "White folks'll never get tired of seein' a black man die in the ring."

Raines had spent all his life trying to find boxers who won. But it was Verne—who, before each fight received an injection of a slow-acting paralytic drug derived from curare, so he only appeared to be dead—who really made the money for him. Who needed a winner when you had a loser like Verne?

"Where to next?" Verne asked.

"Nice little place in Florida," Raines said. "Lotta Klansmen down there." He looked over at Verne and grinned. "They'll just love t'see ya die."

A Bad End

Robert J. Randisi

1

Booth checked his reflection in the mirror once again. No less than perfect. His suit was expertly tailored, his hair impeccably cut, more handsome—possibly—than his own famous brother, who most considered the most handsome man in the theater. He was every inch the Prince of the Stage he was supposed to be. His suit of clothes was all black, as befitted the occasion. He sat on the bed to pull on his calf-length boots, and then applied his new spurs.

He walked to the window of his room at the National Hotel and looked out. He was in room 228, and was able to look down on Pennsylvania Avenue. The hotel was but six blocks from the Capitol.

He reflected upon his actions of the day so far, to make sure he had given nothing away. . . .

For a man who rarely slept, he had slept remarkably well that night and was amazingly refreshed upon waking, considering the task he had set for himself that day.

That morning he had left the hotel at 9 A.M., had his breakfast in a nearby restaurant, then went to have his boots shined at Booker and Stewart's barbershop on E Street, which was near Grover's Theater. He then returned to his room, and did not leave again until 11 A.M. He then

went to Ford's Theater on 10th to retrieve his mail. At that
time his clothes were also dark, along with the tall silk hat
he wore. He was also clad in a gray topcoat, kid gloves,
and carried a cane. It was when he reached the theater that
he determined that the President of the United States
would be attending that evening's performance of the play
An American Cousin.

After that he spent some time in the theater, walking
around, looking at it with a new eye. He had spent many,
many hours in Ford's Theater in the past, both on and off
the stage, but tonight would be totally different from any
other day or night he had been there. Never before had his
planned exit from the theater—or any theater—been
thought of as an escape.

He also knew the play very well. He knew the time it
would start, went through the play in his mind, and realized that the best time to do the deed would be at 10:15 P.M.

Upon leaving the theater he went to a livery stable on C
Street and rented a horse. He deliberately asked for a fast
horse, and was shown a roan that he approved of. He informed the liveryman that he would be back to pick up the
animal at 4:00 P.M.

His actions during the ensuing time were of no conse-
quence to anyone, visits with friends for idle chatter to
while away the hours. At precisely 4 P.M., he returned to
the stable and picked up the horse. He stopped at Grover's
Theater and went upstairs to Deery's tavern to have a
drink. It was there, while nursing his drink, that he wrote a
letter to the editor of the *National Intelligencer,* explaining
his intended actions of the day. (They were "intended" at
the time of the writing, but the deed would have been
"done" by the time the editor read the letter.) He signed the
letter with his full name.

After that he left the theater and walked the horse down
14th Street. While passing Willard's Hotel he happened
upon a friend, an actor who would be performing in that

evening's rendition of *An American Cousin*. Enjoying the irony, he handed the letter to the man and asked that he deliver it to the editor as a favor to him. Once the man agreed to perform the favor, Booth mounted the horse and rode back to Ford's Theater, where he had a drink with friends at Taltavuk's Star Saloon. Afterward he went into the theater and paced off the evening's planned actions. He drilled a small hole in the back wall of the box where the President, First Lady, and whatever guests they would invite would be seated. This would enable him to look in and see the President sitting there, if the need arose. When this was all accomplished he left the Ford Theater, had dinner and returned to the National Hotel to rest.

Satisfied that nothing he had done that day—or had been seen doing—had been particularly suspicious, nor had they given away his plans, he picked up the single-shot derringer he would be using that night and checked to be sure it was loaded with a .44-caliber bullet. He also picked up a Bowie knife and stuck it inside the left leg of his trousers. In addition he pocketed a compass, which would be necessary for making his escape in the dark, once he made it outside the city limits.

At 8:45 P.M. he left the hotel.

He arrived at the theater at about 9 P.M. He found an employee of the theater and asked him to hold his mare for him in the back of the theater. He paid the man a dollar, and the man agreed.

Next, Booth went into a tavern next to the theater and ordered a whisky and water. Seated there alone he thought about his brother and the arguments they'd had in the past about the war. Their allegiances were on different sides and this—among other things—had caused a rift in their relationship. He realized that what he planned on doing tonight would reflect badly on the entire Booth family: his mother, Mary Ann; his sister, Asia; his brothers, John and Junius, Jr.; and the memory of his father, the great actor Junius Brutus Booth. There was no help for it, though. He hoped that when they heard the news, they would understand.

Perhaps this action would not have been necessary if a previously planned kidnapping of the President had been successful, but the man had cancelled his trip at the last minute, after all the planning had been set in motion.

He had given this plan a lot of thought, and had finally decided that he had no other choice. Sometimes the depression was so bad he thought he would die. This act—this assassination—would, he hoped, lift the depression not only from him, but from the shoulders of all who still suffered the bitter defeat of the so called "War Between Brothers." The apparent, inevitable slide since the crushing defeat at Gettysburg two years before had culminated in the surrender just five days ago, on April 9, 1865.

He was convinced that it was his fate to be the sole savior of all those who felt the same way he did.

This war was not over.

Booth walked into the Ford Theater lobby at 10:07 P.M. He went up the stairs to the next floor and approached the white door that led to the President's State Box. He opened the door quietly and entered the darkness at the back of the box. On an earlier visit he had hidden the wooden leg of a music stand there, and he now used it to wedge the door shut behind him. He recognized the voice of the actor, Harry Hawk, speaking his lines on stage, and knew the time was near. It was by Hawk's lines that he was timing his action, and at precisely 10:15 he stepped forward, opened the inner door to the box where the President was sitting. He pressed the barrel of the derringer to the back of the President's head, behind the ear, and fired the gun.

The sound the derringer made could not be heard

throughout the theater, but it was certainly heard by those in the box. The First Lady gasped and turned her head to look at her husband as he slumped forward. The President's bodyguard reacted quickly and began to wrestle with Booth, who produced the Bowie knife and stabbed the man in the arm. He then stepped to the front of the box and leaped down to the stage below. As he did so his spur caught on one of the flags hanging from the box. He lost his balance and the eleven-foot leap, which should have been accomplished without difficulty, resulted in his left leg breaking just above the ankle.

The adrenaline of the moment was pumping so strongly, however, that he barely felt the injury as he rushed across the stage to make his escape by the stage door.

Up in the box the First Lady was holding her husband's head in her lap as soldiers pounded on the door to the box. The bodyguard, holding his own wounded arm, managed to kick the wooden leg away and open the door.

The bodyguard, an avid theatergoer himself, shouted to the men, "It was Booth. My God, Edwin Booth has shot President Jeff Davis!"

AUTHOR'S NOTE

I am indebted to the editors of this anthology for allowing me to finish this story severely under the number of words they had originally requested. It was my intention to do something I have never done before, and that was to write a story with entirely no dialogue until the last line. I am, to say the least, usually quite wordy when I attempt to write short stories, so that they are rarely actual "short stories" in the true sense of the term.

This is, but there are still some points to be made to aid in the (hopeful) appreciation of this story.

Before I go into that, though, I must give thanks to Gene Smith for having written American Gothic: The Story of America's Legendary Theatrical Family—Junius, Edwin and John Wilkes Booth. *It was only because of this book that I was able to construct this story.*

When I conceived the idea of Edwin Booth assassinating President Jefferson Davis as a result of an alternative ending to the Battle of Gettysburg, I wondered, first, if Edwin's politics and personality would allow such an extrapolation. I was able to find the following material to support my premise in Mr. Smith's book.

While Edwin did not relish arguing the points of the "conflict" with John, he was indeed a supporter of the North, and of Abraham Lincoln, though not fanatically so. However, Edwin had personality problems that lead me to believe that—had the war ended differently—he might have become more avid in his support of the Union.

Edwin drank heavily and, as much time as he spent in the limelight of the stage, he spent much more in the gloom of his own life. He was subject to great bouts of depression, during one of which he had said to a friend that he had evil hanging over his head and would someday come "to a bad end." And while Edwin was thought to have mental problems, it was something of a well-known fact that his father was genuinely insane.

Most of the depiction of Edwin's day was taken from descriptions of how John Wilkes Booth spent his day prior to the assassination of Abraham Lincoln. I chose, however, to make the assassination of Jeff Davis a single act, and so did not involve any coconspirators.

Again, my thanks to everyone involved.

Lazarus

Jim DeFelice

Gettysburg

The bullets came at him like thick bunches of gray lightning, leaping from the billowing steam at the base of the
hill. They spit through the air, blurs he couldn't separate.

Except for one. That ball he saw, large and perfect, nos-
ing against the wind so gracefully that he stared in wonder,
arms and shoulders slack, legs loose. The bullet flashed silver, then glowed red, growing larger than the sun. It went
from red to blue to dark black, a perfect sphere without in-
dentation, without nick or imperfection. It became so large
that it consumed the entire world.

And then Private Jeptha Aarron saw the lead slug slam
hard against his chest. As if snared by the talons of an
angry eagle, Jep soared upward over the thin line of his fellow sharpshooters at the summit of Big Round Top. He
saw his commander, Major Homer R. Stoughton, point at
the Confederates in the wooded tangle on the slope. He
saw the gray mass of Rebs streaming through nearby
Devil's Den, saw the Union line along Cemetery Ridge,
saw the town of Gettysburg, saw an endless array of fields
and trees. He saw lakes with their blue water marble-
smooth, unrippled by wind or man's intention. He saw
green hills lying undisturbed, oblivious to war.

Then he felt a terrible pain in his chest. A black geyser

erupted around him, soaking his body with wet, numbing darkness.

Jep woke to the wails of dead men rising around him. There was Thomas, who'd joined the sharpshooters the day he had; he'd been gut shot. There was Helmut, the German who had killed a Reb captain at over two hundred yards with a flintlock he'd rifled and converted to percussion himself; his eye dangled from its socket and his left arm was missing. A hundred other men stood, naked, gore hanging from their wounds, a few missing limbs and one his entire head. Men from both sides joined the procession, tromping down the hill, avoiding the rocks and trees as dogs nipped at their flesh, urging them on. The dogs were two or three times the size of normal beasts, with fangs that hung almost to the ground and claws the size of a good hunting knife; they yapped and slobbered and slashed, prodded forward by the whirling whip of their master, Charon, who seemed to be everywhere behind them, laughing and snarling and urging them on.

This cannot be, Jep thought to himself. I cannot be dead.

In that moment the dogs descended on him, snorting and growling. Two took his right leg; a third pulled his left. As he reached to beat them off, Charon put his face to Jep's. The devil's sneer contorted until it transformed into the face of a massive pig, blistered snout wheezing, saw-teeth snapping. Jep screamed and tried to move his arms to fend off his enemy; the earth rolled around him and once more he returned to the black lake of unconsciousness.

Dirt woke him up. It fell on his boots first, then his legs, then his waist. When the first shovelful hit his chest, he realized he was being buried alive; before he could move, another load landed on his face. But he caught his breath and kept quiet, hearing the slurs and curses of the men

above. They were from the South. It did not take much to
sense they hated their work, nor was it hard to guess they
would kill any corpse that dared to show it was alive. Jep
might have been wrong in that—he wavered, considering
what he might do if he were in their position, if a corpse
pushed off the dirt and rose like Lazarus before him. But
the heavy clump of a rock or some other great weight
against his chest pushed all thought away; for a moment,
perhaps longer, his mind fell back into darkness. When he
returned to himself, dirt lay thick over him. He began to
push at it, slowly at first, thinking he would sneak from the
grave. Then, as he realized how great the weight was, he
became desperate. Gasping for air, he flailed upwards,
striving for the surface like a swimmer caught in a river's
undertow. He felt air with his hand, but still couldn't see.
Desperation went to panic, turned to something beyond despair; he flailed wildly, pushed, and only when the blackness cleared with a burst did he realize that the top part of
his body had been covered by another corpse.

Helmut's. His face, sad-eyed, dark with soot, fell into
Jep's lap as he pushed himself up out of the ground and
caught his breath. A low mound of dirt ran to his right, edg-
ing along the hillside in a furrow like seeds in a family gar-
den—Union dead planted for Judgment Day. Jep stumbled
from his grave. Legs wobbly, he somehow conjured
enough sense and momentum to begin running toward the
woods. There was a shout in the distance. Jep ran so hard
he thought he imagined it all, dreaming the field that gave
way to the woods, trees thickening as he ran, rocks spring-
ing up before him. He crossed a narrow brook and found
himself at the edge of a fallow, weeded expanse, a thick
roadway in the distance. Jep collapsed about three steps
into the field, head spinning.

No one had followed him. He couldn't be sure now that
he had heard a shout or that it had even been directed at
him. But he was sure he was behind the Confederates'

lines—an open wagon passed on the roadway a short distance away, accompanied by several men in gray uniforms on horseback. They were heading north, moving with the ease of men who had just won a great battle.

Washington, D.C.

This dream was worse than the one a few days before, the one with Tad and the pistol. An immense black eagle swooped from the sky and grabbed the young boy, carrying him screaming from his mother's side in broad daylight as they walked in Philadelphia.

Lincoln bolted upright, pounding his fists against the bed, even though he knew it was only a dream. To lose Tad now, after Willie, would be unbearable.

As he caught his breath, his thoughts turned to Gettysburg. The dispatches all day yesterday and all evening had been horrible. Meade had not sent word. The early rumors of a rout and the disintegration of the army had proven true; the question now was what would Lee do next. It was not beyond possibility that he would march all the way to Philadelphia.

They had been defeated before. He could withstand yet another and another if need be. He could withstand a million deaths, even his own—whatever was necessary to preserve the Union, to preserve the dream of democracy and justice. That was his task and his fate; if he ended drenched in blood and tears, so be it.

But if Tad died, and Robert, too—if all of his sons were laid below the ground?

The President got out of bed and slowly began to dress despite the darkness. In the hallway outside his bedroom, he found his young secretary, John Hay, leaning off a chair against the wall, his body suspended in sleep. In one of his hands was a telegraph note.

Lincoln put his hand against the wall and lowered himself until he could gently pry the note from Hay's hand.

"Philadelphia threatened. All safe," said the message.

it was meant to assure him about his wife and son, who had gone to the city a few days before. But as he read the words, the shadow of his dream fell across his eyes. He turned back toward the stairs, realizing now that the dream was not about Tad or Willie or Mary or any one person dear to him; it was his country being snatched away.

Lincoln folded the note carefully, then he set out for the War Department to see what news had come.

Near Gettysburg

Jep lay in the tall weeds as it grew dark, clouds mounting as the sun fled. He thought of his mother, mooning over a pie he'd eaten when he wasn't supposed to; he thought of his father drinking with his uncle Jimmy in the corner of the summer room near the stove, whiskey thick and sweet in the air. He wanted to think of other things—Betty Stern especially—but his mind wouldn't congeal around any image but memories of his childhood. Gradually those also faded, his consciousness bumping along with the wind. Shapes and colors, vague sensations of hot and cold, drums and cannon in the distance—his mind skeetered along without rest.

Finally he gathered enough courage to feel for the wound at his chest. His right middle finger found the edge of tattered fabric in his uniform just at the edge of his rib cage. He moved his hand slowly toward the center, surprised by the soft down at the edge of the hole. He felt something hard, then realized he was feeling the packet of letters stuffed in his belt and the Bible Reverend Horton had given him before he'd gone off to war. He laughed, or tried to—he'd opened the Bible perhaps once his whole time in the army. If it had helped stop the bullet, the Reb who'd shot him had put it to more use than he ever had.

As he thought that, it began to rain. The first drop stung his forehead, the next his neck, then his legs. A tumult followed, the heavens pounding him relentlessly. He absorbed the blows until they became part of him. The water soaked through his skin as if he were a piece of dried peat, saturating every inch. Black became gray became hazy white, and still the rain continued. He heard sounds—wagons, horses, voices—whether from the road nearby or his own imagination, he could not tell. Consciousness turned to dream turned to consciousness. He got up several times, each time numb from head to toe, each time lying back down, whether in dream or real life he couldn't say.

At last the sun pushed off the clouds and the rain ceased. Jeptha heard the dull rhythm of foot soldiers sloshing through the mud on the road nearby. He pushed through the weeds quietly, getting within five yards before seeing they were one and all Confederates, gray mismatched uniforms plain against the green field beyond.

Oh, to have his precious Winchester in hand! Sixteen men would have fallen in half a minute! He mimed the action unconsciously, pulling at the trigger and lever, chambering and firing, chambering and firing. Several other men in his company had procured the rifle from Indiana friends; they would have made short work of these rubes.

There were more than a hundred of them. Two hundred. Three. The line seemed endless. As Jep watched them parade, he realized the magnitude of the Union failure—of his failure—in the battle. His commander had warned of what might happen if Round Top were taken: A handful of cannons pushed up the steep woods to the summit could sweep the heart of the army's position, breaking it in two. The prophecy had come to pass.

When the Confederate army had finally passed, Jep pulled off his soggy outer clothes leaving only his long

shirt and trousers. Blood had caked from five or six small
wounds near the top of his shoulder. His whole chest was
black with bruises. There were scratches on much of his
body, and when he touched his face, he felt a jagged welt
across his temple and forehead. But given that he had
found himself in the grave, he did not seem badly off.
Though shoeless and soaked to the bone, the thing he
needed most was food. His legs were stiff when he started
to walk, but his toes actually felt liberated—his boots had
been about two sizes too small.

He walked south for what he judged was a half-hour.
Then Jeptha cut across the road to the east and started
down a narrow, well-rutted and muddy lane that lay between two wooded fields. He'd gone only a few yards
when the head of a soldier appeared above a bush just
ahead; Jep threw himself off the road, rolling and holding
his breath as he found a log to flatten himself behind.

Waiting for the soldier to come, he saw that he was hiding not behind a log but behind the back of a dead Reb infantryman. Maggots crawled around the corpse's neck.
Bile gurgled in Jep's throat and he wretched helplessly,
overcome by the spasms, which produced mostly phlegm
and yellow mucous. He curled up in a ball, spit leaking
from his mouth, tears flowing from his eyes. The heaves
grew more and more powerful, his insides spewing themselves out.

When he finally managed to stop puking, Jep looked
upward, expecting to see the sentry with his rifle standing
over him. But no one was there. He rose slowly; the picket
was no where to be seen.

Jep bent back and grabbed at the dead man's thin coat
from behind, fingers gnawing open the buttons. He slid off
the coat and rolled his arms into the sleeves, then tumbled
toward the dead man's feet. The Confederate did not give
up his boots easily; Jep finally had to push his foot against

the dead man's groin to lever them off. But they fit him a good deal better than his own had.

The man had a knife and an ancient pistol in his belt. Jep took both, then went down along the muddy path, expecting at any second that the Reb sentry would jump out at him. In a few minutes the white base of a church steeple loomed over a row of evergreens on his right. The roof of the steeple itself was missing; it appeared never to have been built, for the church was otherwise intact, and in fact a loud chorus of voices announced that a service was in progress as he approached.

The song was familiar, very familiar: "The Battle Hymn of the Republic." It drew Jeptha toward the building, exquisite voices rising like the righteous thunder of angels above the tiny hamlet that appeared beyond the trees. The church was full to overflowing, with men and women and children crowded down the steps and onto the small front lawn. A few turned and looked at him as he walked, then looked quickly back inside, singing louder. Suddenly the most important thing in the world to Jep was to hear the song; he walked through the edge of the crowd as if drawn by magic, people silently parting, making way. He reached the narrow narthex just inside the open door as the song ended. The silence broke the spell. He realized he must smell and look horrendous; his hunger returned and he tried to shuffle backward and get out. But the preacher at the front began to speak. His words riveted everyone in their place, including Jeptha Aarron.

"Cain was a sinner! The greatest sinner, a man who killed his brother over jealousy and bore the mark of a murderer 'til the end of his days, the Devil's own mark. Did he regret his sin? Did he regret his great evil?

"I tell you no, brothers. I tell you that in his pride, he could not fathom how great, how evil, how vile was his deed.

"We have such men among us now. Even here. Here! Here! In God's house!"

The minister fixed Jep with his eyes. Jep didn't understand, then remembered that he had put on the Confederate's coat.

"They are arrogant, they are Godless, they are agents of the Devil himself," said the reverend, his words shaking the floorboards. "But look not to them—no, my friends, we look not to the Devil but to ourselves. Evil walks wide in the world. What is our own fate? What is our own purpose?"

As he spoke, the minister drew the upper half of his body half over his rickety wooden podium, as if pulled there by his words. He drew back, recharging himself like a crew packing a twelve-pounder.

"Lazarus rises for a purpose!" he said harshly. His loud voice suddenly descending to a hush that barely carried to where Jep stood. "Everything that happens, happens to God's will. That is the meaning of the passage we read earlier. God is allowing the Devil to triumph today. Why? What is it that we must do? What is *our* destiny?"

Jep waited for the answer with the rest of the congregation. The preacher scanned the church again, then turned to the back, once more fixing his eyes on the Confederate who had wandered into his midst. "You tell me, sir," he said. "What is our fate?"

Jep felt the eyes of the others boring into him. Why did the minister imagine Jep would have an answer?

"Tell me, sir—our fate. What is it? Peace? Eternal damnation? At what price do you value our souls?"

Jep wanted to say that he was from Connecticut and for the Union, against slavery, for freedom—but his tongue would not move.

"Fate is God's will; it cannot be undone," shouted the preacher. He made a gesture to the rest of the congregation, then turned back to Jep. "Our sins must be expiated, and they shall be. What is our fate?"

To die and rise and die again?

"What is our fate?"

"I don't know!" shouted Jep, the words exploding unexpectedly from his throat. As everyone turned, he ran from the church, fleeing down the steps, running to the street, tripping but still running, the preacher's voice ringing in his ears. He ran until he collapsed over a rail fence in front of a squat gray building, exhausted.

"Come and have something to eat," said a kind voice above him.

Jep smelled the light scent of rose water and caught a glimpse of a brightly colored dress. He turned, expecting a young girl, but instead found a woman twice his mother's age, bent nearly at the waist, her face thin parchment stretched over knobby blue branches. She placed her curled, yellow fingers on his sleeve, then gently pulled him with her inside the small house beyond the fence, over the dirt threshold, to a small chair before an open hearth. She fetched a kettle, then a plate and a cup. Prodding the small log at the bottom of the fireplace, she coaxed a few embers upward, then opened a black pot and spooned out some food onto the plate. Jep took several bites before realizing it was turkey stew, or a close proximity—in truth it had little taste, but his hunger provided spice more powerful than any in India, and he quickly worked through three full helpings.

"You're the enemy, I suppose," said the old woman.

"No," said Jep.

"Oh, yes," said the woman calmly, as if recording a fact. "Your coat gives you away."

"I stole it," he blurted. "I was wounded on Big Round Top and buried for dead by the Rebs. I escaped and pulled this coat off a dead man."

The woman twisted her head, as if a fresh perspective might tell her whether to believe or not.

"I swear to God I'm from the Union. Hear my voice. I'm Connecticut, born and bred. I lived in New York City three months before joining the army."

"There's riots there," said the woman. "Riots this very day. John Fairchild heard it from the telegrapher. Riots in Philadelphia, too. And many other places."

"What's happened to the army?" Jep asked.

The old woman scowled. "Dead, or run away."

"I didn't run away."

"You ain't dead." She took a towel and grabbed the handle of the kettle to make him some tea.

Washington, D.C.

Lincoln knew every inch of the oilcloth and boards in the hallway floor outside the War Department telegraph office, every smudge, every nail, every tobacco stain. He knew the wall exceptionally well—the slight sway in the plaster about two feet from the doorway, the several jagged hairline cracks on the left side, the slight gloss hiding a repair. He had spent hours and hours here studying the surface, waiting for every hint and rumor that Meade had finally succeeded in drawing his ragged army together. Stanton had suggested several times he relieve Meade of command; last night Lincoln had replied that he might, if Meade only had something to command.

In truth, it seemed of little difference who commanded the army now. Too many men had lost the will to fight. The slaughter of Gettysburg had terrified them, blotting away their courage. If only the flank had been defended, if only the senior officers had been more aggressive, if only he had found a better commander sooner or prodded McClellan more effectively at the start of the war. . . .

The President pushed his mind back to the present, narrowing his focus on a knot in the wall. Grant had won Vicksburg in the West, giving the Union the Mississippi. But the chaos of Gettysburg and riots in the Eastern cities had shaken the Northern states so severely that the Cause teetered on the brink, perhaps over it. Several state legislatures had passed bills withdrawing support for the war. Just this morning the city of New York had declared itself "an open city," calling on its natives to lay down their arms and return home. Mutiny was widespread. Grant and his troops could be counted on, but his army was too far away to attack Lee or reassure the East. Stuart's troopers were reported to have ridden down the streets of Philadelphia. Lee was said to be within a day's march, with nothing but ragtag militia before him.

Exaggerations, perhaps. But soon they would be true enough. Even Stanton counseled for negotiation. *Stanton.*

To negotiate would be to surrender. To bind hundreds of thousands of men and their children to unholy slavery for generations. Whites themselves would suffer—there would be tyranny for all now, the South ruled by generals and aristocrats, perhaps the West as well. The North would surely follow as the ties between the remaining states continued to unravel. The dark shadow of the black eagle rose before his eyes, mocking him for his failure to preserve democracy.

A door crashed open at the end of the hall. The President jerked his head around—*Willie, dead Willie, coming to see him.*

John Nicolay.

"I've just gotten word," said his trusted secretary, half shouting as he ran. "The ambassador from Great Britain—the bastard English are going to recognize the Rebels. The ambassador is on his way."

Pennsylvania

The old lady gave Jep clothes as well as food, then let him sleep in a corner of her room. A unit from A. P. Hill's army marched through the town that afternoon and early evening. If the townspeople had any notion of hunting down the strange Confederate who had come to mock them in their church, Hill's men surely distracted them. The jangled hush of the troops moving through town conjured shadows in Jep's mind, monsters passing behind a dark screen. He dreamed of his death, found himself buried again, rose, stood alone in the town church. They called him Lazarus and asked what he would do. Words filtered into his consciousness—the old woman reading her Bible over him, praying to herself. "A righteous God will smite down your enemies." He became an eagle, tangled in limed lines laid down for sparrows; he freed himself only with great difficulty, losing half of his feathers yet flying still, soaring over the countryside. "A righteous God will choose your champion." The grass turned brown and a gray figure appeared on horseback, gaunt yet proud, three times the size of a normal man, sitting majestically on a horse that strutted over the countryside. Jep's eagle claws tensed and he knew he had been raised, knew he had been created, for this one moment—he flashed from the sky, talons grabbing for the neck of the man, who changed instantly into the many-headed beast, fire and ice spewing from every mouth, embers covering the sky. Cannon balls melting into running metal.

"Ashes thou art. Ashes."

Jeptha held to the demon as the whirlwind continued, evil flailing him with a thousand whips of steel, piercing his skin with hot knives and pounding his head with the force of a fleet's full broadside against his skull.

And then water rushed over him, and he plunged over a great waterfall. Jep gasped for air but continued to hold on,

certain now of victory. Water pushed into his lungs and the
demon flailed with all its might, steam hissing as they
tumbled over and over, tumbled through cold and then an
inferno, the sound of a thousand steam engines roaring
around him.

Then silence.

Then warm, shallow water lapping at his side.

Then peace, his body whole, aches and bruises gone.

Jep opened his eyes. The afternoon sun played pink-
blue light across the walls, small bits of dust fluttering in
its rays like angels watching over him. He raised his head
slowly from the bed. The old lady was bent over in the
chair near him, sleeping.

Dead.

He laid her down in the bed, her body no heavier than a
cat's. Her Bible had fallen on the floor. Jeptha placed it in
her hands, open to the page she seemed to have been reading—Lazarus being raised from the tomb.·

He felt like Lazarus, truly. His body seemed whole
again. And if he was Lazarus, if he truly had been raised
from the dead, what should he do? For all that happened
did so with a purpose, as the preacher had implied. A man
had a certain fate on earth, which he could not escape, even
with death.

Two hours later, as Jep walked along the road south of
town, still debating things in his head, a horse approached
him from across a mowed field. The animal had a full saddle and kit, complete with a rifle lashed against its side. It
came right to him, nuzzling Jep in the chest as he stood
stone still in amazement.

The weapon the animal carried was an extraordinary
gun, so shiny it might have come from a factory that very
hour. Jep examined it closely: a Henry repeater, it could
hold twelve cartridges and fire them in quick succession,
thanks to a lever that ejected spent casings, loaded a new
shell and cocked the gun's firing hammer, all in one mo-

tion. Jep had heard of the rifle but never seen one before; it had a light, well-balanced feel in his hands and was easily aimed. He found eight rim-fire cartridges in a bag tied to the saddle and loaded them one by one, fingers trembling as he pushed the bullets inside.

It was too much coincidence that the horse and gun had come to him. Providence was preparing him for his fate.

If it was to kill Confederates, there were plenty to choose from. The gray stream that had coiled its way northward had metamorphosed into a vast river that flooded the countryside with Rebels. Confederate units, some well organized, others not, were everywhere. Northern sympathizers, in some cases including blue-clad infantrymen who'd deserted their own army, were thick in their ranks. The world had turned upside down in the space of a few days—hours, really. Johnny Reb was now in control.

Control was not quite the word. Chaos reigned; the fact that Jep had a horse and a good gun as well as a Confederate jacket kept him from being molested, but it was clear that others might not be so lucky.

When night came, Jep stopped in a small inn near the Pennsylvania border. Within five minutes he heard there had been riots in many Northern cities, including Boston. Philadelphia had given itself to Lee as an open city. A man well into his cups claimed Delaware had ceded from the Union.

The others at the overcrowded inn left Jep alone. People nodded or tipped their hats, but always moved on, ignoring him as if he were a ghost to them. He spent the night in a thick chair in the corner of the main room, absorbing the conversations. A good number of the men here were from the South—journalists, businessmen, and others doing work for the army. Washington was still protected and there was news that Grant had won in the West, but clearly, the war had been lost.

If that were true, what was he to do? Why had he been taken from the grave? What mission could be accomplished in a dead man's shirt, with a horse and a rifle sent by God?

"Lee will be the president now," said a man at the far end of the room, his voice breaking through the buzz of the room. "Lee will be the master of us all."

Jep raised his head to catch a glimpse of the man, but all he could see was a haze of cigar smoke.

"A good master," said another man. "A good president."

"I'd make him emperor," said the first man. "What we need is a good leader—strong. Not like the one we've now, for damn sure."

"Lee would never take that."

"Another would."

"Make him president, with real power. A fist to back up his words."

"Not like the one we've now."

Perhaps Lee was his destiny, Jep thought. He sat in the chair, waiting for another sign.

Washington, D.C.

A blue ghost looked at him from the mirror, eyes pushed deep in his skull, cheekbones dagger-sharp. Mary moaned from the other room, as if in grief.

Death would be almost welcome now.

Lincoln pulled his collar into place and stepped away from the mirror at the hallway. There was much work to be done after the cabinet meeting; best get it underway.

The President had thought of resigning, but decided that was the coward's way. There was no precedent besides, and in all honestly, Hamlin wasn't up to the task ahead, not even for the few months before the end of the term. Lincoln would not stand for reelection, of course. A new

leader would need to be chosen, though it would be difficult to find a competent man who would want the thank-
less job of trying to hold what was left of the Union
together.

He shut all of that out of his mind as he strode toward
the stairs. A number of men were waiting at the bottom of
the steps, undoubtedly hoping to make some last-minute
suggestion or recommendation. Justice Noah Swayne,
James Speed, even the scoundrel Willard Saulsbury, undoubtedly here under some cover or other to hide his glee
at Lincoln's downfall.

Stanton would be inside his office, waiting with the others. At least there'd be no job seekers this morning. They'd
all be in Richmond, most likely, bothering Davis.

The notion brightened Lincoln's mood ever so slightly.

He would have Bates and his clerk work up the terms,
but the President had the broad outline of his plan ready:
active hostilities to cease unilaterally; the states—all the
states, North and South—invited to join a special session
of Congress to consider the calling of a Constitutional convention. He expected the Confederates would not attend
this convention; in some ways that would make the future
easier. Lincoln saw that the eventual result would be three
nations, not two—the Northern states in a smaller Union,
the Confederates in theirs, and then a loose amalgamation
of states and territories to the west of the Mississippi, most
likely governed by Grant, who presently had them in his de
facto control. Lincoln foresaw much more; he saw tyranny
and a loss of freedom and chaos rising amid chaos, but he
could not concern himself with that dark future. He had to
concentrate on the task before him, which was to restore
order and law to as much of the nation as would accept it.

He had thought his fate grander. He had thought God
himself had chosen the people of the United States to show
the way to freedom for the entire world. But events had
proven him wrong.

Did only fate determine what happened, or did chance play a role? If the dice were thrown a hundred million times, if some small event were to be misplaced, some key moment changed, what would the outcome be?

And if his job was to preserve the liberty his forefathers had established—if that vow went beyond the one to simply uphold the Constitution, as he had long ago decided it did—what should he do now? Should he make himself a martyr, an example to others in the river of time? If it would take more than a wild gesture to reverse this war, might one not suffice to influence the future? Or was his task now simply to be an impotent loser?

Lincoln had considered riding out alone to meet the Rebels, guns in both hands, throwing himself into the howling wind as the crazy man John Brown had done. He'd wondered if such an act might inspire others years hence, show them what freedom and justice were worth. But it was a crazy, vain thought, and in the end he'd dismissed it.

As the President reached the bottom of the stairs and turned toward his office, a middle-aged man with a bird-like face approached him. He grabbed Lincoln by the arm as the others in the crowd milled forward. The President looked down toward the man's other hand wanting to see the gun that would kill him.

"Mr. President, I heard there was an opening in the treasury department and I wish to apply," said the man. He had nothing in his hand. "I am broke, sir, and in need of a job."

Lincoln began to laugh. "The man shoveling dirt on my coffin will pause and ask for a job," he said.

Virginia

There were no signs, no voices, no shining lights. Jeptha Aarron wandered southward, at times aiming for Richmond, at times aiming for nowhere at all. He heard different things when he stopped; Grant was coming eastward with his army, Meade had regrouped his men, Lincoln had fled to Massachusetts. The newspapers were filled with stories of Northern army units surrendering, of cities gone mad. A group of congressmen had turned up in Richmond to sue for peace. As Jep traveled, he found himself in a no-man's-land between the two armies, or rather between Lee's forces and what was left of the Union army. Knots of blue-coated pickets stood near stone walls at crossroads, eyeing passersby. Once or twice a Union soldier shouldered a gun and took aim in Jep's direction. But no one fired or even challenged him. Confederates treated him much the same; a few shouted questions which he answered only with nods or grunts, fearing his Connecticut tongue would give him away. Mostly what they wanted was news, information that he didn't have about rumors they had heard: Had the Yanks truly given up? Was Lee really riding back to Virginia with Meade in chains?

What amount of time passed, Jep couldn't say. There were days and nights, yet he didn't feel the need to sleep. He stopped at times for food but tasted nothing. His horse never seemed to get hungry or tired; she drank slowly when he watered her and when she rode, she seemed equally content to gallop or walk, whichever was his pleasure. At times Jep thought he had truly died and was only passing through the countryside as a figment of someone else's dream.

And then one afternoon he rode into a small farming town in Virginia. People flooded into the street ahead of him, surging from the stores and hotels. His horse hesitated, but the flow was irresistible; they were drawn along the street toward a large green near a railroad line. Dust swirled in a great wave beyond the grass, and Jep knew that an army approached even before he reached a spot where he could see it. People shouted and screamed; a band played somewhere, drumbeats reverberating off the clapboards of the nearby building. The crowd ahead stopped, but Jep's horse kept going, treading slowly as the people cleared a path. He found himself standing on a knoll overlooking the green where the vanguard of an immense gray-jacketed army was just marching in. Officers on horseback rode back and forth, paying scant attention to the onlookers as they checked the echelons of soldiers.

Was this the army that had defeated the Union? Their uniforms were rags and their lines uneven.They were smiling and whistling and joking, jubilant as opposed to disciplined.

"There he is!" yelled someone behind Jep. He turned to his right and saw the dust cloud parting, a group of men on horseback following the straggling train of the advance guard. A thick knot of cavalrymen trotted together in perfect formation and dusty dress, flags held erect from the saddle. Behind the first line rode a man waving another ensign, this one upside down on its pole—Old Glory turned on its head, tattered and torn.

Other troopers followed. Officers. A wagon. Then one man alone on a gray horse, erect.

Lee.

Now Jep knew he was alive, for his heart pounded in his chest and sweat ran from every pore in his body. His heart stuttered but his eyes were hard and clear; the scourge of the Union, the devil himself, rode on his mare not fifty yards away, now forty, now thirty. In a minute he would pass directly in front of Jep, ten yards away at most, a clear shot even if he stood still.

Jep's hand slid down to the rifle slung in the holster at the side of the saddle. His horse took an easy step down the slope.

None of the Confederate soldiers was close enough to stop him. Lee was fifteen yards away, turning in his direction, taking off his hat, his steel eyes picking Jep out of the crowd.

Lift the gun and fire. Fire now.

His heart stopped. Jep's fingers touched the rifle, then froze, paralyzed by Lee's eyes, steel eyes that took hold of each side of his face.

"Watch out! Watch out! The bastard's got a gun!"

The world whirled. Thunder exploded in Jep's ear. Flames shot everywhere and he felt himself being hurtled to the ground, lightning sparking in his eyes. Men stampeded around him, over him. He pushed his mouth into the grass, blood streaming onto his tongue as he lost consciousness.

Washington, D.C.

To have gone into Richmond itself would have been too humiliating, and in any event not even Lee could have guaranteed his safety. So the emissaries agreed on a small town near Manassas Junction in Virginia, not far from the ignoble Union defeat that in many ways foreshadowed the rest of the war. Lincoln had decided he would go himself, trailing Halleck and a few members of the general's staff. A cavalry company would escort the President, but he had turned down his cabinet's offers to accompany him. Too big a procession would set an improper tone, he thought, not to mention fuel numerous political fires. Besides, Stanton and Chase had already resigned, and while he thought he might like Blair or even Speed along for company, choosing just one man to go with him would slight the others.

Not that accepting peace was in any way an honor.

Lincoln walked across the lawn toward the small black carriage and its pair of horses. The sun had just edged over the horizon, alone in the blue sky. It was too beautiful a

day to surrender, he thought. He remembered the day they
had put Willie to rest, the harsh rain.

"Papa, can't I please come?"

Tad launched himself, landing in his father's arms as he
twisted around. Lincoln hugged him for a moment, hugged
him a second time for Willie's sake, then set him down.

"I will be back by sundown," he told his son. "Where's
your mama?"

"She's in bed still."

"Well go cheer her up." Three young privates from the
Bucktail regiment who'd been milling around nearby came
forward. Lincoln pushed Tad in their direction, then
boarded the carriage.

Fate was inevitable. He had misjudged its intentions,
and now there was no escaping it.

Virginia

"They say you saved Lee. Wait, no, don't get up. Just keep
your head back. Please. You're not well. You fell from the
horse."

Jep heard the voice but couldn't see where it came
from. He couldn't see anything beyond a jamble of yellow
and black, the blurred shadows of a ruined photographic
plate.

He lay on something soft. A heavy weight pressed
against the left side of his chest.

"You've had a fever. You've been delirious these twelve
hours."

Cold fingers touched the middle of his forehead. Jep
tried to jerk away.

"Ssshhhh," said the voice.

The shadows turned darker. Jep heard a buzzing in his
ears.

"Lazarus, rise."

The weight pressed against his ribs. The force doubled, then doubled again. He flailed upwards, remembered the body on his face, pushed it away.

"Why did you say your name was Lazarus? It's not, is it?"

Jep opened his eyes. A young woman's face hovered a few inches from his, floating in the yellow light of the room. He stared at the pale, perfect skin, at the auburn hair pulled back at her forehead. Slowly, he became aware of her dress and the rest of her body. Her fingers reached to stroke the side of his forehead—cold, cold fingers, but gentle, gliding just at the surface of his skin.

"My name is Jeptha Aarron," he said.

"Yes, I know. You said so several times in your fever. You're from Connecticut."

Her hand pressed gently against his forehead as she explained that after the tumult of the attempt on Lee's life, he had been taken here, to her mother's hotel. The officers who had brought him explained how he had wheeled his horse at the last moment, blocking the man who had rushed through the crowd with the gun to assassinate the general. In the confusion Jep's horse had been shot and Jep thrown to the ground. They thought he was a Confederate from Georgia because of his uniform; she was the only one who knew he was a Yankee.

"Mary," she said, as if he had asked her name. She continued to stroke his face.

He had saved Lee, not killed him. He was the Union's greatest traitor.

Had he been torn from the tomb for this? Then it was the devil who had restored him to life, the devil who had led him here.

"I must go." Jep pushed up from the bed.

"You're not strong enough," she said.

He winced as her hand caught him in the chest, but

slipped out of bed nonetheless. His legs were naked. He didn't recognize the nightshirt.

"They left a fresh uniform for you," said the girl, reluctantly pointing to a wooden chair near the doorway. "With boots and all."

"A pistol?" he asked.

"No. A pistol? Did you lose it when you stopped the assassin?"

Her hand gripped his arm as he reached for the uniform, and in that instant Jep saw his future, or a future that could be his—this girl, a family, a small farm in the new Confederacy. A modest pension or at least a stake for saving Lee.

Success and peace. At the price of his soul. Or had he already given that up?

Her eyes and hair and skin were more beautiful, ten times, than any he had ever seen before. The curve of her hips swayed him, pulled him toward a future he had not wished for.

He grabbed for his pants.

"Colonel Taylor wished to see you when you recovered. He is with Lee at the farmhouse," said Mary. Her voice was resigned, as if she had been able to overhear the struggle of his thoughts.

"Yes," he said, sitting and pulling on the clothes.

"You should rest before you go there. You have wounds that haven't healed."

Jep forced himself not to look at her, not to linger, moving so deliberately as he left the room that the papered walls and bright yellow wainscoting seemed to stand back as he walked. He'd been foolish to rely on providence and fate, mistaking it for his own desire. But could he reverse it?

An officer challenged him as he neared the parlor door.

"Colonel Taylor has ordered me to report to him," snapped Jep.

"Where are you from, soldier?" demanded the captain.

"Virginia, sir. But before that, Connecticut. My mother . . ." He let his voice trail off, calculating that it would make it sound as if his mother had dragged him north, calculating that the admission and hint of shame would be enough to convince the officer of his sincerity. The man glared at him a few moments more, then let him pass.

Twice he was stopped in the street, once for failing to salute. The confusion he had witnessed after Gettysburg had been replaced by an almost supernatural adherence to discipline. Armed units were everywhere in the tiny town, with well-ordered checkpoints and suspicious officers. Colonel Taylor's name had power, but still there were questions, and Jep passed only because he mustered a supreme self-assurance directly at odds with the fear coursing through his veins. By midday, he had learned where Lee's headquarters were; he was in fact only two miles from it. He immediately began walking in that direction, still unarmed, without even a hat. He did not even have a plan, except to get as close to Lee as possible, and then to find some way to kill him, with his bare hands if necessary.

Riders thundered by him on the road, dousing him with dust. Soldiers were everywhere—on the road, in the woods, even up in the trees. He ran the gamut of three more checkpoints before being stopped at a fourth within sight of the house. Here, Taylor's name seemed to count for little; the captain who stopped Jep turned him over to a colonel, who folded his arms and rocked before him, his right leg clearly a peg beneath ill-fitting trousers.

"I saved General Lee from an assassin," Jep told him. "Colonel Taylor ordered me to report to him personally, without delay."

"Why should I believe you?" asked the colonel.

Jep said nothing. The colonel stared at him for a good

minute, then turned to a sergeant standing nearby and told him to search him. The man practically punched him, running his hands harshly over his shirt and pants though it was clear Jeptha had no weapon. When he was done, Jep started toward the house, only to be stopped by the officer's sharp call.

"Who said you could go anywhere?" demanded the colonel. "Tell me, July 2—where were you?"

"Big Round Top, sir. At Gettysburg. We beat back the Yanks, then wrestled the guns into position. We chewed up their flanks as our fellows overran them."

"And then?"

Jep looked down. "Wounded and left for dead."

That seemed to mollify the colonel. He told the sergeant to accompany him to the house where Colonel Taylor was with Lee. "Be respectful," he added. "Even of the devil."

The sergeant pushed him toward the house, but after a few steps his mood and manner changed. "Ol' Jeff Davis is inside," the sergeant told him. "With Lee and the others. General Halleck and his staff are there licking their boot heels. Lincoln is due within the hour. Half his escort's already arrived. You're witnessing history, kid. You'll have a front-row pew."

Well-dressed civilians and high-ranking officers of both sides crowded the front yard. Men had climbed all over the house. The sergeant pointed toward a knot of men, indicating that one was Taylor. Then he said something about getting a good vantage from the roof of the porch and disappeared. Some horsemen and carriages were arriving down the road; the crowd turned as one, craning to see who it was. Jep stood near the porch of the house, unsure what to do, until a cane smacked hard against his shoulder and broke the spell of his trance.

"You. I saw you in Washington. You're a Yankee."

Jep jerked around. "You're mistaken."

He had the voice of an actor and the manner of a dandy,

but he was quite obviously drunk. He must have been famous or important to get here, but he seemed to have come alone; the others nearby looked away, embarrassed. Jep turned back toward the road but the man swung the cane again, this time smacking his ear so hard it felt like it was on fire.

Jep whirled and grabbed the cane; the man held on and fell toward him, stumbling.

There was a small gun in his belt. As the man fell past him, Jep whipped the cane up and managed to smash his head with it. Then he dove on the man, punching with one hand, grabbing for the gun with the other. The weapon was so small he palmed it in his hand.

There were shouts behind him. A boot caught him in the ribs. Jep pushed backward, blood rushing around his temple. He flailed, desperate, expecting everyone to jump on him. But except for a single man who pulled him off his assailant and then let him go, no one bothered with him. They were turning, surging toward the roadway, toward the line of gray soldiers and the phalanx of blue-clad horsemen, which gave way to a black surrey. The carriage rode forward, coming halfway up the lawn before stopping. A lone man sat in the vehicle.

Meanwhile, two men appeared in the doorway of the house. One wore a shiny brown suit with a gold vest on the left, his face red—Jeff Davis, it seemed to Jep.

The other walked across the porch on legs that seemed too short for his upper body. His manner was regal; he rose above the others though he was not especially tall, striding ahead as a small group of blue- and gray-clad generals trailed out of the house and lined the lawn.

Lee.

Jeptha Aarron pushed forward. No one stopped him, or even seemed to see him. He moved toward Lee—ten feet, eight, his heart beating, the red shadows of the grave descending over his eyes, the cannons' thump drenching his

ears, a thousand balls passing through the air. To have held
that hill five more minutes, to have turned back the tide of
Rebs one more time—fate stood at the apex, balanced by
chance, balanced by the anger and determination of one
man rushing forward, gun in hand. Jep's target stopped
right before him, six feet away.

He leveled his arm to fire. As he squeezed the trigger a
black cloud rose from his left; he felt a moment of doubt
and jumped to his left, then felt nothing at all, forever nothing.

Lincoln saw the man approaching from the corner of his
eye as he walked toward Lee. The gray uniform the man
wore flared, as if he had wings. Lincoln saw the man's
hand moving upward and caught sight of the gun. In that
instant Abraham Lincoln acted as he had always acted,
moved by the impulse of his convictions, driven by the un-
changeable core of who he was. He threw himself forward,
aiming to grab the assassin. But the man stopped short, firing without stretching out his arm for aim.

Lincoln felt a thud at the back of his head, a pain more
emotional than physical and not at all unlike what he had
felt the night Willie had died. And then he felt not the sorrow he had traveled here with, nor the weight of his country's horrible future: He felt something more like peace. As
his body stretched down toward the dust, he realized fate
was a star, waning and waxing, shining into a thousand
broken mirrors, each image different, each perceived by
one person at one time, each equally true though different
in its particulars. A great warmness fell over him. He had
presided over the greatest catastrophe his country had ever
known. He had failed to protect those most in need. Yet he
felt peace as his long arms groped in the dirt, felt a shudder of contentment even as the blood poured like a flood
from the gap in his skull. He had been true to himself and

met fate on its own terms; what others would make of it, what future would come, was no longer in his hands.

ABOUT THE AUTHOR

Jim DeFelice is the author of a trilogy of historical fiction set in the Revolutionary War: *The Silver Bullet, The Iron Chain,* and *The Golden Flask.*

A Gun for Johnny Reb

Simon Hawke

Excerpted from *A Soldier's Life: The Memoirs of Colonel Bruce Edward Hamill, First Virginia Mounted Rifles, CSA*

A philosopher once noted that a critic is one who watches from the safety of a hilltop while a fierce battle is being fought in the valley below, and when the battle is over, he then goes down and slaughters the survivors. In the aftermath of the War for Southern Independence, and in particular of its high-water mark in the Gettysburg Campaign, there was certainly no shortage of such critics, primarily armchair generals who had never commanded troops in battle, and most of whom had never even *seen* a battle, yet somehow they nevertheless felt themselves eminently qualified to expound at considerable length upon the decisions made by the commanders on both sides. I was not in command at Gettysburg, but I can at least claim that I was there, serving under Lieutenant General J. E. B. "Jeb" Stuart in the capacity of a second lieutenant on his staff. As such, I was in a unique position not only to observe most of the key events and personalities of the campaign, but to participate directly in what was undoubtedly the pivotal event of the entire war.

As the month of May in the year 1863 drew to a close, no one had any doubts, at least upon our side of the conflict, that the war had reached or was about to reach its turning point. We had just achieved an important victory at Chancellorsville against superior odds, and the Federal army seemed demoralized. "Old Marse Robert" had taught "Fighting Joe" a lesson and, in the end, Joe Hooker had failed to live up to his bellicose *nom de guerre.* But then, we had not really expected any more from this particular commander of the Union forces than we had seen from all those who had preceeded him. We had heard about the lax discipline under his command and the numerous camp followers he had allowed to attend upon his troops, women of easy virtue who became known as "Hooker's girls" or simply "Hookers." There was not much to be thought of such a man, and so it followed suit that we did not think much of him. He was overmatched and General Lee had whipped him, pure and simple, as indeed, he had whipped every Yankee general who had come up against him since the beginning of the war. Well, in truth, I suppose that Sharpsburg could be called a draw, but Chancellorsville was yet another in a long string of Federal defeats, although it did not come without great cost, and word had reached even those of us out in the field that a "peace party" had been formed and was gaining momentum in the north. One more significant victory could gain us the European recognition that had thus far eluded us, with England in particular, and the time was surely right to press home our advantage.

Much blood had been shed at Chancellorsville, but the single greatest loss we had incurred was the death of the valiant Stonewall Jackson. In General Lee's own words, "Any victory would be dear at such a price." There was no man alive who could possibly have taken Thomas Jackson's place, and so General Lee determined upon a reorganization of the army. Instead of our previous organization into two corps of infantry divided into four divisions each, we would henceforth have three corps, each made up of three divisions. In effect, a new division was created by taking two brigades from A. P. Hill's command and combining them with new troops brought up as reinforcements. To command this new division, Henry Heth was promoted from the rank of brigadier to major general, and to further fill out the newly formed Third Corps, one division each was taken from the First and Second. "Old Pete" Longstreet would remain in command of the First Corps, composed of the divisions of McLaws, Pickett, and Hood. Richard Ewell was appointed to command the Second Corps, composed of the divisions led by Early, Johnson, and Rodes. The Third Corps, composed of the divisions led by Anderson, Heth, and Pender, would be commanded by A. P. Hill. These new dispositions, it should perhaps be noted, were not received with unanimous favor, as indeed, few command decisions are. Writing well after the fact, Longstreet was later to observe that there was perhaps "too much Virginia" on the roster of command, but whatever objections may have been voiced at the time were certainly not voiced strenuously and the reorganization stood as General Lee had ordered it.

Prior to the opening of the campaign, there had been some disagreement as to how best to proceed against the Union at that point. While we in the Army of Northern Virginia had enjoyed repeated success against the Federal troops, the same could not truly be said of our forces in the west at that time, which were being sorely pressed by Grant at Vicksburg. There was concern that if Vicksburg fell, the Mississippi would irretrievably be lost. There were several strategies advanced, by Generals Beauregard and Longstreet among others, that involved sending troops out west in order to strengthen our forces there, but General Lee opposed them, fearing justifiably that weakening our forces in the east by taking troops from them and sending them out west would mean certain disaster in Virginia. We were already outnumbered by the Army of the Potomac, and they had also the advantages of superior supply lines and industrial support. In short, we were both outmanned and outgunned. What we had not been, to that point, was out-generaled, but there was only so much that any commander could do in the face of overwhelming odds. General Lee, perhaps better than any man alive, had understood that and he succeeded in making President Davis understand it, also. Hooker, after all, was far closer to Richmond than were either Grant or Rosecrans.

General Lee proposed instead to launch an invasion of the North, taking the war home to them on their own soil. Those officers with whom he shared his plan were enthusiastically in favor of it, as indeed were all the Southern newspapers. Let the Yankees have a taste of what it felt like to be invaded, they all wrote. Let them experience the war in their own backyard for a change. A push along the Blue Ridge Mountains, across the Potomac and into Pennsylvania would put us in position to threaten Philadelphia or Baltimore, and in Washington, President Lincoln would find himself suddenly quite vulnerable, cut off from the remainder of the Union which he so wanted to preserve at any cost.

Hooker would be forced to give pursuit and come to the relief of Washington, thereby giving Virginia much-needed relief at harvest time. We would not require extended supply lines in support of our invasion. We would live off the land as we moved, taking advantage of the Pennsylvania harvest season, although General Lee had insisted from the start that we pay for everything we took from Yankee civilians as forage and supply, and that we refrain from any depredations such as had been practiced in the South by Union troops. The Army of Northern Virginia would only make war on soldiers, he said, not civilians. When Hooker came after us, as he would have no choice but to do once we moved north, he would find us ready and waiting for him on ground of our own choosing. And Lee would beat him there, just as he had done before. It was a fine plan, and President Davis wholeheartedly approved it.

Thus, on the third of June, General Lee embarked upon his Pennsylvania campaign, with the division of McLaws moving out along the Rappahannock River towards Culpepper. Rodes would follow with his division on the following day, with Early and Johnson departing on the fifth. Hill would cover the rear with his three divisions. Hood and Pickett were already encamped in the vicinity, as were those of us in Stuart's cavalry.

We had, in fact, been at Culpepper for about two weeks at that point, getting ourselves in shape for action while we awaited further orders. Jeb Stuart was never a man given to idleness, and he had given orders for a grand review to be held at Brandy Station for the sake of discipline and to boost the morale of our troops. Five brigades of cavalry passed in review in front of grandstands the general had especially built for the occasion and, much to the delight of the audience composed of both military and local civilians, we staged a cavalry charge upon our own guns, which had been loaded with blank charges, the better to provide an atmosphere of actual battle conditions.

Not a few of the young ladies in the audience swooned at the impressive spectacle of our troopers charging at the guns with sabres drawn, filling the air with the sound of Rebel yells while the cannons boomed and blanketed the field with smoke. It greatly raised the spirits of our troops, and General Stuart was very pleased with the way it all came off. He was even more pleased when, after General Lee arrived, he received permission to restage the review for his commander's benefit, although General Lee directed that the mock charge on the guns be dispensed with upon this occasion, the better to conserve the strength of our horses and our supplies of powder. This was a wise decision, as things turned out, for on the ninth of June, we played host to General Alfred Pleasonton and his eight brigades of Union cavalry, with whom we were to exchange courtesies a number of times over the next several weeks. Reports in the newspapers would describe it as the greatest cavalry engagement of the war, and it was certainly the largest, although our most significant engagement was yet to come, outside the town of Gettysburg.

It had been raining hard as the army started its march, and many of the troops, of both the cavalry and infantry, resorted to the use of carpets for their raingear. Our supplies were low, as always, and many of the men marched barefoot, having worn out their shoes. We in the cavalry were able to maintain at least some semblance of military spit and polish, but it was certainly not of the sort that one would have found at West Point. Some of us were fortunate enough to have oilskins, but many had to resort to carpets that had been sent from home to use as blankets or cloaks. The men cut holes in them for their heads and arms, making colorful, makeshift ponchos that gave the army the appearance of an ambulatory quilt. General Stuart, like General Lee, eschewed the use of houses for his lodgings, even in inclement weather, not wishing to have the advantage of comfortable quarters while his men were forced to sleep exposed to the elements. All throughout the war, in fact, General Lee always used tents, and on numerous occasions, I saw General Stuart take cover underneath the leafy canopies of trees and wrap himself in blankets and oilskins against the rain where he could easily have commandeered a comfortable house that stood nearby. Those who were so fond of criticizing him for his plumage and flamboyance should have been there to see him upon those occasions, so that they might have judged whether they would have subjected themselves to such discomfort in his place rather than enjoy an advantage denied to the men under his command.

The bad weather had held, and the condition of the roads left much to be desired. It did not take much rain to

turn the roads into a quagmire, especially with so many
men, horses, wagons, and caissons churning it all up. It
therefore became important to take quick advantage of any
breaks in the weather to make the most effective progress.
On the morning of June 9, General Stuart waited at Brandy
Station with his entire command, consisting of close to
10,000 troopers, ready to screen the movements of the
army as they marched through the Shenandoah Valley.
However, we received an unpleasant surprise at the hands
of the aforementioned Alfred Pleasonton, who struck us
hard and unexpectedly with six brigades of Federal cavalry, supported by two brigades of infantry, who had
forded the Rappahannock shortly before dawn and wasted
little time in demonstrating to us that their intentions were
decidedly unfriendly.

Taken by surprise, we were forced to withdraw to Fleetwood Hill, where General Stuart rallied us and we were
able to mount an effective countercharge. Word of the attack was sent back, and General Lee sent up some infantry
from Culpepper, but by that time, we had exchanged
charges with Pleasonton a number of times, losing Fleetwood Hill twice and retaking it twice in the sort of ebb and
flow that is not uncommon in cavalry fighting. It was a
harbinger of similar action to come, albeit on a considerably smaller scale, at Aldie, Middleburg, and Upperville
over the next two weeks.

Those who have never seen cavalry in combat and
whose perceptions of same are dictated primarily by the
drawings published in the newspapers and the vivid ren-
derings on canvas which became so popular soon after the
war, and in fact remain so to this day, have little inkling of
what the reality was truly like. Indeed, some painters captured very realistic images in their portrayals of the glamorous charges, but these were only momentary fragments
of a vision which all too often had a nightmarish aspect of
chaos and confusion in totality. Often, the cavalry com-

mander is depicted at full gallop out in front of his troops, with saber drawn, hair flying, and head thrown back as he exhorts his men to charge. In fact, Stuart on occasion had been known to lead his men in such a fashion, but it was not a very common practice and, indeed, could even be called foolish. There was only one cavalry commander to my knowledge who lived up to these stirring paintings in most respects, although he did not live very long. But then I am getting ahead of myself.

The truth about a cavalry engagement is that it is, comparatively speaking, very brief compared to an infantry engagement. It is also not often decisive, in and of itself. It is quite fast and furious, as the newspapers have reported, but then so is a knock-down, drag-out barroom brawl. In most cases, there is usually a much higher number of wounded than killed, primarily from saber cuts, and although pistols are employed on such occasions, it is a rare man, indeed, who can shoot with any accuracy from the back of a galloping horse, especially with a smoothbore. For this reason, Stuart was particularly fond of his Le Mat, which had both a pistol and a shotgun barrel that made it eminently suitable to close-quarter cavalry engagements.

Now, while the Southerner is in most respects a better horseman than the Yankee, who often does not know which end of the horse to face unless somebody shows him, they had a slight advantage over us in that some of them had been equipped with the new Spencer carbine. This new rifle caused some consternation when it first appeared, for it was of a unique design known as a "repeater." It fired metallic cartridges, so that you didn't have to worry about keeping your powder dry, and you could load it in the morning and shoot it pretty near all day. In practical terms, in the time it took a good marksman with a musket to get off about four shots, a man armed with a Spencer could get off about twenty. Now, it should probably be noted that under ordinary circumstances, anyone

planning to fire off a weapon from the back of a mount un-
accustomed to such practice should be prepared to do a bit
of traveling, quite possibly even through the air. Cavalry
horses are, of course, generally accustomed to the sound of
gunfire, but even so, they have been known to shy and bolt
upon occasion, and no trooper ever knows for certain just
when such an occasion might arise. For this reason, in
most engagements, the cavalry trooper on both sides usually fought dismounted. One out of every four men would
hold the horses for himself and for the other three while
they moved up to shoot like infantry. For our troopers in
particular this was a necessity, for while we felt ourselves
superior horsemen to the Yankees in every respect, it was
not really possible to reload and fire a musket while on
horseback.

In any event, the glamorous spectacle of a cavalry
charge, the opening moments of which are what the
painters normally depict, becomes considerably less glamorous very quickly upon the point of convergence with the
enemy. And this Napoleonic nonsense is not, by any
means, the most effective use of cavalry in modern warfare.

The primary purpose of the cavalry is to screen the
movements of the troops that it supports, gather intelligence about the enemy's movements and dispositions, and
cause damage to the enemy, particularly to his lines of
communication and supply, whenever practically possible.
And it is upon this very point of tactics that scholars of the
Gettysburg Campaign—most of them civilians, I might
add—often focus their attention in their analysis of General Stuart and his actions in the closing days of June.

General Lee had sent orders to our headquarters which
arrived by courier on the rainy twenty-third of June. He
had seemed particularly anxious that his intentions be
made clear, as General Stuart received several dispatches
from his headquarters.

General Stuart's orders were to determine what the enemy was doing and interpret his directions subject to those movements, for General Lee wrote, "If you find the enemy is moving northward and two brigades can guard the Blue Ridge and take care of your rear, you can move with the other three into Maryland and take position on General Ewell's right. Place yourself in communication with him, guard his flank, and keep him informed of the enemy's movements, and collect all the supplies you can for the use of the army." Then, in a following dispatch clearly intended to clarify the first, General Lee added, "You will, however, be able to judge whether you can pass around their army without hindrance, doing them all the damage you can, and cross the river east of the mountains. In either case, after crossing the river you must move on and feel the right of Ewell's troops, collecting information, provisions, etc." Little did any of us know it at the time, but it was how General Stuart interpreted those orders that would make all the difference in the world.

Earlier, in June of 1862, when General George McClellan was in command of the Army of the Potomac during their Peninsula Campaign, we had ourselves a bit of fun with the dashing "Young Napoleon." When it came to combat, McClellan was a great general in bivouac. He was about as slow as blackstrap molasses on a winter day, and General Stuart had achieved great notoriety throughout the nation by riding all the way around his army, like a horse-fly buzzing round a heifer. Here, then, was an opportunity to do the same again with Hooker (or Meade, as it turned out, for we later learned that "Fighting Joe" Hooker was about to be relieved of his command, to be replaced by General George Meade, who was not "Fighting George" or "Dashing George" or "Handsome George" or any kind of George at all other than methodical, deliberate, and stead-fast, which made him a damn-sight better general than anyone the Yankees had up to that point). On the twenty-fourth, therefore, the brigades of Wade Hampton, Fitzhugh Lee (General Lee's nephew), and John Chambliss (commanding the brigade of Rooney Lee, General Lee's son, who had been wounded at Fleetwood) moved out from Salem, heading east beyond the Bull Run Mountains. The brigades of William "Grumble" Jones and Beverly Robertson were left behind to screen the army's advance, as per our orders, and then follow.

Our problems began soon afterward when we emerged at dawn on the twenty-fifth from Glasscock's Gap to find our way blocked by a large column of Union infantry on the march. It appeared that an entire corps was moving across our front, and so it was, for it was the command of Winfield Scott Hancock. Unbeknownst to any of us, Hooker (still in command of the army at this point) had started moving northward toward the Potomac with his whole army. Although our previous actions against the Union cavalry had helped to screen the movements of our troops, Hooker had deduced that Lee was launching a campaign and moved to interpose himself between our army and Washington.

It was later revealed that "Fighting Joe" had considered letting Lee continue northward unmolested while he swept down with his entire army to attack Richmond. The theory, presumably, was that Lee would then find himself forced to turn around and come back to the aid of Richmond. Ironically, Lee had thought that Hooker would be forced to do the very same in order to protect Washington as we advanced. (As Lincoln, in fact, ordered him to do.) Many have since speculated about what might have happened had Hooker marched on Richmond, and whether or not Meade would have continued with that plan when he found himself appointed to command, or what might have occurred if Meade had never taken Hooker's place and it was "Fighting Joe" who led the Army of the Potomac at Gettysburg. Such speculations, fascinating as they might be to some, are not my purpose here, however. My purpose is to recount what happened and, perhaps, to give some insight into those events. At any rate, what we discovered on that day when we came out of Glasscock's Gap and saw the Union army on the march across our front, was that the Union rear which we had meant to ride around had, in effect, reversed itself to become the Union front, which was now moving northward and placing itself squarely between us and our own army. We were, effectively, cut off.

Stuart gave Hancock a few salutations with our six cannon, but it would have been foolhardy in the extreme to attempt any further engagement with so large a body of troops, and so we turned south, intending to make a wide swing around the enemy and thus rejoin our army. We camped for the night near Buckland, but at dawn the enemy had moved on, presumably further north, and we could catch no sight of him. We continued on our way, through Bristoe and Brentsville, camped at Occoquan Creek and crossed it on the morning of the twenty-seventh. Throughout all this time, we did not see the enemy and did not know where he was. We could but guess.

I recall having a conversation with the general while we were biovouacked on the night of the twenty-sixth. It was cool, a breeze was blowing, and we stood upon the bank of the Occoquan, discussing what to do. His anxiety, at this time, was considerable. His blue eyes were deeply troubled and he kept nervously stroking his voluminous beard as he stared off across the creek, into the dark distance.

"We should have rejoined our army three days ago," he told me. "General Lee has to be wondering where the devil I am, and I am in no position to assist him."

"Sir, we are making every effort to rejoin our troops," I told him. "The blame does not sit with you. General Lee had no way of knowing when he sent his orders that Hooker would move north so quickly."

"I know that, Hamill," he replied. "I did not anticipate

it, either. But with Hooker somewhere to the west of us and the forces defending Washington to the east, we are caught squarely in the middle. I have but two choices: turn around and go back south the way I came, which would only increase our risk of exposure and place even more distance between us and our troops, or else continue on a northward course and get around the Federals."

"It does seem to be our only choice, sir," I replied.

"It is no choice at all, Hamill," he replied, tensely. "We are being blown upon the winds of fate. We can but ride the wind and trust to God to guide us."

We continued on toward Fairfax Station, where we caught a detachment of New York cavalry napping and captured most of them, giving them parole after confiscating their arms and their supplies, for prisoners would only slow us down at this point, and it was difficult enough to make good speed. Our horses were tired and hungry, as were our men, some of whom were sleeping in the saddle. We had to complete our swing around the Federals, but we did not know exactly where they were. Worse still, we did not know where General Lee was. Our orders had been to place ourselves on Ewell's right as soon as possible, and Stuart reasoned that Ewell would be moving toward the Susquehanna. We had no choice but to press on.

As we made our way toward the Potomac, we began to see signs on the road of the Union army's passage. They were very close, for their campfires were still smoking. We stopped at intervals to rest our horses as we pressed on toward the Potomac, only to discover that most of the fords we could have used to cross were well guarded. The Federals knew that we were out there somewhere, and they were doing what they could to inconvenience us. We were forced to continue north and effect a crossing at Roswer's Ford, which I judged impassable when I first saw it. The river was wide at that point, and the water was high and flowing very fast. Most men, I think, would never have attempted it, but then, Jeb Stuart was not like most men. No more difficult achievement was accomplished by the cavalry during the war than the crossing of that ford.

The ammunition for our guns was distributed among the men, so that they could hold it in their arms and keep it above water as we crossed. The horses plunged into the Potomac, far from eagerly, neighing and snorting with alarm, their eyes rolling with fear, and many of our men were no less wide-eyed at the task that was before us. The guns disappeared completely below the surface of the rushing water and for a few nasty moments, I feared that we might lose them, as well as the unfortunate horses pulling the caissons, but men and beasts both pulled alike and we managed to make it through. We completed the crossing several hours before the first gray light of dawn broke over the horizon and sprawled upon the Maryland shore, wet, cold, miserable, and utterly exhausted, grateful just to get a few all-too-brief hours of sleep before daybreak. And sleep we did, wet clothes and all, giving our worn-out horses a much-needed opportunity to rest and graze. We had at last crossed the Potomac. All that remained now was to become reunited with our troops.

The question still remained, however . . . where were they?

After an all-too-brief respite, we set out once more, making our way to Rockville, which was only about nine miles from the outskirts of Washington, D.C. It felt peculiar, to say the least, to be so near the Federal capital, within striking distance, and yet be without our army. Not a few of us reflected on the irony of it. Here we were, within a stone's throw of Washington, and yet we were too few to do anything about it, for we could not prevail by ourselves over the strong Federal defenses there. Nevertheless, mindful of our orders to inflict as much damage as possible upon the enemy and disrupt his communications, and perhaps in some respect as well spurred on by a sense of frustration, we destroyed telegraph lines, damaged some track, and seized what supplies we could. (It should perhaps be noted here that our tearing up of railroad tracks did not result in train wrecks, as has been reported with much exaggeration. Any such derailments were very much the exception rather than the rule, for the trains did not travel very quickly and had more than enough time to brake safely to a stop and then reverse themselves before they reached the torn-up track, which, incidentally, did not inconvenience the railroads for much more time than it took to bring out a repair crew. It did, however, cause delays, and in warfare, such things often add up. A shipment of supplies that does not reach its destination at the proper time can make all the difference in the world, as both we and the Federals were shortly to discover.

As we rode into the town of Rockville at about midday on the twenty-eighth of June, we created a bit of a stir among the citizenry, many of whom were just getting out of church as we arrived. One may well imagine their surprise as they looked down the road and beheld a dusty column of Confederate cavalry coming into town! We were greeted warmly and excitedly, with applause and even cheers, for there were many Marylanders friendly to our cause, and although we must have looked a sight, young girls came running up to us and begged to cut souvenir buttons from our uniforms. Not surprisingly, they all wanted to see General Stuart, who swept his hat off to them with a courtly bow, charming each and every one of them. We did not have long to take advantage of this pleasant welcome, however, for as we were entering the town from one end, we spotted a Federal supply train of wagons approaching the other end of town on the main road, from the direction of the capital. At a glance, I estimated the number of wagons in the train to be at least one hundred, but it turned out that my estimate was short. It was closer to 150. After all we had been through, this was indeed a windfall.

Our spirits already considerably buoyed by the warm welcome we had received from the residents of Rockville, we became fired up at the sight of all those new wagons, drawn by well-fed mules in fresh-stitched harness leather. Thinking of all the provisions those wagons must have contained, we wasted no time. We all set spurs, drew sabers, raised a yell and charged hell-bent for leather, our hungry stomachs growling in anticipation of a truly splendid feed.

Without a doubt, the last thing these Yankee teamsters had expected to run into so close to their own capital was a screaming horde of Rebel cavalry. They were taken completely by surprise. The guard was easily overwhelmed, and the front wagons were all captured before they even knew what hit them. Once the wagon drivers in the rear of the supply train realized what was afoot, however, they wasted little time in turning around and lighting out of there as fast as their teams could pull them. We at once gave chase, leaving behind some of our troops to keep the captured wagons and the prisoners in custody. Our horses were spent and winded after all their exertions, however, and the wagons in the rear of the train had a good head start. We feared those wagons just might get away, and most of them might have made good their escape had it not been for one of the wagons overturning, which brought about a pileup and a jam not unlike one that we had seen before, back at the beginning of the war, when all of the civilians came out from Washington in their fine carriages, bringing their picnic lunches with them to watch the first battle of Bull Run as if it were a Sunday outing. I could well recall how they had panicked when, against all their expectations, the Federal lines broke and their soldiers started running. Their wild exodus down the road back to Washington was much like the sort of sight that now confronted us, as their carriages ran into one another, colliding with military wagons, causing a hopeless tangle, and trap-

ping all those who were behind them. We had caused quite
a stir back them, when our "black horse cavalry," as they
had called us, had ridden almost to the streets of Washington, and it looked as if we were about to do so once again.

All told, no more than twenty-five wagons managed to
escape the mess, and our troopers pursued them nearly to
the city limits of Washington, when they pulled up and decided against taking the risk of going any farther. Though
it was tantalizing to consider keeping up the pursuit right
into the streets of Washington and giving those folks a real
scare, General Stuart wisely refrained from the temptation.
We watched those wagons disappear into the distance,
knowing they'd raise quite a scare themselves when they
got back to tell the story of how Stuart's cavalry had pulled
a raid right under Lincoln's nose. And what a raid it was!
All told, we had managed to capture 125 wagons, 900
mules, and 400 Yankees, but the most significant prize that
fell to us that day became revealed when we rode back to
find some of our men gathered excitedly around one of the
wagons that had turned over.

As we rode up to the tangled mess of wagons that had
overturned and collided in the road, we gazed down and
saw that one of them had been loaded with wooden crates,
most of which had fallen out when it turned over. A few of
these crates had broken open, spilling out their contents in
the road. They were Spencer repeating rifles.

Of the 125 wagons we had captured, we soon learned
that only twenty-two had been loaded with provisions,
such as hams, feed for horses, whiskey, beans, sugar,
crackers, bacon, and so forth. Of the rest, all 103 wagons
were loaded chock full of the same large wooden crates,
each of them containing two dozen brand new Spencer rifles and boxes of metallic cartridges which had been
bound for the Army of the Potomac. And now they were
ours.

This seizure suddenly changed everything and gave

added urgency to the necessity of rejoining our army. Just as we realized the importance of our troops getting those rifles, the Federals back in Washington, who would be alerted by those wagons which had escaped, would quickly realize the importance of stopping us at any cost. There was no time to lose. We had to make tracks and find our army and we had to find it quickly, but the speed which gave our cavalry its advantage would be greatly reduced by the necessity of having to travel with all those captured wagons. Night marches would be necessary, which we were not looking forward to, but we understood that there truly was no other choice.

General Stuart had planned to strike at the Baltimore and Ohio railroad near the town of Harper's Ferry, tearing up as much track as we could and disrupting the flow of Federal supplies, but that plan now had to be abandoned. Time was of the essence. It was far more important that our troops be supplied with the wonderful new rifles we had captured. We paused only long enough to feed and rest our horses and enjoy a much-needed repast ourselves before we made way with all possible speed toward Westminster, where we were set upon by Union cavalry. It turned out to be several detachments from the First Delaware, but they were inferior to us in number and we managed to disperse and drive them off without much trouble. We then stopped to rest once more and see to the condition of the wagons. They were all newly built, but we wanted to keep a close eye on them, for we could not afford to have any of them break down. Most of our prisoners we had paroled, as previously, because such a large number would have been an impediment to us, but we did keep a few to drive the wagons, as well as some ordnance men to acquaint us with the operation of the new repeating rifles.

They were hesitant at first, but we prevailed upon them by offering them a simple choice: They could educate us about the rifles, and then be paroled, or else refuse and accompany us until we could get back home and drop them off at a convenient prison camp. We found that it was not at all difficult to become proficient with the new guns very quickly, as the little carbines were vastly superior to the smoothbore muskets and pistols most of our troops were equipped with. Especially impressive was the accuracy that could be achieved with them, and the lightning-fast follow-up shots made possible by the seven-round capacity and the repeating action mechanism. The old cumbersome and time-consuming method of reloading a musket with a measured powder charge, a patched ball, a ramrod, and a percussion cap had been rendered obsolete. We had been impressed with the rifled muskets we had captured from the Federals before, but these little beauties could even be reloaded while on horseback, so long as the mount was standing still or at a walking pace, and with some practice, it seemed that a good horseman could even manage it while his mount was at the gallop. The design was truly revolutionary. Our own weapons suffered greatly by comparison. The different this could make for our army in combat could be considerable.

On the morning of the twenty-ninth, General Stuart was faced with a difficult choice. If we made for Hanover, from there we could turn toward either York or Carlisle, depending upon what news we received of our troops. Thus far, we had heard nothing, and we had no idea where Ewell was, although we assumed he would be somewhere in that vicinity. Otherwise, we could instead take the Hanover Road to a town called Gettysburg, which would bring us closer to the mountains and our army's probable route, although that way might also bring us closer to the Federal army as well, if they were still moving north, as they appeared to be. What bothered General Stuart more than anything else was the knowledge that without our presence, General Lee was moving blindly, doubtless unaware of where the Federal army was. That, more than anything else, decided him. We made for Gettysburg.

Along the way, we had one more encounter with the Union cavalry. We had heard that Kilpatrick was in the area with several brigades and it had been our hope to avoid him, but word must have reached them about our capture of the wagons and they had deduced the route that we would take. With the wagons in our train, there was no hope of running. We could only stand and fight. We now had our first opportunity to see what a tremendous difference these new rifles could make in the hands of men who had grown up hunting to put meat on the table.

I spoke before of the paintings of battles and cavalry charges that have since become so popular, even if most of the scenes that are depicted in these paintings have more relation to fancy than to fact. Here, however, we were suddenly presented with a scene as stirring and dramatic as any ever depicted in these paintings. The general in command drew up his brigade and charged us in as fine a fashion as any I had ever seen, and he led the charge himself, by God, well out in front of his troops, with his saber drawn and raised high in the air. And what a picture he presented! He was dressed from head to toe in tailored black velveteen, with a wide-collared blue sailor's shirt, high boots, a bright red bandanna, and a rakish cavalier's hat. His name, we later learned, was Custer, and he looked so pretty, it was a shame to shoot him. Shoot we did, however, and the devastating, withering fire we poured into them broke up that charge as if they had run into a brick wall. Custer and his horse went down and plowed a furrow in the ground and his charging troopers fell behind him like stalks of wheat cut down by a scythe. I had never seen anything like it.

"My God," said Stuart softly as he watched it all with awe. He could say nothing more. He just stared and slowly shook his head.

What followed, of course, is well known to all students of the war. We linked up with General Lee at Gettysburg on the thirtieth of June to discover that the Federal army, now under the command of Meade, had secured all the high ground south of the town, taking up well-fortified positions on Culp's Hill, Cemetery Hill, and Cemetery Ridge. On the following day, they strengthened their position further by occupying the rocky hills of Round Top and Little Round Top, emplacing guns along strategic points along their fishhook-shaped defensive line. For a change, they had a commander who seemed to know what he was about, for Meade had taken full advantage of the ground, reversing our roles so that this time, it was the Army of the Potomac that was in a firm defensive position, inviting us to attack them, to fight their fight, just as Lee had always done to them. And prior to our arrival, that was just what General Lee had planned to do.

But the rifles we had brought changed everything.

General Lee had positioned his three corps with Ewell's Second Corps nearest to the town and the Federal position on Culp's Hill, Hill's Third Corps lined up roughly parallel with Cemetery Ridge, and Longstreet's First Corps down by the Round Tops, across the Emmitsburg Road. Deprived of his cavalry to gather intelligence for him, General Lee had never realized until almost the last moment that the Federals had been coming up behind him all along, on the east side of the mountains. With little in the way of supplies, he had felt he had no choice but to strike the Federal army hard with everything he had and defeat them on this ground, once and for all. "The enemy is there," he had said, indicating the strong Federal positions, "and I am going to attack him there." However, once he realized the significance of the rifles we had brought him, Lee altered his plans.

General Longstreet had already observed that Meade seemed vulnerable to being flanked upon his left, and he had suggested just such a maneuver, but General Lee had rejected the suggestion, for while it was true that Meade seemed vulnerable to a flanking maneuver on his left, the disposition of our forces made such a tactic a risky proposition. Because Ewell had been en route to strike at Harrisburg when Lee had received word that the Federal army was at hand and sent couriers to recall him, he was now at the northernmost position of our lines, southeast of the town. If Longstreet were to begin his flanking maneuver on the Federal left, Hill would have to come down behind him with his Third Corps, and Ewell would have to turn to the west and then come down behind Hill. This, however, would leave him vulnerable all along his left flank as he moved, unless he were to swing wide to avoid it, which would add much time to his maneuvers and give the Federals time to move against him.

Alternatively, Ewell could have swung around to the east in an attempt to flank Meade on his right while Longstreet and Hill flanked on his left. The trouble with that strategy was that it would divide our army, which was a risky proposition in itself. General Lee had done it before, but not in such unfavorable conditions. He felt that it was doubtful Ewell could hold off a Federal advance all by himself if they came down off the heights and moved against him in force. On the other hand, with Ewell's forces augmented by Stuart's, with the new Spencers distributed among them, holding a Federal advance seemed possible.

To the best of our knowledge, most of the Federal army did not have the new repeaters. Buford's cavalry were equipped with them, but the rest still carried rifled muskets. The advantage in firepower that had been meant for them had now fallen to us, and General Lee now intended to make the most of it. Therefore, he changed his plans.

On the second of July, our guns began shelling the Federal position on Cemetery Ridge from the wooded slopes of Seminary Ridge, making it seem as if we were soften-

ing them up for an attack. As the Federal artillery returned
fire and the entire countryside became blanketed with
smoke, Longstreet began moving his First Corps on a
swing around the Round Tops and the Federal left flank.
General Lee had always placed great faith in "Old Pete"
Longstreet, but had often felt that he had moved too
slowly. Such was not the case upon this occasion, however.

Stonewall Jackson himself could not have marched his
troops more efficiently or speedily. As the intense bombardment continued on both sides, Hill began to follow
Longstreet south, moving roughly parallel with the Emmitsburg Road. So furious was the shelling, and so quickly
did Hill and Longstreet's forces move, that Hill's troops
were on the Emmitsburg Road, moving towards the peach
orchard west of the position that had been held by Sickles's
Third Corps, before any of the Federals realized that they
were in the process of being flanked.

The risk this strategy entailed was that it left our artillery behind to cover the flanking maneuver, thus exposing them as Hill left his position, but General Lee had felt
that the flanking maneuver would present the greater threat
to the enemy, as indeed it did, and that they would not concern themselves about our guns, but instead concentrate
their efforts upon blocking Hill and Longstreet. And that
was precisely what they did. Here, however, was where
our cavalry under Stuart and our Second Corps under
Ewell came into play.

As Longstreet advanced and swung wide around the
Round Tops, Hill moved in his wake and encountered
Union Major General Dan Sickles, whose Third Corps was
on the far left of the Federal line. Sickles was a former
politician, not a military man, and an excellent argument
for why command staff officers should not be politically
appointed. It seems he had believed himself exposed in his
position on the southernmost end of Cemetery Ridge. The
ground was considerably lower there, and opposite his po-

sition, the Emmitsburg Road ran across slightly higher open ground, just west of the peach orchard. Apparently fearing that Confederate guns emplaced there would be able to shell him at will, Sickles had advanced his troops to hold a salient over a half a mile to the west of the main Federal line, so that presumably he could occupy the higher ground from which he believed he could be threatened. Any gunner could have told him that if we had been incautious enough to place our cannons in that position, on completely open ground, we could easily have been shelled, but it seems that General Sickles did not ask for any qualified opinion, either from his subordinates or from his commander, who surely could not have authorized such a foolish move, for it placed him squarely between Hill's advancing divisions and Longstreet's flanking ones.

Too late, Sickles realized his blunder as he was caught in enfilading fire on both flanks as he reached the Emmitsburg Road. McLaws's division, bringing up the rear of Longstreet's flanking movement, raked his left while Anderson, advancing in the vanguard of Hill's corps, pitched into his right. As Sickles's unfortunate command retreated in disorder, McLaws continued to swing around their left, punishing them with flanking fire as they retreated through the wheat field while Anderson's advancing troops moved up to occupy McLaws's previous position and Pender's division came up to hasten Sickles on his way.

Meade quickly realized Sickles's disastrous predicament and ordered up Sykes's Fifth Corps from reserve to reinforce the position Sickles had abandoned and prevent the rout of his command from collapsing the entire Union line at that point, but Sykes saw that to advance his troops to the attack where Sickles's decimated forces were retreating would not only expose them to the same predicament, but would also allow Longstreet to continue his now-exposed flanking maneuver unmolested, for by this time, more than half his forces had already advanced wide around the Federal left, well to the south of Round Top.

This put Meade in a difficult predicament. He had positioned his troops extremely well along the high ground of Culp's Hill, Cemetery Hill, and Cemetery Ridge, with Sykes's and Sedgwick's Corps held in reserve. However, Sykes already had to be brought up to reinforce the Union left where Sickles had blundered so badly, and Sedgwick at this time was still making a forced march to reach the scene. Longstreet was his immediate danger, but to pull any more of his forces to his left to meet that threat meant weakening his center, which would then become vulnerable to Hill, who could still turn and strike in that direction if he perceived a weakness. And to pull any of his forces from his right would weaken Meade's position there and leave him vulnerable to Ewell, who could advance and seize the high ground at Cemetery Hill, emplace guns there, and leave Meade's entire line vulnerable to enfilading fire from artillery. Meade at this point still believed that Lee was moving to the attack, using tactics similar to those he had used successfully before at such engagements as Bull Run. What Meade did not suspect was that *Lee had no intentions of attacking him at all.*

Except where combat had essentially been forced, such as when Sickles had imprudently placed himself directly in the line of march, General Lee had no intentions of committing his troops to a general engagement. Instead, with our newfound advantage, he was repeating what he had done once before, dividing his army into two separate bodies, one being the combined corps of Hill and Longstreet, the other Ewell's corps, supported by the cavalry under Stuart. For as Ewell and Stuart moved around the Federal right flank, getting behind them and heading toward the Baltimore Road, Hill and Longstreet were marching straight toward Washington.

Meade totally misread the flanking maneuver on his left

as an attempt to get around him, not *away* from him. As a result, he did everything he could to strengthen his center. By the time he realized how badly he had misjudged General Lee's intentions, it was too late. Hill and Longstreet were on the march to Washington and Ewell and Stuart had placed themselves squarely in between the corps of Hill and Longstreet and the Federal army. Meade had no choice but to abandon his position and pursue, but in his pursuit, he was severely hampered by the newfound firepower of Ewell's corps and Stuart's cavalry, who had learned, in fairly short order, to shoot on the run from horseback with the Spencers. We thereby became a very dangerous and versatile mobile force, able to hit and run with devastating effectiveness in our support of Ewell's efforts to stem the Federal pursuit.

Panic had set in at Washington when they learned of Lee's approach and a disorganized exodus of the city quickly followed. There were no forces to help protect the capital except those already placed there for the defense, and these were totally inadequate against the combined corps of Hill and Longstreet. The city fell, and along with it, all of its resources, which enabled General Lee to rearm and resupply his army to face Meade, who would now have to attack Washington in order to dislodge us. As we all know, however, no such attack would follow and Meade instead pulled back.

I can still recall that vividly dramatic moment when General Lee, General Stuart, General Longstreet, and myself, along with several other officers, came into the White House, where we encountered not President Lincoln as we had hoped but his secretary, Mr. Hay, who then informed us that the President had been evacuated, along with his cabinet, and had proceeded by shipboard to New York, which would become the Union capital. Washington and Maryland had fallen to the Confederacy, while Vicksburg had fallen to Grant, although in a few months, it was retaken. We had gained industrial support that we had not previously possessed, a new ability to manufacture weapons, and in time, and perhaps despite themselves, the Europeans and in particular the British gave us the recognition that they had so long withheld. The war was to continue for another ten long years until a weary North would sue for peace. In the long run it was to take a serious threat to both our nations in order for the two separate Americas to reunite, but then, that is another story, and one that our children are perhaps best qualified to tell.

—Colonel Bruce Edward Hamill, ret.
Richmond, Virginia

Born in Blood
Denise Little

November 1872

Sometimes, the most mundane and ordinary things can be revolutionary. As I stand in line with my ballot in my hands, I can hardly believe it. It seems strange that so much effort has come down to this—a folded piece of paper with names on it and a few checkmarks. I wait for my turn to drop the slip of paper into the slot on top of the lockbox. I will vote, legally, for the first time in my life today. My choice will be counted, as we, the people of the United States of America, elect our president.

That may not seem so revolutionary to you. But this great election in the year of 1872 is the first one in which all the people of this country—in all their infinite variety, those of every color and kind—will have the right to participate. I understand at what cost these rights have been secured, and I will never forget how much I owe to those who fought beside me to procure them and to all those who died so that I might live to see this day.

Ours is a country born in war and baptized in blood. And even after the British surrendered at Yorktown, we had not finished our fighting. A scant few years later, in August of 1814, red-coated soldiers marched upon our capital, ate the President's dinner, sacked the White House, and put it to the torch. All that was left after the Brits were through was the portrait of George Washington that Dolly Madison cut from its frame and took with her as she fled, and the blackened stone walls of the building, an empty and desolate shell. America was shaken by the destruction, but the bonds of nationhood endured, and the city of Washington was rebuilt.

Terrible as those days were, the threats we faced then were from outsiders. Our battles to survive united us—though not enough and not forever. By the time I was old enough to be aware of such things, it was clear that war was looming once again, but that this time the enemy was within. The conflicts separating North and South were too great, and the bonds uniting them too weak, to hold the union together. I've always wondered whether, if we'd known that the cost of attempting to dissolve the Union would be so high, we couldn't have come to some agreement before the first shots were fired.

But the Washington Peace Convention failed, the Confederates took Fort Sumter, and the bloodbath began. I was fifteen then, and innocent. My notions of war were all misty visions of heroes and victory, and my greatest fear was that the fighting would be over before I had a chance to take part in it. Since I knew my mother would be horrified and I was sure she'd refuse to give me permission to enlist, I never even bothered to ask her. One of my brothers had gone to West Point and then out to serve the army in a fort at the far edge of the world in some sleepy little place called Los Angeles. There'd been talk that they would recall his regiment once the war started, but it would take months for them to return. His old clothes almost fit me—I was tall for my age, and my brother had been thin then, before all that officer-style sittin' around padded him up a bit. Late one night I stole some of his old uniforms, put one on, rolled up the pant legs, tightened the belt, took an apple pie from the pie safe and a hunk of cheese from the pantry, rounded up a rifle and a couple of old wool blankets and all the money I had, and headed out into the night to look for somewhere that I could join up.

I knew better than to sign on with my hometown regiment. Everybody knew me. Despite the fact that I was the best shot in the valley and a crackerjack rider, they'd never let me go off to war. Everybody in that town was more afraid of my mother than any Confederate army—and with good reason. They'd seen Momma in action. It takes a strong woman to raise a passel of kids and run a farm hacked out of the wilderness, all without a husband around to help. Mother had managed for the last thirteen years on her own, with only the help of her children—Indians killed my father when I was just a baby. Most women would have caved in, given up, and gone to live with relatives back East until they found a handy man to marry. But Momma'd just tightened her resolve, dug in, and beat the odds. She taught us all to shoot straight, work hard, and think fast. She'd made a success of her life, the farm, and all of us. Now the war was looming, and all my brothers were involved in it, one way or another. The farm was surviving thanks to whatever help I could give and the labor of a few hired hands, men too old or too feeble to enlist. But the war was coming and I wasn't about to be left out.

So I took my horse, Buster, from the barn and rode through the woods, swatting at bugs and cussing a blue streak, until I reached the back road from town. It was a relief not to have Momma nearby to tell me to mind my language, though I knew I'd miss her something awful. And I didn't want to think about how she'd take it when she found the note I'd left her. She worried enough about my brothers—and I was the baby of the family. But I figured it couldn't be helped. Young fool that I was, I was so eager to fight that I was willing to break my mother's heart to do it. After some hard riding and some fast talking on my part, and a bit of money under the table, I finally found a regiment willing to take me on as a lieutenant. It was no great accomplishment—in those days the Union army would make anyone an officer. I was posted to the First division of the Cavalry Corps, Pleasonton.

That was how my saga began. Like so many others, I came of age surrounded by the crack of gunfire and the boom of cannon blasts and the groans of the wounded and the dying. And, for the first two years of the war, I have to tell you that the Federal cavalry was one of the biggest jokes of the Union army. Jeb Stuart and the Rebs thrashed us so many times we had a hangdog look about us on our best days. Those Southern boys knew a thing or two about fighting—and Robert E. Lee a few more things about how to use them. The Rebs beat the tar out of us far too often.

It took those of us in the Union cavalry some time to find our place in things. Too many of us were city-bred, with no idea how to live off the land or use the countryside around us to the greatest advantage. That wasn't my problem—but the fight to keep myself and my men well fed, well mounted, and in one piece still consumed my every waking hour, and I was only partially successful. As I rose steadily through the ranks amid the slaughter and defeat all around me, I seemed to be bulletproof—never a nick or a musket ball found me. I didn't know whether to feel guilty or relieved. Why was I so blessed? And why were soldiers falling like flies in every fight when I took chance after chance, fought like a fury for the cause, and yet never seemed to draw my share of enemy fire? It made no sense, though I thanked God every night for my deliverance. I didn't exactly relish what would happen if I ended up with too close an acquaintance with a lead slug or cannon blast.

But as June ended in the year 1863, when I said my nightly prayers, I had no idea that the luck—all our luck—was about to change. The big news around then was that we had a new commander in the Army of the Potomac. General Joseph Hooker had finally offered his resignation once too often to President Lincoln. This time Lincoln had taken him at his word. Hooker was out, and General George Meade had inherited the mess he'd made. While Hooker waffled and waited, Lee had snuck out of Virginia and hightailed it to the North. He was loose in the Union, and nobody seemed to know where he was heading. It seemed likely the Rebs were marching to take a big bite out of some tasty Union target—maybe Baltimore, or Philadelphia, or even the nation's capital, Washington, D.C.

So now the Confederate army was on Union soil, and headed for glory. Those Southern boys hadn't lost a battle in so long it was getting hard to remember when the Union had won one. We'd chased them since they'd left their encampment on June 3, but hadn't caught up with them. But we knew that they'd brought the war to us. By God, we were going to give it back to them, right in the teeth, if possible.

All of us officers were hoping Meade was the man for the job. Under Hooker, every time we faced the Johnny Rebs, things fell apart. The old man seemed to lose his mind or his nerve in the middle of every battle. We figured Meade could only be an improvement. His men reputedly called him a "damned goggle-eyed snapping turtle," but nobody had ever said he was a gutless coward or a madman. We had called Hooker all those things and worse after the disaster at Chancellorsville. A turtle was mean and tough, more likely to take a defensive position than to run. So Meade's nickname had to be a good sign, even if it was all we knew about the man. Still, whether we were ready or not, and even though the man holding our fate in his hands was almost a total unknown to us, everything we could glean pointed to this: The Confederate army was close, and the time to fight was near. So when Meade gave us our marching orders, we went out with butterflies in our bellies but a gleam of hope in our hearts. Maybe this time we could finally put the Rebels in their place.

Our commander, General John Buford, rounded us all up and told us what was expected. Meade's orders were clear. We were headed out, all two thousand and seven hundred of us in the cavalry, to see if we could find Lee and his army. If we found them, we were supposed to tie them up and hold them off until reinforcements arrived.

By that last day of June, it seemed to us that we would never find them. We'd heard rumors, talked to civilians who'd seen hordes of butternut-and-gray-clad soldiers march by, but we hadn't found their encampment. Then, that evening, we ran flat into them. We rode up a hill into the Gettysburg Cemetery with General Buford at our head. Far in the distance, down Cemetery Hill and about a mile away, we could see a red brick building—the Lutheran seminary we'd been told about. Moving around it, we could see a few Rebs on some kind of raiding party. As I sat on my horse and looked more closely at the enemy through my spyglass, I could tell that this was no ordinary raiding party. I could see the flags of at least six different companies. We'd found the Rebels, all right, and they'd found us. They fired shots at us, silhouetted as we were on the ridge of the hill. We were much too far out of range to be in any danger, so those first shots of what would become the Battle of Gettysburg were harmless. But I felt in my heart that the coming fight was going to be a bloody one. Our few men were about to mix it up with a big old mess of Lee's army.

Then those Rebs did the strangest thing. As the evening shadows deepened, they started forming up and moving away from us, off into the distance. We figured that they were looking for the rest of their force, and when they found them they'd return to demolish us. We'd been in this situation once before. Way back in Thorofare Gap in Virginia, we'd once held off nearly thirty thousand Rebels for most of a day with a force of three thousand. It hadn't been pretty, but we'd held our ground then, and we'd learned some hard lessons since. This time, we could prepare for the coming fray, and we made the most of the opportunity. As night fell, General Buford sent for reinforcements and told us to place ourselves at a good defensive position. Our job was to hold the high ground before Lee could seize it, so that our infantry would be able to take control of the best places to fight from when they arrived. As our general put it, we would have to "fight like the devil" until the rest of our army could come to our aid. The fate of the Union itself was in our hands.

I wrote a note to my Momma, just in case I didn't live through the coming fight. With that in my pocket, I made my peace with my Maker and set about digging the damndest hole to fight from that anyone had ever seen. Shielded by a wooden fence on the top of what all the world would come to know as McPherson's Ridge, I rested in the hollow I'd constructed and awaited the coming dawn.

It was clear that this fight was going to be no place for the horses, so we had every fourth man at the back of our lines, holding our mounts in whatever shelter we could find for them. We might be cavalry, but this fight was going to be an infantry battle, and we were the only soldiers handy to be the infantry at the moment. No gallant charges for us—we had to stand and take it until the fight killed us or help came. We waited and prayed, unable to sleep, and thought about what would happen once the sun came up. All of us figured it was going to be pretty bad. As the night crawled by and dawn broke, we found out just how right we were.

The early light picked out what seemed to be many thousands of Rebels, all of them headed straight at us, a sea of butternut-and-gray uniforms. We'd heard shots in the distance before dawn, the sound of our outposts exchanging fire with the vast column of men marching up the Chambersberg Pike. Now we could see at last what our men had been firing at. So many men. And in the midst of the marching men, the early morning sunlight struck gleams off the metal of their artillery pieces. The battle that was to come became all too clear then. We were outnumbered by at least two to one, and our few cannons were no match for what the Confederates were bringing to the party. But it was our duty to hold the line, so we waited for the enemy to approach.

The deadly quiet that precedes a great battle fell upon us. Finally all hell broke loose—a fury of gunshots and cannon blasts. The first shots had been fired. As a haze of black powder smoke engulfed us, we took aim as best we could and let them have it. We would either hold our ground, or die trying.

The din of battle is impossible to describe to those who have never heard it—a terrible sound composed of exploding shells and gunfire and the drummers beating cadence and the screams of the wounded and dying men and the shrieks of the wounded horses all merging into some impossible noise. The smell of it is even more overwhelming—the odors of flowers and grass and pine trees gradually overcome by the burnt-powder smell, the copper tang of blood, the scent of unwashed bodies and horses and excrement and then, all too soon, the stench of burned flesh and bodies decaying in the summer heat.

An explosion sounded so near to me that my ears rang and I could feel fragments from it rain down on my back. As my vision cleared and my hearing returned, I became aware of my best friend's screams from his position next to me. He was one of the first to be hit. I crawled over to try to help, but his leg was nearly torn from its socket. Nothing I could do would staunch the flow of blood from his wounds. He begged me to tell his mother he'd died facing the enemy, not running from them. Such was our reputation in the cavalry—my friend's last painful words were defending his honor as a fighter. He bled to death in my arms. I closed his eyes as he passed on, and set back to my task of felling as many of the enemy as I could.

The next few hours were a never-ending nightmare—even now I can't remember events in any sort of sequence. I know we fell back as the Johnny Rebs pressed us, once, and then again. Good friends and bitter enemies died all around me. We ended up back where we'd started, on Cemetery Ridge and Culp's Hill, pressed by wave after wave of Confederate soldiers. But we held our ranks and continued fighting. We had repeating rifles—along with our position, they were our only advantage—so we were able to fire much faster than the men opposing us. The Rebs said later that it was like we could load our guns on Monday and fire all week. Musket balls were flying over us so fast and furiously that they stripped the leaves off the trees, then cut through the wood until even the trunks were severed by the gunfire. Finally, after hours of crashing hell, when our numbers were greatly reduced and our ammunition was running low, reinforcements arrived.

General John F. Reynolds brought in the infantry just as we reached the end of our ability to hold on. The battle would have been lost if he'd been even a few minutes later. Once the new men joined our lines, the fight became fiercer. We were determined not to lose the advantage of our strong position. Thanks to the incoming regiments, including the grim-faced and battle-hardened Iron Brigade, we were able to hold out even when it seemed impossible that we could do so. The slaughter was appalling—many units would be blown to shreds by the time nightfall approached.

As the skirmish raged on, I lost all ability to understand what was happening around me. All I knew was the sound of the gun in my hand. I fired until I could fire no longer, stopped to reload and let my gun cool, then fired again. When word passed down the line that General Reynolds had been killed, shot off his horse and dead before he hit the ground, I cried but I kept firing.

Finally, just after midday, there was a lull in the fighting. Our army re-formed and regrouped, and the cavalry was pulled back, the better to let the infantry do what they do best. As I looked at the men who had fought so bravely beside me and thought of the many who were missing— some dead, some wounded—I resolved that this battle would not be fought in vain. I wanted to live to see that the world changed forever because of what had gone on that morning at Cemetery Ridge. On a personal level, I never wanted anyone to go through what I did then.

Through three more terrible days of fighting, the Union army battled fiercely on around Gettysburg—often on the point of losing to Lee's brilliant generalship and his hard-ened Southern troops, frequently driven back to the high ground that we in Buford's cavalry had seized in those opening moments of the battle and held at the cost of our lives. On the third day of the fighting, Pickett's charge even rammed a force of Confederates all the way up the hill to the center of our line on Cemetery Ridge and breached it. The attack only failed at the last because so many of the Rebel force had fallen to our guns as they climbed. Had Pickett been reinforced just then, it might have succeeded. Pickett's charge would later come to be known as the high-water mark of the Confederacy—the closest that the Rebel forces came to winning the war.

But we in the cavalry only found that out later. At the moment that Pickett was marching to his failed glory, we were several miles away and busy with a battle of our own against Jeb Stuart's cavalry. We managed to fight them to a standstill, preventing them from rushing to Pickett's res-cue. Stuart and his men broke off, so our battle was incon-clusive, but we had saved the rest of the Union army from the havoc that those Rebs could wreak.

In that last battle, the thing I had dreaded most from the

day I had run away from home to enlist finally happened. I was shot in the leg, a terrible wound. I was able to persuade my men to take me to a farmhouse in the town where several of the ladies of Gettysburg were caring for the injured, rather than the Union field hospital where they would amputate first and ask questions later. There I met the woman I would eventually call my wife, a woman widowed early in the war with two small children to raise, who knew my secrets, fears, and dreams, and who nursed me back to health most tenderly despite everything. But it was months before I was fit to return to the field, and I was never again able to take my place in the cavalry. Even today, I still limp from that wound, and am rather pale and frail compared to most of the men of my acquaintance. I ended up as an officer on General Grant's staff and saw out the war from the rear, buried in requisitions and orders.

After Appomattox, after Grant accepted Lee's surrender, events finally fell into place to enable me to make my vow on the battlefield at Gettysburg come true. When Ulysses S. Grant became president, he asked me to join his government. And as a member of his cabinet, I was able to help in the drafting and passage of the Fifteenth Amendment. Which is what, in essence, brings me to this moment in November of 1872, ballot in hand. I had a strong hand in the wording of the document that passed Congress in February of 1869. I watched it ratified by the secretary of state in March of 1870. Of course, mine wasn't the only hand that worked on it. I had much help, from President Grant and his advisors, as well as from many outside forces.

The amendment said:

1. The right of citizens of the United States to vote shall not be denied or abridged by the United States or by any state on account of race, color, gender, or previous condition of servitude.

2. The Congress shall have the power to enforce this
article by appropriate legislation.

I helped make the change that revolutionized this country,
a fitting memorial to all the men who fought so hard and
to those who died so bravely on those first three days of
July, 1863, at the battle of Gettysburg. And I added a twist
of my own to it, a memorial to all that I endured and sacrificed in the war years and beyond.

I smile today as I cast my vote. Though I have voted
many times since I came of age, today's vote is my very
first to be counted legally. For, you see, I have a secret,
kept at great risk in all those days when I fought to save my
country. I am, despite my attire and my accomplishments
and my occasional lapses into blue language, not exactly
the man that all my acquaintances think I am. Though they
know me well, there is one small fact that I have kept from
nearly everyone since the day that I ran away from home
to join the army.

I'm no man at all, but a woman in a man's disguise. I
had no choice but to enter my charade. My country would
never have let me serve under my own name, in my true
guise. Despite the fact that I knew my service would be as
useful, and that my sacrifice was as real as any man's, despite the fact that my actions were in many ways instru-
mental in saving this country, even now I would be
denounced and subjected to every imaginable form of public ridicule if the truth were known.

After the war years, I had planned to retire somewhere
and fade into obscurity, where I could once more return to
my family and begin life again as I once was. But when it
came to doing it, I was unable to persuade myself to go
back. I feared that I would never again be able to assume
the proper maidenly blushes and deferral to masculine au-
thority. Besides, it seemed to me that the opportunity I was
offered by General Grant upon his entry into politics at a

time of such tremendous social upheaval in this country was too good to turn down. I have never once shirked from my duty to my country, regardless of the cost to me personally. And I know that this country can only benefit from the input of all its citizens—white, black, red, yellow, male, or female—when the time comes to choose the leader of this country. I feel very sure that, once everyone has a voice in government, never again will this country see repeated the slaughter that was the Civil War. Brother will never again face brother over loaded muskets, and the dead at Gettysburg will rest in peace. And finally, born from my own sacrifice of blood and bone, I hope that I can buy for future generations of women the choice that I could only make by disguising my true self—the chance to serve God and country whenever the need arises.

I cast my vote now, legally this time, and walk off to where my "wife" awaits me. She, too, voted. The ballot box is a quieter weapon, perhaps, than a rifle or cannon, but it is far more powerful. Together, we walk off into the future.

AUTHOR'S NOTE

This story, though speculative, has its roots in fact. Several women served notably in uniform during the Civil War—on both sides. Often, their identity was discovered when they were wounded, and they were sent home in disgrace. But at least one woman survived the war with her disguise intact. Her secret was revealed years later, after her death, when the undertaker readied her for burial.

The move to add the emancipation of women to the fifteenth amendment was also quite real and discussed seriously at the time, though it threw male white society into even greater dismay than the thought of letting men of every race vote. Elizabeth Cady Stanton and Susan B.

Anthony pushed hard for it, saying that women deserved not only the vote, but also the same rights of self-determination and opportunity for individual advancement as American men had. The matter of female suffrage went as far as constitutional amendments in Massachusetts, Iowa, Michigan, and Maine, though failed to pass those legislatures. Female suffrage actually passed and was enacted in Wyoming and Utah Territories in 1869. Some members of Grant's cabinet were surprisingly open to the possibility, but the proposal never made it to Congress at the national level at that time. After another great and terrible war, the Nineteenth Amendment was ratified in 1920, giving women the right to vote in America.

Well-Chosen Words

Kristine Kathryn Rusch

The Gettysburg Address has become an authoritative expression of the American spirit—as authoritative as the Declaration [of Independence] itself, and perhaps even more influential, since it determines how we read the Declaration. . . . By accepting the Gettysburg Address, its concepts of a single people dedicated to a proposition [that all men are created equal], we have been changed. Because of [the Address], we live in a different America.

—Gary Wills
Lincoln at Gettysburg

I

Lincoln set his lap desk on the cushioned seat across from him as the train went over a rough patch in the rails. The desk bounced once but held its place. Fortunately, Lincoln had capped his inkwell and placed his pen in its holder. Only the papers on top of the desk slid.

He caught them with one hand. The page on top, with "Office of the Executive," embossed across the parchment, was covered with his chicken scratchings.

Phrases leapt up at him in mute apology for their inadequacy. *Neither party expected for the war the magnitude or the duration it has already attained. . . . Fondly do we hope, fervently do we pray, that this mighty scourge of war may speedily pass away. . . .*

He grabbed the sheet and crumpled it. Around him, conversation ceased. His personal secretaries, John Hay and John "Nico" Nicolay, stared at him over the bronze railing separating their seat from his. William Seward paused in the middle of one of his ribald jokes. John Usher, the newest cabinet member, who was sitting across from Seward and Montgomery Blair, looked relieved. Apparently Usher wasn't used to Seward's biting sense of humor yet, and Seward knew it.

Blair's gaze went to the crumpled paper in Lincoln's hand. Monty Blair had been a friend for years now, as well as Postmaster General. Lincoln had wanted him on this trip not so much for his expertise as for his company, despite his volatile temper.

"Troubles, Mr. President?" he asked.

Lincoln forced himself to smile. "I should have finished the speech before we got on the train."

John Hay made a small *tsk-tsk* sound and Lincoln gave him a cautionary look. Hay had warned him that the train would not be conducive to writing.

"Join us for a bit of conversation," Seward said. "I have some jokes I don't believe you've heard yet."

This time, Lincoln's smile was real. "I have no doubt of that," he said. "But I promised David Wills that I would speak at the dedication, and so I had best finish my speech."

"Finish?" Blair said. "Looks like you haven't even started."

"Oh, I've started," Lincoln said. "Too many times."

"What do you wish to speak about?" Usher asked timidly.

"That is the problem, John." Lincoln set the crumpled sheet near all the others. "There is simply too much to say."

II

David Wills watched the workers put the finishing touches on the makeshift platform. It was long and wide, just as he had asked, covering a large tract of ground. This evening, his assistants would put the chairs in place and festoon the area near the speaker's podium with flags.

The November day was unusually warm. Gettysburg was having a spot of Indian Summer. He hoped it would last throughout the morrow. The last thing he wanted was rain on his ceremony. This place was dismal enough.

He tried to shake off the thought. But it had been part of him since July. In the past, he'd found Cemetery Hill a pleasant enough place. He had even thought he might be interred there, decades from now.

But ever since the battle, this area had lost its pleasantness. The seventeen acres he had purchased from the Evergreen Cemetery Association still showed its scars.

He had tried to hide them, but the work had been too great. Bodies remained half buried or, in the case of Devil's Den, not buried at all. From his vantage near the road, he could see pieces of artillery wagons, and on his way into the cemetery, he had found yet another canteen, this one punctured by a bullet.

He tried to imagine the site as it would be, years hence when William Saunder's landscaping plans would be complete, the bodies buried, and monuments covering the earth. But he couldn't see it. In fact, at times he did not see the land as it was at all but as it had been on July 23 when he had finally come to it for the first time since the battle ended.

Hogs had been rooting bodies out of their shallow graves and devouring them as he had walked this road. Other bodies hadn't been buried at all. The stench had been unspeakable, the sight unforgettable.

Wills had come here on behalf of Governor Curtin, who

had visited a week after the fighting. Curtin had wanted to do something with the dead. Initially, Curtin had decided that the State of Pennsylvania would pay the expenses to have the dead shipped to their respective homes. But that undertaking was too great and too difficult. Most of the bodies were beyond repair.

Instead, Wills had called a meeting of various Northern state agents, and somehow—he still wasn't sure how exactly—the idea of the Soldiers' National Cemetery was born.

The Northern states had agreed to finance it, but he had become the organizer, the man everyone turned to, the one who made sure this daydream became a reality. It was, he knew, a sacred task and one he had to carry out with great solemnity. He had designed the cemetery so that soldiers would be buried by state and the size of the lots would be determined by the number of troops each state had lost.

The central idea—his central idea—was that he wanted the cemetery to convey a sense of equality.

The way his home and all the familiar landmarks had changed seemed strange to him. Five years ago, as he had been setting up his law practice, he had had no idea the Southern states would secede. He couldn't have imagined how the ground shook when armies met, the way artillery fire could be heard from miles away. He had never seen anything like the plumes of smoke that hovered over his small town for days after the battles ended, and the feeling of threat which had yet to leave him.

The Battle of Gettysburg had proven to be the pivotal battle of the war. General Meade chased the traitor Lee to the shores of the Potomac. Heavy rains had swollen the river, making it impossible to cross. Meade took his advantage there and finished off Lee's army.

Lee had surrendered near the raging waters, and the Army of Northern Virginia was done.

Around the same time, General Grant had recaptured

Vicksburg and moved south into Tennessee. Word was that he would again divide the remaining Confederate troops, leaving the false president, Davis, unprotected in Richmond.

It would take little to finish off the Confederacy. It was clear that with Lee's surrender and the fall of Vicksburg, the North had won the war.

But no one felt elation, perhaps because so many places in this once-great land looked like Cemetery Hill. The dead were strewn from Pennsylvania to Louisiana, men he had known and men he hadn't, who had lost their lives defending all he held dear.

The least he could do was offer them a place to rest.

III

Lincoln stood near the front of the car. The seats were empty here. His staff rode farther back. The conversation continued, softer now. His mood had obviously affected the rest of the train.

He resisted the urge to pace. That would simply draw attention to his unease. If he walked through the other cars, as was his normal bent on a long train trip, he would be forced to stop and converse with the others who had come along for the ceremony. Wills had invited foreign dignitaries and senators, governors and great orators. Most of the Washington contingent was on this train.

John Hay had chastised Lincoln for his melancholy just this morning. *We have near won the war,* Hays said. *We should be celebrating.*

But Lincoln would not celebrate until all of the rebel states had returned to the fold.

The conversation had gotten even softer behind him. He stared out the window at the Maryland countryside, brown with the approaching winter. Part of his problem was that he hated winter—its bleakness and its gloom. Since his son Willie had died in February nearly two years before, the winters had gotten harder.

A hand fell on his shoulder. He glanced beside him. Seward stood there, slightly stooped as he always was. His gray hair was mussed from his hat—he still hadn't straightened it, although they had been on the train for hours—and his thin face, usually lit by a smile, was serious.

"It's not like you to be unprepared," Seward spoke quietly so that none of the others could overhear.

"I have a dilemma, William." Lincoln sat, knowing that his voice would carry if he continued to stand.

Seward sat beside him, leaning toward him, arm on the brass rail in front of him so that anyone passing would think twice before joining the conversation.

"If I have learned nothing else in this administration," Lincoln said, "I have come to realize that history is about timing."

"This is an inconsequential speech," Seward said. "It is certainly not worth the time you are giving it."

Lincoln shook his head. "Presidents do not make inconsequential speeches. Wills wrote to me that he expects the town to be filled with visitors. That is why we are staying at his home. I'm sure among the visitors will be the reporters, and they will give the speech its due."

"You believe they have expectations of you?" Seward asked.

"Of course they have expectations of me," Lincoln said. "They expect me to speak of the war, or perhaps of its aftermath. Since Lee has surrendered, many of the Northern papers believe that we have won the war. They do not understand that there are still battles continuing. And we have not yet captured Richmond."

"It is only a matter of time," Seward said.

Lincoln nodded. "And therein lies my dilemma. If I

speak as the victor, then I risk reigniting flames that have become embers. I have not forgotten how our Southern neighbors reacted to my inaugural address."

"You could have read the entire text of the Bible and they would have reacted in the same way," Seward said.

Lincoln glanced out the window. The countryside remained brown and dark. "I do not believe that. Words have power, William."

"It is not the expectations of others that worry you, is it?" Seward asked. "It is your own expectations."

This was why Lincoln liked Seward. The man had a clarity of thought and a way of going at the heart of the matter which Lincoln valued. The other members of the cabinet worried that Seward was converting Lincoln to a more conservative view. But what existed between the two men was a friendship, one that Lincoln sorely needed. They might not agree on everything, but Lincoln could trust Seward to help him analyze the situation and find the solution closest to Lincoln's heart.

"I want to speak of the future," Lincoln said, "and I cannot."

"The future?"

Lincoln turned away from the window. "After the war ends. We are a house divided, William, and somehow we must heal the rift. And since we issued the Proclamation, we have a responsibility to the former slaves as well as their former masters."

He ran his hands along his trouser legs, smoothing the wool. It was a nervous habit that Mary had been trying to get him to quit.

"The years ahead of us will be much more difficult than the years we have just lived," he said. "How we approach those years is vital to the future of our nation."

Seward leaned back in the seat. "Am I understanding you correctly? You wish to address all of this in one speech?"

Lincoln nodded. "But I must choose the right time for this speech. It cannot come too soon or I will create a deeper divide than the one we now have. But it cannot come too late either, or it will look like political opportunism. We have a campaign to start after the first of the year, and then, more than now, every one of my words will be measured against my ambition."

"So," Seward said slowly, "you look at this speech in Gettysburg as an opportunity."

"I must start laying the groundwork for our lives after the war ends."

"It seems a mighty task for a ceremony dedicating a cemetery."

Lincoln stood again, the restlessness back. "I suppose it does."

IV

Wills grunted as he set down the desk. He had moved more furniture this afternoon than he had done in months. Still, the second-floor bedroom where the President of the United States would sleep was spotless and comfortable. Wills had moved all the best furniture into this room, adding an area for the President to work if he so chose.

Wills had not expected to be this nervous. He was generally a confident man, one who dealt with all equally. But President Lincoln had surprised him when he had accepted the invitation to come to Gettysburg, and by then there were no more accommodations in the town's handful of hotels.

Wills felt he had no choice but to invite the President into his home.

His wife had gone into a frenzy. She had been cleaning for the last two weeks. When he had seen her a few moments before, she had still been wearing her cleaning bonnet and had had a smudge of dirt on the tip of her turned-up nose. He had reminded her that she had to change before the train arrived with their guests, and she had looked at him with the same panic he had been seeing all month.

She had not believed it possible to make this place presentable, and yet she had done an admirable job. Three weeks ago, the floors were still stained with blood. The house had been a makeshift hospital during the battle, and boys had died on this very floor.

Perhaps that was why Wills worked so tirelessly for the cemetery. He had not enlisted, feeling that, at thirty-two, he was too old to be a soldier. His wife had discouraged him as well. He was better suited to solving problems in Gettysburg than he was to carrying a rifle.

Or so he had thought until the battle raged near the house. By the middle of the afternoon on July first, Union troops were driven into the streets of town. Everything became a disorganized mess. Artillery and ambulances tried to get through, but nothing moved.

He had thought of getting his rifle and joining the mêlée. Then he realized that he would be better served helping the injured. He and his wife and several friends diverted ambulances to his home and, once the beds were filled, laying the wounded like cordwood on the floors and the stairs.

Sometimes he still heard the soldiers crying for help. He would wake in the middle of the night to the screams of pain, only to realize they were coming from his memory.

He slipped his hands in the pockets of his waistcoat and walked to the window. The street was full of strangers, most of them well dressed, milling about as they examined the town where the battle had taken place. Soldiers from the Fifth New York had arrived. Their military band was to play that night and they were scouting out the proper positions.

He recognized few others. Since the battle, Gettysburg had been filled with homeless veterans, injured soldiers, and drifters. Some filled the streets now, mingling with the women in their afternoon finery.

One man in particular caught his attention. He stood behind the soldiers and stared at the house. He was gaunt, his black beard untrimmed, his clothing tattered. The crowd flowed around him, as if no one wanted to get close.

His gaze met Wills's and held it for a moment, and in his eyes, Wills saw something. Anger? Despair? Wills wasn't certain. But it made him shudder nonetheless.

Wills turned away from the window and contemplated the room. The President would be here shortly. Then the first national cemetery in the United States would be dedicated and the crowds would go home.

But the work would not be done. Indeed, the work was only beginning.

V

With a whistle of brakes, the train came to a stop at the Gettysburg station. Through the thick glass windows, Lincoln could hear the cheers of the crowd and the cadence of a military band. He stiffened his shoulders, folded the paper he had been scribbling on, and shoved it in his pocket. Then he set aside the lap desk and handed the remaining sheets of paper to Nico.

As he stood, John Usher handed him his hat. Lincoln thanked him and placed it on his head as if he were putting on a crown. It was time to become presidential.

The cabinet secretaries left the car first. Lincoln followed a moment later, pausing to wave at the top of the stairs.

It was dusk and cool, but not cold as it had been in Washington. The air carried the odor of burning leaves.

The railway station was modern and new—two stories of elaborate stonework with a cupola and large arching windows. It was an impressive building for such a small town.

People were gathered in front, the military band to his right playing a raucous marching tune. There were soldiers scattered among the crowd, more than he had expected, many of them waving. There were also a lot of ladies, many of them wearing widows' weeds and holding the hands of small children. It was to them, and them alone, that he nodded. Some of the children ducked behind their mothers' full skirts. But the women returned his acknowledgment.

Then he made his way down the stairs, followed by his secretaries, and headed into the fray.

A thin, serious-looking young man stepped before him and extended his hand.

"Mr. President," he said, "I'm David Wills. Thank you for honoring our small community with your presence."

Lincoln took his hand. "It is you who honor me."

Governor Curtin stood off to his left, and slightly behind him stood Edward Everett, the well-known orator.

Lincoln greeted them warmly, but his attention returned to the widows and their children watching him from the fringes of the crowd.

His sense had been correct: It was wrong to speak of the future before the ghosts of the past had been laid to rest.

VI

David Wills was shaking, his hand still tingling from the President's firm grip. He had been warned that the President was a tall man, but he hadn't expected such an imposing figure. Wills had never come up to another man's shoulders before. The President had to stoop slightly to look him in the face.

Although the walk from the rail station to his home was a short one, Wills had brought his carriage around so that the President would not be inconvenienced. He was glad he had done so now. The crowd pressed forward, eager to catch a glimpse of the man who towered over them all. Wills had never been in such a crowd, and he wondered how the President managed it.

Yet Lincoln moved calmly forward, shaking hands and leaning toward people who were attempting to speak with him. Wills turned, saw his assistant, and sent him toward the carriages, just as they had planned.

A woman grabbed Wills's arm. She was slight, dressed all in black, her face covered by a thick veil.

"Beg pardon, sir," she said, her voice husky, its accent carrying the soft cadences of Virginia, "but I would like to petition the President. Is there a moment at which I might speak with him alone?"

"I'm sorry, ma'am." Wills patted her gloved hand and gently removed it from his arm. "The President is here for less than twenty-four hours and his schedule is quite full. Perhaps if you had contacted me sooner—

"I hadn't heard of his appearance, sir, until I read of it in the New York papers last week. I have traveled a long way. Surely you can accommodate me."

"I'm sorry," Wills said again. "There will be a receiving line after the speakers have finished. You might be able to make your case then."

At that moment, the carriages arrived—Wills's family carriage for the President and two he had borrowed for the other dignitaries. The woman slipped into the crowd before he had a chance to ask her name.

He searched after her but didn't see her. It wasn't until after he had joined President Lincoln in the carriage that he caught a glimpse of her.

The slight woman looked up at a hard-faced red-haired man. He held her gloved hands in his own. Her veil was

off, but Wills could not make out her features. Still, he had
the impression that she was older than he had initially
thought—not a young widow at all, but a woman full-
grown, perhaps mourning for a soldier son.

For some reason, his misperception made him uneasy.
He pulled the carriage door closed and tried to shake off
the feeling as they drove off into the night.

                              VII

William Seward pushed his plate away from the table. He
grabbed his glass of red wine and cradled it in his hands.
Wills had promised coffee, but it was too late in the
evening. Seward would have his wine and then retire.

The dinner had been elegant, a treat after a long day of
travel. The conversation had been interesting—Governors
Curtin, Seymour, and Morton had held forth on the diffi-
culties of governing a state in these unusual times. Edward
Everett had described in great detail his tour of the battlefield, and from across the table Seward had seen Lincoln's
eyes light up. Something Everett had said had obviously
inspired him.

Seward was worried about Lincoln. He had always
been a melancholy man, but his melancholy had deepened
this last year. The death of his son had been a heavy blow,
and since it, his wife, Mary, had flirted with madness.

Lincoln had adored Willie and had grieved deeply as
well, although he did not mention it much. He had to remain clear-minded so that he could conduct the war. Besides, he had once confided to Seward, he was not the only
man to lose a son in these past two years.

The burden of governing weighed heavily on him, and
the speech he had made on the train worried Seward all the
more. If Lincoln was right—and he usually was—the tests
to the nation would only increase after the war ended.

Somehow they would have to get this man reelected so that he could use the force of his indomitable personality to keep the country together.

Lincoln was right: Timing was everything. But how was a mortal man, wrapped in the events of the day, to know which action to take? Seward had lived sixty years and with each passing one, he grew more convinced that man could not triumph over the whims of fate.

Outside, a military band struck up "The Battle Hymn of the Republic." Seward was growing heartily sick of the tune, new as it was. Some said it captured the spirit of the war. He felt that it was too militaristic, too judgmental, and each time he heard it, he felt shades of darkness within it.

Everett places his linen napkin on the table. He was an elegant white-haired Bostonian with a booming voice and a strong sense of propriety. "They play for you, Mr. President."

Lincoln nodded. In the candlelight, his eyes looked sunken. He was obviously tired.

"I think we should acknowledge them." And then, without waiting for the President, Everett pushed his chair away from the table and walked toward the door. The others waited for Lincoln, who shot Seward an annoyed glance. Then he stood, careful not to hit the chandelier brilliant with the light of dozens of candles.

Seward made his way to Lincoln's side. "If you go to the door, they will expect you to speak."

"I shall not," Lincoln said.

"A few well-chosen words would lift their hearts."

Lincoln looked at him. "This is what we discussed on the train. Better that I say nothing."

Seward shook his head. He had been thinking about this all evening. "A man's silence may be interpreted a thousand ways, misconstrued by his enemies, misused by his friends."

Lincoln gazed at him fondly. "I won't be completely

silent, William. Mary says it would take an act of God to still my voice."

Then he stepped through the door and clapped his hands, acknowledging the band. The crowd roared its approval, and Seward's heart lifted.

Perhaps the next election would not be so difficult after all.

VIII

The bedroom Wills had given him was large and warm. The bed looked soft and inviting, covered with thick quilts and pillows. Lincoln set his lamp on the desk. His secretaries had already placed his stationery there, and his clothing for the ceremony was airing beside the fire. Outside, the military band continued playing, and there were shouts of laughter as the crowd danced into the night.

Lincoln did not feel like celebrating. He was tired to the bone and he had not finished his speech. He pulled the final draft from his breast pocket and stared at it.

With malice toward none, with charity for all, with firmness in the right as God gives us to see the right, let us strive on to finish the work we are in . . .

He crumpled the paper. *Firmness in the right as God gives us to see the right* was too judgmental. He was here to dedicate a cemetery, not give a major policy speech.

The widows in their black reminded him of Mary. She would never, he knew, recover from the death of their son. It had forever changed her, just as it had forever changed him.

All of this death. He could feel it in the air around him. This place still resonated with the souls sacrificed for two causes: one he believed in and one he did not.

He could not impugn the souls of the Confederate dead. Everett had said he had seen their bodies in the Devil's

Den and still scattered about the battlefield, untended because their people could not come north and bury their own.

Soon that would change, he hoped. But that did not alter what he had to do the following day. He had to honor the dead. They had given their lives that a nation might live. His nation. The one conceived in liberty and, if his idol Thomas Jefferson were to be believed, dedicated to the proposition that all men were created equal.

That was it. Those were the concepts he had been searching for. The idea that all men, black and white, were created equal and as such, should have equal treatment under the law.

He would use Jefferson's language to articulate a new position. It would be a simple position, spoken without judgment, yet still managing to respect the brave men, living and dead, who had struggled in this place.

He uncapped the inkwell, picked up his pen, and proceeded to write a speech suitable for the dedication of the national cemetery, a short yet pointed Gettysburg Address.

IX

The morning was clear and warm for November. The sun, a pale shadow of its summer self, had graced the ceremonies with its presence, taking away at least one of David Wills's worries.

He had had many that morning. The President had breakfasted alone while he finished his speech. Before Wills could confirm the schedule with him, the President had borrowed a wagon and toured the battlefield with Secretary of State Seward. When they had returned, the President had again closeted himself in his room making final touches.

The President's secretary John Hay had assured Wills

that such behavior was normal and that the President would meet his obligations. Still, Wills had worried until he had seen the President mount the chestnut bay Wills had provided for the occasion. From that moment on, Wills hoped, things would go as planned.

So far, they had. He had watched as the President had ridden through the streets of Gettysburg. Just outside the cemetery, the military escort—one squadron of cavalry, two batteries of artillery, and a regiment of infantry—had formed a line and saluted the President as he had passed.

The night before Edward Everett had expressed surprise at the number of military units here. Wills had been about to answer when the President had spoken up.

"Mr. Wills requested the regular funeral escort of honor for the highest officer in the service. Secretary of War Stanton and I believed that such an escort was appropriate."

The President's answer had startled Wills. He hadn't realized that his requests had gone to the highest office. Indeed, until yesterday, he hadn't realized just how involved the President was in the national cemetery. Obviously, the President felt this was important enough to grace with his presence. Perhaps he saw it as the first symbolic step marking the end of the war.

After making certain that the President's procession was going well, Wills took a back way into the cemetery. He wanted to make sure last-minute details had been finalized.

People swarmed around the platform. Women, their skirts trailing in the mud, found places to stand near the front. Men continued to move about, as if uncertain about where the speakers would be.

A wagon, abandoned near one of the flagpoles, was surrounded by people. It was tilted on its back wheels, the buckboard extended high in the air and the harnesses empty. Wills sighed. It would take too much work to move it now, so he decided to let it stay.

The military band, standing near the cemetery's entrance arch, began to play a marching tune. It meant they had sighted the President's procession. The last of the infantry regiment and the generals lined up from the arch to the platform and watched as the first of the horses entered.

Reporters moved closer to the platform, trying to shove some of the women aside. The men would not allow it. Wills caught a glimpse of the red-haired man he'd seen the night before with his arm around the veiled widow, ushering her toward the wagon and the slight protection it provided.

President Lincoln was easy to see. He sat tall on the chestnut bay, his height exaggerated by his silk hat, rising high above the others. The soldiers saluted him as he passed, and he returned their attention.

He followed the other guests to the platform, where they dismounted. One of Wills's many assistants lead the horses away.

As the President walked toward the platform, a man hurtled out of the crowd. Wills's breath caught in his throat. It was the ruffian he'd seen out his window the afternoon before.

Wills hurried forward, hoping to stop the man, but two of the soldiers reached him first.

"Mr. President!" the man shouted.

The President turned just as Wills reached his side. Up close, the man seemed even scruffier than he had through the window, his beard and hair untrimmed, his clothing torn and smudged with dirt.

"Let him go," the President said.

"Sir," one of the soldiers said, clearly in protest.

"Mr. President," Wills started. "I don't believe this is wise."

"Let him go," the President said again.

The soldiers dropped the man's arms. He stepped forward, then bowed his head. "Forgive me, sir, for taking this moment of your time."

"It's quite all right," the President said.

Wills threaded his hands together. He watched the man carefully, alert for sudden movements.

The man raised his head. His face was clean and his eyes were bright. "I simply wished to thank you, sir, for the kind words you sent to my wife. It was a condolence on the death of our son. He died at Antietam, sir. You said he acted with unusual valor."

The President's face softened.

"During my wife's last days, she clung to that letter. Your words gave her enormous comfort, and I wished to tell you so."

"What is your name, sir?" the President asked.

"Thomas Dewsbury."

"Mr. Dewsbury." The President held out his hand, and as if were in a trance, Dewsbury took it. "My condolences on the loss of your wife."

"Thank you, sir."

The President nodded over Dewsbury's head at Hay, who hovered nearby. After the President finished shaking Dewsbury's hand, he turned away and Hay came forward, taking Dewsbury by the arm.

The President mounted the platform and Wills let out a small sigh, feeling relief. He was worrying too much about this event. He would be glad when it was over.

Wills mounted the platform as well, making certain that everyone took their seats. The President sat between Seward and Everett, with governors and dignitaries on all sides. Before Wills took his chair at the very edge of the platform, he signaled the military band to begin a funeral dirge.

The ceremony had begun.

X

As the dirge ended and Reverend Stockton stood, the crowd grew silent. Lincoln removed his hat, placing it beneath his chair. All of the other men did the same. The solemnity of the event seemed to affect them all.

"Let us pray," Reverend Stockton said.

Lincoln bowed his head. His hand still ached from the shake Dewsbury had given it. The man had startled him. In fact, the man had startled everyone. So much talk of assassination over the years—particularly at the inaugural—had left them all jumpy. The talk had subsided in the last year, but clearly not the nerves it had generated.

When Lincoln turned, he had seen that the man, although he had fallen on hard times, had a good face. Lincoln did not remember the letter he wrote—there had been so many letters over the past year, written to families whose sons had exhibited uncommon valor in the face of great danger—but it would take little to discover what Dewsbury's son had done.

Hay would discern all he could about Dewsbury and whether or not there was a way the government could help him. There were too many men like him now, their families gone, their homes destroyed, their memories the only thing remaining.

This place still had the feel of death. Some of the souls hadn't yet left the battlefield, perhaps because so many bodies were improperly buried. Lincoln could understand Governor Curtin's desire to heal this place, and David Wills's hard work in making that vision come about.

After those three days in July, Gettysburg would never again be the same.

". . . they are all with thee, and the spirit of their example is here." The reverend's cadence had changed, his voice booming, signaling he was near the end of the prayer. "It fills the air, it fills our hearts, and as long as time shall last it will hover in these skies, these landscapes . . ."

That caught Lincoln's attention. Apparently everyone here felt the power of the dead, as if they were listening, as if they were part of the ceremony in heart as well as in mind.

". . . and pilgrims of our own land and of all lands will thrill with its inspiration and increase and confirm their devotion to liberty, religion and God. Amen."

"Amen," Lincoln repeated, then lifted his head.

His gaze caught that of a red-haired man sitting in the buckboard of an up-ended wagon. The man had a clear view of the entire proceedings. Their gazes held for a moment and Lincoln saw something in the other man's. Defiance, perhaps, or anger. Or perhaps it was simple grief. He couldn't quite tell from this distance.

After a moment, the man looked away. Reverend Stockton returned to his seat and Edward Everett stood, making his way toward the edge of the platform.

As he stepped into place, Lincoln studied the crowd. He would wager that most of them were here not out of simple curiosity but because they shared with him a loss. The loss of the country and its stability, yes—although he hoped to regain that within the next month—but also a deeper and more personal loss. The loss of a son, a husband, a brother, entire families and homes gone.

The depth of the nation's grief was something else he would have to acknowledge within the next few months. The toll the war had taken on the young men of the nation was greater than could ever be calculated.

The red-haired man was looking at him again. Perhaps he had never seen a man quite as homely as the President. Lincoln smiled inwardly, careful not to let the reaction show. People were always startled at his appearance.

But when he stood to give his little speech, he would show the man—and the rest of the crowd—that there was more to Abraham Lincoln than a bony, mismatched face and wool suit that was proving itself too warm for this November afternoon. He would show them that he was not just the President whose election had divided the country. He would show them that he could bring together that which had been torn asunder.

He would show them that he was a man of his word.

XI

Two hours and counting. Seward resisted the urge to sneak a look at his watch yet again. The last time he had peered at it, the President had craned his long neck in the watch's direction.

Everett may have been considered one of the country's greatest orators, but he had overstayed his welcome by at least an hour as far as Seward was concerned. The speech had managed to quote Sophocles and Pericles as well as reenact the entire battle at great length. Some of the anecdotes Seward had heard at dinner the night before, almost verbatim, and many of the descriptions he had witnessed just that morning in his wagon ride around the battlefield with the President.

The crowd, at least, seemed entranced by the great Everett. Most of them had stood during the entire oration and had not spoken a word. And, to Seward's great surprise, none of them had left.

Perhaps they were all waiting for the President.

Everett was extending his arms in an all-encompassing embrace. His voice rumbled, rich and full with an actor's flare. "But they, I am sure, will join us in saying, as we bid farewell to the dust of these martyr-heroes that wheresoever throughout the civilized world the accounts of this great warfare are read . . ."

The President sighed and bowed his head. Seward resisted the urge to roll his eyes.

". . . there will be no brighter page than that which relates *the battles of Gettysburg*." Then Everett brought his hands together in a prayerlike pose, and bowed.

The applause which greeted the end of his oration was long and loud. The President applauded for a moment, then reached into his pocket, removing a single sheet of paper. Seward could not make out any of the words on the page.

"I promise," the President whispered, leaning toward Seward, "that this will take no more than a minute."

"After all that discussion about proper language?" Seward whispered back.

Lincoln kept his head bowed so that the crowd couldn't see his puckish grin. "If a man chooses the right words the first time, he has no need to embellish."

Seward had to bring a hand to his face, faking a cough to cover his own smile. The grin was the first sign that Lincoln's mood was improving. Good. Perhaps they would laugh on the train trip home. Lord knew, the President needed some relaxation before taking up his Washington duties again.

The applause was finally dying down. Everett had taken his final bow and had returned to his seat. David Wills was standing at the edge of the platform, holding up his hands for silence. Then he announced that the next speaker would be the President of the United States.

Applause began again as Lincoln unfurled himself from his chair. He clutched that sheet of paper in his right hand and headed toward Wills.

They shook hands, and Wills returned to his seat. Lincoln opened that single sheet, but did not glance at it.

"Four score and seven years ago," he said, his reedy voice carrying better than Everett's deep one had, "our fathers brought forth, upon this continent, a new nation, conceived in Liberty—"

A shot rang out and for a moment, time paused. Seward considered launching himself from his chair and knocking the President aside, but in the instant it took to have that thought, the bullet hit its target with a sickening thud.

Lincoln staggered, a hand going up toward his face, and then he fell backward. The crowd began screaming and running in all directions. Beside Seward, men pointed, but he did not look where they pointed. Instead, he went to the President's side.

Even before he arrived, he knew it was over. Lincoln's eyes were open and sightless, a single bullet hole in the center of his forehead.

Seward moaned, then cried out for a doctor. No one seemed to hear him; the screams of the crowd were so very loud. He looked over them, saw women scooping up their children, men running toward the cemetery arch.

The soldiers were chasing a wagon driven by a red-headed man. A woman in widows' weeds sat beside him. As they reached the arch, a soldier dropped to his knees, pointed his rifle and shot. The man fell backward, the woman reaching for the team of horses. A second shot rang out and she tumbled from the wagon while the screaming continued.

A man had reached Seward's side. "I'm a doctor," he said.

Seward beckoned toward the President, hands shaking. He had no words for this, no way of telling this poor doctor that his services were not needed.

What they needed now no man could give. A vision, a hope for the future. Vice President Hamlin wasn't up to the task. He was antislavery, hard-line, and frightening to the South. He would make a terrible president.

And then there was Mary. Poor, sad Mary, who hadn't wanted Lincoln to leave on this trip at all. Had she known?

Seward shook his head. At least he would not be the one

to tell her. It was probably already on the telegraph lines: *The President was dead.* All was lost.

Even, perhaps, their victory. The South's defeat wasn't finished. Richmond still stood. Jeff Davis still lived. This would breathe fire back into the embers that Lincoln had worried about.

He had been so right, and Seward hadn't seen it. History was about timing. And on this occasion, the timing couldn't have been worse.

XII

The assassins were dead. Their bodies lay where they had fallen, twisted and ignored. The wagon they had brought—and to which they had somehow managed, during Everett's speech, to hook their team—was in a ruin near the arch, the horses gone as well.

Wills wondered if he was responsible for those bodies, too. He had no idea what to do with them.

His sacred project was once again drenched in blood. Parasols, discarded hats, and ruined programs lay on the ground before the platform. Several people had been injured in the riot after the shooting, and they had been carried off.

Others paced the grounds as if they could find something to turn the clock backward. Edward Everett still sat in his chair, staring at the scene before him.

The other dignitaries had gone. The soldiers were searching the town to see if more assassins remained.

It was clear that they had been Rebels. The woman had held the Confederate flag as the wagon started its escape. Wills had stared at it in horror, wondering how he had missed all of this when he had spoken with her the night before.

This felt like his fault. It had been his idea to invite the

President, his plan to set up the platform in full view of the crowd. He had made the man a target as easily as if he had painted an X on his chest.

Wills climbed onto the platform. Lincoln's hat remained under his chair. He reached for it, a long silk top hat. He had admired how the man had not tried to hide his great height.

He had admired so much.

The hat had blood spattered on its front. Wills tried to brush it off, but the blood did not wipe away.

His movement seemed to catch Everett's eye. The man shifted, as if coming out of a trance. He stood, took a stumbling step toward the great stain of blood and brains that marred the platform, and lifted a piece of parchment from it.

Everett studied it for a moment, then turned toward Wills. Everett's face was speckled with dried blood.

"His speech," Everett said, shaking it at Wills. "It is his speech."

Everett bowed his head over it, read, and Wills watched as if the very act of reading could bring the President back. Everett blinked hard, then shook his head.

He looked at Wills. "He would have said more in two minutes than I said in two hours."

The paper was rippled with blood. The words were hard to make out, the handwriting long and spidery.

Everett's finger brushed the center of the page. He read, "The world will little note, nor long remember, what we say here, but can never forget what they did here."

His voice carried over the ruined grounds, out to the shattered artillery wagons, the dented canteens, and the unburied bodies. Wills tried to imagine the words spoken in Lincoln's reedy voice, and could not.

Wills thought of the line Everett had just read. The words would vanish, but the deeds remain. Now no one would remember this cemetery as the site of a valiant battle, but as a place where a great man had died at the hands of a suicidal madman.

Everett handed Wills the paper and sighed. Then together the two men stepped off the platform and disappeared into the silence.

APPENDIX

* * *

The Gettysburg Address

Abraham Lincoln

Four **score and** seven years ago our fathers brought forth on this continent, a new nation, conceived in Liberty, and dedicated to the proposition that all men are created equal.

Now we are engaged in a great civil war, testing whether that nation, or any nation so conceived and so dedicated, can long endure. We are met on a great battlefield of that war. We have come to dedicate a portion of that field, as a final resting place for those who here gave their lives that that nation might live.

It is altogether fitting and proper that we should do this.

But, in a larger sense, we cannot dedicate—we cannot consecrate—we cannot hallow—this ground. The brave men, living and dead, who struggled here, have consecrated it, far above our poor power to add or detract. The world will little note, nor long remember what we say here, but it can never forget what they did here. It is for us the living, rather, to be dedicated here to the unfinished work which they who fought here have thus far so nobly advanced. It is rather for us to be here dedicated to the great remaining task before us—that from these honored dead we take increased devotion to that cause for which they gave the last full measure of devotion—that we here highly resolve that these dead shall not have died in vain—that this nation, under God, shall have a new birth of freedom—and that government of the people, by the people, for the people, shall not perish from the earth.

The Battle of Gettysburg: An Overview

Steve Winter

Before the Battle

Gettysburg, a placid Pennsylvania college town, seems to have no particular attraction that would draw armies and cause them to shed blood over it. One must look at a map to see why the place became a battlefield. The town lay at the intersection of nine major roads radiating out to all of south-central Pennsylvania. It was a natural concentration point, a magnet for any army.

On the heels of his victory at Chancellorsville, Robert E. Lee launched a second invasion of the North. In the last week of June, 1863, the invasion seemed to be going extremely well. The Rebel army fanned out through south-central Pennsylvania, forming a sixty-mile crescent from Chambersburg in the west to Carlisle in the north and penetrating as far as York and the Susquehanna River in the east. At the focal point of that fan lay the road hub of Gettysburg.

The only dark cloud was the absence of legendary cavalry commander Jeb Stuart. Recently humiliated by Federal cavalry at Brandy Station, Stuart took open-ended orders from Lee and set off on a wide-ranging ride to raise hell and assuage his pride. When Meade moved his seven corps northward through Maryland, Stuart was cut off from his commander, leaving Lee blinded by the lack of cavalry reconnaissance at a critical time.

Meade's army was two to three days behind the Confederates. Ahead of the army rode General John Buford's cavalry division. On June 30, they entered Gettysburg from the south. The townsfolk were greatly alarmed at having seen Rebel infantry approaching along the road to Chambersburg, but having spotted the cavalry's approach, the Confederates—Pettigrew's brigade—withdrew without a fight.

An experienced campaigner, Buford quickly assessed the situation. The Rebel army lay to the west. Also west of Gettysburg rose three ridges, like the crests of three waves rolling outward from the town: distant Herr Ridge, McPherson's Ridge, and the commanding Seminary Ridge. An enemy approaching from Chambersburg would have to cross all three ridges in succession, a difficult task if the advance was opposed by a mobile force. Buford arranged his two brigades along the ridges, posted pickets well ahead, and settled in.

To the west, Lee finally had information regarding the whereabouts and intentions of the Union army, received not from Jeb Stuart but from a spy. Correspondingly, he ordered the army to concentrate where the roads converged.

Day 1: July 1, 1863

With first light, Confederate skirmishers engaged Buford's outlying and widely scattered vedettes. A. P. Hill's Third Corps was strung out on the Chambersburg Pike headed toward Gettysburg, Harry Heth's division in the lead. When the first resistance was met, it was assumed to be militia, easily brushed aside by a show of force.

Southern skirmishers pressed the cavalry screen back aggressively, unaware that they were facing veteran, regular army troops. The pickets fell back onto Colonel Gamble's First Brigade, strung thinly along Herr Ridge. Heth marched ahead, still in road column, with lines of skirmishers on his flanks. Fire from a battery of horse artillery backed up by dismounted troopers armed with breechloading Sharps carbines quickly dispelled the notion that the enemy was a rabble of shopkeepers sporting flintlock muskets and shotguns.

Faced with a real scrap, Heth deployed a brigade and attacked again, this time with artillery support. The cavalry was eventually forced to fall back to McPherson's Ridge, where it joined Devin's brigade. Here they had woods for cover and excellent fields of fire into the swale between McPherson's and Herr ridges. Attackers would be forced to slow down while crossing Willoughby Run, and any flanking threats would have to cross the exposed ridge to north and south. Armed with repeating carbines, the cavalry could hold out until ammunition ran short or they were outflanked. Still, outnumbered almost four to one, it was only a matter of time before Buford's position would be flanked and he would have to withdraw again.

The moment the Rebels materialized, however, Buford sent for help to General John Reynolds, whose First Corps was moving up the road from Emmitsburg. Reynolds, a thorough professional, rushed forward to support the cavalry.

Reynolds himself arrived ahead of his corps and conferred with Buford, then rode back to hasten his men onward. As Confederates of Archer's brigade moved into flanking positions in McPherson's Woods, they ran into Reynolds's lead element: the hard-fighting Iron Brigade. For the second time that morning, the Confederates found themselves fighting a greater foe than they had expected. This time it was not just a cavalry division but the Army of the Potomac advancing in force. Archer's men were driven back and the situation stabilized again.

For hours the battle raged on the ridges, assaults surging forward and back. Again and again the Rebels probed for an open flank only to find it suddenly manned by yet another freshly arrived brigade of the Union First Corps extending the line to the right and to the left.

Meanwhile, the Eleventh Corps, commanded by Major General Oliver O. Howard, was advancing behind the First Corps. Learning that General Reynolds had been killed, felled by a sniper or perhaps a stray bullet, Howard assumed battlefield command.

As the line continued to stretch, Howard ordered his own divisions into positions on the First Corps's right. North of town the ground was open, rolling farmland. Confederate guns had begun booming on that end of the line, almost certainly signalling an assault. The attacks came from Major General Robert Rodes's division at about 2 P.M., but they were poorly coordinated and fairly easily repulsed with heavy Confederate losses.

By early afternoon the Union position formed a sharp angle, with the First Corps deployed north to south along McPherson's Ridge and the Eleventh Corps aligned east to west north of Gettysburg. The First Corps had suffered tremendously in very hard fighting. The Iron Brigade alone lost over 1,100 men from its starting strength of about 1,800. When they were assailed yet again by Pender's veteran division, they broke and fled McPherson's Ridge.

As the First Corps crumbled, in the north a maneuver was developing. Answering Lee's call to concentrate, Dick Ewell's Second Corps was marching south on the Carlisle and Harrisburg roads, converging directly onto the Eleventh Corps's position. With their left exposed by the First Corps' retreat and a fresh Confederate corps to their front and right, the Eleventh Corps's line collapsed like a row of dominoes. One after another regiments abandoned the fight and escaped through the streets of the town.

It looked as if General Lee had his victory, at a time and place chosen by providence.

The Union forces, however, were humiliated but not beaten. South of the town, the shattered regiments were being re-formed and redeployed on the final line of high ground—the "fishhook" that began east of the town on rocky Culp's Hill, swung around the bend of Cemetery Hill, and ran south along the gently descending crest of Cemetery Ridge. South of the ridge, two miles from the town, stood another pair of hills: Little Round Top and Big Round Top.

The situation for the Union troops at this point was precarious. They were tired from a long day of marching and fighting, disorganized, hungry, badly rattled by defeat, and confused by officer casualties and changes in command (five different general officers had been in overall command that day).

The Confederates, too, were feeling the effects of a hard and bloody fight. A. P. Hills's Third Corps, in particular, had been through the ringer. Ewell still had fresh units, however, and should have been able to press the attack, but he did not. He had no orders to attack from General Lee, and prospects for flanking the hills effectively were not good. Late in the afternoon, orders from Lee finally arrived: Take the high ground south of Gettysburg "if practicable." Ewell deemed it not practicable, and the best chance that the Army of Northern Virginia would have to win the battle and sweep the Federal army from the field was lost.

Day 2: July 2, 1863

Overnight, General James Longstreet, commanding the Confederate First Corps, urged Lee to swing around the Union position south of the Round Tops, find good defensive ground between the Army of the Potomac and Washington, D.C., and make the enemy attack them. Lee refused. He hadn't come looking for a battle at Gettysburg, but once he had it, and had nearly won it, he was resolved to finish it.

Early morning reconnaissance discovered that the Round Tops were completely undefended and the southern end of Cemetery Ridge was held only by skirmishers. Lee saw an opportunity to roll up the Union line from the south.

Longstreet's was the only force that had not seen heavy action the day before. Even though one of his three infantry divisions, General George Pickett's, was not on the field yet, Longstreet was ordered to maneuver to the south and attack "in echelon" up the Emmitsburg Road. After several delays, Longstreet's corps began marching about mid-morning toward its jumping-off positions at the southern end of Seminary Ridge. But the chosen route, behind and across Herr Ridge, turned out to be exposed to view from the Union position. If the corps moved south under enemy observation, any chance for surprise would be lost. Longstreet ordered the corps to back up and alter its route to follow Willoughby Run. This preserved some air of secrecy, but cost several critical hours' delay. The First Corps would not reach its final attack positions due west of Little Round Top and the gap between it and Cemetery Ridge until mid-afternoon.

From General Meade's point of view, his position on the northern hills and Cemetery Ridge was weak but not terrible. Short of withdrawing overnight, however, there was little he could do but reinforce and shore up his defenses. He believed that the bulk of the Rebel army was to his north, and that was where he concentrated his own force.

Meade's preoccupation with Cemetery and Culp's Hills was a dangerous case of oversight. Little Round Top, with its clear fields of fire across the entire Union position, was the real lynchpin, and portions at least of Lee's army were already becoming aware of it.

In fact, Meade was aware of it, too, but did not give it a high priority. He had ordered Major General Dan Sickles to position his Third Corps at the far left of the Union line and cover the Round Tops. On inspection, Sickles feared the position was dangerously weak. At its southern end, Cemetery Ridge is so slight that it's barely noticeable, no military obstacle at all.

Ahead of the position, however, was higher ground topped by a peach orchard. Sickles wanted to occupy that rise and asked for permission to do so. No response came. Finally, at about 3 P.M., without permission from Meade, Sickles ordered his corps to advance and occupy what he considered superior ground.

The Third Corps's advance was dangerous because it left the Union's left flank swinging without an anchor and exposed it to fire from two directions. For the moment, however, it threw the Confederates for a loop. Lee's plan depended on the presumption that the enemy was thinly spread and on Cemetery Ridge. General John Bell Hood, at the southern tip of the Rebel line, could plainly see that if he attacked as ordered, his open right would be subjected to murderous flanking fire from the Peach Orchard. The Round Tops, however, were still wide open and from there, he would be the one enfilading the Union line instead of the other way round.

Hood was a good soldier. Three times he sent messages to Longstreet explaining the situation and asking permission to alter his axis of advance, and three times he was refused with an identical reply: "General Lee's orders are to attack up the Emmitsburg Road."

For the first time in his career, Hood disobeyed orders. He did not attack up the road, but instead launched his brigades straight toward the Round Tops. If they could be seized immediately, possibly without much of a fight, the victory would fall into Lee's hands.

First they had to battle their way into and through a maze of boulders called the Devil's Den, at the foot of the hills. Then Federal snipers were cleared off the wooded slope, and finally, Big Round Top was in Confederate hands.

Then word came that Hood had been wounded and carried from the field. His replacement, Brigadier Law, sent orders forward that Little Round Top, not Big Round Top, was the target.

Four regiments filed into the narrow hollow between the hills and once more started up, moving between the trees. The slope appeared deserted. Suddenly, from less than fifty yards away, an enemy force rose up from behind a low stone wall and opened up the "most destructive fire I ever saw," according to one Confederate officer.

The Union soldiers behind that fusillade had arrived just ten minutes ahead of the attacking Rebels. Their presence was the work of Meade's chief engineer, Brigadier General Gouverneur G. K. Warren. Dispatched by Meade to check on the troop placements at the southern end of Cemetery Ridge, Warren had instantly appraised the value of Little Round Top with an engineer's eye. He was shocked to find it manned only by a signaling station and further alarmed on seeing the glint and rustle of enemy movement in the woods across the Emmitsburg Road. Instantly he sent riders in search of whatever troops they could find.

They found Colonel Strong Vincent commanding the Third Brigade, First Division, Fifth Corps, waiting in reserve behind Cemetery Ridge. Vincent rushed his four regiments into positions across the hill. At the far end of the line, the most vulnerable spot and the first the enemy would hit, was Colonel Joshua Chamberlain and the Twentieth Maine regiment.

The battle on Little Round Top raged for an hour and a half, with Confederates charging up the hill time after time, only to be driven down again by intense fire from behind the stone wall. The fighting was confused, chaotic, and at very close quarters. Eventually, with their ammunition almost exhausted and the Confederates coming on again, the Twentieth Maine surged across the wall and charged downhill. The Rebels fled before the unexpected onslaught and Little Round Top was saved.

Meanwhile, a fight every bit as desperate raged in the Devil's Den. As Longstreet's echelon attack developed, the Peach Orchard and the adjacent Wheat Field became the scene of ferocious attacks and counterattacks. The Wheat Field changed hands six times, and each time the new owners paid a heavy price in blood. Blue-coated reinforcements were rushed to the scene from all directions, eventually forcing the attackers to withdraw.

Still the Union's troubles were not over. Longstreet's southern attack had played out, but the initiative passed to Hill's corps, deployed along Seminary Ridge. The fighting in the Wheat Field and the Orchard pulled in Federal troops that had been protecting Cemetery Hill, leaving dangerous gaps in that position. Brigadier General Cadmus Wilcox's brigade was headed straight toward one such gap. With no other troops available, the tiny First Minnesota regiment with only 262 men was ordered to counterattack Wilcox's entire brigade. They did, and although the Minnesotans suffered over eighty-percent casualties, the Confederates turned back and withdrew.

It was Brigadier General Ambrose Wright who achieved the greatest success of the day for the Rebels. His 1,400 Georgia men actually seized a foothold on Cemetery Hill, although they did not quite make it to the top. They broke the line at a critical point, where it bent from the south toward the east. Before they could be reinforced, a counterattack by the Second Division of the Second Corps threatened to envelop the Confederates, who gallantly cut their way out of the trap and withdrew in good order.

All that was left was Ewell's attack from the north against Culp's Hill. Coming far too late to prevent troops there from reinforcing other sectors, his efforts were wasted. One Louisiana brigade managed to set foot on the crest of Cemetery Hill, but was driven off almost immediately by coordinated counterattacks.

Day 3: July 3, 1863

Believing that Meade would strengthen his flanks after the near-disasters of the second, Lee aimed his renewed assault at the Federal center. The only fresh division in the Army of Northern Virginia was that of George Pickett, who arrived too late to take part in the second day's fight. Ewell would attack again from the north to draw in and tie down reinforcements.

An early-morning Union counterattack against Confederates still occupying portions of Culp's Hill threatened to upset Lee's timetable. The fight lasted three hours and ended any possibility of Ewell's participation; his brigades were exhausted.

But if Ewell's men were spent, reasoned Lee, so too must be the enemy. The attack would proceed.

Three divisions formed behind Seminary Ridge: Pickett's, Pettigrew's, and Trimble's. Pettigrew and Trimble had assumed division command to replace Heth and Pender, both of whom had been wounded the day before.

The target of the advance was a plainly visible clump of trees near the northern end of Cemetery Ridge. All units were to converge on that point, break through, and scatter the enemy line.

But getting to that point meant crossing half a mile of largely open ground and ascending a hill, all the while under fire from Union batteries. To make such an approach possible, 170 Confederate guns were arrayed along the crest of Seminary Ridge. The ensuing bombardment was the most colossal cannonade of the war.

Gunners were instructed to concentrate their fire against the Union artillery. The Federal guns, exposed along the open skyline of the ridge, made excellent targets. But before long, smoke from both armies' batteries made accurate sighting and ranging all but impossible. When, at about 3 P.M., Federal fire seemed to slacken, it had as much to do with both armies running low on long-range ammunition as with any destruction of guns.

At that point, the order passed through the army: Advance! Long lines of gray-and-butternut-clad men stepped out of the shadow of the woods into the bright July sunshine and marched through the long grass toward the enemy-held ridge.

As the cannon smoke drifted away to reveal the snapping flags and glinting rifles of Rebel infantry, Northern gunners relaid their ten-pound Parrotts and their three-inch rifles, their twelve-pound Napoleons and their six-pound smoothbores. Within minutes, shot and shell was plunging and bursting through the Southern lines. Batteries blazed from Cemetery Hill to Little Round Top. All three divisions suffered horribly, losing men in ones and twos, then in fives, and tens, and twenties. Occasionally they halted to close up the gaps where clumps of men had fallen before resuming the implacable, awe-inspiring advance.

Within a few hundred yards of the blue line, small arms fire from thousands of muskets joined the crashing cannons.

Along the northern portion of the Federal line, a low stone wall followed the ridge. About eighty yards north of the clump of trees, it veered westward for another eighty yards, and then turned south again. This dubious bit of cover would shortly become notorious as "the Bloody Angle."

With the Confederates coming grimly on through the hell of artillery and musket fire, General Alexander Hays, commanding the Second Corps, seized an opportunity. His line overlapped gaps in the enemy's line. Wheeling forward, the audacious Northerners began pouring murderous enfilading fire into the Confederates' exposed flank.

South of the clump of trees, men of the Third Division, First Corps, were doing the same thing to Pickett's division as it passed.

This awful fire coming from both flanks drove the Confederates more and more toward the center, where they formed an ever more compact mass directly in front of the Angle. In places fifteen to thirty men deep, the Rebel column was a target that could not be missed. Cannons firing double canister blasted gaps as wide as roads through the throng. But still they kept coming.

At last the wall itself was reached. General Lew Armistead, one of Pickett's brigadiers, waving his hat at the end of his sword, leaped the wall yelling "Who will follow me?" Immediately he was shot down, but his men did follow, swarming across the wall and charging ahead to the copse of trees with the Rebel yell in their throats.

At the trees they were stopped cold by a volley from the Sixty-Ninth Pennsylvania regiment. Moments later they crossed bayonets with three Union regiments in a mad, swirling, choking, clubbing mêlée. But the men who had made that long uphill march, under fire the whole way, were too spent, too outnumbered to hold this ground. The gray line fell back in pockets and clusters. Careful not to turn tail or leave behind a man who might be saved, they fought their way out and retraced their steps across that awful, shot-churned, corpse-strewn field to the shelter of Seminary Ridge.

Three thousand Confederate dead stayed behind. Only

one field officer of the fifteen attacking regiments was un-
hurt. Entire companies had disappeared; some regiments
suffered eighty-five percent casualties.

The Day After: July 4, 1863

There was no pursuit, no counterattack of frenzied Union
infantry screaming down from their hills and ridges to
harry the beaten Rebels from the field. Both armies were
used up. One out of every three of the 160,000 men who
had marched over those hills had become a casualty.

At four o'clock that afternoon, the long gray lines of
survivors in Lee's army began snaking away from the
blood-soaked hills. Ten days later, they were once again
across the Potomac and back in Virginia. Never again
would the Confederacy challenge the Federal army on
Northern soil.

Gettysburg and the Politics of War

William Terdoslavich

"War is nothing but the continuation of policy by other means."—Carl von Clausewitz.

So what does this have to do with the Battle of Gettysburg?

The American Civil War was begotten by political failure to resolve disagreements over slavery in the United States. Past compromises papered over differences and maintained a crude balance of political power between North and South that failed over time as the North grew. As long as the number of slave states and free states remained even, deadlock would prevail in the Senate and slavery would be untouched. The pending admission of Kansas and Nebraska threatened the indelicate balance, and the Supreme Court's ruling in the infamous Dred Scott case extended slavery throughout the United States, further raising tensions over the issue.

Presidents, senators, representatives, and Supreme Court judges could not square the circle of slavery in a free country. The result of this failure was war, as both sides picked up their guns to finish an argument that words could not win.

But war is a slippery thing.

Nations may turn to war as "a continuation of policy by other means." A nation can start a war, claiming it seeks one objective only to see the war change into a different struggle with different objectives, and battles are the currency of war, adding up to victory or defeat over time.

Gettysburg takes its place in that continuum, and the political outcome was more than a brief speech by Abraham Lincoln to dedicate a cemetery. The Battle of Gettysburg may stand as the dramatic high point of the Civil War, but its political ramifications may not seem as great as Antietam, a draw which yielded the Emancipation Proclamation, or Atlanta, which secured Lincoln's reelection in 1864.

Yet Gettysburg affected the North's will to continue the struggle, the political debate over Emancipation, the election of governors in Ohio and Pennsylvania (which marked a preview of the upcoming presidential race in 1864), and the command arrangements of the United States Army. Moreover, for the South, Gettysburg was one of several defeats that dearly affected its morale, its chances for securing a negotiated ending to the war, and also shook its confidence in the generalship of Robert E. Lee.

Long after the last shot was fired in the Civil War, Gettysburg continues to be a political football. Benignly at first, the battlefield became a ground for reconciliation between veterans Blue and Gray. Lately, it has reflected the myopia of the war, as the conflict's politics are ignored for the narrow focus of military history. The war's professed object—the abolition of slavery—is nowhere to be found on this museum-battlefield.

BATTLE IS THE CURRENCY OF WAR

Abraham Lincoln and Jefferson Davis relied on success on the battlefield to justify their politics and their presidencies. For Davis, victory would mean an independent Confederate States of America, recognized by foreign powers and making safe the institution of slavery. But for Lincoln, the war was first fought to preserve the Union. Lincoln won his election campaigning for slavery's limitation to the South and not for its abolition.

The South enjoyed an early winning streak, and recognition of the CSA by England and France was becoming a distinct possibility that Lincoln could not ignore. The Battle of Antietam, which saw McClellan check Lee's invasion of the North, was considered a draw, if not a moral victory for the South. But for Lincoln, this was good enough to issue his Emancipation Proclamation. England was historically at the forefront of the battle to ban the slave trade—now it became politically impossible for the world's greatest empire to side with the Confederacy. England's moral outrage over the slave trade could not be contradicted by an alliance with a CSA supporting slavery. France, embroiled in putting Maximilian on the throne to rule Mexico, was arguably too busy to intervene. (Lincoln later approved a campaign up the Red River, sadly ill-executed, that was intended to establish a United States military presence in Texas to forestall any French interest north of the Rio Grande.)

Antietam allowed Lincoln to change the Union's objective in the war. With the stroke of a pen, the goal of restoring the Union became a crusade for freedom. Slaves would now flee their owners and cross the lines wherever Union armies stood. The South would lose a major source of cheap labor, and in turn lose some economic power needed to fight its war. But Antietam was not enough for the North to win its war, too.

Battlefield victory justifies policy. The "victory" at Antietam was enough for Lincoln to change policy, but that policy certainly didn't get any further backing from subsequent Union defeats. Fortune again favored the South. Confederate victories at Fredericksburg and Chancellorsville checked two Northern invasions of Virginia, keeping the strategic stalemate alive. The Union needed to win its war to make its policy fact. All the South needed to do was keep the stalemate going in the hopes that the North would quit.

Jefferson Davis placed most of his confidence in Robert E. Lee, and Lee's combat record justified such judgment. Upon taking command of Confederate forces the year before, Lee had fended off McClellan's offensive to take Richmond, fighting a week-long series of battles that drove the Union army back upon its base on the Peninsula. After that, Lee had won three more major battles and suffered one draw. His reputation was stellar.

Meanwhile, Lincoln had gone through three generals since Antietam, discarding McClellan, Burnside, and Hooker in just a nine-month span. The Union was starved of a clear-cut victory that would put it firmly on the road toward victory. After seeing the command of the Army of the Potomac spurned by Reynolds, Lincoln gave the top job to Meade. He would have to do. Meade had acquitted himself well in prior commands, showing competence at the brigade, division, and corps levels.

Events would not give Meade much time to become acquainted with his command, as Lee moved north shortly after his counterpart received his commission. Meade moved the Army of the Potomac north, keeping himself between Lee and Washington. Lee's invasion north of the Mason-Dixon line received a sharp check at Gettysburg.

THE NORTH WINS BIG

Meade won a defensive battle against a better general. Others can argue in hindsight whether Lee failed to win or Meade failed to lose. But Meade got credit for "whipping Bobby Lee." The Confederates were no longer ten feet tall. Gettysburg boosted Northern morale immediately, given that news of a victory did not have to travel far to reach the newspapers in Baltimore, Philadelphia, and New York.

Meade issued a proclamation thanking the soldiers of the Army of the Potomac for the victory at Gettysburg. But Meade then followed his thanks with a reminder that the job was not yet done. The troops still had to "drive from our soil every vestige of the invader." This did not sit well with Lincoln, and marked the beginning of his annoyance with Meade. Ten days after Gettysburg, Lincoln's secretary, John Hay, recorded in his diary Lincoln's exasperation with Meade over the note: "Will our generals get that idea out of their heads? The whole country is our soil."

The drought of Union victories then turned into a flood as news finally reached east of Grant's victory at Vicksburg. Marking the trio was the bloodless victory at Tullahoma, where Rosecrans outmaneuvered Bragg's army, forcing it to exit central Tennessee. Union hopes rode much higher while Southern morale tanked.

Unfortunately, Meade was not allowed much time to rest on his laurels. Victory at Gettysburg only brought more problems to Meade. Armies typically were spent after battle, and he did not think the Army of the Potomac was in any shape to pursue Lee, given the lack of supply and transport to enable the move. Lincoln was gladdened by news of Gettysburg, but he now pressed Meade to pursue Lee's army and destroy it.

Lincoln's desires were not unfounded. A Union cavalry raid destroyed Lee's pontoon bridge across the Potomac, isolating the Army of Northern Virginia from its home ground. Lee had to find new crossings to bring his army home while the Army of Northern Virginia had its back pressed against the Potomac. This crossing had to be managed while a hostile army hovered nearby. One good push by Meade and the Army of Northern Virginia would truly be no more.

Meade failed to drive the blade home. Heavy rains

began on July 4, and lack of transport complicated such a pursuit. On July 7, Lincoln felt that the Confederacy was on the ropes, and one good hard push would be enough to bring it down. By July 12, after giving Lee a two-day head start, Meade finally had the Army of the Potomac ready to march. But the attack slated for the thirteenth was postponed as Meade opted for caution in light of false information provided by a Confederate "deserter" who said that the Army of Northern Virginia was in "good shape to fight." The Army of the Potomac's corps commanders also counseled Meade to postpone the attack. When Meade finally advanced on July 14, he found only a rearguard facing him.

"Our army had the war in the hollow of their hand and they would not close it," Lincoln said when he heard the news. To Lincoln, it was another opportunity blown, with Meade re-creating McClellan's slack pursuit of Lee after Antietam. Lincoln could not fire Meade after he had won at Gettysburg, but at the same time, his confidence in Meade was less than rewarded. On July 14, Lincoln sat down to write a letter to Meade, expressing his heartfelt gratitude to Meade for the Union victory at Gettysburg. But Lincoln then expressed his misgivings, arguing that had Lee's army been destroyed in pursuit, the war would have ended. Lincoln thought better after writing the letter and did not send it. (His spirits were later buoyed upon hearing the news of Vicksburg and Tullahoma.)

In the coming months, the political fallout from Gettysburg would dog Meade. A later fall offensive into northern Virginia proved abortive when Meade came upon Lee's defensive positions at Mine Run. Meade was not stupid— he would not go forth with a Northern version of Pickett's Charge. The Army of the Potomac retreated back north as Meade left a bad battle unfought.

Knowing when to pass a fight did not endear Meade to his political enemies. Hooker, who had commanded the

Army of the Potomac at its defeat in Chancellorsville, and Sickles, who had fought at Gettysburg under Meade, both used their influence to persuade Congress to investigate Meade's conduct at Gettysburg and the subsequent campaign. Meade survived the scrutiny with his command intact but his political reputation tarnished. It was this kind of second-guessing by politicians that hung many albatrosses around the neck of the hapless Army of the Potomac. It was a political price many commanders of the Army of the Potomac paid, given the army's proximity to the national capital after all.

(Note that distance was kind to the Army of Tennessee under Grant. Far from Washington's prying, the taciturn Grant subdued Vicksburg and further burnished his reputation by securing Chattanooga in a chaotic, unplanned fall victory while Meade sulked away from Mine Run. Battles are the currency of victory. Grant was flush with victory, so Lincoln had no trouble betting on a sure thing compared to Meade's also-ran performance. The political climate after Gettysburg cut Meade no breaks.)

SOUTHERN FORTUNES HIT THE SKIDS

Davis had pinned high hopes on Lee's invasion of the North.

Confederate Vice President Alexander Stephens was already on his way to Norfolk under a flag of truce to meet with Union officials there and proceed to Washington. Stephens was going to bank on his prewar friendship with Lincoln to obtain a meeting about prisoner exchange and use that venue to see if the North was willing to talk peace (hopefully while Lee was invading Pennsylvania and racking up another victory—this time on Northern soil).

News of the Stephens mission reached Lincoln at the same time as he got news of Gettysburg, and as a result,

Lincoln refused his request for a pass through the lines, closing for the time being any chance for discreet peace talks between the two belligerents. The Northern president was not going to talk peace while bullets were winning his argument.

While the victory of Gettysburg slowly soured up North, things went from bad to worse for the South. Lee tendered his resignation to President Davis within a month of the battle's close. Davis, of course, could not accept this from his best general. Nonetheless, Lee came in for criticism from Southern newspapers and senators after his winning streak was broken. It appeared that victory had protected Lee from the second-guessing that dogged the Union generals.

Confederate congressional elections were slated for the fall of 1863, after the losses of Gettysburg and Vicksburg were fully digested by the body politic. Political tools like patronage and appeals to party loyalty were not available to Davis as they had been for Lincoln. Party affiliation and patronage bound Northern Republican governors to the war effort and provided measures of discipline to both Democrats and Republicans alike in the Northern Congress. Since the South had no formal political parties, many of these features were lacking.

Issues like conscription, impressments, taxes paid in goods, and war finances were all issues at play in the Confederate off-year election in 1863. Opponents to Davis's policies ran as individuals, and Davis did not have the supportive political means to oppose them. His opposition crystallized behind General Joseph Johnston. Davis had blamed him for the failure to stop Grant from taking Jackson, Mississippi, during the Vicksburg campaign. Johnston kept up correspondence with many Davis opponents, and behind him they rallied to criticize Davis's handling of the war. He could not argue against Davis, but he could persuade his allies to do so.

After the Confederate house elections, the number of anti-Davis representatives shot up from twenty-six to forty-one in the 106-member Confederate House. Of the Confederacy's twenty-six Senators, twelve were aligned against Davis. Prewar Whigs captured the governorships of Mississippi and Alabama. Georgia and North Carolina would be the epicenter of the opposition, fielding sixteen of their combined nineteen representatives in the opposition. Yet these two states had yet to feel the harsh sting of the war's lash.

Davis maintained his grip on House and Senate in the fallout after Gettysburg and Vicksburg, but only by extraordinary means. His supporters were senators and congressmen from states and districts under partial or total Union control, like Tennessee, Arkansas, Louisiana, Mississippi, and part of Virginia. The Confederacy could not hold elections where Union armies stood, so the congressmen simply continued serving, or were elected in token fashion by the few refugees that could be found. These representatives were free to vote for higher taxes and the draft, knowing full well that their districts would not be coughing up cash or levying manpower. This was the closets thing Davis had to a war party in Richmond.

Religion also played its role in boosting and later undermining Southern morale, which put further spin on the political situation. What is casually referred to as the Bible Belt today has deep roots in the South of the Civil War. So long as Southern armies fought and won battles, God was on the side of Dixie. This opinion was reinforced by Sunday sermons and articles in the religious newspapers of the time. Even President Davis had a long record of beseeching the Almighty for battlefield victories and thanking Him whenever he got one.

But the loss at Gettysburg, on top of the setbacks at Vicksburg and Tullahoma, brought the South's religious beliefs into a deep funk. God rewards the good with victories, but scourges the wicked with defeat. Had the South done something wrong? Could the Confederacy be punished by a just God? These worries nagged the South as defeat after defeat brought a worsening war to the doorsteps of states yet untouched by Northern armies. Davis would ask the Almighty for strength and deliverance as the South's trials became heavier with defeat. Gettysburg started into motion this growing spiritual doubt.

Lincoln was also deeply religious, and did not hesitate to thank the Almighty for the Union victory at Gettysburg. Lincoln, however, did not pretend to know what God's plan was for the war, "though we erring mortals may fail to accurately perceive them in advance. We hoped for a happy ending of this terrible war long before this; but God knows best, and has ruled otherwise."

GIVE WAR A CHANCE

The Union's sagging fortunes in the first half of 1863 strengthened the hand of peace Democrats in Northern states, better known by their perjorative nickname as "Copperheads." Clement Vallandigham got the Democratic nomination to run for governor of Ohio, even though he was in exile in Windsor, Canada. State Supreme Court Judge George Woodward got the Democratic nomination to run for governor in Pennsylvania.

These nominations were made prior to Gettysburg, when the war was going badly. If Vallandigham and Woodward won, they could unite with New York Governor Horatio Seymour, also a Copperhead, to find a way to pull out of the war. New York, Pennsylvania, and Ohio together added up to roughly half the Union's population.

Union victory at Gettysburg undercut the peace Democrats, who suffered further blows by the public fallout following the New York draft riots and the valiant failure to take Fort Fisher by the all-black Fifty-Fourth Massachusetts regiment. Both events triggered a backlash against the "race card" being played by Copperheads, where they tried to raise white fears of being inundated by freed blacks. "You say you will not fight to free Negroes . . . Some of them seem willing to fight for you," Lincoln contended in a public letter he penned on August 26.

Again, the notion that battles can drive politics just as surely as politics can drive battles received its proof in November, just five months after the fight at Gettysburg. Just as Davis's hand was weakened by defeat, Lincoln's grip on war policy was strengthened by victory. In Ohio, Vallandigham got trounced as his Republican rival took sixty-one percent of the vote. Woodward, the more moderate of the two Copperheads, was beaten by a 15,000-vote margin as the Republicans captured the Pennsylvania governorship with fifty-one point five percent of the vote.

On November 19, after election day, Lincoln paid a visit to Gettysburg to dedicate a cemetery where the Union dead had been laid to rest. Edward Everett of Massachusetts, one of the finest orators of the day, spoke for two hours. Lincoln followed, and in three minutes said more than Everett.

Lincoln was no doubt sincere when he gave his 269-word speech to the small crowd at Gettysburg that November. But the President was a political realist. He got a good preview of his chances for reelection in the coming year with the Republican victories in Pennsylvania and Ohio. So it was with one eye on 1864 that Lincoln gave his modest speech, standing on a battlefield success had purchased dearly with much blood the previous summer. He reminded the nation that the war was not over, but repeated the reason why it was being fought and how that reason was justified by victory at Gettysburg.

War is not just about armies fighting on battlefields. It is fought just as well in legislatures and in cabinet meeting rooms. Winning battles justifies the policy a nation pursues through war, while losing quickly undermines it. The Union and the Confederacy were not exempt from this iron law. Whoever won the war would dictate the political future of this country—united and free of slavery, or politically and socially divided. This was war as policy by other means, making the Civil War no different in political tone than the Napoleonic Wars witnessed by Clausewitz. The victory at Gettysburg was a large weight placed on the scales that measured the fortunes of war in the Union's favor. Alone, it did not guarantee the Union's victory over the Confederacy. But taken together with the Union victories at Tullahoma and Vicksburg, Gettysburg helped mark the beginning of the end for the South, militarily and politically.

Union and Confederate Social Convictions Surrounding the Battle of Gettysburg

Paul A. Thomsen

Confederate President Jefferson Davis and his now-legendary military commander, General Robert Lee, knew their meager forces could not long match the Union Army blow for blow, but the steadily rising number of Union casualties from battles like First and Second Manassas, Shiloh, Antietam, and Chancellorsville (as well as the resulting conflicting public opinion over the war's prosecution) gave the Southern Rebels one last chance. With the scarcity of Union victories and the rising tide of dissension among several Northern states over Lincoln's heavy-handed policies, by the onset of summer in 1863 it seemed the Union's precarious balance of national support and Federalist actions might be encouraged to tip toward the Confederacy's favor, bring England into the war, and successfully arbitrate a negotiated peace. With a dwindling chance of foreign intervention and a rapidly evaporating stockpile of both supplies and soldiers, Lee had little time to lose.

Marshalling his forces, General Lee audaciously invaded Union-held Pennsylvania. Venturing farther North than the Confederate Army had ever gone, Lee knew it was only a matter of time before Union General George Meade's rather large force would be brought to bear upon his steady advance. The numbers were daunting. According to the United States Army Center of Military History, prior to the clashing of forces outside Gettysburg, the Union Army of the Potomac numbered 115,256 officers and enlisted men with 362 guns, while the Confederate Army of Northern Virginia retained only 76,224 men and 272 guns. Still, Lee took heart in his men's recent accomplishment at Chancellorsville. If 60,000 of his finest soldiers had managed to turn back the Union's forces 134,000 strong, his army might yet turn back their seemingly insurmountable enemy one last time and compel an end to the hostilities dozens of miles *above* the Union capital.

President Lincoln's personal endurance was beginning to wane . . . and a great deal rested on the events of the next few weeks. Plagued by bad dreams, Lincoln had "drooping eyelids, looking almost swollen; dark bags beneath the eyes; the deep marks about the large and expressive mouth" a White House visitor observed. In restraining the disparate factions of his own party with a bit of cajoling, chicanery, and common-sense erudition, Lincoln had traded one set of domestic problems for another. The President had been effective in curbing the secession of the Border States and suppression of potentially sympathetic insurrectionists among the Northern populace since the war's onset, but his curtailing of certain constitutional rights, such as suspending the right of habeas corpus and the placement of limitations on the freedom of speech for the sake of neutralizing a few Copperhead factions had not gone over well with the general public.

Facing a steadily escalating Union debt, soaring prices, deep losses of skilled laborers to the war effort, and several violent worker–employee altercations over the unionization of certain key industries, Lincoln and his Republican Congress had likewise failed to garner sizeable public support when they instituted corrective measures to forestall a potential labor shortfall and bankrupt economy. In providing certain incentives for businesses to attract immigrant labor, many industry workers began vocally criticizing Lincoln's domestic policies. With poorly paid urban workers gathering into key unionized labor groups in New York and elsewhere, demanding better wages and safer conditions, it seemed the secessionist crisis, which no one had expected to last more than a few months, would not only roll into its fourth year, but would also divide urban workers from their brothers on the battlefield threatening to send thousands over to the "Peace" Democrats and their call for an immediate cessation of hostilities.

Furthermore, when Lincoln had released the Emancipation Proclamation the previous year, unequivocally freeing roughly 3.5 million Southern slaves remaining in bondage, the act was seen as too little by certain Republicans and Abolitionists and far too much by others. Lincoln's Secretary of the Treasury Salmon P. Chase, a past and future potential candidate for the presidency, had forwarded the opinion that, "Emancipation could be much better and more quietly accomplished by allowing [Union] Generals to organize and arm the slaves." Others, among them a number of Northern laborers, fearing the loss of their jobs to the industrialization of industry, the importation of immigrant labor, and implementation of brutal means to break strikes, sided with the secessionist view.

With blood being spilt on and behind the Union's lines, the Republican's Federalist reforms were weakening the Union's popular resolve. Not even the news of black troops being massed to support the defense of the Union seemed to sway public opinion back toward the Republicans. As one governor astutely warned his black troops, "Keep very quiet lest a democratic convention, then in session, should have its attention drawn to the fact of black soldiers being in town." Their presence was drawing further criticism from Lincoln's opposition that the war was not only a costly protraction of an unpopular political disagreement, but that at its heart resided the Abolitionists' re-

solve to free the Southern slaves and flood Northern industries with vast numbers of newly emancipated un-
skilled laborers. As Lee's force drove over land to meet
Meade's forces among the hills and fields of Pennsylvania,
some felt Postmaster General Montgomery Blair's fear
might yet come true. Lincoln's policy against slavery, he
said, "would cost the Administration the fall election."

The Republicans had barely managed to hold control of
Congress in 1862. "After a year and a half of trial and a
pouring out of blood and treasure, and the maiming of
thousands," one Republican wrote, "we have made no sen-
sible progress in putting down the rebellion . . . and the
people are desirous of some change." Having suffered several poor Army commanders and incurring staggering
losses under their direction the past few years, the party of
Lincoln was coming under close scrutiny by their Democrat adversaries. If the Republicans were to maintain control of Congress, it would be only by the slimmest of
margins and the support of their soldiers.

Placing his last hopes for a restored Union on General
Ulysses Grant, the hero of the West, President Lincoln
grew more restless with each passing day. As he had not
heard a word from Grant on his campaign against Vicksburg in weeks, Lincoln, desperate for news, eventually
began writing the region's local commanders, asking, "Do
the Richmond papers have anything about . . . Vicksburg?"
and "Have you heard anything from Grant?" Still, little re-
liable information was forthcoming. With a pending presidential election the next year against the Democrat George
McClellan (one of the generals the President had previously sacked), Lincoln and his Republicans desperately
needed a decisive victory. By the time news reached him
of Grant's victory at Vicksburg, President Lincoln was
deep into his appraisal of Meade's actions at the little junction of roads defining Gettysburg.

With a year remaining before the '64 election, Abraham

Lincoln might have felt compelled to ride close upon Grant, thus restraining and second-guessing his Union commander as Davis had Lee throughout the war to disastrous results. Regardless of whatever victories the future might have held for the Union, Lincoln knew the blood spilt at Shiloh, Antietam, and Gettysburg would be a powerful influence on the minds of many Conservatives as they cast their ballots, as it would be on the Radicals in realizing how far short their leader had fallen in abolishing slavery, not throughout the Border States, but only among the Rebel South; and as it would strengthen the Peace Democrats' resolve, remembering the burnt shells of cities and towns left after the rioting against the butcher's waste would soon spark violence in the largely Democratic state of New York.

With the Union's ranks decimated at Gettysburg, there would be no reserves to put down the New York insurrections nor keep the antiwar movement from spreading to similar pockets of resistance throughout the Union. Though most of the Copperheads had been sequestered early in the war, new ones would rise and take their place to fight against the perceived acts of tyranny. Likewise, with few soldiers surviving the campaign, had Lincoln somehow managed to survive the Republican nomination process, he would have been soundly defeated by now-citizen and presidential hopeful George McClellan.

Still, the President, rather than humiliate the fledgling Republican Party, would have more likely bowed out of his bid for reelection so that the next likely candidate, his now former Treasury Secretary Salmon P. Chase, might make a successful bid for the White House. Money had been the main issue keeping Chase from the presidency and with Lincoln out of the way, he would have had the coffers of the Radical Republicans laid open to him. In all likelihood, however, he too would have faltered before McClellan. The Civil War would end as Jefferson Davis and his colleagues had hoped from the start: a negotiated peace and a nation divided.

Lee's and Meade's armies met on the afternoon of June 30, 1863. Deprived of timely intelligence and at a critical loss of the area's high ground to Union cavalry and artillery, the bulk of Lee's Confederate army was sent to its death, crossing open fields and charging up steep well-defended hills. After three days of battlefield carnage the likes of which even the bloody fields of Antietam (according to one estimate 5,000 men died in a single day at Antietam) paled in comparison, General Robert Lee, telling his soldiers, "It's all my fault. My fault," withdrew the remains of his now-tattered army from the Pennsylvania town.

Although Lincoln leapt when he received the news of both Grant's victory at Vicksburg and Meade's steady triumph, proclaiming, "[the] great success to the cause of the Union . . . That on this day, He whose will, not ours, should ever be done, be everywhere remembered and reverenced with profoundest gratitude." Still, when Lincoln was eventually fully briefed on the battle, he glimpsed a fatal flaw in Meade's execution. The escape of Lee's army into Virginia, of course, meant an indeterminate lengthening of the conflict, but far worse than this realization and the number of American lives spent on both sides of the battlefield was the galling fact that Meade could have captured his Rebel adversary had the Union general pressed the initiative.

Lincoln was furious. Shouting at the air, he cried, "Our army held the war in the hollow of their hand and they would not close it!" In a letter to Meade he wrote, but never signed nor sent, Lincoln said, "My dear general, I do not believe you appreciate the magnitude of the misfortune involved in Lee's escape. He was within your easy grasp, and to have closed upon him would, in connection with our other late success, have ended the war. As it is, the war will be prolonged indefinitely . . . Your golden opportunity is gone and I am distressed immeasurably because of it."

The social consequences of the Gettysburg battle for the divided country were equally as grave. A few days after the battle, on July 11, New York City, the Union's center of finance and social tolerance, was reduced to a state of anarchy as long-brewing animosities and misgivings spilled out over the first United States draft. Although many of New York's prominent politicians (including Lincoln's own Secretary of State William H. Seward) had long decried slavery in the South as "incompatible with all . . . the elements of the security, welfare, and greatness of nations," its largely Democratic constituency, backed by Governor Horatio Seymour, had been a thorn in the Union's side. An infamous Lincoln critic, the governor had protested both the administration's 1862 policy of Emancipation and its new Conscription Act as unconstitutional, but his rhetoric had failed to make an impact until a steady stream of lengthy war-casualty lists began filtering into the city.

Though largely considered "barbarians," a number of Irish, Germans, and Italians from the New York area had already voluntarily entered military service and served in some of the war's fiercest battles. In a city where the largely immigrant poor lived in ramshackle firetraps, worked under sweatshop conditions at low wages, and often endured religious oppression and widely corrupt political machines, fire departments, *and* police departments, the idea of mass conscription into a perilous, irregularly paying job at a poorer wage than the local factory's offering met with heated opposition. As news reached New York of the bloody Gettysburg victory, the escape of Lee, and the 779 New York Excelsior Brigade casualties suffered during the battle, it was learned that a provision in the act allowed exemptions for residents who could either pay $300 or provide an acceptable substitute, a fee that only the wealthy could afford. The Daily News further polarized the issue, printing, "the people are notified that one out of two and a half of our citizens are to be brought off to Messrs. Lincoln & Company's charnel house."

Three years of economic strife, slave rights, and Federalism suddenly erupted into violence across the city. Stores were looted. Telegraph wires were cut. Buildings were set ablaze. Entire blocks were razed to the ground, and a number of the community's meager black populace, despised as strikebreakers and labor usurpers, were beaten to death or lynched, then set ablaze. Crying, "Rich man's war, poor man's fight," "To hell with the draft and the war," and "Tell Old Abe to come to New York," the rioters called for a recognition of their troubles, an end to the war against slavery, and sweeping changes made to their corner of the Union.

"I know that many of those who have participated in the proceedings," answered Governor Seymour, "would not have allowed themselves to be carried to such extremes of violence and of wrens, except under an apprehension of injustice; but such persons are reminded that the only opposition . . . which can be allowed is an appeal to the courts . . . Riotous proceedings must and shall be put down. The laws of the state must be enforced . . ."

The rampant violence was a heavy blow to the Union President. Despite their recent victories, it seemed the war was beginning to surpass his every measure to contain and eliminate the insurrectionist sentiments. Deeply troubled at one cabinet meeting, he told the attendees, "he did not believe we could take up anything in cabinet today. Probably none of us were in a right frame of mind for deliberation—he was not." Lincoln immediately dispatched five Union regiments, fresh from the fighting at Gettysburg, to subdue the city and contain the insurrection. Although Holmes County, Ohio; Rush and Sullivan counties in Indiana; areas in Milwaukee, the mining districts of Pennsylvania, and several other parts of the country actively resisted attempts to carry out the conscription act, none were as violent as New York. When the riots finally ended, over one-hundred civilians were dead, and pressure was being brought to bear on the President to appoint a special commissioner to investigate the riots' causes, but Lincoln thought better of it. "One rebellion at a time is about as much as we can conveniently handle."

The conscription act of the North had actually added little to the Union's military reserves as had its Southern legislative counterpart which had been enacted a year prior. However, President Lincoln had gambled correctly on several fronts. With a string of victories from Grant and Meade, the soldier vote would secure his reelection in 1864, topping McClellan even in the heart of New York. Congress would remain firmly in the grasp of the Republican party. Fast running out of troops and supplies, the Confederate army would eventually surrender when its commander did. The Confederacy, on a steady slide into oblivion, would never again cost the country the lives it had lost at Gettysburg.

Both Union and Confederate appraisals of the Gettysburg battle's importance had been well founded. The distance Lee's Confederate army had come, the farthest North the Confederacy would ever march, had not only placed Washington, D.C., in strategic danger, but the move had also managed to bring fear to the hearts of military men and civilians alike with questions of how much farther might they yet proceed and what would be the point in continuing the war fought over the issues of federalism and slavery? The losses to both sides had been devastating. According to *The Civil War Society's Encyclopedia of the Civil War*, the Union force of 85,000 soldiers had suffered more than 23,000 dead, wounded, and missing, while the Confederacy's military ranks of 70,000 men had lost 20,000, facts which would be revisited through the endeavors of yellow journalism and contribute to the narrow number of seats by which the Republicans would retain control of Congress in the 1864 election. Moreover, General Lee had gotten away, ensuring a continuation of the war for more than a year to come. Each factor had contributed to the New York Draft Riots and the near loss of Republican control of Congress, but the fires of disharmony and outrage had burned only briefly across the Union. The acts were condemned, the dead were counted, and the spirit which had spawned them went away.

Still, had one single element of the Gettysburg battle been altered by time, luck, or fate, the entire landscape of the war would have changed. A resounding Union victory at Gettysburg may well have shortened the conventional war by years, but the jaded peace of reconstruction under Lincoln's 1864 running mate, the arrogant Andrew Johnson, would have been akin to bliss when compared with the ensuing grassroots movements of unconventional resistance that would have come to light as Confederate President Jefferson Davis had hoped.

In a May 2, 1865, message to his brigade commanders, with the Confederacy's demise now certain, Davis had written, "It is time we adopt some definite plan upon which the further prosecution of our struggle shall be conducted. . . . Three thousand brave men are enough for a nucleus around which the whole people will rally when the panic which now afflicts them has passed away." Though his words were slightly vague, the Confederate President, who would soon try to escape to Mexico, had intended the war to now be waged on a new level: guerilla warfare.

The Confederacy, although poorly managed, had survived far longer than their Union counterparts had guessed. Bereft of clothing, food, and ammunition, thousands had held to their Rebel vision of America until their commanding general, Robert Lee, surrendered his sword at Appomattox Courthouse. Others, like William Clarke

Quantrill and his raiders (among them Frank and Jesse James) had held on to their Rebel beliefs until the bitter end. Still more took their personal crusades against changing times under the white sheets and hoods of the Ku Klux Klan. Following their misguided hearts and deriving their tactics from such fellow Southerners as American revolutionaries Francis "The Swamp Fox" Marion, Harry "Light Horse" Lee, and Francis "The Carolina Gamecock" Sumter, the South could have turned into a militarized zone with an army of occupation in similarity with the ancient Roman subjugation of Jewish Palestine, Ireland after the 1916 Easter Uprising, and modern day northern Israel/Palestine.

Either way, John Wilkes Booth would like have not assassinated the President *at* Ford's Theater. The cost of Confederate blood throughout the war, the ensuing invasion of Virginia, and Lincoln's initial recommendation of limited black suffrage had, indeed, sent Booth over the edge of sanity, declaring "That means nigger suffrage. That is the last speech he will ever make. . . . By God, I'll put him through." Booth had been plotting for some time with his fellow Southern conspirators to abduct the President as a means of forcing the North to capitulate their war efforts, but the armed conflict had ended before the actor's idea could be set in motion. Settling on assassination, Booth and his colleagues had lucked into a series of events (learning at the theater box office that the President would be attending Ford's later that evening, that Lincoln had not cancelled the engagement due to fatigue, that no guard had been chosen to stand watch over the door to the President's box . . .) which allowed them time to plan and execute their self-imposed mission of terrorism.

A swift demise dealt to the Confederacy in 1864 and impending full black suffrage throughout the conquered South would have granted Booth not only ample reason and motive to fix his rage on Abraham Lincoln, but as in our history, in 1864 more than one proper vantage point from which the second-rate actor might assassinate the President. On March 4, standing in the Rotunda as Lincoln passed through the portico to briefly outline his Reconstruction plans at his second Inaugural Address, Booth might have acted on the thoughts he'd later confessed to having. Instead of remarking to a friend how easily it could have been, Booth might very well have pulled out a pistol, shouted "Sic semper tyrannis" (Thus always to tyrants) and shot at the President of the United States at the Inaugural. Should his aim have proved as lethal as his demonstration at Ford's Theater, Andrew Johnson would have stepped into Lincoln's place and therefore, with the President's demise, Reconstruction would have had to wait nearly another hundred years and several more martyrs before the process would be completed in the Civil Rights era.

The Union could not have endured a loss at Gettysburg. Neither, as history has shown, could the Southern Confederacy. The Confederacy, though unaware of the exactitude of the number of casualties which had awaited them, had been willing to gamble over the outcome of Gettysburg. Other than surrender, they held no other choice. If Lee's forces had not been stopped at that sleepy Pennsylvania town, or had the number of casualties been less severe, or had Lee actually been captured, the face of the war would have changed. A stalemate or Confederate withdrawal to better ground would have eventually lead the United States down the same paths of steadily rising casualties and nascent tactics of modern warfare, but for the North, Gettysburg and every battle thereafter would have taken on the resolve of a war fought for the Union's survival to be secured, retribution to be exacted.

The conflict was fought over unquantifiable terms. Both sides paid the price with their dearest blood, but the actions of certain social forces defined Gettysburg as more than a strategic military turning point. It became a polarizing lens through which past animosities would be magnified. Whichever way the Battle of Gettysburg would have gone, one point is certain: The crisis would have perpetuated itself as the loser, as a united nation, or as separate resistance cells furthered their own ends through social means. The wounded, dying, and dead Union and Confederate soldiers lying among those grassy Pennsylvania fields would not have been the last to suffer or fall in America's Civil War.

Lee's Victory at Gettysburg . . . And Then What?

William R. Forstchen

William Faulkner's famous quote—that it is again the afternoon of July 3, 1863, and all things are still possible—reveals the long-cherished dream of the "Lost Cause": that all things were indeed possible, and if the game had played out just slightly differently, the South could have won the Civil War.

Center stage for this dream of victory is the Battle of Gettysburg. Even without the speculations about Confederate victory, Gettysburg holds the national imagination. It is the most visited of the National Battlefield Parks and still the most written-about battle in American history, with this book being but one more addition to hundreds of works on the subject.

When it comes to the speculations, there is the famed Longstreet controversy, with passionate devotees arguing that "Old Pete" lost the battle, or could have won it if only Lee had listened to him. We have the failure by Dick Ewell to advance against Cemetery Hill and Culp's Hill on July 1, and of course the disappearance of Jeb Stuart and his late arrival on the battlefield as other turning points.

On the Union side there are the dozens of what-ifs, such as the diversion of Joshua Chamberlain's regiment to Little Round Top or the advance of Dan Sickles into the

Peach Orchard which, if played out just slightly differently, might have changed the course of history.

On both sides we have a grand cast of characters to work with: the stubborn Longstreet, the strangely detached Lee, Hancock the Superb, and Sickles the slightly crazy. In the real history of the battle they are fascinating to study; in the realm of alternate history they become yet more possibilities to play with.

I write this essay from what I think is a rather interesting dual perspective. I am a science fiction writer who works in the realm of military SF and alternate history, but I also hold a PhD in history with a specialization in the American Civil War, and I teach a course on the Civil War at my college. The one side of me loves to toy with the "what-ifs" of history, the other side of me rebels at the thought of accepting anything that is not solid fact, backed up by the proper sources, properly footnoted.

Yet, as an historian, I do believe it is worth considering the great "what-if," of the Civil War, which is: Could the South have won the war if victory had been achieved at Gettysburg? For tied into this question is not just an entertaining speculation but also a serious historical point in terms of how the South perceived its loss and created an heroic mythology to explain their defeat.

So, as a departure point, let us accept any one of several scenarios considered in this book and say that Lee did win at Gettysburg. It is not a half victory such as Second Manassas where the Union army is sent reeling in retreat but nevertheless escapes relatively intact. Instead it is an Austerlitz or Cannae, a battle of near-total annihilation.

Such an overwhelming victory, if it had happened, would most likely have occurred on the second day of the battle. A full victory on the first day, with a triumphal Ewell pushing up over Cemetery Hill, might have finished off the battered remnants of the First and Eleventh Corps, and perhaps even caught the Twelfth Corps, but the rest of the Army of the Potomac—four full corps—most likely would have disengaged and fallen back on Washington.

A third-day victory, with Pettigrew and Pickett's gallant brigades punching through the line at Cemetery Ridge, might have triggered a rout, but yet again a fair part of the Army of the Potomac would have been able to disengage, especially the parts of four corps holding the Union line south of where the great charge hit.

It was the second day that truly offers the prospect of a crucial victory, so for the sake of a scenario, let's say that Hood did swing around Big Round Top and plow into the Union reserve supplies parked behind the hill. In a coordinated assault, Ewell pushes around the flank of Culp's Hill and somewhere out on the Baltimore Pike the two flanking forces link up and close the trap in a classic double envelopment which then triggers a panic in the Union army.

Here is the moment that would be the fulfillment of every Southern boy's dream: The victorious Lee riding forward to the ringing cheers of his ragged hard-fighting veterans. A humbled Meade offers up his sword to Lee, and the ever-gallant Lee refuses the blade, returning it and then, before all, bowing his head in a prayer of thanksgiving. Stuart sets off in pursuit of the few who escaped. Hancock is dead, Chamberlain is dead, a broken remnant led by John Sedgwick of the Sixth Corps manages to break out and flees toward Taneytown and Westminster.

Then what?

Even in victory it would have been a deadly fight for the victor. The very nature of Civil War combat, with the newly introduced rifled musket, placed a ghastly premium on a successful assault. The Army of Northern Virginia suffered at least six thousand casualties in the first day's battle, and it is fair to assume they would have suffered at least as many, and probably more, in the battle of encirclement of the second day.

Regardless of the general panic, many heroic regiments

of the Army of the Potomac would never go down to defeat without one hell of a fight at the end. One can picture Chamberlain on the slopes of Little Round Top holding out till the last man, and Hancock rallying his shattered brigades for a final desperate stand on the crest of Cemetery Hill, holding his corps's flag aloft until struck down. Many a cut-off regiment would rally around its colors and defend them to the death, and thousands of Southern boys would fall while taking those colors in the hour of victory.

Thirty thousand men or more, North and South, would lay dead, wounded, and dying in the fields and woods around Gettysburg on that night of Confederate victory, while inside the pocket over forty thousand prisoners would need to be rounded up, disarmed, fed, guarded, and eventually paroled.

At the earliest it would have been sometime on the afternoon of the third of July before any serious pursuit could have been launched against the survivors fleeing toward Washington.

At this juncture it must be remembered that war is not simply a matter of what happens at the moment of battle, it is first and foremost a question of logistics and of such simple things as feeding men, getting clean water, and resting them before they can march. In the realm of real history, a valid argument can be set forth that Chamberlain held the flank of Little Round Top against five to one odds because the Confederate troops had not been allowed to stop and get water prior to the attack and thus had charged up the steep slope with empty canteens. Fifteen miles of marching in ninety degree heat in wool uniforms had sapped their strength, a quart canteen of water might have made all the difference that day. In our scenario, two days of hard fighting in the July heat would have left the Confederate army nearly as exhausted as the men they had defeated.

Nevertheless, let us give to the Confederates their moment of glory and picture them setting forth in triumph, heads held high, an eager fire in their eyes as the red banners of the Army of Northern Virginia advance on Washington. During the previous night the relatively fresh division of Pickett's is pushed through the lines and on to the Baltimore Pike, followed in turn by Pettigrew and Pender, who though mauled in the first day's fight will now take the vanguard.

They set off in hot pursuit, pushing twenty miles or more, following the wrecked and demoralized remnants of the Army of the Potomac who were able to slip out of the cauldron of defeat. The road before them is littered with abandoned equipment, upended caissons, burning wagons, and prisoners rounded up by Stuart's cavaliers.

And then it rains.

We can play with the what-ifs of history, but there are certain things that go beyond the actions or inactions of men and one of the unchangeables in alternate history, at least for this historian, are the acts of God; and on July 4, it rained.

It rained, and it continued to rain on and off for days, raining so hard that in the real history of that war the Potomac River and every other creek, stream, and river in southern Pennsylvania, Maryland, and northern Virginia flooded. Along with the rivers flooding, the roads turned into quagmires.

The triumphal pursuit against the defeated Army of the Potomac would, within thirty-six hours, turn into a crawling march through rivers of mud. It creates a grim picture, not of sunlit fields filled with red banners held high, but instead it's a brutal murder match, exhausted and sick men stumbling from the line of march, bitter rear-guard fights in the pouring rain, horses driven to exhaustion collapsing into convulsive death, men dying by the roadsides covered in mud and filth.

His army strung out along fifty miles of road, Lee

would have pushed the advance on Washington without
respite, but it would have been an advance at a crawl. To
try to take Philadelphia was absurd, even the taking of Baltimore would give but a temporary advantage. The Civil
War was a political war, and the taking of Washington was
the key.

Granted, some of Jeb Stuart's men might have been into
the suburbs within forty-eight hours, cutting telegraph
lines, perhaps even swinging north around the city to cut
the rails, but there would have been no weight behind
them, and they would have arrived on mounts exhausted
from a deadly battle and a grueling pursuit. It would take
at least five days, perhaps a week or more, for Lee's infantry and artillery to come upon to the capital city.

And waiting for them would have been roughly forty
thousand Union troops manning the fortifications around
the city. This is one fact more than any other that is over-
looked by the dreamers of Confederate victory: the regiments of heavy artillery, such as the First Maine and First
Massachusetts, who garrisoned the city. Ten months later
they would be the reinforcements to beef up Grants drive
on Richmond, but in the summer of 1863 they sat out Gettysburg, manning the rings of fortifications guarding the
city. The equipment they manned within those fortifications were not light, ten-pound field pieces, they were
heavy, twenty- and thirty-pound rifled guns that could tear
apart any charge.

North of Gettysburg, in the capital of Pennsylvania, another force, under the veteran corps commander Couch,
was forming up. Granted it was primarily militia, but it
would number well over ten thousand men before being
disbanded. As a fighting force it was not much, but it was
a presence nevertheless that Lee would have to shadow,
forcing him to divert at least a division to cover his flank
while another division remained in Gettysburg to handle
the wounded, guard the supply lines, and sort out the pris-

oners. Removing nearly a corps from the advance and given the casualties suffered in winning Gettysburg, it is doubtful if Lee could have advanced towards Washington with more than forty thousand combat effectives and the bulk of his artillery would be strung out far to the rear of the advance due to the roads.

Finally there is the issue of supply. Lee's move to the southeast would pull him farther away from his main supply line which weaved its way up the Shenandoah Valley, into Pennsylvania to Chambersburg, and then over the South Mountain range to Gettysburg. This long serpentine chain would be stretched beyond its limits by the advance on Washington. Supply depots would have to be packed up, vast trains of hundreds of wagons moved, and all of this mad tangle then shifted along the one road coming out of Chambersburg, through Gettysburg, then down the Baltimore Pike to Westminster and from there to Washington.

Granted, supplies would have been looted from the captured Union trains parked behind the Round Tops, but both sides had fought a bitter two-day action. To support another assault, or worse yet a direct attack on the massive fortifications around Washington, required refitting and resupplying far beyond the amount captured at Gettysburg, and the feeble Confederate system would be stretched to the breaking point.

As for the captured Union supplies, yes there was the beginning of a pileup of rations and ammunition at Gettysburg by the morning of the second day, but the bulk of the army's equipment was actually being stockpiled in Westminster, twenty miles to the southeast, and far outside the scope of the battlefield. It goes even beyond the stretched plausibility of some alternate history stories to give to Lee not just the victory at Gettysburg but all the supplies held twenty miles away as well. As soon as word reached Westminster of the debacle, the stockpile would have been evacuated by train to Washington, or destroyed.

So we have Lee in front of Washington with forty thousand triumphal but exhausted troops, enough artillery to sustain at best a hard two-day fight, confronting a sprinkling of veterans who had escaped the encirclement, but behind those veterans upward of thirty thousand garrison troops who history would show did indeed have guts, for these same regiments would charge with fanatical bravery and be bled white in the real campaigns of 1864.

Given the accepted ratio of a minimum of four men attacking in order to defeat a single determined defender behind fortifications, the task of taking Washington would have been impossible in that summer of 1863, real or imagined.

Lee might have tried, in fact he would have definitely tried, with the goal so close, the half-completed dome of the Capitol visible just a few miles away. The fortifications around Washington, however, were massive, far exceeding what the Union army bled itself against the following year in front of Richmond, Petersburg, and Atlanta.

It is easy to see here a legendary Pickett's Charge on Washington, a flag bearer screaming, "Home, boys, home. Home is just on the other side of this hill," with Armistead, sword held high, scrambling up to the crest of Fort Stevens . . . and then the battered remnants retiring after the doomed assault of July 13, 1863.

Lee might linger in Maryland for the rest of the month, living off the land, perhaps making a lunge on Baltimore or even trying a second assault on Washington using reinforcements taken from Braxton Bragg's army in Tennessee, but in the interim Union forces would continue to pile into Washington. Even if Confederate raiders did cut the rail lines north of town, there was still the sea, and Union garrisons at Fortress Monroe and from as far away as the coast of South Carolina would be pulled in to confront the crisis. In a final irony, there might have even been an exchange by this point, paroling back the Army of the

Potomac for the Confederate army captured at Vicksburg so that the hearty veterans of the First Minnesota and Sixty-Ninth New York would again be on the battle line.

On August 15, the last of Lee's men would be across the Potomac and back into Virginia, boasting of victory at Gettysburg but realizing in their hearts that no matter what was done, the war would continue to drag on.

Some of you might cry foul at what you've just read, wanting to believe that somehow The Dream was indeed possible, that the Gray Fox would have found a way.

Sorry, but the numbers, logistics, and the reality of the grim new form of industrial warfare argue against it.

In a matter of weeks, if need be, a whole new army could have been created, armed, and put in the field, this time commanded by the hero of Vicksburg.

Let us even concede a successful raid into downtown Washington, as the great author McKinlay Kantor did in his *If the South had Won the Civil War.* Kantor pictured a victory at Gettysburg and Stuart riding up to the White House to capture Lincoln. It is the stuff of good fiction by a great writer, but all rather doubtful for a hard-case alternate history. Lincoln was too cagey a president and politician to be so caught, and it was but a ten-minute ride to the docks at the Annicosta Naval Yard and safety aboard a river ironclad which an entire division of cavalry could have ridden around all day without much effect. Within a day the unsupported raiders would have been driven back outside the city, for the worst place for cavalry to be caught is in a hostile town, cornered by infantry.

What about the political ramifications such as the historic draft riots in New York flaring into a national outcry? Again doubtful. The riots in New York were put down with brutal effectiveness, nailed in part by some regiments which had left the army just before and after the Battle of Gettysburg, their two-year enlistments having ended. To counterbalance Gettysburg there was the great victory at

Vicksburg, and the spin masters of the day would have balanced out the two and pointed to what Grant would ac-
complish once he came east. In fact, Grant most likely
would have come east, bringing with him part of his victorious army, and chances are he would have sought a fall
campaign to reestablish control in the eastern theater. As
for elections, the big one was still a long year away.

What about England and France? Maybe France might
have taken a stab at breaking the blockage given that it was
run by a very erratic leader, but Napoleon III already had
troubles enough in Mexico, and the French fleet was, in reality, a minor player when compared to the largest fleet in
the world in 1863, the fleet of the United States Navy.

Finally, and this is a grim statement for this historian
who admires and loves the Army of the Potomac, even the
Army of the Potomac, in the long-term scheme of things,
was expendable. In fact it was expended the following year
in the brutal Wilderness Campaign. Grant bled it out, losing over sixty thousand men in less than two months. Hard
as it sounds, the men who would have been lost in an alternate Gettysburg were doomed anyhow, to be lost in the
inferno of the Wilderness and the suicidal charges of Cold
Harbor. They died, yet the Union endured.

So let us give Lee his victory at Gettysburg, but by August he would have been back in Virginia, the status quo
returned, Grant most likely would have come east earlier,
a new army would have been built, and the bloodletting
continued.

It might, at that point, have even shaken Confederate
morale, for here was a complete victory won on Northern
territory, and yet an Industrial-Age phoenix rose up again
anyhow, ready to seek yet another battle, and another, until
the chivalrous preindustrial armies of the South were battered into submission.

So in every Southern boy's heart there is The Dream.
And that is the interesting point of this speculation: The

Dream, the what-if, and the creation of a mythology that victory was just on the other side of the hill.

Even though my pro-Northern sentiments are obvious, I will pick an argument with anyone who dares to insult the valor of the Southern armies, and that is not just because I live in the South and must be respectful (and cautious!) when it comes to the sentiments of my neighbors.

The story of the Southern armies is like a beloved tragic novel, where we know the ending, that the hero will die, or the lovers separated forever, and yet every time we reread it there is a voice in many that whispers a wish for the ending to be different. We know it won't be, but just once we want the words to change, our hearts filled with admiration for the wild, mad, Celtic-like spirit of Southern infantry, who will forever be unmatched for sheer raw courage.

In the world of our reality the war was barely over before the myths started—that victory was so close, and if only Ewell had gone forward at Gettysburg, or Jackson had not gone forward that night at Chancellorsville, or Longstreet had been listened to, or the three cigars with the orders wrapped around them had not been lost, and then how different it would have been. It is fascinating how quickly the myths formed, and how fervently they have been embraced across a hundred and forty years.

Yet I maintain that a grand and noble result came out of this dream. It was this mythology of the Lost Cause, that I believe contributed to the healing of the wounds and the reunification of our nation. It was a balm on the soul of the South, a dream that said that all could have been done was done, and the will of the Almighty had simply decided differently. But if only He had allowed but one moment to be changed, then victory would have been achieved.

This romantic myth allowed the veterans of the fallen side to stand proudly in spite of defeat, and the victors to eventually nod and grudgingly say it was a darn close call and then extend a hand in friendship to equals, rather than a conquered and dishonored enemy. It said that the inferno of the Civil War was not the vanquishing of a detested foe but rather was the testing of steel against steel, and the re-forging of that steel into a true United States of America.

And yet, regardless of the reasoning behind the argument I've presented, I know that for so many there will always be The Dream, that it is again a summer day in Pennsylvania in 1863 and all things are, indeed, still possible.

Contributors' Information

Harold Coyle graduated from the Virginia Military Institute in 1974 with a BA in history and a commission as a second lieutenant in Armor.

His first assignment was in Germany, where he served for five years as a tank platoon leader, a tank company executive officer, a tank battalion assistant operations officer, and as a tank company commander. Following that he attended the Infantry Officers Advanced Course at Fort Benning, Georgia, became a branch chief in the Armor School's Weapons Department at Fort Knox, Kentucky, worked with the National Guard in New England, spent a year in the Republic of Korea as an assistant operations officer, and went to Fort Hoof, Texas, for a tour of duty as the G-3 Training officer of the First Cavalry Division and the operations officer of Task Force 1-32 Armor, a combined arms maneuver task force.

Harold's last assignment with the army was at the Command and General Staff College at Fort Leavenworth, Kansas. In January, 1991, he reported to the Third Army, with which he served during Desert Storm. Resigning his commission after returning from the Gulf in the spring of 1991, Harold continues to serve as a lieutenant colonel in the army's Individual Ready Reserve. He writes full-time and has produced the following novels: *Team Yankee, Sword Point, Bright Star, Trial by Fire, The Ten Thousand,*

Code of Honor, Look Away, Until the End, Savage Wilderness, and God's Children.

Doug Allyn is an accomplished author whose short fiction regularly graces year's-best collections. His work has appeared in *Once Upon a Crime, Cat Crimes Through Time,* and *The Year's Twenty-Five Finest Crime and Mystery Stories,* Third and Fourth Editions. His stories of Talifer the wandering minstrel have appeared in *Ellery Queen's Mystery Magazine* and *Murder Most Scottish.* His story "The Dancing Bear," a Tallifer tale, won the Edgar award for short fiction in 1995. His other series character is veterinarian Dr. David Westbrook, whose exploits have been collected in the anthology *All Creatures Dark and Dangerous.* He lives with his wife in Montrose, Michigan.

William H. Keith, Jr. is the author of over sixty novels, nearly all of them dealing with the theme of men at war. Writing under the pseudonym H. Jay Riker, he's responsible for the extremely popular *SEALS: The Warrior Breed* series, a family saga spanning the history of the Navy UDT and SEALs from World War II to the present day. As Ian Douglas, he writes a well-received military science fiction series following the exploits of the U.S. Marines in the future, in combat on the Moon and Mars. A former hospital corpsman in the Navy during the late Vietnam era, many of his characters, his medical knowledge, his feel for life in the military, and his profound respect for the men and women who put their lives on the line for their country are all drawn from personal experience.

In a full-time writing career that has spanned a couple of decades, **James M. Reasoner** has written in virtually every category of commercial fiction. His novel *Texas Wind* is a true cult classic, and his gritty crime stories about contemporary Texas are in the first rank of today's suspense fiction. He has written many books in ongoing western series, including the Faraday, Stagecoach, and Abilene novel series. Recent books include The Civil War Battles series published by Cumberland House.

Brendan DuBois is an award-winning author of short stories and novels. His short fiction has appeared in *Playboy, Ellery Queen's Mystery Magazine, Alfred Hitchcock's Mystery Magazine, Mary Higgins Clark Mystery Magazine,* and numerous anthologies. He has received the Shamus Award from the Private Eye Writers of America for one of his short stories and has been nominated three times for an Edgar Allan Poe Award by the Mystery Writers of America.

He's also the author of the Lewis Cole mystery series—*Dead Sand, Black Tide,* and *Shattered Shell.* His most recent novel, *Resurrection Day*, is a suspense thriller that looks at what might have happened had the Cuban Missile Crisis of 1962 erupted into a nuclear war between the United States and the Soviet Union. This book also recently received the Sidewise Award for best alternative history novel of 1999. Visit his website at www.BrendanDuBois.com.

He lives in New Hampshire with his wife, Mona.

Jake Foster is a full-time mystery, horror, western, and science fiction writer who lives in Iowa.

Robert J. Randisi has had over 370 books published since 1982. He has written in the mystery, western, men's adventure, fantasy, historical, and spy genres. He is the author of the Nick Delvecchio series, the Miles Jacoby series, the Joe Keough novels, and is the creator and writer of The Gunsmith series, which he writes as J. R. Roberts and which presently numbers more than 250 books. He is the founder and executive director of the Private Eye Writers of America.

Jim DeFelice's recent techno-thrillers include *Brother's Keeper* (2000) and *Havana Strike* (1997), both currently available in paperback from Leisure Books. His first novel, *Coyote Bird*, was reissued in paperback by Leisure in February 2001. Jim has also written more than a dozen works of fiction and nonfiction for young people, including an A&E biography of the Beatles published by Lerner Books in 2001. He lives with his wife and son in upstate New York, and can be contacted by Email at JDchester@aol.com.

Simon Hawke has been writing professionally for over twenty years. He has published over sixty novels, among them the popular Time Wars series, the Wizard of 4th St. novels, and The Reluctant Sorcerer trilogy. His latest book, *Mystery of Errors,* is available in hardcover from Forge Books. He lives with his wife and stepson in Greensboro, North Carolina.

Denise Little is a writer and editor who has worked on multiple anthologies, including most recently *Alaska* and *A Constellation of Cats.* Her fascination for the Civil War began when she was growing up in Texas, and never abated—though she draws the line at attending reenactments in full costume when it is over a hundred degrees outside. She is absolutely certain the women were tough back then the thought of living in the South without air conditioning, and in *those* clothes, is enough to bring on hives without even factoring in the war.

Kristine Kathryn Rusch is an award-winning fiction writer. Her novella, *The Gallery of His Dreams,* won the Locus Award for best short fiction. Her body of fiction

work won her the John W. Campbell Award, given in 1991
in Europe. She has been nominated for several dozen fiction awards, and her short work has been reprinted in six
year's-best collections. She has published twenty novels
under her own name. She has penned forty-one total, including pseudonymous books. Her novels have been published in seven languages, and have spent several weeks on
the *USA Today* bestseller list and *The Wall Street Journal*
bestseller list. She has written a number of Star Trek novels with her husband, Dean Wesley Smith, including a
book in this summer's crossover series called *New Earth*.
She is the former editor of prestigious *The Magazine of
Fantasy and Science Fiction*. She won a Hugo Award for
her work there. Before that, she and Dean Wesley Smith
started and ran Pulphouse Publishing, a science fiction and
mystery press in Eugene, Oregon. She lives and works on
the Oregon coast.

Copyright Information

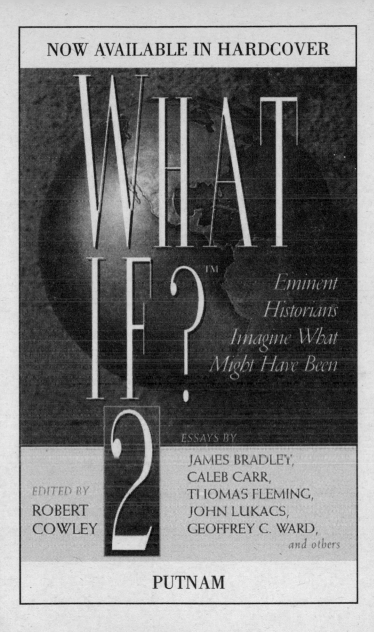

NOW AVAILABLE IN HARDCOVER

WHAT IF?™

Eminent Historians Imagine What Might Have Been

2

ESSAYS BY

JAMES BRADLEY,
CALEB CARR,
THOMAS FLEMING,
JOHN LUKACS,
GEOFFREY C. WARD,
and others

EDITED BY
ROBERT COWLEY

PUTNAM